T0039399

# Family.....

## GOD'S GREATEST GIFT TO MANKIND

# Family.....
## GOD'S GREATEST GIFT TO MANKIND

## TOKMAN

PARTRIDGE

A Penguin Random House Company

**To order additional copies of this book, contact**
Toll Free 800 101 2657 (Singapore)
Toll Free 1 800 81 7340 (Malaysia)
orders.singapore@partridgepublishing.com

www.partridgepublishing.com/singapore

Family-God's greatest gift to mankind

Family is probably today the oldest human social institution. The need to communicate, to share experiences and laughter, to illicit sympathy and comfort, to love and be loved are lasting needs for majority of us.

---

"Love, I find, is like singing. Everybody can do enough to satisfy themselves, though it may not impress the neighbours as being very much."

Zora Neale Hurston – American anthropologist (1891- 1960)

# CHAPTER 1

Room No. 9, in the condominium at Bukit Pinang was filled with the exciting sound of the popular group, the 'Westlife', the singing sensation, belting one of their top hits 'Flying Without Wings'....

Alan Tan, a mirror image of the famous actor, Kevin Costner, had earlier entered his living room and automatically switched on the CD near the sofa. But this time around he was not really listening to the song but lost in the world of his own. His mind ran berserk due to the incident in the Boardroom that fateful morning. He was a very worried person for letting down a man he most loved and respected, Datuk Khalid, Executive Chairman of Bibi Sdn. Bhd, or popularly known as the 'Taipan'. He was the man responsible for what he is today. He could not accept that it could happen to him….a very meticulous person that was most trusted by the Chairman for his wide international experience in the corporate world. It was close to 6.30 pm and the living room was dark. His two boys, the twins, Michael and Alex, with some resemblance of the famous actor, Brad Pitt, were in a boarding school in London, England, pursuing their studies at a Secondary School level. His wife, a career woman, was on the way home. Sonny, 8, his youngest son, with the striking image of Daniel Radcliffe (of Harry Potter fame) was out playing football with his friends. Alan had a very bad day in the office when nothing seemed to be right. Mawi, his Executive Director, the sly looking character like the movie actor, Al Pacino, had been after his scalp since he joined the company. Mawi felt a person like Alan had no place in the company as this was a family bumiputra business. Mawi at any single opportunity will try to put Alan down in front of Dato' Khalid but fortunately just ignored by Dato'. Dato' used to say, "As humans we err from time to time and only the Prophet Mohammad SAW was perfect…..so we must always forgive each other and learn from these mistakes." That made Mawi mad and more adamant to find faults with Alan. This morning Alan had been accused of incompetence and sheer negligence in handling the billion-dollar bid with a foreign investor. He wanted Alan out of the company dishonourably and worse still to leave the company in shame.

Earlier, Alan was given the task of securing the billion-dollar contract for the company with a reputable firm overseas. The deal fell short due to the inadequate information tabled at the meeting held in Kuala Lumpur that morning. He could not convince the clients as his presentation was rather sketchy and lacked the relevant data that the clients requested. The foreign company who flew in to listen to his briefing in front of Mawi accused Alan of being secretive, not transparent and unprofessional in his presentation.

"I am very confused with your presentation. You were very evasive and the figures to us are to me, fictitious and unrealistic. Those figures do not make sense to me and I am sure from the look of my Accountant here he looked very puzzled. I did not fly all the way from Europe to hear this......this rubbish. This is a waste of time and money," said Mr. James, the team leader from Holland, who stood up immediately, mad, ready to leave the room.

"I thought I could close the deal with your company today as I trusted you Alan.......our past business relationships made me made choose your company and take this trip to Malaysia. Your country has so much potential for business venture......your government and economy attract so many businessmen to this part of the world. Besides China and India all eyes of foreign businessmen are on your country. In fact I came down here because of our long trusted friendship! We had so many offers from other countries but I managed to convince the Board of Directors that your company was the ideal choice. A few African countries invited us and besides this project they have in line to offer other lucrative projects on joint-venture basis. I am disappointed, really amazed that the man that I used to respect and look forward to work together can change so dramatically. Today, you are not the person whom I use to know….you…..you…..seems you are not convinced of this project......are you Alan? You fail to convince me too…. Alan. In fact I am very sceptical and really disappointed with your presentation!"

# CHAPTER 2

Alan, who was the Manager of the Foreign Investment Department knew he had been sabotage by his colleagues, either by his deputy Nasir, a look alike of American actor, Andy Garcia, or by Manjit, the Assistant Manager, who always reminded him of Rafael Nadal, the tennis sensation. Alan had meticulously prepared the project paper 3 months ago with Nasir. The Chief Accountant, Wong checked the costing meticulously with Nasir and Manjit for almost a week. Alan knew the project paper was in good hands but he remained cautious because he had a very nasty experience at his former employment. His previous working experience in Europe taught him never to trust anyone in the company. "It is a very positive working attitude as others are just waiting to pounce on you for the slightest error.....be always hands on".......said his lecturer. He still remembered vividly the incident that nearly costs his reputation and career while working in an oil and gas firm. Being very meticulous and cautious he prepared personally a very important document for the Board members to approve. He had gone through the papers time and time again to the extent that he knew the subject matter like the back of his palm.

A few weeks before the Board meeting he passed the papers to his Accountant to check on some figures and his Secretary to compile his papers. Fortunately for him he kept a copy of his papers and during the Board meeting he found most of the figures had been manipulated by his Accountant who had a grudge against him for his promotion. The Accountant hoped that by doing so the Board members would realised that they had promoted a wrong man to run the project division! Alan found the discrepancies as soon as he opened the file and immediately called his Secretary to photostat a new set based on his own copy. While waiting for the new set of figures he explained and apologised to the Board members who was convinced and appreciated what he was doing. The Accountant left dishonourably the very next day. That bad experience taught him to never ever trust anybody in his work no doubt his boss always emphasised the importance of teamwork.

# CHAPTER 3

$B$ack to this current project he had asked Nasir to go through the papers to be back in his office 12 days before the presentation. Alan, as always being hands on, was anxious to review the papers earlier in case of any need for amendments. He was not only a workaholic but also a perfectionist. Further, he needed to get the papers approved by both Datuk and Mawi before the presentation to the clients. 10 days before the meeting Alan was informed by Nasir that the project paper could only be ready in about 5 days time, as they had to verify some data and technical specifications with a third party. However, after a few days Alan was notified that the papers could only be ready 2 days before the meeting. There had been a delay, yes, and a long delay, due to the breakdown to the office's fax machines. Alan met with both Datuk and Mawi and explained of the delay and both gentlemen appreciated that it was not his fault and anyway being a very competent person trusted him to give a very good presentation to their potential partners.

On the morning of the meeting, Alan became worried, as Nasir had still not given the project papers to him. Nasir informed Alan late that afternoon that the photostating machine had again some mechanical problems but was confident the papers would be ready first thing the next morning. He would be working overnight to get the papers ready. Early the next morning Alan intercom Nasir and was told that he would send it to the Boardroom before the meeting. Alan, however, had to inform both Datuk and Mawi about the delay but Mawi refused to accept any excuses. Mawi angrily left for the boardroom. The Chairman who had left it entirely to Mawi and Alan to seal the USD 2.6 billion deal advised Alan to do his best as he was scheduled to meet the Minister of International Trade that same morning. Alan proceeded to the Boardroom and saw Mawi seating there looking disgusted while waiting anxiously there.

Mawi, looking irritated, asked Alan for the papers as soon as Alan entered the meeting room. He was upset when told it was not ready. "What? The papers are not ready? Do you know that our clients will be here any time minute now and here you are telling me the papers are not even ready? I don't want to attend this meeting unprepared with an open mind. This is very amateurish and Datuk had been trying to impress me about your impressive international experience. You can't even prepare a project paper in time......do you know that this is a very big project, at least for our company......what international experience are you talking about? I can't help you here.....not without any relevant information." He continued to insinuate that Alan wanted to keep all the information to himself in his bid to gain personal glory. He kept on stressing on the importance of teamwork, a culture practised by them before Alan joined the company. Alan's action smacked of misconduct according to him. A few minutes before the clients arrived, his secretary sent the papers to Alan and he gave a copy to Mawi. Alan was browsing through the papers when James arrived with his two assistants; an Accountant and a Chemical Engineer at 10.00 am. Mr. James, who had the look of the tough movie hero, Charles Bronson, and his team were in a very jovial mood.

# CHAPTER 4

"We had a very adventurous night with some clients last night. Kuala Lumpur not only offers good food and accommodation but excellent 'hospitality'," he joked. "The first time I was here years ago I stayed at J.W. Marriott but this time around they put us up at the P.J. Hilton. But our clients brought us to a 'secret' rendezvous somewhere in a 5 star hotel in the city…marvellous place," he added. "We will put you up at the Istana Hotel or Shangri-la the next time you drop in, James," said Mawi. "By the way Datuk apologised for his absence as he has an urgent meeting with the Minister of Trade," Mawi added. "I hope to catch up with him later if he is free," said James. After an exchange of pleasantries they got down to serious business….. Alan gave his proposal to the clients. During the discussion with the clients he realised somewhere along the line he had been sabotaged probably by Nasir. Some vital information was missing in the project paper. Cold sweats appeared on his forehead in spite of the room being below room temperature. He felt lost and desperate as the figures just did not tally and the bottom line was not very impressive. How was he going to convince the delegation on this proposed joint venture? During the presentations there were many questions left unanswered which made the clients uncomfortable and suspicious. Alan was seen as uncertain and full of doubts in replying to all the queries posed by the delegation. In fact he had no solid data to back his statement. James looked at his delegation, whispered to each other for a while and soon stormed out of the Boardroom in disgust when they realised the meeting was not making any headway after 20 minutes. Mawi stared hard at Alan and said,

"You are a failure and incompetent. You have sabotaged the company. I want your resignation letter now!" and he too left the Boardroom.

Alan was left stunt, speechless and feeling down. Losing the USD 2.6 billion project was a big blow to him personally as Datuk was confident he could secure the contract. He was in total confusion and had no idea what to do next.

James and his colleagues immediately left the office without making a courtesy call on Datuk Khalid. Initially, he promised to see Datuk who invited him for lunch the next time he was in Kuala Lumpur. On entering the limousine that was waiting for them at the porch James uttered some remarks to his colleagues, which was inaudible to them. He sat in the limousine deep in his own thoughts. While travelling back to the hotel he said,

"You know, I have this feeling that Alan was unprepared for this meeting or he could have been sabotaged by his staffs. Look at this proposal that he submitted to us......it is so amateurish......the data are all nonsense's..... nothing for us to evaluate and make a decision. This not definitely not him as I knew him previously to be a very meticulous and efficient bloke."

"I believed whoever prepared the proposal had no intention to see the proposed joint venture go through, James," interjected his Chief engineer, Sebastian. "I wanted to brief them on this proposed project as it is new and very technical to them," Sebastian added.

"We have wasted this long trip coming to this company, we should be more prudent in choosing our partners in the future.....that company in Singapore or Hong Kong would be an ideal partner I think. Anyway, I made this decision because of Alan, whom I knew when we were both working in the same company in Amsterdam. I found him a very intelligent and a reasonable person. I was impressed with him.....he was a workaholic and gave tremendous contributions to that company," said James.

# CHAPTER 5

$S$uddenly his cell phone rang. "Yes….hello….who is this? Who? Alan…..sorry, your voice is breaking up…..the telephone reception is not too good. Yes…..I am disappointed…..really disappointed with the meeting this morning….. yes, I am leaving tomorrow night for Hong Kong on the 7.30 pm flight. What is that…..you want to meet me…. today? We are not free today but let me check with my colleagues. Just hold on for a few minutes okay?" said James. He informed his colleagues that Alan wanted to meet them before we fly off to Hong Kong tomorrow. "What do you all think….should we?" Nixon, the accountant, a very quiet person by nature, suddenly spoke out, "This project is very viable and we need a partner from here who is reliable and trustworthy….. you know Alan and Datuk, so I suggest we listen to what Alan has got to say….. we have nothing to lose. Why don't we invite him to join us for lunch tomorrow after the meeting with Felda Global- FGV." "Agreed," said Sebastian.

"Okay Alan….can you join us for lunch at the P.J. Hilton hotel, say, by 12.00 noon tomorrow? Good. Give me a call when you arrive. I am in Room 2020. Make sure you come alone or with Datuk…..not that Mawi please. By the way send my regards to Datuk as I do not think we can see him tomorrow before we leave. Right, see you tomorrow for lunch Alan," said James while switching off his cell phone. "I am glad he called as we are very close friends and I do not like our friendship to end in a sour note," remarked James to his colleagues.

# CHAPTER 6

$A$lan joined the company, Bibi Sdn. Bhd. Almost two years ago. Datuk Khalid knew him well being one of the best orphans that 'graduated' from his orphanage. Alan, to Datuk Khalid was not a Chinese but a true Malaysian who loved this country like any other Malaysians. Datuk Khalid, who can easily pass as the elder brother of Microsoft boss, Bill Gates, invited him to help build the company to explore and expand into the international market. Coming from a very humble family of three boys and two girls, Datuk Khalid, now 60, was a man of vision. Datuk Khalid related to Alan over dinner one evening about his early days,

"My father had no opportunity when he was young and remained illiterate earning his living as a padi planter. You know Alan during the British era we were categorised by our professions....the Malays were padi planters, Chinese were tin miners and Indians working in the estates as rubber tappers. My mother helped him to bring additional income by doing odd jobs in the village. Both were from a very small village near the small town of Batang Berjuntai in the state of Selangor. Their joint monthly earnings could barely support the family. Being the eldest, I had to earn additional income for the family by working at a food stall after school. I remembered my siblings and I had to stay away from school for a few months, as my parents could not pay the school fees. We were financially down. The sad thing was that it was common among the poor families in the kampong. We were scared to face our Form teachers so we skipped school. Our parents could do nothing about it so my brothers and I got a part time job to tap the rubber trees in a small holders plot to earn extra income and my young sisters helped at a food stall. It was after two months that the headmaster came over to our house together with a few caring teachers. They told us to come back to school as they promised that all the fees would be taken care of. I did not know how they did it so my father urged us to go back to school. Walking for about 6 kilometres daily to school was our routine. We could not afford to pay for the school bus. I pity my siblings especially during the rainy days, as we could not afford any umbrella and were always drenched to the bones whenever there was a heavy downpour, which was often then. Sheltering under the trees or shop houses did help but we were scared to be late for school. Our shoes were always dirty because of the road which was either dry or dusty during the dry season or muddy when it rained.....so we walked bare footed to school to keep our shoes clean.

School canteen was alien to us as we had no pocket money. Only when the school served free food on special occasions that we get to eat in the canteen. My mother could not even afford to prepare any food for us to take to school but we normally had some 'cucur pisang' and coffee for breakfast. Free milk was unheard of for the underprivileged children then. To stop thinking about hunger during the recess time we kept ourselves occupied by talking together with the other underprivileged children under the trees near the school field. At certain times I past my time playing football with the others during the break. That kept our minds from thinking about food. Tap water in the toilet, which was clean and tasty to us, was good enough to quench our thirst daily. Sometimes we do get to enjoy some biscuits or chocolates given by some of our caring classmates. It was like getting gifts from Santa Claus! We always looked forward to the bulan Ramadhan (fasting month) as everyone were then equal."

# CHAPTER 7

$A$lan asked how he and his siblings can cope with life without proper food.

"Frankly, going without food for a day was a normal thing in our household, but we managed to sustain our energy for the day without much effort. It's all in the mind, they say and a question of getting used to it! Having food on the table for dinner is a rare thing. Anyway, fasting during the Ramadhan made us very resilience, so having one good meal per day was an accepted norm in the family. We were trained to fast by our parents during the month of Ramadhan when we reached the age of 5 and fasting came naturally to us as we fast about 10 days every month," Datuk replied.

He completed his Form Five with straight As, but had to forgo his dream of tertiary education to help his siblings. Both his parents died in a freak van accident just after he sat for his 'O' level examinations. Fortunately or unfortunately, none of us followed them to attend the wedding as the trip was meant for adults only.

"They were coming back from Morib after attending a wedding of our relatives. It was in the late evening and everybody was tired. Most of the occupants were sleeping when the van, at a very sharp blind corner, crashed into an oncoming timber lorry. 7 of the passengers died on the spot including my parents. Only 2 of my relatives survived the crash and I was told by the survivors that they did not realised what hit them. I was informed of the accident two hours later and taken to the hospital in Klang by one of my uncles. The untimely death of our parents was very traumatic. It left us in a state of dilemma and complete distress. I was naive then and got extremely upset with Allah SWT for depriving us from the love and protection of our parents at this tender young age. I was in rage with the world around me. However, one day when I attended the Friday prayer at the mosque I realised it was very wrong to blame Allah SWT for what had befallen my family was fated.

# CHAPTER 8

The 'Khatib' (Preacher) quoted the relevant verses from the Quran, which asked mankind to always have faith and be thankful to God when facing hardship or triumph. Whatever happened to us is the will of Allah SWT...... fated! We got to remain strong and positive as whatever misfortune or calamity we endure now there is always a silver lining ahead of us. I cried and repented in the mosque and made a pledge to work hard to keep my family together. I was the eldest in the family and I had to take over the responsibility of my parents....as a surrogate father, so to say," said Datuk, who appeared deeply emotional and depressed when he related the incident to Alan. He was very quiet for a few minutes and had teary eyes. Alan too was touched by the story. Datuk looked down and after wiping his tears he smiled at Alan and continued his story, "It was not easy to keep my siblings together. They were all so demoralised due to the sudden loss of our parents and were psychologically down for the first few months. Nobody wanted to continue their schoolings and everybody insisted on getting some odd jobs to support the family. I had to be patient but at the same time stood firm and put my foot down. I told them they must continue going to school and complete at least their 'O' levels. 'O' level then was the minimum qualification that can unlock the door for young man and woman in the country to get a respectable job. With 'O' level we can use it later as the platform to progress further in our lives. I knew there were many others out there who achieved success without any education but I told my siblings to complete their education in memory of our parents that we love so much. Our parents would be very proud of what we are doing."

Datuk added, "I was young and knew I could not do it by myself and help came from our Quran teacher, an Ustaz, who instilled into us the importance of education and keeping the family together. We knew strong religious foundations would help in giving us strength to face the challenges ahead."

Few of our relatives wanted us to move into their homes and it meant that we would be separated but Datuk knew he had to keep the family together at whatever costs.

"We were fortunate that our parents had this small hut, which we proudly can call our home. That was the only property we inherited. Until today that hut has been kept in the family and today one of my sisters lives there after we renovated the hut into a proper house," said Datuk.

# CHAPTER 9

Datuk got a job as an Accounts clerk in a small Chinese construction company before his examination results were out. With his meagre salary and assistance from the Welfare Department he managed to keep his siblings in school until they completed their studies at 'O' level. His brother, Mawi and one of his sisters became college-trained teachers. The younger brother, Zamani, joined as an interpreter with the court and later did an external degree in law. It took him much longer than those who got to go straight to the university but it was much cheaper. His work in the court gave him a better understanding of court procedures and the law. It was only for his final examinations that he had to go overseas for a year to complete his law studies with the help of a loan from an institution. He successfully completed his Certificate of Legal Practice and did chambering with a law firm in town before he became a lawyer. The other sister became a trained nurse at one of the local hospitals in the city.

While working in the Chinese company Datuk Khalid 'learn the trade' of how to run a small enterprise. Being exposed to the accounts of the company helped him to better understand the company's financial affairs, which was crucial to ensure of success in the business world. His boss, Ah Soon, was not well educated but managed the family company well in his own style. He was very helpful and one of the few Chinese who was not 'selfish' to impart his knowledge to those who were keen to learn, like Datuk Khalid. Almost every day after closing the shop he sat down with Datuk Khalid to guide him on the fundamentals of running a small business and keeping accounts. He treated Datuk as a friend rather than as an employee or competitor. Datuk found running a business firm very intriguing and stimulating so after 9 years with the company he said goodbye to his boss when he decided to start his own small operation with some savings he had. Ah Soon's advised was simple,

"You will be a big 'Taipan' one day if you stay humble......share your profit with your employees and they will take good care of the company. Remember, it's better to think negative on anything, than think positive on nothing."

Datuk Khalid stuck to that philosophy in his business approach. Ah Soon became his 'consultant' and he was always there to advise him. The company, Suria Sdn. Bhd. with a class F certificate, started as a small family business, with two casual workers, repairing and renovating offices, mosques and other small urban and rural projects. The government was, however, impressed with the company as all the works were done diligently and completed on time. Suria Sdn. Bhd. made a reputation as a very reliable bumiputra company. He set up a small plastic factory and with the help of Government the company became the vendor for one of the airlines in the country supplying plastic items. Datuk could never forget his mentor, Ah Soon. Whenever he could, some of the jobs offered to him were subcontracted to his 'sifu'. He offered Ah Tan, the eldest son of Ah Soon, to work in his company to expose him to new management ideas that would one-day help him to run his father's company in the near future. He always reminded himself and his employees,

"I am here today because of my 'sifu'. He is my mentor and I will never forget that."

# CHAPTER 10

Datuk first met his wife, Datin Bibi, at the Welfare Department where he was given a job to repair some defects in that building. The moment he stepped into the building he saw the most beautiful lady he had ever set eyes in his life. He liked what he saw and made a vow that he must get to know her before his job was done there. Being young and beautiful, Bibi did not notice, or show any interest in him. He was just another small time contractor, moving about repairing the office with two of his men. Shabbily dressed in his working clothes she hardly noticed him working there. He tried his best to get her to notice him but to no avail.....she was just too busy with her work. He thought probably she was married or engaged to one of the hotshots in town. He came to know from those working in the office that her name was Bibi. She went about doing her work like a clock and refused to get distracted by anybody. When they met along the corridor or the lift she refused to acknowledge his presence or even glance at him. Khalid was always ready with a smile. On one occasion he even tried to strike a conversation with her by asking her where the toilet was located.

Without looking at him she said, "Straight on and first door on the left."

Fate played a big role on the last day of Khalid's presence at that building. An incident at the office brought Bibi to take notice of this young man who was working conscientiously at her office. Khalid had almost given up hope of getting to know this young lady. That morning a man and a woman came to inquire about some welfare aids that they had requested. The discussions soon turned nasty when the man lost his temper. The woman could do nothing and the enraged man started throwing abuses at Bibi and throwing the files in the office. Khalid was right near the door of the meeting room when he heard the commotion. He immediately opened the door and saw the man throwing verbal abuses at Bibi. The enraged man looked at him and asked what he wanted. "What do you want.....get out!" he reacted. "Eh.....eh....I just want to check the ceiling that they said was leaking," answered Khalid. "What leaks are you talking about.......get out," He then started tormenting and threatening Bibi with a pen knife. Datuk knew he had to act fast and so he stepped in and tried to cool down the man who turned more aggressive. Khalid, being an exponent of 'silat', the Malay art of self-defence, initially tried to cool him down by talking to him calmly. When the man became aggressive, Khalid had no alternative but to subdue the man to control the situation. He managed to secure the pen knife, twisted his arm and dragged him out of the office before the security guards took him away to the Police station. Khalid left the office after the incident as he had completed his contract there. Bibi was traumatised for a few days and did not get the chance to thank the young man who came to her aid. It was almost 2 weeks after the incident that he received a call from Bibi. He was having a meeting with his men in his office when the call came in.

# CHAPTER 11

"Hello? Is that En. Khalid?" he heard a sweet female voice on the phone. He tried to remain cool and said, "Khalid here…..may I know who is on the line?" "You may not remember me….I am Bibi….Bibi, the woman at the Welfare Department here. You came to do some repairs here?" said Bibi. He immediately stopped the meeting and politely asked his men to leave the room as he needed some privacy. He pretended not to remember her but was so happy to hear her call. "Sorry, Puan Bibi, I cannot recall, which one was you…..are you the one wearing the scarf? Anyway, was my repair work unsatisfactory? If it is defective I will come back to remedy the defects immediately….today?" said Khalid. "No….no….your repair works are excellent….. Perfect. Yes…. no….I am Cik not Puan Bibi….the one wearing the scarf is Puan Murni…..it's nothing like that…..It was about the incident at the office," said Bibi. "Oh…. Sorry Cik…..Cik Bibi…..what incident was that? I am sorry if any damage has happened."

"Oh, no…this is regarding the incident in my office two weeks ago when you help to control that man who went beserk….out of control," said Bibi.

"I hope the lady is okay now…..it is such a pity it had to happen to such a beautiful polite lady….I heard she was traumatised by the incident. Are you one of the office staffs……sitting near the entrance in the main office?" Khalid pretended not to know.

"No, no….that is Salmiah…..I was the one in the meeting room whom you rescued when the man went berserk and started throwing abuses at me. You suddenly stepped in and subdued the mad man….remember?" Bibi replied.

Khalid kept quiet pretending to contemplate for a while.

"Hello…hello…are you still there En. Khalid….hello….." called Bibi, who sounded very desperate.

"Yes, I am still here, trying to recall the incident…you know a small contractor like me, I get abused by people in power everyday….so many things happened all the time to me almost every day. You must be the lady who came with that man then," said Khalid.

"No, no, no.....I was the lady being harassed by that rogue....I work here... at the Welfare Department."

"Right....ok...now I got it ......you were the lady officer in that room. Are you okay now? Are you calling me about my payment cheque.....is it ready for collection?" asked Khalid.

"Yes....no.....no.....it is like this....ok....I was traumatised by the incident for almost a week and I did not have the chance to say thank you to you personally," answered Bibi.

"Ooh...that was nothing...anybody would had done the same thing on instinct....nobody likes to see a lady in distress what more being verbally abused.....anyway, when can you post the payment cheque Cik Bibi?" Khalid asked.

"Why don't you come tomorrow personally to collect it....it will be much better," Bibi replied.

"I am bogged down with so many repair works....I may ask my clerk to collect it tomorrow...okay?" said Khalid.

"No....no...I mean...it's better for you to come personally.....so I get the chance to thank you personally, En.Khalid," said Bibi.

Datuk knew he had made an impression of himself on Bibi....now it was a question of sealing the relationship and he had to make the next crucial move.

"Ok....if you insist. I......maybe I can be there if I can complete my work at the surau......I will call you first before I come in...okay?"

"Okay....fine....I will be waiting for your call tomorrow, En.Khalid," replied Bibi.

# CHAPTER 12

$K$halid had a plan. He had to come out with a strategy to see whether she really wanted to meet him. He did not call her for the next few days nor did any of his men go to collect the payment cheque. Each day Bibi was waiting eagerly to meet Khalid and was desperately hoping he called her. On the fourth day the waiting became unbearable and Bibi had no choice but to call him. "Hello, En. Khalid….how are you?" asked Bibi. He decided to pull a fast one on Bibi to see how she reacted. "Sorry, Bibi…..I was down with high fever….. some unknown virus hit me and only today I am out of the bed and back at the office….I could not even call you….did my office call you?" Khalid asked. "No? Nobody from your office called me. By the way….sorry to hear about your sickness…are you alright now? Can I help you in any way? I can send over the payment cheque to your office if necessary….would you like that?" asked Bibi. Khalid was delighted and kept smiling to himself. Now he had caught her 'in his net'. "I don't want to impose on you just for the cheque….. you are such a busy officer and needs to attend to more important matters at the office. It's too much trouble for you," said Khalid. "I will be attending a meeting near your area in the morning, which should end before noon, so I will drop in your office on the way back," replied Bibi. "In that case…why not? that's a brilliant idea….we can have lunch near here if you don't mind……I will see you before 12.00 noon then…..tomorrow? You know where my office is located right? Anyway if you get lost give me a call okay?" replied Khalid who was jumping with joy. When his secretary came in he was dancing about in his room and lost in a world of his own. "Did you get more new projects, En. Khalid?" asked his secretary. "Better than projects, Bedah, much better, in fact…..it is my ultimate achievement in life," he laughed.

His secretary, Bedah, was confused and left the room bewildered. Bibi came to Khalid's office the next day and was entertained by his secretary who was instructed to deliberately delay her in the reception room…..as he was supposed to be very busy. Bibi was curious about Khalid and she discreetly asked the secretary about his family background and his marital status. Bedah, being a very smart secretary painted her a picture of the most perfect boss in the world as she had the feeling that this pretty lady was interested in her boss. Bedah liked her as she was polite, pleasant and now realised why her boss was smiling 'from ear to ear', yesterday after this lady called. He must be in love with her and, probably, her with him. After half an hour the secretary entered Khalid's room and invited Bibi in. He was waiting enthusiastically, flashing his big smile as she walked into his room and quickly ushered his secretary out of the office.

"Sorry, I was busy on the line with a client....you know the usual 'kow tow' I have to do to keep my clients happy," said Khalid.

# CHAPTER 13

After 15 minutes Khalid left the office with Bibi for lunch. On the way out he left the payment cheque brought by Bibi on his secretary's desk…..he was in an extremely good mood. Bedah thought to herself that, "If the lady is not around I would have asked for an immediate pay raise…I am sure he will agree!" He just could not help himself from grinning and before he left his office he raised his eyebrows in triumph, like Mr. Bean, to his secretary. The lunch at the posh hotel lasted for almost 4 hours and they had to leave as the hotel was preparing for Hi-tea.

It was the beginning of a torrid love affair between the two. They started dating almost everyday and within three months they were happily married. Khalid renamed his company to Bibi Sdn. Bhd. as he believed the name would bring him more luck and prosperity……..and it did indeed!

With some savings they had, Khalid went for the pilgrimage to Mecca with Bibi after 8 years of blissful married life. "Everyday was like a honeymoon," said Datuk smiling, "and rest of the story, Alan, you have heard from Datin!"

Datin continued working as an officer at the Welfare Department until Datuk established the orphanage. She then decided to devote full time at the foster home to make it a success. Bibi Orphanage as it was known was for all races and ages. 2 boys and 3 girls below 3 years old, including an abandoned baby were the first batch of orphans they took care. The building was initially a makae shift two dorms house…….one for the males and the other for the females with separate toilet facilities. After a few years with an increase in the number of orphans the building was renovated to cater foor the bigger numbers. Datin loved her job and she found complete satisfaction and complete joy taking care of the children. Datin was inspired by so many stories that she read in the Readers Digest and motivational books. The famous writer and motivator, Robin Sharma, in his book "The leader who had no title" stated that a person can lead others even without a title. Dr. Martin Luther King Jr. said that, "If a man is called to be a street sweeper, he should sweep streets as Michelangelo painted or Beethoven composed music, or Shakespeare poetry. He should sweep streets so well that all the hosts of heaven and earth will pause to say, "Here lived a great sweeper who did his job well." True strangers who hold no official posts in the government or corporate world can play a big role in this modern world. They maybe strangers to us initially but later became friends. Angelina Jodi, Jet Li and many other celebrities are helping to make Africa a better place to live by spending millions of dollars for its development.

# CHAPTER 14

In Philippines one young man helped in making tremendous changes to the lives of the poor on an isolated island. He admitted that he just wanted to help the best he could and, "I didn't imagine how it would open a whole new world of opportunities for the entire community so quickly." It had never ever crossed anybody's mind that some kids had to endure hardships and danger just to get to schools daily. These were students in primary schools. The article appeared in the October 2011 issue about Jay Jaboneta, an ordinary Filipino, who discovered and revealed the hazards the school kids from a small isolated island, Layag Layag, in the Philippines had to go through to get to schools. The kids had to swim 2 kilometres and walked another 5 kilometres to reach the schools. The islanders were too poor to build a boat for the kids but knew the importance of education for their children. Most of the island had no basic amenities such as fresh water and electricity. Jaboneta spread the news through his face book and the mass media which supported him in his good cause and soon donations from the public came in which were used to help the islanders. His first action was to build a boat to ferry the school kids to get to school daily. That boat has lifted an enormous burden from the shoulders of the parents. Nur-Ma Hamsan a mother of two kids and a number of stepchildren had his to say "I didn't go to school but I knew how important it was. I used to stand watching them swim away with the younger ones clinging to the shoulders of their bigger siblings when the waves were high. When they had to stay in school later than usual, I worried about all the children swimming in the dark."

Many other groups came to join in to help Jaboneta such as the Tzu Chi Foundation, Dr. Ofelia Sy and many social media experts including face book headquarters in Palo Alto in California. They provided boats to ferry the school kids in many isolated islands in the Philippines. While the children are in school the boats are used to transport goods and produce of the islanders to the market. The government too soon realized the importance of giving education to isolated areas and makeshift schools were built on the islands as an immediate step. Dr. Sy aptly said about Jaboneta that, "He reminded us that as citizens of this country, we can empower ourselves by helping each other." This is a case of strangers who came to the aids of the islanders as friends without waiting for the government to step in.

With some help and donations from well wishes the orphanage survived until today with about 50 kids under her care. Childless couples adopted a number of the orphans legally. Datin Bibi administered the daily operations of the orphanage with the help of Datuk Khalid's sisters, 4 helpers and volunteers. Datuk Khalid was conferred the Datukship for his contributions in social work and nation building. Alan was one of earliest baby to the orphanage. He was found, abandoned by the parents, wrapped in a 'sarong' with a bottle of milk one morning, near the entrance, with a short hand written note, 'Please take care of my baby. God bless you.'

Some of the babies were not adopted so Datin Bibi saw to it that they get proper education. Alan made it good up to tertiary level. He was a success story to Datin Bibi. Alan recalled vividly his early days at the orphanage. He did not realise that he was staying in the 'home' until he started attending the primary school. He was a happy child when he was in the 'home' being loved by everybody as he was a cute little baby. Having so many other kids to play with everyday was fun. It was all play initially. As the kids understood their environment better they were taught to be independent and be helpful around the 'home'. He remembered celebrating Hari Raya (Eide Day), Chinese New Year, Deepavali and Christmas at the home together with the other kids. To him and the rest of the kids each festival was a day of celebration with no significance to any religion. It was only much later that he knew what those celebrations were all about. He did not know about parents and the role they played in their children's lives. It was on his first day in school when he saw men and women sending the children to school, whispering and smiling trying to give them confidence to face the new world that he realised he was missing something. Some of the kids were crying and others tagging behind the men or women. A few were not ready to enter the classes during the first few days and it took plenty of coaxing from the parents to get them into the classrooms. Alan saw most of the children had a mother or father accompanying them to school for the first few days. Datin Bibi sent him and a few others from the 'home' to the school and soon left when the school bell rang to signal the start of the school session.

# CHAPTER 15

However, he was confused when he noticed some mothers or fathers, concerned for their kids, waited along the corridors, watching their kids from the distance. During the breaks they escorted their kids to the canteen......it was very comforting to the kids having their parents around for the first few days in school. The children, however, felt rather shy to be seen with their parents when they have their own friends in school.....the parents were asked to leave once they reached the school gate! Alan and those from the 'home', however, adjusted quickly to the school environment as they were used to be independent. He went about in school on his own confidently. At the end of the school session he watched with curiosity the parents taking their children from school to their own homes. He listened to the other kids talking about their homes, families and holidays they went together. He could not comprehend what they meant until the teachers explained to the class on the importance of the institution of family.

The teachers explained about homeless children and the wonderful things these foster 'homes' had done for them. "Family is everything…. the greatest gift from God to us, it is sacred and you are a lost soul without a family," said a teacher. Only then did he realised he was from one of these 'homes'…that he had no family …a lost soul…without a mum or dad to share his experience. He felt sad and lost in this big world. The day when he knew about the institution of family he skipped lunch when he returned from school. He felt dejected and rejected from society. Realising Alan was missing at lunch; Datin Bibi went looking for him and saw his lonely figure on the bed. She sat on his bed and asked him softly what was wrong. Alan was withdrawn and kept silent. He refused to indulge in any conversation with Datin. All the children in the home were just like Datin's own and could not bear to see any of them feeling sad.

She said to Datuk, "We set up this 'home' to give hope and happiness to these unfortunate children and it is always a bad day for me to watch just one sad face amongst them. Just giving education, food, clothes and shelter are not enough to me.....I want to see radiant and happy faces......accepting and loving us as their own parents." Datin wanted to hug Alan so badly and she just stretched her arms and hugged the young child, holding him tight. With her arms around him she whispered a promise to Alan that no matter what the future holds, no matter what the odds were, she would do everything she could to make sure Alan attained happiness in life. She felt tears onto her shoulders as he hung on to her. He was sobbing uncontrollably and unable to say a word to Datin. Later after he was able to control his emotion he decided to confide to Datin whom he realised was the only one in this world who really cared for him from the day he came to this world. She had always been by his side whenever he felt low. She was like an angel to him. She took him in and gave her undivided love to all in the 'home'. Her presence almost always cheered him up....she was after all to him....the only mother he knew! He always felt secured and well protected around her. He took courage and after he had calmed down he started asking questions about his parents and why they were not there for him. Datin was at a lost, initially, as to how best to answer his questions and knew she had to come out with the right answers, as children like Alan were very sensitive.

# CHAPTER 16

$\text{D}$atin delicately explained to Alan about how he and the others in the 'home' came under her care. She explained that some parents were very poor and could not give their children the best care, education and home. Some of these parents who lived far below poverty level, in short extreme poverty, could not even afford to give food and clothes to their children. It was fated and so they decided the 'homes' were the best place to see that their kids get the best opportunity to face the world. Alan was one of the fortunate kids to come to her 'home' and she promised him equal opportunity like other kids under the care of their biological parents. The future for him to change his destiny was there and like other kids it was up to them to make that change. Furthermore, she promised that Alan would get the chance to look for his biological parents, if he wanted, when he was of age and ready to face them. "Make your parents proud and happy by taking this opportunity by becoming a useful citizen in society," said Datin.

After listening to her, Alan remained a bitter young boy, angry at the unfairness of what his parents had done to him. He felt a sense of betrayal and abandonment and could not help but felt that his parents were very irresponsible.

"What kind of parents were they?" he said to himself.

For reasons known only to his parents Alan could not forgive them for leaving him at the 'home'. He wanted to run away but he had nowhere to go and knew he was too young to do so. He knew Datin and Datuk loved him and they were his 'guardian angels', the only parents he knew. Alan was like their own son and they hoped that one day Alan grow up to be a responsible young man and come back to help them run the family business. However, unlike some kids his anger lasted just for a few days. Soon his days of rage were gone and he found peace in himself and a sense of purpose in his life under the guidance of Datin. He recollected seeing babies brought to the foster homes and others adopted by childless parents when he was there. He was sad to see these babies and young children crying for their 'mum' when they had to part from the foster home. Their 'mum' to them was no other than Datin who was the motherly figure at the 'home'. Being amongst the older kids in the 'home' he was like a big brother to all the children there. Alan knew all of them well as he loved children and kept them happy during his free time. He felt depressed and sad whenever one of the children left the 'home' with their adopted parents.

For the first few years he was in school he and those from the 'homes' were the targets of ridicules and insinuations by some of the mischievous kids in school. They labelled them as 'Anak haram' (illegitimate kids) because they had no biological parents. It was such a cruel remark for the innocent young children to bear and some of the boys got into fights with those kids, while others like the young girls, just cried silently. Some of the kids were traumatised for a very long time. Alan kept away from such boys and was determined to prove to them that without a parent did not make him a lesser person. He knew he had no parents to turn to, but unfair remarks towards his friends and himself from the 'home' bonded them stronger to each other. Their high performance in the school both in the academics and extracurricular activities made heads turned and they not only gained respect but also were accepted as equals in school. Most of the students from the 'homes' put more effort in their studies as they knew they had to survive on their own or be left behind in this competitive world. Alan remembered what Datin used to tell them, "Education is the most powerful weapon which you can use to change people's perception of you."

Volunteers at the home played a major part by unselfishly helping the children at the 'home' in their studies in the evening. Those in the homes were more 'regimented' and 'disciplined' than those staying with their parents. The routine chores had to be done by them once they are of age. Chores like making their beds, washing their clothing, keeping the toilets clean, sweeping the floor were some of the chores every single child staying in the homes had to do. The disciplined lives they led in the foster home made them very resilient and competitive in school. Alan was very active in the school boy scouts' movement. He took up badminton early and before he reached 10 years old he was able to match his more senior schoolmates. He was selected to play for the school team at the age of 12. At the age of 13 he was accepted into one of the government boarding schools and that gave him added advantage to advance further in education besides boosting his exceptional skills in badminton. At 'O' level he was representing the state at national level. There were others who represented the state in soccer and hockey.

# CHAPTER 17

Obtaining a place in a boarding school did not keep him away from the foster home because he was always back helping Datin during the school holidays. Alan was awarded a place and scholarship in the local varsity due to his scholastic achievements, his sports prowess and a school prefect. He recollected an incident in the school when he was in level 7 he was told by the teachers that the school would be building a special laboratory for computers and Internet. He was so excited and so were the rest of his schoolmates. The building and the computers should be ready within a year. However, it took the contractor longer than that as the building collapsed on completion. It was fortunate that there were no students in the building when the roof and ceiling gave way during a heavy rain. The computers and components had to be replaced as many were badly damaged. A new contractor was invited to repair the building as the old contactor had been black listed. It was after another 2 years later that the project was completed and the students were able to use the facility. Alan said to Datin that the computer laboratory was such a great idea as it allowed the students to explore, with the guidance of their teachers, the intriguing world of computers. Students with initiative were able to surf around the world in search of knowledge. "I could surf any information overseas just by clicking the mouse of my computer. It was so thrilling to be part of this technology," said Alan to Datin. "However, there are many senior teachers who are still illiterate about computers. Some are willing to learn just like us," added Alan.

"Of course, computer is a new technology….even for people like Datuk and me, both in the business sector….we had to attend this short intensive course on how to operate the computers, we have to be competent in the soft skills and the complicated software. Fortunately we are English literates…..that helps and being computer literate, life can be so simple. All the information is in your laptop! The laptop would replace the 'brief case' soon, Alan. When you enter the university you will noticed that the Professors would be carrying laptops instead of briefcases. In the business world almost everybody would have laptops just like the cell phones today. Banking, paying income tax, renewing road tax and many more can all be done from your home. You can even purchase items from overseas through the internet," said Datin.

"Is it safe Datin?" asked Alan.

"I can't answer that as from what I see in the movies there are many unscrupulous hackers out there. Even in Malaysia millions have been siphoned out from companies and personal accounts. We used to get free monthly statements from the banks whereby we can check our balances and expenditures for the month. Today all that have stopped and the customers have to pay the banks to get the monthly statements.....that I do not understand until today. "Banks are getting smarter and want to charge the customers double every cent they have to spend," added Alan. "Exactly, without the consent of the customers they get the approval from Bank Negara and implement what is best to the banks not to the customers. They completely forget their social obligations to the customers....with the customers the banks are nothing, right?" said Datin. Alan just nodded in agreement. "I remember reading somewhere that cyber crime is on the rise internationally and it is said the Romania is the centre of this crime. The town of Ramnicue Valcea in Romania once a dead town now has transformed into a busy city and that country has become a dirty word in the world of online commerce!" explained Datin. "Really.....so everything is not plain sailing in the world of internet.....it can be very costly," added Alan. "I still prefer conventional banking, Alan.....it is the most secure system. You know what you are doing and you sleep well at night after every transaction. The Judiciary and lawyers too would refer the case laws using the laptops in the courts. They would develop software for the art directors, engineers, architects and probably doctors to help in their work. Fantastic isn't?" replied Datin.

"So...so...are you going to install Internet Wifi here Datin?" asked Alan cheekily.

"You are one smart elite, Alan.....I knew you are leading me down to this.....okay, I will install a few computers and Internet Wifi in our library for the common use. You, Alan as the eldest here are in charge.... anything goes wrong with these computers you will answer to me...okay?" asked Datin.

"I accept Datin....yes....I accept....hurray!" shouted Alan.

# CHAPTER 18

$\text{T}$he computers and Internet Wifi were installed within a few days in the small library of the foster home. It was of great help to the orphans who were computer savvy in doing their home work and improving their general knowledge. They were exposed to the world around them and were trained to think outside the box. Among them they discussed about the countries freely that they goggled and tell their friends as if they had been there before. There was a kind of friendly and healthy competition between them to be one or two steps ahead of their friends. Many of the orphans who benefitted from the computers installed at the foster home were successful in their lives and voluntarily came back to contribute financial assistance to the orphanage. They spend their free time on weekends to help the kids. Jimmy and Shah, his close friends, became successful corporate executives. Nantha and Jenny Cheah opened a law firm, while Ah Chong, now Dr. Albert Chong worked at the National Heart Centre as a surgeon. Norman who aspired to be a politician became the political secretary to one of the Ministers.

There were many success stories from the 'home' and Datuk and Datin now have a very big extended 'family' who helped to run the 'home'. They were very proud to be associated with the orphanage. Datuk and Datin never felt happier when the 'kids' came back to celebrate some festivals with the children at the foster home especially during Aide, Chinese New Year, Deepavali and Christmas' celebrations.. They brought along their spouses and their children to cheer up the kids at the 'home'. Many of the more effluent parents 'adopted' the children by sponsoring their education and paying for monthly expenses until they completed their education. A number of the children went for a few days to stay with their foster parents during the school holidays or went on organised day outings, picnics and visits with the other kids. They were motivated not to feel inferior but as equals with other kids in Malaysia, able to achieve what they dreamt for. Others had done it and they became role models to others in the 'home'.

However, there were a few who just did not appreciate the opportunities that came their way. Zaki, a very intelligent and bright child who rebelled to any form of discipline was one who could not forgive his parents for putting him in the 'home'. From young he was a problem child and grew up influencing others to go against the rules and regulations at the 'home'. In school he was aggressive and turned out to be a bully. Extorting money from the other younger kids and at times even threatening the teachers were some of his bad habits. He started smoking at a very young age in the school toilet. The school disciplined him with public caning but that only made him a 'hero' amongst the problem kids in school. At the 'home' he refused to do the chores and had to be daily closely monitored by the helpers. Datin was strict at the 'home' but found Zaki incorrigible. He was sacked from school at the age of 10 for bullying a year three student. Datin pleaded to the school to give him a second chance but it was turned down, as Zaki was not a first offender. His difficult childhood set him on the path of delinquency. That led to his downfall. The school could no longer tolerate his actions any longer as sufficient advice and warnings had been given to him. Datin had on numerous occasions advised him to change his ways and to stay out of trouble. Datin knew Zaki's aggressive attitude came from a broken home....both his parents abused and neglected him at a very tender age. He was homeless and a lost young soul at the age of 3 when his parents divorced and his young mother left him at the 'home'.

Poor innocent young Zaki grew up not trusting anybody in this world, including Datin. Growing up in the home 'alone' was tough and affected him psychologically. To many, he was a hopeless case. Datin did not give up hope but paid close attention to him hoping he changed his ways. He was not one to accept love readily and he never did from anyone. At the age of 15, he and another two kids disappeared from the 'home'. The matter was reported to the Police and Datin received news that they were involved in housebreaking, extortion and eventually became drug addicts. She felt so sad and disappointed when she received the reports from the Police about Zaki and the other kids because she had failed in helping them to be useful to society. She knew she had lost them forever. One morning while Datin was helping the others to clean the 'home', the security guard escorted a beggar to the doorstep. The security guard informed that the beggar wanted to meet Datin. Datin, who was busy helping her workers, came to the door and saw a man standing unsteadily at the doorstep. He had an unkempt long beard and moustache with dirty unruly hair. He wore a ragged torn T-shirt and trousers. Datin called one of her helpers to bring her purse to give him some money but he stopped her and said,

"Don't you recognise me Datin?"

Datin immediately stopped as the voice was familiar to her. However, this was the voice of a tired and sick person who needed help.

"I need your help.......Datin...," he suddenly collapsed.

Datin was shocked and taken aback and immediately asked some helpers to carry him up into the 'home'. One of the helpers quickly brought a glass of water. Zaki, who was conscious, grabbed the glass and quickly gulped it down. He had not had any food for the past 5 days, just tap water. Datin looked into his eyes for a long time and soon realised that the man in front of her was none other than the young boy who ran away from the 'home' many years ago..... Zaki. Overcame with joy she hugged Zaki who cried with happiness as he realised after what he had den Datin was still willing to accept him into her home. The 'prodigal' son had returned. The security guard and the helpers just watched in disbelief at what took place right in front of their eyes. When everything had calmed down Datin explained to those present that Zaki was once in this foster home but left the place on his own accord to look for greener grass. That was before their time.

# CHAPTER 19

Datin informed Datuk on the phone and led Zaki into her private office where they had a long private talk. Datuk, on hearing of Zaki's return rushed to the 'home' to meet him and was grateful to God that Zaki had found his way 'home'. Zaki related to them about his 'wayward' life after he ran away from the 'home'. He wanted the life of luxury, fun and not bogged down with rules and regulations. 'Work' was a dirty word to him as he never believed working an honest living to survive in this world. He wanted to get rich quick by robbing the wealthy and ATM machines. He was involved in drug trafficking, initially on a small scale. He sold to school kids and before long with the blessings of the Drug Kings he started to smuggle in drugs on a large scale. Thailand was his main supplier of opium, heroin and other drugs. He kept company with thugs and drug addicts and was soon trapped in the dark world and activities of lawlessness. The long arms of the law, however, caught up with him and he was thrown into the jail a number of times. As he was also a drug addict he was sent to the rehabilitation centre and fortunately he was among the few drug addicts who were able to kick that bad habit. He realised the folly of trying to rebel in life and that some house rules had to be obeyed to survive in this concrete world. He was jailed for one year for robbing a petrol kiosk. En. Zamani, appointed by the court, was his attorney as Zaki could not afford a lawyer. Zamani immediately recognised him and after the Judge sentenced Zaki to a one year jail term he advised Zaki to meet Datin after his release. On his release from the jail he wandered around and contemplated on what En. Zamani had advised him to do. He was ashamed to face Datin and Datuk after what he did to them. He had enough of going against establishment and wanted to make a fresh start……..he believed only Datin and Datuk can help him make that change. He did not know what happened to the other kids who ran away from the 'home' as he lost contact with them along the way. After hearing his story, Datin and Datuk left the room for a while to discuss privately regarding the future of Zaki. Both of them out of compassion decided to give Zaki a second chance to turn a new leaf.

# CHAPTER 20

Datin strongly felt he must have repented for his wrongdoing to have the courage to come back here. Datuk agreed with Datin but said that he must be closely monitored for at least for the first six months… "kind of probationary period," said Datuk. Datin said she could arrange for that. He, however, was sent to the hospital for a thorough check-up in case he suffered any ailment. Zaki was offered initially, a job as a worker in the 'home' and soon became a 'counsellor' to the problem kids. Alan, who also heard Zaki was back at the 'home', came over in the evening to give to Zaki some of his shirts, T-shirts and trousers. Alan, who knew Zaki well, had a long chat and stayed until late at night and promised to help Zaki to build a new life. Datuk also contributed some 'sarongs', shirts and money for him to start a new beginning. The next morning after having his hair trimmed by one of the helpers, shaved his moustache, beard and dressed in a clean pair of shirt and trousers, Zaki was a totally different man. Datin was impressed and so were those at the 'home'. Zaki kept to his words and became an exemplary worker at the 'home'. He was a very obliging and obedient worker and later Datuk agreed to employ him as a supervisor at Bibi Holdings.

When he was working here one of his 'old friends' from his 'dark past' came over seeking for his help. Zaki sought the help of Datin to give his friend a job at the home. Datin, initially, was sceptical about the idea but Zaki was persistent and promised he personally would be responsible to his friend. Datin agreed, in the hope that she could yet help another lost soul returned to the right path. His friend, Jamil, was employed as a worker at the 'home'. Zaki and his friend stayed at one of the huts at the 'home' and in the evening helped the foster kids with their homework and advised them to grow as productive young men and women in life.

Datin who had children much later in her marriage, had a son Aqiel and a daughter, Wawa, who were currently studying overseas. But that did not kill their enthusiasm to love other kids at the home.

# CHAPTER 21

During the boom of the construction industry, the company was awarded as subcontractor to Sime UEP and Selangor Development Corporation. That was the turning point in the history of the company. However, Datuk Khalid realised early that he couldn't sustain the company for long without diversifying into other local business and venturing overseas. He needed to diversify fast. Recession later dented his construction business badly. The construction industry came to a standstill. Business in the domestic scene looked gloomy and things turned complicated for contractors without any political affiliation. Datuk, though not highly educated, was a smart and shrewd businessman. He did not want to succeed through political patronage but through self-perseverance and good networking.

He idolised, Howard Hughes and Bill Gates, the billionaire businessmen in America for their business acumen. On the local front he admired Robert Kuok, the 'Sugar King', who had expanded his business world-wide. Datuk Khalid was an avid reader, reading books ranges from novels, classics to business magazines. He was a die-hard fan of renowned writers such as, Graham Greene, Ernest Hemingway, Sir Arthur Conan Doyle, Alistair Maclean, Sidney Sheldon, Jeffrey Archer and many others. Books by well-known economists like David Ricardo, Adam Smith, and John Maynard Keynes, who propagated Keynesian economics, ignited his business instinct. Magazines on new technology and business were also part of his readings. He spent much of his spare time in the office on the Internet browsing on latest development in the business world. He passed his time watching 'Discovery' and 'National Geographic' channels on the Astro when he was resting at home.

He had missed out to pursue his ambition to be an Engineer but he knew knowledge could be acquired in many other ways. He realised his company had to go global to survive and to pursue his dreams, he had to find alternative means to achieve it as he had no confidence to do it on his own. His brother, Mawi, with no exposure on international corporate affairs was of no help. Overseas business, though said to be very lucrative, was alien to both of them. He needed someone he could trust to take his company beyond the shores of Malaysia. When he discussed the problem with his wife, Datin Bibi, who sat as a Director in the company, she suggested Alan as her first choice to which Datuk agreed. Alan, an MBA graduate from London School of Economics, in his 30s had by then over 7 years of experience working abroad in a multinational company in Europe. He was the ideal candidate. Many multinational companies in Malaysia would love to have him in their team. He was very familiar with the 'corporate culture' in Europe and United States, and Bibi Sdn. Bhd. needed someone like him to venture and succeed overseas. Venturing overseas can be very costly without experienced staffs in your company. Datuk said to his wife,

"There are so many vultures out there ready to grab good money from unsuspected companies. I have seen so many companies in the red but the 'vultures' left the companies filthy rich."

# CHAPTER 22

$A$lan, at the meeting with Datuk in Brussels, said he agreed to come back to help the company but he needed to beef up the company with a few qualified people to be competitive. The company then had 6 permanent employees, mostly junior executives, when Alan joined the company with its turnover well over MR 1.3 million per annum. The employees were kind of 'Jack of all trades', as they had to do almost about anything.

Mawi, the Executive Director, was against the appointment of Alan in the company. He had never like Alan since he was at the 'home' and knew he could never accept Alan as his working colleague. He had the prejudice against Alan who came from the orphanage. To him, coming from the orphanage, made Alan a third class citizen. He did not like what he saw as Datuk paid too much extra attention to Alan. Mawi wanted a 'bumiputra' to run the company. He was from the old, obsolete, Malay school of thought and in short a racist. As a teacher he was active in politics, and aspired to be a political leader. However, he failed to get grassroots support, as he did not pay much attention to them….. but only to his bosses! Alan was not his choice. He had planned to employ a Malay friend as the Manager (Foreign Investment) when Datuk brought up the matter with him on his proposal to expand the company overseas. He told Mawi,

"Now it was timely for the company to open its door to outsiders, if we are to survive. You and I are not capable and able to sustain this company to a higher level in time to come. It is so competitive out there. We need help from outside, people who are qualified but most importantly, loyal and trustworthy. It crossed my mind that a person like Alan is most suitable…" Dato' was interrupted by Mawi, "Alan? That boy who was in our orphage before?" "Yes, Alan, that orphan that we brought up and who is now a very responsible corporate personality in Europe. Do you have any objection if I appoint him as an executive in this company?" answered Dato'. Mawi looked down and did not answer. After a few minutes, "Right…..before I was rudely interrupted……subject to if he agrees to come back. He, hopefully, can transform our floundering family company into a big corporation. If necessary, you and I may have to let go of the daily operations, hiring and strategic planning." He looked at Mawi.

Mawi was not in agreement but he kept his thoughts to himself. Datuk Khalid had planned to get the company public listed on the second board of Bursa Malaysia initially and later on the first Board if things business expanded as he envisioned. He needed to move fast as the business world changes every time the clock ticks. He had to come out with some projects to qualify the company to be listed as one of the prerequisites of Bursa Malaysia.

# CHAPTER 23

$A$lan was glad to be in Malaysia. He owned a condominium and two semi-detached two-storey houses he invested here with his earnings from Europe. He knew his home was in Malaysia and had never thought about migrating overseas. They rented out the semi-detached houses in Subang Jaya. He hoped his two sons would stay there when they come back to work in Malaysia later. These houses were good investments as the prices then was reasonable. He had no intention of joining any multinational companies as he believed in the principle of 'growing with the company', especially with a small operator. "You get that sense of belonging and loyalty to the company. The initial monetary reward was small but the experience was priceless," he told a friend.

He knew he was 'home' at last. During his 7 years in Europe he had identified a number of business Malaysian companies should explore. Oil and gas was one area where most companies were interested to invest. So when he joined Bibi Sdn. Bhd. he briefed Datuk Khalid about his business plan and vision. He had met up with many businessmen to explore the possibility of joint ventures both overseas and in Malaysia when he was working in Europe. A group promised to come down to Malaysia to discuss on a proposed USD 2.6 billion project with Alan as soon he was settled on his new job. He recruited Nasir, an MBA graduate from University Utara Malaysia, and Manjit Singh, an Economics graduate from University of Malaya to assist him in his quest to explore overseas market. His advice to them was,

"Always put your company's interests your number one priority when negotiating with your clients. Be a diplomat not a businessman when you reject ideas".

Mawi had felt insecure and threatened when Alan joined the company. Mawi had five children, two boys and three girls. The eldest, Anwar, was sitting for his final examinations in Political Science at the local university and he intended to join the Malaysian Diplomatic Service, if given the opportunity. Nina, second in the family, was working in a 5-star hotel, and Nadia was studying medicine in Ireland. The rest were in the secondary schools in Kuala Lumpur.

Back at home that night Alan had no choice but to prepare his letter of resignation. His wife, Judy Pandian, of Indian descent, image of Keira Knightly, the leading actress in the 'Pirates of the Caribbean', whom he met during his student days, came back at about 6.30 pm. She found the room was dark and the CD was on. She switched on the lights and saw Alan lying on the sofa looking listless. She merrily chatted about her office colleagues' antics at work and suddenly realised Alan was extra quiet this time around. She came over to him and asked,

"What is wrong, honey?" Alan was in a dazed and said, "I had a bad day at the office...I...I have been asked to quit!"

She was shocked. She knew he had never been happier since joining the company though he never mentioned of his problems with Mawi. She immediately went to sit beside him on the sofa, trying to console him. She put her arms around him and held his head close to her chest. He was on the verge of sobbing, not able to control his emotions anymore.

# CHAPTER 24

"What happened, darling, talk to me please.... talk to me," she said softly, concerned. "My assistants.....They sabotaged me. There was this presentation..... this morning, that I told you earlier, it was a complete disaster. My assistants...... did not prepare the project paper as I requested. Lots of vital information was..... missing. I was not able to convince my clients to accept the proposal. They walked out.....walked out of the Boardroom before I could complete my presentation! I threw that contract of more than USD 2.6 billion just like that." Judy was silent, not knowing what to say to her husband. "It was my mistake.....my mistake for being too trusting to my assistants. My two assistants deliberately delayed the project paper. Those papers should have been on my table a week before the presentation for our final internal discussions first. I needed to brief the Chairman and Mawi for their approval. But the papers were handed to me a few minutes before the presentation with all sorts of excuses. I can do my presentation off the cuff to our clients but I needed the important data that were deleted by my assistants. I did not realise it was a conspiracy against me. Mawi, you know him well, my Executive Director, wanted my resignation letter immediately." "What then, honey? I mean....... What are you going to do?" she asked. "What can I do? I messed up the 2 billion dollar deal...I have prepared my resignation letter to meet the Chairman, Datuk Khalid, tomorrow, before I leave."

Kissing his wife on the cheek he went into his bedroom took a cool shower and rested on the bed before joining his wife for dinner. It was a quiet dinner, though his son, Sonny, kept on rambling about how he scored two goals for his team.

"The first goal was a free kick, dad....I scored just like Ronaldo, it was incredible, right at the top corner of the goal post. The goalkeeper was caught on the wrong foot as he stood there shaking his head. He was completely confused, dad! The second goal was brilliant! It was a header from a corner kick. My friends said I executed it just like Zinedine Zidan, you know, dad, the famous former Real Madrid striker. My close friend, Chin Aun dribbles the ball like Figo. Mokhtar, who plays in the centre half is just a superb player. He plays like Eric Cantona, dad!"

He kept on endlessly talk about his soccer game and Alan could only nod his head in appreciation but Judy kept the mood of his son going. She said and hoped that one day Sonny would become a professional player.

"Yes, mum...that's my dream, not in Malaysian football anyway, but in England or Europe, hopefully. I want to retire as a millionaire mum!"

They all had a good laugh, and Alan quipped,

"Then I do not have to pay for your PS station games in future, Sonny!"

Sonny smiled with satisfaction and excused himself to do his homework. Alan said to Judy that he hoped Sonny achieved his dream to be a professional soccer player in England. After dinner Alan helped his wife to clear the table and washed the plates before retiring early to bed to try to relax his tired mind. Alone in the dark Alan could not sleep. He had difficulties closing his eyes, not because of the sound from the TV room but the recurring nightmare of seeing Mawi each time he closed his eyes. He appeared in his sleep accusing him of sabotaging the company,

"You are incompetence, you have sabotage the company. I want your resignation letter.....Right now!"

# CHAPTER 25

$H$is wife knew her husband wanted to be left alone, so she tried to watch some movies on the Astro while Sonny slipped into his bedroom to do his homework before retiring to bed. However, Sonny came out of his room and asked his mother, "What's wrong with dad tonight mum? He is not his usual self." "I thought you did not notice, but its good you keep it to yourself until now. He is having some problem at the office, I suppose. There's nothing to worry about," replied Judy.

'Okay' said Sonny, "I know, dad knows how to fix anything.... goodnight mum!"

She was unable to concentrate on the movies, as she could not bear to see Alan in a trouble state of mind. He was always a happy person ever since she knew him. Her mind kept flashing back to their happy days working overseas. There was no tension or pressure, though there was responsibility and accountability to their bosses. She was very worried for Alan, as he had hoped to work and grow up with the company and repay Datuk Khalid for what he had done for Alan. She got bored after a while for she never did like to watch the TV alone. When she turned in at 10.33 pm her husband was already asleep like a baby – looking very exhausted and restless.

He got up early and went jogging around the lake in front of his house. His son left for school on the school bus. He was back by 7.30 am, had a quick bath and took breakfast with his wife. His wife hugged him before he left and wished him lucked.

"I need that, I love you", he said.

Always an early bird he was in his office by 8.00 am though the office operated from 9.00 am. He checked his computer to extract some important data for his discussions with his foreign clients later whom he had contacted in the evening before he left for home. The foreign clients reluctantly agreed to his request to meet them at the hotel the next day. The meeting was scheduled at 12.00 noon at the P.J.Hilton. He needed to clarify the situation. The clients agreed for the discussion as they knew Alan personally and had established a good working relationship when he was overseas. At 9.30 am the Chairman's secretary informed Alan that the Chairman was in. He plucked up his courage and went to the Chairman's office. The secretary told him that the Executive Director just entered the room. He sat in the waiting room anxiously, browsing through the morning papers. After half an hour the Executive Director came out and saw Alan....glared at him, murmured something to the secretary, and soon left the room.

# CHAPTER 26

Alan stepped into the Chairman's room and saw the old man looking out of the window, deep in his own thought.

"Good morning Datuk."

"Morning, take a sit", said the old man, who was still standing, staring blankly out the window.

He was always polite and a gentleman. His room overlooked a beautiful view, on the left was the jogging track lined up with assortment of trees and on the right the man-made serene, blue lake. The old man always reminded Alan,

"Your mind must be like the mirror, it must always be clear and clean. Then you make good decisions."

The Chairman took his seat and looked at Alan. He looked tired and sad.

"I do not know what to say, Alan. Anyway, what really happened in the Boardroom yesterday? Mawi told me his version but I need to listen to yours before I make a decision. I know Mawi's dislike for you started way back from when you were in the orphanage. I cannot believe you want to sabotage the company….me…no, not you. Now tell me truthfully what made our clients walked out of the Boardroom."

"Thank you Datuk for giving me the opportunity to see you before I leave. The Executive Director told me yesterday to tender my resignation because of the aborted deal with our clients."

"I know," Datuk replied.

Alan continued, "I would like to clear my name before I leave as I felt there is a conspiracy to get me out of the company."

"What do you mean?" the Datuk was shocked.

"I am not able to divulge any names right now but I am certain our own staffs are involved. However, I have contacted our clients yesterday and they agreed to see me at about 12.00 noon at the hotel with your permission. Allow me to meet them as I hope I can rectify the situation, Datuk. I want to leave the company with the USD 2.6 billion contract sealed with Bibi Sdn. Bhd. En. Mawi had requested for my resignation, here is my letter, Datuk."

He gave the letter, which the Datuk put into his drawer without even looking at it.

"By the way James apologised to you for not dropping to see you after the meeting yesterday and was wondering whether you would like to join the meeting?" said Alan.

"I understand, Alan, but I suggest you try to resolve the matter…you know him well," replied Datuk.

"I will keep you posted after my meeting with the clients and later inform you in detail why the meeting was aborted, Datuk. I have to leave now to meet the clients."

"Is Mawi joining you for the meeting?" asked Datuk.

"No, Datuk, Mr. James specifically told me to come alone or with you."

"Do whatever you need to do. Good luck and I pray for your success," he said.

Alan knew the old man meant well.

He left the room leaving the old man who was like a father to him, a father, whom he never knew. Datuk Khalid who sat as Chairman at the orphanage and the other Directors sponsored the orphans' education, and Alan was his favourite 'son'. Alan, a bright student, completed his first degree locally and his MBA overseas. Datuk Khalid encouraged him to gain working experience overseas and hinted to him to come back to work in Malaysia some day, during a dinner in Copenhagen. Alan was happy working overseas not so much because of the monetary rewards but the business exposure he gained there. His wife, Judy, a financial analyst, too had a good job with one of the local banks. It was only after 7 years serving overseas that he and his wife decided to come home. Alan felt obliged to repay the old man for what he is today.

# CHAPTER 27

$A$lan arrived at the P.J.Hilton at 10.45 am. He gave a call to Mr. James, who was in his room, and was told to wait downstairs. While waiting at the lobby he saw his Executive Director came to the lobby and immediately strides across the lounge with a red face. He came straight to Alan. "Why are you here?" Mawi confronted Alan. "To meet with Mr. James", Alan replied. "You better leave now. I am trying to have a meeting with him before he leaves. Do not hassle my clients anymore!" said Mawi.

"I have an appointment with Mr. James and his team at 11.00 am", said Alan.

"He is no more your client and you are no more an employee of Bibi Sdn. Bhd.! I am trying to meet with my clients and secure the deal," retorted Mawi.

Alan said, "Datuk Khalid gave his permission to proceed with this meeting and….".

Before he could explain further Mawi blew his top, and shouted at the top of his voice,

"You idiot….. Can you understand English? Leave before you do more damage to us!"

Everybody in the lobby turned around and froze…anticipating Mawi's next move. The lobby, which was buzzing with laughter and greetings between clients, was completely silent except for the pipe music rendering an instrumental hit of 'Heart Break Hotel'. The Manager of the Hotel, who was at the lobby, whispered to his Security personnel to move in quickly to try cool the situation. The Hotel Manager was concerned as the reputation of the hotel was at stake. He did not want to lose his regular clients and the hotel branded as 'The Wild, Wild West!'. Mawi was insistence and kept on shouting at Alan. The Security personnel decided to withdraw when Mawi stared at him. From past experience the Hotel Manager decided it was best to persuade Alan to leave the lobby and go to his private office rather than talk to the aggressor. Mawi was not about to cool down from the look of it. The Security personnel will only use reasonable force if Mawi turned violent. Alan, by then, was about to lose his patience. He stood up and took a few paces towards Mawi with his fists clenched. The Hotel Manager was about to intervene when suddenly Mr. James and his team appeared. He walked briskly passed by Mawi without acknowledging him and greeted Alan.

It seemed Mr. James had been watching the 'drama' at the back of the crowd for quite a while and decided to intervene before things turned nasty. He completely ignored Mawi. Mawi was stunned and furious. He had been snub by Mr. James in front of the other businessmen in the lobby. Mr. James quickly pulled Alan into the coffee lounge leaving Mawi in a very foul mood. He stood there all by himself uncertain of what to do next while the crowd in the lobby was watching him. At long last, red in the face, he kicked a porter's chair near the entrance and stormed out of the hotel. He shouted at the top of his voice calling for his driver to pick him at the entrance. He created a scene unbecoming of a corporate figure in public.

Someone in the lobby remarked, "Typical show of arrogance by an idiotic corporate figure!" Everybody laughed.

# CHAPTER 28

$A$lan had a long discussion with Mr. James and his team before they adjourned for lunch. Alan apologised to James about the way the whole presentation was conducted by him.

"That was not you, Alan. I know for sure that something was amiss. I have known you for more than 7 years as a working colleague, and you have never failed to impress me with your presentations…..you are so talented and not only such an excellent corporate man but a very good salesperson! We came to Malaysia because I have full confidence you are the man for this joint venture, without you it will not succeed. That's the reason I have decided to give you a second opportunity to convince me that we should jointly go ahead with this project" he said.

"Actually, James, the project papers were not ready when you came due to our, well…....that's our internal problem," replied Alan. "Anyway, thank you for giving me a second chance to make another presentation to your team today. I am glad you are all impress with the new figures I presented and those were the real figures…..not fictitious, James," Alan quipped. James and his team looked very relieved and they all were so glad that they had given Alan a second chance!"

By the way your Datuk gave me a call after you left his room and he thanked me for giving you time for this meeting. I like your Datuk, very intelligent and sharp in his line of thinking. He is quick, fast and very decisive…I like those attributes…..very good for business deals!" said James. "He did that? That was a very awesome gesture of Datuk. You know James……when a boss is slow, they say he is very meticulous, but when his subordinate is slow they say….. he is lousy!" added Alan.

"But Datuk is fast and sharp…that makes him a genius!" interjected James.

They all laughed over it. Alan paid for the lunch telling James,

"This is my territory…..here I pay for everything, including your hotel bills okay? The hotel account's department does not accept your Euro, they only accept Malaysian ringgit," Alan jokingly told James.

"Thank you, Alan, my best regards to Datuk." Before they parted Alan promised to meet them in Amsterdam in two weeks' time to finalised the project.

Mawi, back at the office, stormed through the office of Datuk Khalid. He was about to relate the whole incident at the hotel when the Datuk said,

"Shouldn't you knock before you enter anybody's room?" remarked Datuk. Mawi looked stunned as Datuk had never been so crossed with him. "Anyway what is it that you want?" asked Datuk. "This is about Alan…..I have told him to resign for making a very big blunder this morning in front of James and his team! I met him at the PJ Hilton today during lunch hour making a fool of himself," Mawi explained. "I met Alan before he left for PJ Hilton…..he was there with my blessings. James phoned me about your stupid behaviour at the lobby…..it was not Alan. You should be ashamed of yourself for creating such a scene out there. That was bad for the corporate image of our company. For your information the deal for the USD 2.6 billion has been sealed by Alan. Now leave my room before I decide on something drastic. I have many urgent matters to attend to."

# CHAPTER 29

Mawi left the room feeling dejected and humiliated as his brother was not supportive of his actions. He sat at his sofa thinking how best to inflict revenge on Alan. He called Nasir through the intercom but he was then out of his room. Nasir was nowhere to be found as he had gone out for lunch break. At 2.15 pm Nasir walked into Mawi's room. "You did well yesterday, Nasir. Alan will soon resign and I am recommending you to the Chairman as the new Manager, Foreign Investment. Alan must go as he is very incompetent." Nasir said, "Thank you En. Mawi, but I am not ready to shoulder that responsibility yet. Further, what I did was wrong and........."

"Shut up!" retorted Mawi. "This is the problem with Malays. You get an opportunity but you are scared to grab it. Other races are clamouring for such posts. There was nothing wrong with what you did. It was for the good of the company. We do not need him. Power struggles between top executives are common features in all companies. It is a global phenomenon. We do not want non-Malays to manage this company...we have our pride and dignity."

Nasir could no longer control himself and spontaneously responded,

"What is wrong with other races working together with us. They are Malaysians. We should stop looking at others as Chinese, Indians or whatever. They are our friends, humans. They can contribute to our progress. We do this to other races; they do this to us. Everybody loses. Everywhere in the public and private sectors I hear about social integration but ironically nobody practised it….that includes you! The so-called experts blamed others, the policy makers blamed the public…..the society is confused because after 57 years we are still talking about social integration. The unrest and mistrust could end today if we treat all Malaysians fairly and just. 'Special privileges' and National Economic Policies for the Malays are the two main issues. Delete these 2 items in the government's agenda, then, all our problems are solved. Deserving Malaysians should be given the chance to enter universities with scholarships, jobs and promotions in the public and private sectors. We want to go places globally, together, and we need all the good brains to do that."

"Ah…. You are too naïve to understand all these……too young.……you do not understand nationalism. This is our country, we fought hard to gain independence, so we must be the leaders not only in the public but private sectors! Anyway, what do you say to my recommendation?"

"No offence, En. Mawi.….but what I understand from the history textbooks all races were jointly involved in the fight for independence….not just one race or one political party. The fight for independence started way back during the early days before we even know about politics. It started way back during the time of the Malacca Sultanate, before the time of 'Mat Kilau', the killing of J.W.W. Birch in Perak by a Malay warrior, Maharaja Lela and the exiled of Sultan Abdullah who was implicated in the murder depicted the early rise of nationalism in Malaya. Others races that migrated to the Malay Peninsula then also played their roles in supporting the Malays to fight against the 'foreigners'. Anyway, our forefathers fought hard for independence not you or me. We are just trying to take a free ride on the effort of others. You can s***f your offer up your a***," replied Nasir, who was contemplating of resigning rather than accepting the offer.

"I will not wait too long as Manjit is just waiting for the offer….he will be your boss!" said Mawi.

"Good luck to him for a having you as a boss!" replied Nasir.

# CHAPTER 30

Nasir went back to his room regretting what he had done to Alan but felt most satisfied he had summoned enough courage to face Mawi. He knew what he did was rude and cruel to his immediate boss. He had no choice but to follow orders from his Executive Director. He was told to delay the project paper and submitted erroneous figures so as to ensure the proposal failed. Nasir decided to make amend for his wrong doings, even though he had to resign. He was undecided whether to meet Alan or Datuk Khalid. It was a tough decision as it would be his words against Executive Director and also the brother of the Chairman. He knew he had to do it to put things right.

Alan came back from his meeting with Mr. James and went straight to meet Datuk Khalid. He briefed Datuk Khalid that Mr. James had agreed to the proposal. Datuk Khalid was very happy with the outcome and told Alan that he had rejected his resignation letter. He wanted Alan to stay focus on the job and not to allow internal office politics to cloud his mind. Alan immediately went back to his office and convened a meeting with Nasir, Wong and Manjit. He briefly mentioned the blunder he created at the meeting with the foreign clients and that the company was given a second chance to make a presentation in two weeks time. Whatever that needed to be done were in the computer. "Extract and compile the data systematically and give me your full co-operation...the USD 2.6 billion project must go ahead!" He did not even mention about being 'sabotaged' by someone in the office. After the meeting Nasir requested for a private meeting with Alan. "What do you have in mind, Nasir? We are running short of time now. It is best we focus on getting the project papers done."

"Mr. Alan.….I would like to apologise to you about the project papers that were handed to you yesterday. Manjit, Wong and I did a thorough check on the papers two weeks before the meeting. On the day I was to hand over the papers to you En. Mawi called me to his room and requested to check the papers. He instructed me to delete some major portions of the papers, especially on the data. He told me to randomly change the figures to make you look ridiculous at the meeting.…. which did happen, I understand. I am sorry...I should not have done it and I have decided to tender my resignation first thing tomorrow morning".

"You don't have to do that. You are a very competent officer and I need your assistance now. Anyway, you were only following orders from the Executive Director. Everything is back in place again. We do not need to take the matter up with the Chairman. I think he knows what is happening. I am not going to have a stand-off with En. Mawi, it would be just a waste of my time. There is no need for that. As a Christian I believe God is always there to protect us from evil. I know you as a Muslim believed in Allah who will protect you all the time. Just do your job but report to me directly if you face any problem".

Nasir left the room a very relieved person with a clear conscience at last.

# CHAPTER 31

The first thing the next morning Mawi marched into Alan's room when he heard Alan was back in the office. "Why are you still hanging around here. You have no authority to be in this building. Leave now or I will call the Security guard to escort you out of the building."

"You do that and I will make an official report to the Chairman. Go ahead…..Please! Why are you doing this? Check with the Chairman first before you come in barging into my room. Have some courtesy to knock before you enter my room the next time! Don't make yourself look silly in front of all the employees. Now please get out before I call the Security!" said Alan. Though he had a lot of respect for Mawi, Alan lost his temper as Mawi had overstepped his jurisdiction.

He looked around and saw many of the employees were watching him from outside the glass room. He hesitated, glared at them and soon left.

Alan was so upset by the persistent harassment by the Executive Director but he had one major task to do for the company…..to see the USD 2.6 billion contract becomes a reality. Mawi was nonexistent right now as far as he was concerned. Within 3 days the amended project papers were ready and Alan together with Najib, Wong and Manjit were deeply engrossed in discussing the paper. Alan confirmed the meeting with Mr. James within a week to be held in Amsterdam as agreed. The Chairman requested Alan and Nasir to represent the company and finalised the matter. Mawi was instructed by the Chairman to attend to some other matters in Singapore with Manjit. It was actually a diversion so that Mawi was kept out of the meeting. Datuk Khalid had earlier received e-mail from Mr. James that he would not agree to proceed with the discussion in the presence of Mawi. Datuk Khalid agreed to the request in the interest of the company.

While in Europe, Alan e-mailed to the Chairman that all was well and that Bibi Sdn. Bhd. was officially awarded the USD 2.6 billion project. Back at the office a few days later he went directly to Datuk's room to brief him on the presentation. Datuk was very pleased with Alan's effort in securing the contract and decided to give some incentive for his magnificent effort. At the management meeting the next day the Chairman announced that Alan was directly involved to oversee the project and to report to him directly. Alan was promoted as Executive Director for Foreign Investment and Nasir appointed as the new Manager for Foreign Investment.

The move by the Chairman was seen as a way out to avoid unnecessary confrontation between Mawi and Alan that can have adverse effect on the growth of the company. Mawi was kept out of all overseas investments. Mawi was fuming with disgust but there was nothing much he could do now. Alan was now beyond his control and he had to accept that fact. Nasir had to spend more time in Europe to oversee the new project. At lunch with the Datuk one day, Alan decided to explain what transpired during the first presentation to their clients, Mr. James and his team.

"You don't have to explain anything, Alan. Nasir, before leaving for Europe with you, came over to my room and explained everything to me. I knew Mawi did not agree with us to take you in…..but I did not think he would go to that extend to sabotage you and at the expense of the company. He would be sacked immediately if he was in any other company but here…..I just did not have the heart to do that……yet. However, I promised this will not happened again and the next wrong move he makes, intentionally…...he will have to go. I am glad the overseas project has now materialised. That gave me the opportunity to make you my Executive Director for Foreign Investment, whereby you report to me only. I want teamwork in the company and I do not want my staffs to waste their energy on internal bickering."

"You know I initially wanted Mawi out, but blood is thicker than water, they say. He has an inferiority complex with well-qualified staffs joining the company and his biggest problem is….a kind of phobia, that scary feeling of not being adequate academically. He thought he would be displaced when you joined us. However, if he caused any financial loss to the company I have no choice but to ask him to go. I will ask him to retire when he reaches 55 soon."

"Thank you, Datuk. I have never had any intention to take over his post. I am very grateful and happy to be part of your team, Datuk. You know when I was overseas, Judy and I always discuss when I could come back to serve you. In fact Judy wanted to join your company but I told her not to……..as I felt it was not a very healthy kind of arrangement. Anyway, now that I am here, you can always count on me."

"Thank you...you don't have to pledge your loyalty. I have known you since you were a baby, Alan, remember that." They both smiled and continued with their lunch.

# CHAPTER 32

$A$fter lunch Datuk cautioned Alan about doing business with the public and private sectors. "Always be wary that in doing business never trust anybody. Whatever projects you intend to pursue keep all the information close to your chest. Never, never give out your detailed feasibility studies to any party.... just give them the outline. I had a very bad experience with a certain agency on my matter. I was naive then, so when they requested for the feasibility study on the proposed project, I gave them whole, stock and barrel. They said they needed to study thoroughly the proposal first before they can consider approving it. After 6 months they replied that the project was not feasible and thus rejected. On appeal they tried to convince us that the project would not be feasible and rather costly to the commuters. We knew the project was good for the community and that the agency had their own agenda. Do you know what the project was about, Alan?" asked Datuk.

"No Datuk," replied Alan.

"It was a shuttle mini bus services linking the many housing estates with the township and the LRT station travelling within the 6-10 miles radius only. It would work out well within the new townships like Subang Jaya, Shah Alam and any other satellite towns. It would considerably reduce the number of cars in town as many would go for this reliable transport system. It was an idea that I saw from my visits especially to the city of London, Paris, New York and Haadyai. London with its reliable Underground and bus services, Paris Metro is unique, New York with its famous subway and Haadyai with its cheap and simple 'tut-tut' transport system. Commuters prefer public transport....it was faster and definitely cost savings. But my proposal was on a much smaller scale to save time to our commuters, especially the housewives. Especially with so many cases of snatch thieves! The housewives need not walk for about 1 or 2 miles to the main road to wait for the buses at the bus stops to go shopping in town. A lot of time is wasted waiting at the bus stops for the buses. The proposed transport project would tremendously reduced the total shopping time for the housewives as the shuttle buses would come into the housing projects right in front of their front gates and stopped at the various strategic points in town. The buses then picked and dropped them right back again at their front gates eliminating security risks and greatly helping the young, old and handicaps," replied Datuk.

"Amazing, how in the name of heaven did they not approve that transport project?" Alan was puzzled.

"Yes.......it is not because the project was not viable but because that project makes sense and definitely profitable. So, many parties were interested after the study was tabled to the committee. I was not surprised as I was earlier warned by one of my friends about my proposal being 'hijacked' but being young and innocent.....and I thought I had powerful friends to help me see the project through. Yes, the committee rejected my proposal. However, after almost 2 years the same project with certain modifications was approved to another party.......and it turned out that one of the board members of that company was my trusted friend!" said Datuk. "Some Directors ride on the ideas of their colleagues and in no time sabotage that company when they see greener pastures!" Alan said. "A business friend told me that about 20 proposals were rejected by the government but implemented by new companies after making a few minor changes! That is what scares most companies to send in proposals to the government," added Datuk.

"It was sad as others benefitted from our ideas and efforts......the study costs money to us as we had to engage a consultant to conduct a thorough study," Datuk lamented.

"I am not surprised Datuk. I have heard about this from my colleagues before but coming from you without doubt confirmed my suspicions," said Alan.

# CHAPTER 33

Upon his return from Europe after sealing the USD 2.6 billion project, Alan took his wife to a posh hotel for a private dinner. Sonny, his son was away camping with friends. He kept his success and promotion a secret from his wife. He gave his wife a red rose and ordered champagne for the dinner. Alan ordered 'Singapore Sling' cocktail drink and Judy preferred the champagne. They ordered prawn cocktails and salad as starters. She then ordered the classic 'bisque' soup while he opted for the French soup 'bouillabaisse'. For the main dish he chose the classic Italian dish of cold poached veal with a caper, tuna fish and anchovy sauce known as 'vitello tonnato'. She ordered the delightful 'paella', a Spanish dish of rice, shellfish, chicken and vegetables flavoured with saffron. They could never understand which wine to go with the main dish. As they understood different dish should go with different wine, but after more than 7 years in Europe they have yet to appreciate it. Normally they left it to the chief waiter to recommend to them and not all chief waiters are really competent to do just that. However, red wine, such as Pinot Noir, Grenache and Tempranillo were all versatile they were told and went well with most dishes. A special French dessert known as 'Peach Melba' (a dish named after the celebrated Australian soprano, Dame Nellie Melba) for both of them was a perfect finale to the romantic dinner. They liked to savour foreign dishes when they were working abroad and it had been quite a while they could afford to indulge in such cuisine. Throughout the dinner they reminisced about their student days and 7 years of sheer bliss when both were working in Europe. They remembered the wonderful times they spend together at the theatre watching musical shows like the ground-breaking American musical 'Hair', 'My Fair Lady', 'West Side Story', 'Madam Butterfly', and many others. They missed all these musical shows when they came back to Malaysia. Alan said there had been some attempts by local producers to stage musical shows recently. One show that was said to be quite successful staged at the 'Istana Budaya', the local opera house, was the musical 'Puteri Gunung Ledang' and 'Broken Bridges'. They missed both the musicals and hoped to see the next time around.

They were able to spend quality time with their kids in spite of their tight schedules.

"It was sad to have to leave them in England to complete their studies," Judy used to say to Alan.

They both knew it was the best option for the kids.

"Darling, thank you so much for your undivided love and for this exclusive dinner tonight, but I think you are up to something naughty....this not my birthday.... Not our anniversary.... So what are you up too.... Tell me... love. I am anxious.... I am waiting...." said Judy and she gave him a kiss.

"I just don't know how to tell you this. This is really a very special occasion for both of us, darling. This was what I had dreamt about before we came back to settle here. For the first time since we came back here I am a very happy man. Okay.... firstly, we managed to seal the USD 2.6 billion deal with Mr. James, thanks to Datuk Khalid for the confidence he had in me. The project is starting next month. Secondly, I was promoted as the Executive Director to oversee all foreign investments. This means I report directly to the Chairman only. That makes my job much easier to handle.....and...."

"And...what else dear?" asked Judy."

"The company has decided to provide me with a company car, E240 Mercedes Benz, a chauffeur and other perks!" replied Alan.

"Wow....that's great news, darling. I am so happy for you. I knew you could do it!" Judy jumped with joy.

"It has been quite a while that I could afford to give you a present, so I bought this necklace, 'murah saja' (very cheap) when I was in Paris." Alan put on the necklace around his wife's neck and gave her a kiss.

The other patrons, without their knowledge, were watching the whole episode between the loving couple, gave them a round of applause. Both Alan and Judy were slightly embarrassed but graciously managed to show gestures of appreciation to them.

# CHAPTER 34

The 'Maasinhon Trio', the singing sensation from the Philippines, that had been entertaining the diners in the restaurant came over to their table and rendered the beautiful song from the movie Blue Hawaii, 'Can't Help Falling In Love', which was incidentally, Judy's favourite song. "Wise men say…only fools rush in….but I can't help falling in love with you…" Alan took her hand and guided her to dance near the table and the other patrons overcame with excitement also took to the floor. The management was so happy with the sudden emotional change in the mood of the patrons, urging the F&B Manager to quickly clear some of the dining tables to allow the patrons more room to dance.

Many couples got sentimental and decided to join the excitement by dancing to the melodies sang by the trio, old melodies such as 'Love Story', 'Feelings', 'I Just Call To Say I Love You', 'Killing Me Softly With His Song'. The tunes kept all the loving couples glued to each other on the dance floor. The lights were dimmed and the dining room was temporarily turned into a ballroom. This was good for the hotel's business as diners wanted something different for a change. Most of the couples danced late through the night and so did Alan and Judy. It was a night they will never forget. The Hotel Manager came over to their table and thanked them for making it such a memorable night for the patrons and the staff's hotel. The Manager whispered to Alan, "Food and beverages is on the house for you two tonight….thank you." "Thank you," replied Alan and Judy…. "We will be back, soon!" they smiled. The Manager accompanied them to the porch and the diners who left with them gave a rousing applause.

"That was great," said Judy. "We never planned it that way," Alan whispered to the Manager.

On the way home in the car, Alan and Judy were on the top of the world. They were in a very romantic mood. Judy sat close to him all the way home. They could not just wait to get home. The half an hour's journey was like forever. They did not say much and Judy kept on snuggling her head on Alan's shoulder.

On the way home Alan recollected how he first met Judy in London, England. He was pursuing his Masters and Judy was in her first year at the same University. He had noticed her when she joined the varsity but initially had no interest to get to know her better because "she was a snob," as most of his friends said to him. In her first year at the varsity she just ignored the male Malaysian students and moved around with the 'Mat Sallehs'. Alan found her attitude irritating, but there is something inside him that made him very curious about her, urging him to get to know her better. Alan mixed well with students of various races, as he felt comfortable in their company. Besides being elected as the President for the Varsity Students Union for two years he was the varsity local hero for being the top badminton player amongst the graduates in England. It was during these two years that Judy took notice of this young Malaysian who commanded respect from all the other students.

One Monday morning in between the lectures they literally 'bumped' into each other. Alan was in a hurry to go to his next lecture and Judy suddenly walked into his path without looking in front. The books in their hands tumbled all over the floor. Alan quickly apologised, scooped his books and left Judy looking stunt by that incident. Slowly she picked up her lecture notes and some books and noticed that Alan had accidentally taken one of her books. She tried to get his attention but he was gone before she could call him. The next day, while enjoying the afternoon sun with some of her friends on the grass near the main building, she saw Alan walking across the main building towards her. She pretended not to notice him and kept on talking with her friends. However, she could not but help admiring the way he walked and smiled. He came right in front of her and said,

"May I sit down ladies?" He knew most of the young undergraduates.

Her friends were overjoyed to meet personally the President of the Students' Union. They knew Judy was very interested in this charismatic young leader..... she had said to them she did not like Alan and to the girls it was a sign of 'secret admiration'. They eagerly welcomed him to sit down. Judy was dumfounded... she suddenly felt dizzy and confused!

"How are you ladies keeping up with your studies? I hope you keep focussing until you graduate in a few years time. Always remember we are the young ambassadors of our country so make our country proud for once. Anyway, actually, I did not come to lecture but to see this sweet lady......to apologise for bumping into her yesterday and return this book which I believed belongs to her……..Judy…...right?" Alan said looking at the name in the book. He was looking right into her eyes without blinking. Judy just did not know what to say or do and the giggling and teasing from her friends made it worse. Judy quickly grabbed the book, stood up and ran back to her dormitory. Her friends were laughing and one of them said,

"It looks like someone is madly in love with somebody!" Alan sat there perplexed.

# CHAPTER 35

He too did not know how to react. The next day he saw Judy sitting alone in the varsity cafeteria. She was having a quick lunch. Alan decided to join her. "Is this seat taken, Judy?" Alan asked. "No," replied Judy, "anyway, I have finished my lunch," she wanted to get up but Alan stopped her.

"Please stay….I just want to say sorry to you for my intrusion and I had no intention to interrupt your study group yesterday….so sorry. I did not mean to be rude, but I just wanted to give back your book which I accidentally took after that collision…….remember?"

She sat down again and said,

"I am so sorry too…......for behaving like a 7 year old kid yesterday. You must have felt so insulted with my childish behaviour."

"Not really, only I was puzzled why you reacted that way. I would like to know you better, Judy. From the first day you came to the campus I was very interested…...to know you…...and help young Malaysians away from home to adjust early in a foreign country. But I noticed you kept away from the company of Malaysian or Asian students but as President of the Students' Union I feel it's just not right. We, as students should get to know everybody in the campus…….it helps to do that. We are all away from home and having a friendly Malaysian here to talk to is very comforting. You never know when you need their help. Once we are home we have to work with other Malaysians when pursuing our careers. Have you had any bad experience with Malaysians before, Judy?"

"Not me but my dad, Alan. He was from a very poor family and joined the government service upon completion of his 'O' level. He was a court interpreter and very proficient in his work. He wanted to be a qualified legal officer….a Magistrate and later a Judge as he loved the job. He proceeded to do an external degree on his own time and money. However, due to financial problems as he wanted his children to be successful in life, he had to forgo his final year. He requested for a scholarship from the government but it was turned down. Many of his juniors were offered scholarship and quite a few failed to qualify," Judy said.

"From that point he was a very disappointed man, dejected and frustrated with the system. He urged us to study hard and not hoped for any government's assistance, as we have to survive on our own merits. It was a very good advice. We all in the family stayed focussed in our studies. I did not get a place in our local varsity so my parents with the educational insurance and some savings managed to had send me here. Most of the Malaysian or Asian students here are all on scholarships so I just want to stay away from them for that reason. I guess what I did was wrong as I should not turned my hatred and frustration towards them. However, most of the Malaysian students too are weird....they stick to their own kinds only.......except you, Alan. You move around freely with all the students," said Judy.

"That's what students should do.....we must develop good networking right now because these students are going to be future leaders in their own countries. You will never know that the guy sitting next to you in your class that you ignored for the past 3 years would be the President or Minister in his country one day. By then it would be too late to tell him that you were the guy that sat beside him for the past 3 years. He won't want to remember you.... for sure. Once we graduate you will never know what our futures are going to be.....some of us maybe Presidents, Prime Ministers or corporate leaders of our countries. Being friendly with them now would bring better co-operation between countries in the future. We can make that change because we study overseas. If we know them well now it would be easy to establish relationships in politics or businesses later," said Alan. "The same applies to our Malaysian students...if we have good relationships with them it would be easier to get things done once we are working in our own organisations. Many business deals are sealed between good friends, Judy. Forget the past, treat it as fate and accept in good faith what God has offered us now."

"Thanks Alan, I accept your advice....it is good and practical," replied Judy.

"I tell you what.....the Malaysian students are organising a get together on Merdeka Day next week, so I suggest you join in the celebrations and put the past behind you, Judy. Our Malaysian students are very forgiving.....one of our Prime Ministers used to say "mudah lupa" (Easily forgets)."

That night the Malaysian students were surprised to see her in the crowd. However, they readily accepted and welcomed her 'home'! From that day Judy changed her attitude and soon she was able to interact with all the Malaysian students in the campus freely. She told Alan one day,

"Now I feel free mentally as I can move around the campus without having to feel being watched or gossiped by certain quarters."

# CHAPTER 36

"I love that feeling of being free and love by everybody, Judy," added Alan to Judy, who became good friends after that and they went their separate ways after graduation. However, it was a few years later when both were working that they accidentally 'bumped' into each other again. They met at an exhibition in London......that triggered the love affair. They decided to meet again for dinner, which led to more lunches, dinners and ended in Alan proposing for her hand in marriage during a special Christmas dinner in London. In February the next year they were married in a simple ceremony in a local church attended by a few friends including Datuk, Datin and Judy's parents. It was that evening that Judy realised why Alan was a 'true' Malaysian. Judy learned that Alan was brought up in an orphanage owned by a Malay couple who helped him to achieve his first degree locally and encouraged him to further his studies overseas. The foster home had helped many children from any religion, race and colour. She realised that not all Malaysians are bad, however, there were some very 'rotten apples', those possibly with 'brain damage' as they used to say!

After 2 years of marriage the twins were born in Amsterdam and when they were of schooling age Alan decided to send them to a boarding school. Judy, however, insisted that they attend tuition on Bahasa Malaysia conducted by a local Malaysian attached to the Malaysian Students' Affairs Department in London. Sonny, who was born much later, stayed with them since they decided to come back to Malaysia. Their combined remuneration overseas was more than enough to give their sons good education there and purchased some property in Malaysia. Initially, they wanted to work in Singapore as they were both offered very good incentives there but Alan wanted to pay back Datuk for his kindness.

That morning both of them woke up late. They rushed together to the bathroom and shared the shower to be in time to the office. Both skipped their breakfast, but just had a glass of fresh orange to keep their tummy happy. Alan gave his wife a kiss and said,

"Thanks for the wonderful night!"

Alan's chauffeur was very worried while waiting downstairs as Alan was never ever late to the office. Now after almost 45 minutes he had still not appeared. Probably my boss is not feeling well today, he thought to himself. Alan and Judy suddenly rushed out of the condominium,

"Sorry Pak Mat, semalam lambat balik…hujan lebat…banjir!" (Sorry Pak Mat, we returned late last night…heavy rain….flooded!), said Alan. "Ini isteri saya, Judy," (This is my wife, Judy).

That was the first day Pak Mat reported for duty to Alan. Judy who was about to enter her car, smiled at Alan and said to Pak Mat

"Semalam dia teringat zaman remajanya! Tak sedar dia dah tua!" (He remembers his younger days! He didn't realised he is old!).

Pak Mat looked more confused, as there was no rain around Kuala Lumpur last night. Before he closed the car door he said to his wife,

"By the way, Datuk Khalid invited us for dinner at his house on Saturday night to celebrate the new billion dollar deal. He is inviting some politicians, corporate friends and their spouses. I'll see you later."

# CHAPTER 37

$A$t Oxford, England, Alex and Michael both excelled in their studies and sports. Following the footsteps of their dad they represented their schools in badminton. However, they were one up on their dad for they also played hockey. They really excelled in badminton and were double champions for 3 years in a row at the county championship. Alex played as full back and his brother, a winger. They were always together at play and work. It was difficult to differentiate the two, but the parents had a way to distinguish them…..the ear was the distinct 'identification' mark. Michael had slightly 'pointed' right ear, "like Mr. Spock of Star Trek" said Alan. However, for whatever reasons, they had different ambitions.

Alex aspires to be a doctor and Michael an architect. Keeping in touch with their parents by e-mails using the laptop was much cheaper than the phone. So almost everyday Judy received their e-mails and Sonny was the one who always replied the e-mails of the twins. That kept Sonny updated with the activities of his two brothers and at times he asked Judy to send him too to the boarding school in London. Judy told him, "You will go there if you do well in your 'O' level examinations….I promise you that." "That's too long….. many, many more years to wait….mum!" said Sonny. "The days and years will pass very fast and before you realise it, you are studying in London!" replied Judy. Hitchhiking had been the hobby of the twins and they went with a few friends during the summer breaks to explore Europe rather than come home to Malaysia. They said, "This is the best time to see Europe….by the cheapest means. Hitchhiking takes you to places you never imagine you can be in your life. Sometimes the trucks could only take you to a certain destination and you have to sleep in a barn or church for that night. Homesteads and motels are too expensive for us but we do get free food from some caring homes. We will have all the time to explore Malaysia when we start working back home". They had so far been to France, Spain and Germany. "There are many more beautiful countries to explore in Europe. Each country had its own unique tradition and culture. We will never get such an opportunity again in our life time".

During their travels they took down notes of the places they visited and photo of interests as they intended to write a book on their 'escapades' in Europe when they returned to Malaysia.

"That would be fantastic reading for students and general readers who intend to hitchhike in Europe. They will get an idea of where to travel, stay and eat cheap. These places we went through do not appear in the travel brochures", Alex said excitedly to Michael.

In Dublin, Ireland, Nadia, with a few friends were busy preparing for their coming examinations in the library. Being very studious she had aspired to be a doctor from schooldays. She did well to obtain a place at one of the medical colleges in Dublin, Ireland.

"I cannot disappoint my family. I need to do well as my other siblings are all looking up to me as a role model", she told her friends.

She did not enjoy playing any games but love to listen to music and watch movies. In London Wawa too was busy preparing for her second year examinations. She was pursuing her studies in Aeronautical Engineering, and hopefully to start her career with one of the airlines locally or as a lecturer in one of the local universities in Malaysia. Being a very meticulous and determined person she also love to read novels and watch soccer. Her favourite soccer club is obviously Manchester United F.C. When she was still in the kindergarten she would pester her favourite grand aunty, To' Mi, to read books both in English and Malay.

# CHAPTER 38

Her younger brother in Los Angeles, Aqiel, had a completely opposite personality to her. He liked to party and have fun but was never into any sports. He was there from his days as a student at 'O' level. Now he was in his final year in Business Studies and Finance. On completing his first degree he intended to pursue his MBA and worked in the States for a few years. By then he was more American then the locals. He completely forgot his religion, Islam, though there were many mosques in America. He kept away from his Muslim friends and was happy to just move around with students of other religions. In his young mind Islam was too rigid and did not give any room to enjoy life. Those who practised Islam religiously like praying 5 times a day, fasting during the Ramadan and abstain from taking non-halal food were extremists. Halal food then was readily available all over America.

Religion to him was non-existent as he completely ignored Malaysians of Malay origins when he was there. He looked down on them as they had very poor command of the English language compared to him. The five times a day compulsory prayers for all Muslims were just ignore and he was never at the mosque for Friday prayers. He drinks, womanising, loved movies and music and given the opportunity he would like to study about filmmaking and sound engineering in USA. He played the guitar and piano and was quite an accomplished singer. In short he was a lost soul as far as Islam is concerned.

His parents had been too liberal with him and never really had time to discuss religion with him. Though from young he attended the religious classes, read AlQuran and pray 5 times a day. They thought everything was well. He had a private dinner with Alan and Judy last year when he was back in Malaysia for a short vacation. "Uncle Alan, I will only come back permanently to Malaysia when I am fully equipped with the necessary experience," he said. "After obtaining your first degree, Aqiel….. proceed to do your MBA and try to get some working experience before you come back. Your dad's expectation is very high, Aqiel….. Datuk wants you to help him and later take over as Chairman of the company. You have a very daunting future ahead of you from rival companies and your dad expects you to bring the company to a much higher level with your qualifications. We won't be around forever, so the fate of the company will depend entirely on you and your new team of management," added Alan. "I heard you got hooked to a sweet petite lady back there. Is it true?" asked Judy. "Nothing serious Aunty.....you know you get lonely out there sometimes....so you find ways to kill your time...." They all smiled.

"Whatever you do, studies should always be your priority. Ok. Life in America may be more glamorous and rewarding but always bear in mind your responsibility to your parents is of utmost importance," Alan advised. Aqiel kept quiet for a while and then said, "My stay in America, uncle, has changed me.......I like to question the rational about every religion. Why Allah SWT created so many religions that have resulted in conflict in the beliefs of the various races. I am a Muslim but I seek answers to many questions in my head. I need to see some learned Ustaz to convince me why I should continue to practise Islam religiously." "That is something thay we are not able to enlighten you......you got to seek truth from your Ustaz as you said," Alan replied. "The problem was, back home when we learn about Islam we were not allowed to question the Ustaz......we must accept everthing as the truth. At the back of my head I have hundreds of questions to ask as to 'why' we need to follow certain tenets but we were trained in schools not to question the Ustaz but just follow the practices. Here in America the Ustaz are more open and willing to explain in detail regarding Islam. I have yet to meet them......I hope to do so in the near future," said Aqiel.

# CHAPTER 39

$I$t was Saturday evening, Alan and Judy dressed up for the dinner date at Datuk Khalid's house. He put on a simple long sleeved blue batik shirt with black pants and she wore a dark blue evening dress with a pearl necklace and matching earrings. Both were looking forward to such a gathering where they would get the chance to meet new friends and clients. Alan drove the car himself, as he did not believe in being chauffeured around when he attended private functions. He felt uncomfortable and guilty keeping the chauffeur waiting for hours at night when he should be free to spend his time with his family. The golf course was another place he refused to be chauffeur driven. He did not want his driver waiting for almost 5 hours at the club when he could spend quality time with his family on weekends. When they arrived at the modest double storey bungalow at Sri Harta Mas there was already a small crowd mingling around the swimming pool.

Datin Bibi was on hand to receive them at the entrance. An elegant and beautiful lady she was always happy to see Alan and Judy. "Hello, welcome Alan, Judy. How are you?"

"Thank you Datin, it is always a pleasure to attend your functions......good crowd and most importantly very delicious food", replied Alan.

"I always make sure your name, besides Mr. Ah Soon, will be on the list at all my functions. You know, Alan, you are like my own son. From a baby I have known and love you. I really wanted to adopt you but Datuk stopped me from doing that as he believed your real parents' might one day come back to claim you. It may cause some complications to your life. Anyway, we can talk about that later. Come in first and mingle with the crowd. Datuk is somewhere out there. I'll see you later, then."

"Datin, can we go into your library to admire your art collections before we go to the pool? Art has always been Judy's first love," asked Alan.

"Correction, second love, Datin," interjected Judy, smiling at Alan.

"Oh, no, those are not my art collections but Datuk. I prefer to collect antics when I am overseas! You will meet some of our guests in the library I think.....they have the same interest as Judy......go ahead, I will see you later," replied Datin.

They chatted for a while with Datin and as more guests arrived, Alan and Judy excused themselves to allow Datin to welcome her guests. Walking through the living room Judy was impressed with Datin's collections of antics....mostly from Indonesia, Myanmar, Middle East and African states. After admiring the unique collections of antics they went straight into the library. There were many guests admiring the art collections of Datuk Khalid. Besides volumes and volumes of books on the shelves, the library was adorned with art collections from overseas and local artists. He had a number of landscape paintings of the Englishman, John Constable; the Italian painter, Giovanni Bellini; a French artist, Lorrain Claude; and American self-taught artist, Grandma Moses, who started painting seriously when she was in her late seventies. She surpassed the ripe age of 100.

"Remarkable lady", remarked Judy regarding Grandma Moses.

Alan joked, "You love painting, dear, so at 35 it is never too late!"

"I should think seriously about that, at least in the year 3000 somebody who walks into the National Art Gallery will remember me as one of the great artist in 21st. Century," joked Judy.

They both laughed at that remark. Further on they saw paintings of the famous portrait painters such as Spanish artist, Francisco de Goya; Dutch artist, Rembrandt van Rijn; Dutch painter, Frans Hals and Italian painter, Pietro Annigoni, best known for his portraits of world leaders, including Queen Elizabeth 11. There was also the remarkable works of Russian painter, Wassily Kandinsky, who was the pioneer of abstract art. There were some collections of the French painter, Claude Monet the leading impressionist of all time including that of Pablo Picasso, the Spanish painter, sculptor, graphic artist and designer. Picasso and George Braque developed the style of 'Cubism' after 1907. Art pieces of Michelangelo, Leonardo da Vinci and Raphael were also displayed. He had a few collections of the local artist such as Syed Alwi, Tan Tong and Hussein. Most of the paintings of the local artists were displayed at the office.

Later, the couple went out to the swimming pool area to meet Datuk Khalid. Datuk was enjoying himself with his guests, laughing and joking at each other. These were Datuk's very close friends, businessmen, politicians and civil servants.

# CHAPTER 40

Mawi and wife, Siti, suddenly appeared in front of them. Alan felt a bit uncomfortable and reluctantly made a gesture to shake hands with Mawi. Mawi just ignored him. Siti, who was looking radiant, quickly took control of the situation by complimenting Judy whom she seldom met. She greeted Alan and complimented him on the new deal with Europe. Mawi, however, remained aloof and unfriendly. He had not put aside their differences after the last Board meeting. After excusing herself from her husband and Alan, Siti invited Judy to meet the other ladies, as Judy was new to that office 'community'. Siti never believed that the wives should get involved in office politics. The two Executive Directors stood together awkwardly, as they just had no idea on how to start a conversation. The night was saved when Datuk spotted Alan. He invited both Alan and Mawi to meet his friends. Holding the shoulder of Alan, he said,

"Here gentlemen, this is the man who actually makes things happen in my company. We are going global due to his effort".

The small crowd gave an appreciative applause. Alan was embarrassed.

"Excuse me Datuk it was your vision, En. Mawi, and the team only implemented it. Without your presence no international companies will take a second look at us, Datuk. You know, whether we like it or not, a CEO is the company's brand and we have a very well known brand internationally, with a very positive image in you, Datuk".

The crowd nodded in agreement to the compliment and Datuk shook hands with Mawi and Alan.

"Come, come, enough of these talks and praises, I am not Julius Caesar and you are not Mark Anthony, Alan, so let's just enjoy the night with drinks and food for now."

Later in the evening Datin Bibi's 13-year-old niece, Lina, demonstrated her skill on the piano playing many beautiful popular numbers to the delight of the crowd. She played a number of classical pieces from Tchaikovsky, J. Haydn, Mozart, Chopin, J. Strauss and Beethoven. The classical pieces reminded Alan and Judy of their time at the opera houses they attended in Europe. A pianist took over to entertain the crowd with local and international songs. Alan managed to make many new friends from the business circles and casually talked about business opportunities overseas. A diplomat from one of the African countries, Mr. Nkrumah, impressed him and he made an appointment the next day to discuss in detail business opportunities out there. Late in the evening Judy who was with Alan remarked to Datuk about the expensive art collections he had in the library.

"Oh, no.....Don't be deceived...those are not originals or authentic. Anyway, I can't afford the originals so duplicates would do...I am happy with what I can purchase. Even Datin's collections of so called antics are imitations....originals are expensive and difficult to come by. Further with originals you can't sleep peacefully," laughed Datuk.

The party ended just before midnight. On the way home Alan spoke to Judy of his sudden urge to seek his real parents after that conversation he had with Datin Bibi. He said he had a chat again with Datin Bibi that evening. She confessed that she had no idea about Alan's parents but the files at the orphanage might have some information for him to follow up. However, she remembered seeing a note that was left by one of 'his' parents when he was a baby. "I kept this note safely in your file because I knew one day you may wish to look up for your biological parents," Datin said to him. Alan thank her and said he would looked up for the note and said, "I am going to frame and hang it in my office to keep reminding me who I am," said Alan. He explained that his search for his real parents was to understand why he was abandoned, and to find out whether he had any other siblings. He knew no parents would want to abandon their babies unless circumstances forced them to do so. He, however, held no grudge against his parents for what they did and said, "It was fated, the will of God".

He dared not asked Datuk Khalid about his past as he felt the time was not right. Alan told his wife, "One day I must try to find time to get to the bottom of his family tree." "Do it, honey....that would be good for you and all of us. You never know maybe your parents are in dire need of your help so the sooner you do it the better. Let us pray that they are all well and healthy. By the way, for tonight, keep your distance okay...I need to be early to the office tomorrow morning," Judy joked to Alan.

"I can't promise anything, dear...no promises as this things happen due to the 'animal' instincts in me........," and he acted as if to wanted to pounce at her like a wild lion.....they both laughed.

# Chapter 41

The project in Amsterdam, oil and gas company, took off without any hitched as scheduled. Manjit, an Accountant and a Biological Engineer were seconded to the project to take care of Bibi Sdn. Bhd. interests. Diana Ng an MBA graduate from Universiti Kebangsaan Malaysia, Kuala Lumpur, replaced him. Her first degree was in Economics. The company recruited Sivaraja, a graduate from University Putra Malaysia, Kuala Lumpur to assist Mawi. Datuk forced Mawi to accept that the company could only grow competitively with the help of all races. He had to forget his racist attitude if he wanted to stay in the company. Datuk Khalid made this clear to him during one of the company's Board meetings. Sivaraja's first degree was the Bachelor of Agriculture and he was with Mardi, a local research centre, for over five years before joining the company. Bibi Sdn. Bhd. intended to diversify into agriculture with special emphasis on biotechnology. Biotechnology was not new to the country but there was no concerted effort from the authority to encourage farmers to explore its potential. Brewing, baking and cheese-making represent ancient forms of biotechnology, but the industry has been revolutionised in recent years by advances in genetics and genetic engineering. Micro-organisms are now used to produce a wide range of drugs and other biological such as enzymes, to refine ores and to clear many forms of pollution such as oil slicks. Biotechnology offers a clean and highly energy-efficient alternative to normal industrial processes.

Datuk Khalid was saddened that the abundant local Malaysian fruits like bananas, pineapples, durian, mangoes, jack fruits, citrus fruits and others were left to rot on the trees. These fruits, rich in Vitamin C should be converted into value added products that can be canned and exported overseas. Today, only about 50% of these fruits are sold in the market while the rest are left to drop and rot in the orchards. Datuk remembered when he attended one seminar on "Strengthening Your Immune System" the speaker said

"Citrus fruits like grapefruit, oranges, tangerines, lemons and limes are all excellent sources of ascorbic acid, the form of Vitamin C found in plants. As a component of food, this nutritional superstar has myriad immune functions, including enhancing the movement of phagocytes, boosting NK-cell activity and building and maintaining mucous membranes and collagen, a tissue that plays a vital role in wound healing."

Datuk was also eyeing the herbal industry that he said could be the 'cash cow' for the company in the future. He said the local market for herb-based products was worth more than RM 6.2 billion annually but 85 % of the products were imported. The world market, however, offered a staggering USD 80 billion to producers of herb-based health supplements, cosmetics and fragrances.

"I am not keen on the concept of direct selling as currently practised by many, but would like my products be sold on the shelves in Guardian, Watson's, George Town and hypermarkets, cheap and easily accessible to all", he continued. "Herbalists take a holistic approach believing that the whole of the plant should be used unlike the pharmaceutical industry that still focus on the creation of extracts with higher concentrations of certain active constituents for more potent effect", he added.

Health food and supplements are now widely accepted globally as people are today getting very health conscious. Datuk spoke at length about the traditional herbal medicine, which was good for the heart, blood circulation, liver, and other vital organs essential to keep us waking up healthy, every morning. He made a special mention on one of commonest and time-tested household remedy known as honey. Honey, with many healing properties, is found in abundance in Malaysia. It replenishes energy, enhancing physical stamina and restore strength to those weakened by illness or stress. Those with indigestion, insomnia, headaches, respiratory complaints and cardiovascular disease can also benefit taking some honey. It helps to disinfect and heal minor skin wounds too. However, Datuk said that consumers must be wary to buy only genuine honey from bees and not contaminated or adulterated with other elements.

He joked, "Some people wake up in the morning and go for their 'moaning' or 'mourning' walk instead of 'morning' walk, that's bad. You should wake up in the morning feeling rejuvenated, happy and not feeling groggy. People all over the world are health conscious today and they want to stay healthy, very fit and kicked the bucket with a smile!"

# CHAPTER 42

$A$ll was well with Bibi Sdn. Bhd. The joint venture project was ready for commissioned and the herbal plantation has started planting the various herbs in the state of Kedah. Datuk Khalid and Alan were on the verge of negotiating for another project in Africa. This was the follow up effort of Alan after his meeting with the African diplomat at Datuk Khalid's dinner party. At the informal meeting at the Embassy the next morning the African diplomat called his Trade Commissioner and they had a lengthy discussion on business opportunities in Africa in general. Alan observed there were huge opportunities to strike rich in Africa with the right contact. Africa is a huge continent and most of her natural resources have yet to be explored or discovered. Datuk said to Alan that Africa had been ravaged and exploited by the immigrants of her rich natural resources. The local natives got only 'peanuts' as hard core labourers. Datuk and Alan decided to visit some of the African countries to personally feel the 'pulse' of the countries, so to say. They flew to Africa a couple of times to determine to which country they should invest. The people, to their surprise were skilful and well educated and it was a question of getting the right mixed to get the results. Doing business in Africa amid political conflict had been a challenge.

Their African partner said, "You need to create loyalty to the company among the workers......Loyalty developed through team building and family-like bonds with the staffs. It's a very alien concept to Western culture where you work for the boss and not with the boss. The risks were high, but so are the gains."

Bibi Sdn. Bhd. decided to take the high risks. Biodiesel project was their goal. The company wanted to build a few biodiesel plants near a port there. This was a much bigger project in terms of financing. The initial cost for the project was estimated at USD 3.3 billion but the return on investment was huge. To ensure of regular supply they had to acquire oil palm estates with local tycoons. They picked Democratic Republic of Congo to establish their plantations. Congo was once one of the world's principal producers of palm oil and Datuk believed that Congo had the potential to grow bigger in the near future under a good stable government.

Meanwhile, Nina got married to her schoolmate, Azli, who works as an Engineer in an airline industry. The 'Kadhi' at the Federal Territory Mosque performed the 'Angkat Nikah' where they were solemnised as husband and wife. Mawi held two receptions, in the afternoon, at his house, and on the next evening at a five star hotel. The receptions were well attended by relatives, friends and her fathers' clients. The Minister of International Trade attended the reception. After the dinner Suki and Jackie, Malaysia's two top entertainers, and a few singers from the show 'Akademi Fantasia', entertained the guests. It was a proud night for Mawi, Siti and the wedding couple. Zamani came with his wife and family. Anwar, who was attached at the Malaysian Embassy in Russia, came back. He was seen with his petite fiancée, Faridah, who works with the Ministry of Finance. Nadia, managed to come back in time for the reception for she just finished her third year medical examinations in Ireland. Aqiel, Wawa and her boyfriend were also present. Both Michael and Alex, the twins were unable to attend the wedding as they were in the midst of their examinations.

Three months later Wawa, tied her knot with her fiancé, Adam, also at the Federal Territory Mosque. Datuk held a grand reception at his kampong for the relatives on Friday and at the Felda Perdana Hall, Kuala Lumpur, on Saturday evening, for his friends and clients. It was typical traditional Malay wedding filled with pomp and grandeur. The Chief Minister and a few Cabinet Ministers were present. The 'Ghazal' group from Johore and the 'Dondang Sayang' troupe from Malacca later entertained the guests. This time around Alex and Michael, the twins, and close friends of Wawa were present. During the short speech to thank the guests Datuk Khalid, among other things advised the couples that,

"Perspective is a changeable thing and the knowledge that differences shunned by some can be embraced by others will help us discover our self-worth."

A very appropriate advised to young couples who were about to share their lives with another and to all those present.

The feud between Alan and Mawi never ceased though it was well over 4 years. Datuk Khalid was at a loss as to how to persuade Mawi to stop the bickering. He knew in his absence from the Board, Alan will leave and the company would fold up. Datuk believed that Alan had the prerequisites to be a good CEO. He was well educated, patience, hands on and above all a man of integrity. Mawi would never be a good Chairman or CEO of a company. He was too impatient and was not prepared to listen to others. Datuk wanted to build a company that can survive when he was not around and remained a preferred employer on a sustained basis. In fact he had built a very reputable company over the years...a company acclaimed by corporate leaders as the 'most competitive company' in Malaysia. He came across in the papers written by Jack and Suzy Welch on why employees would like to be associated with companies with preferred employer status.

"Firstly, the company demonstrated a real commitment to continuous learning. Focus investing in the development and training of the staffs to facilitate the steady path to personal growth. Secondly, pay and promotions are tightly linked to 'meritocracies'. It is all about results. You get the best brains, full of self-confidence and very competitive and aggressive staffs knocking at your door. Third, preferred companies encouraged staffs to take risks and do not penalise those who tries. It is all about creative bold individuals that a company needs in the global marketplace. Fourth, preferred companies understand what is good for society is good for business. Fifth, these companies keep their hiring standards tight, requiring an arduous interview process and strict criteria around intelligence and previous experience. And finally, these companies are profitable and growing, promising future, with career mobility and potential of increased financial reward".

Datuk realised that the company should be identified to Bibi Sdn. Bhd. and not to him. That was the problem when organisations were too closely associated with the CEO.... 'The brand'. It was great while he was around but on his demise the company would struggle to survive. At his age he had to come out with the solution fast. That was the reason he was pushing for the company to be listed on the board of Bursa Malaysia. That move would inject new blood into the Board of Directors and keep the company rejuvenated. Meantime he had to take stock, and review the current management team. Datuk knew that he and Mawi would have to take the back seat if the company was to progress faster. He had to be brave to make a drastic decision about Mawi. That evening he discussed with his wife on the fate of Mawi in the company.

# CHAPTER 43

"I have thought over and over again where I can fit Mawi in this new setup. The company needed to be reengineered to bring it to a new level. Mawi could play a role if his attitude towards Alan and the new staffs can change. The problem is he is too old to change now….what do we do with him, dear?"

"He is your brother who had helped you to build this company…you can't just dump him out of the company!" replied his wife.

Datuk replied, "I know that…but how do we keep the company going without his interference. Alan and most of the senior staffs are contemplating to resign if there is no change. I do not want to lose these good staffs. I have told Mawi time and again to see me if he was not happy with the staffs…..but he insisted to show them that he was the boss! These are very well qualified staffs…they can just resign today and get a job tomorrow! They are here because of Alan, not me or him. They like his 'work culture'."

"Why don't we keep Mawi as a non-Executive Director, like me, as a Board member? You too must sacrifice your executive powers and hand it over to Alan. Our children are now both grown up. Aqiel is working in LA and Wawa now a lecturer with a local university. You should now become the non-Executive Chairman. We can arrange a reasonable monthly remuneration for Mawi so that he does not lose out financially. He can then come to the office during Board meetings only leaving Alan, the Managing Director, and his team to manage the company without interference. His children, Anwar, Nina and Nadia are now working, that leaves only Redzuan and Rozan that have yet to complete their studies," said Datin.

"Excellent! I too feel it is time for me to take a back seat and spend more time with you….what do I do without you?" answered Datuk. "The orphanage can keep you busy….I don't need you to hang around my sarong all the time…." joked Datin.

"I think I like that idea…hanging close to your sarong all the time!" replied Datuk, giving a big hug to his wife. "We now need to persuade our son, Aqiel, to come back…as an executive in the company. I want him to learn all aspects of management before he takes over the reign of the company one day," said Datuk.

"He has his MBA and enough working experience in the States….that should help him to easily adjust quickly to our management system," added Datin.

"I will talk to Mawi tomorrow," said Datuk. "I will e-mail to Aqiel to come home for a holiday, then we can discuss with him about our plans," Datin added.

The next morning Datuk was having a serious discussion with Mawi.

"Mawi, I am contemplating of playing a passive role in the Company as at my age, which is well over 60, I am not able to focus much on the job." Mawi was smiling to himself, thinking he would be the new Executive Chairman and CEO. "So I have decided to restructure and reengineer the management of our company by early next month."

"I think it is a good idea, Khalid. You have done so much for the company and you rightly deserved a rest. There is nothing to fear, as the company will be in good hands and with a team of good managers. I feel I am ready to shoulder bigger responsibility and…." replied Mawi.

"I am glad you concur with me. Actually, both of us do not fit in this new plan. Our days are over….it was very different then, now the challenges ahead are more intricate and complex. We are not equipped or prepared to face these new technology expansions unlike the younger generations. We now have to pass the rein to them whether we like it or not," stressed Datuk.

"You mean, I too…..have no role to play when you leave? I am still healthy and can command respect from the both the staffs and clients….," said Mawi.

"I am saying both of us must move out of the management team. We will remain as Directors. I will remain as non-Executive Chairman, you as non-Executive Director together with Bibi. I intend to promote Alan as the new CEO of the company. Further, I am trying to persuade Aqiel to return and learn the trade of managing a company. What do you think?" asked Datuk.

"I…..I am not agreeable to your proposals….you are too trusting. You can't give your powers to Alan just like that….he is not your son!" retorted Mawi.

"Mawi, Alan may not be my son but I trust him more than anyone else today. I have given you many opportunities to prove your worth to be the Executive Chairman but I found you wanting. You do not respect your staffs or command their respect, the two most important ingredients in managing human assets. Anyway you are now almost 56 years old and time to spend more quality time with your family. Now is the time to let the second generation, our sons and daughters to take care of the company if they want to. I intend to groom Aqiel to be the Executive Chairman when the time comes. Alan will not be here forever, but right now he is a great asset to the company. The 10% share I have given to you is yours and you remain as a Director of the company," Datuk firmly replied.

# CHAPTER 44

$M$awi kept silent for a long-time, not knowing how to response to Datuk's decision. He was unhappy, very unhappy because Datuk had given his staunch 'enemy' Alan full support and confidence'. He had no choice but to abide to Datuk's decision or leave the company. He came home and told his wife, Siti, about his discussion with Datuk.

"That is a very wise decision. We are old and the new employees are well educated to compete on par with other companies. I am happy he made that decision....he has lined up the second generation to take over the business. Not many people are prepared to do that....groom and allow the next generation to run the company. Now you can spend more time at the mosque instead of just attending only the Friday prayers. I am grateful to Datuk for what we are today. It was through his generosity that you become an Executive Director of the company that helped to change our lives for the better.

If you remain a teacher we cannot afford all these luxuries and send our kids overseas. Getting scholarships and even places in local universities are not easy today. At least our children, Anwar and Nadia have completed their tertiary education. Anwar is happy as the Under Secretary at the Malaysian Embassy in Russia and Nadia doing her houseman ship in London. Both of them have achieved their ambitions. I am happy. Accept that decision with an open heart and thank Allah for all that we were endowed with. Datuk and you were young then, but now you have to make way to Alan and Aqiel. They are well prepared and qualified to run a multinational company."

Mawi, being Mawi, was unhappy with his wife's remarks. "You don't understand about pride, Siti," retorted Mawi. He left the room a very unhappy man.

Meanwhile Zamani, 48, was appointed as a Judge in one of the state. He had to resign from his partnership to join the Judiciary. His appointment was based on his past experience as a court interpreter and attorney. He opted to be a Judge as he felt he could contribute positively to enhance the image of the Judiciary.

Aqiel, now all grown up and looking like Tom Cruise, received an e-mail from his mother requesting him to come back for a holiday. He had been in the States since his 'O' level. He was reluctant to leave right now, as he was very much involved with a local American varsity tutor. She was in the same year with him majoring in IT when they met at the varsity. He had many girl friends in the varsity but Daniella, close resemblance of actress Jennifer Lopez, was a totally different species. A mutual friend introduced them at one of the varsity gatherings. Aqiel had for the past two years been trying to get to know her better but without much success. She was then very focus on her studies and did not seem to be interested in any relationship with the opposite sex. Going steady with her classmate was out of question. She knew Aqiel during the karaoke sessions their groups used to organise and Aqiel, an accomplished singer, attracted many admirers. Daniella was one of them but, initially, she tried stay away from him. She was reluctant to be close to Aqiel, a Muslim, who in America then had the stigma of a 'terrorist' attached to him. Aqiel was a very persistent person who kept on meeting Daniella by 'coincidence' or uninvited at the karaoke, the cafeteria and at the varsity basketball games. He appeared everywhere Daniella went and was always around when she needed help. He was one stubborn guy. One day she told her best friend,

"I tried not to entertain or be too close with Aqiel, but with that boyish look of the famous Tom Cruise, who can turn him away.....Not me."

It was during the summer camp organised by the varsity that got them together. Many students from the varsity went for one-week picnic near a beautiful lake. Neither Aqiel nor Daniella realised that both had enrolled for the same summer camp. Aqiel thought that she should be home with her parents for the holidays. He reported at the camp in the morning with a busload of his friends. He was told that another 3 buses of students were on the way and Daniella's group arrived just before lunch. Aqiel was about to go for his lunch when he saw Daniella alighting from the bus. It was a delightful and pleasant surprise to him. He sure was glad she came. They were allocated separate summer lodges 'to keep the summer camp peaceful' said the camp warden. The summer camp was conducted by the varsity to develop their endurance and teamwork when they pursue their vocations in the competitive world after graduation. Besides the routine motivational talks in the evenings they went trekking in the morning, mountain climbing, kayaking and map reading while at night they relaxed at the campfire before they retire for bed. It was at the campfire by the lake that all the students enjoyed themselves. They sang and dance to the strumming of the guitar, ukulele and the sound of the harmonica played by the students. It was during the campfire that Daniella noticed that Aqiel was not only an outstanding guitarist but also a talented singer. She loved the way he sang and played the guitar. Aqiel did his best to impressed Daniella and most of the love song he sang was dedicated to Daniella. The one-week summer camp changed Daniella's opinion towards Aqiel and she gradually learned to like this young man from Malaysia. She was ready to let him into her life and be part of her family.

There were many young Americans interested in courting her, but she was not ready to be tied down to one person and further "the relationship just did not have any 'chemistry'" she told Aqiel. They went on their own separate ways after dating a few times. She had many friends but she just did not have any interest in anybody until she met Aqiel who had that certain charisma which appealed to her. Aqiel had a great impact in her life during the summer camp and from then on they were inseparable. Daniella invited Aqiel to meet her parents over the weekends, which Aqiel obliged. Her parents apparently liked Aqiel from the moment they met him. From then on he was a regular visitor to her parents' home. Daniella's parents, was open-minded, and did not object to their relationship. All they wanted to see was that their daughter was happy and they knew she had made the right choice. Her father, Mr. Bush, an Accountant, said to Aqiel,

"You cannot condemn the whole nation just because of a few terrorists from there. Just like me not all Bushs are 'terrorists', maybe one or two," he laughed. Monica, Daniella's mother just smiled.

"Yes Sir, now most Americans identify all Muslims as terrorists after September 11 because of Osama Ben Laden…. Actually the terminology 'terrorists' depends on who flips the coin. To Osama Ben Laden, President Bush is the 'terrorist' and to the President, Osama Ben Laden is definitely the one," added Aqiel with a broad smile.

# CHAPTER 45

After graduation they became lovers and the relationship was one heading for marriage eventually. Aqiel needed the blessings from his parents to fulfil his dream. Anyway, when he received the e-mail, he knew he was called back to discuss important family matters. He met Daniella and told her about his intention to take a few days break back in Malaysia. Daniella wanted to see Malaysia and meet Aqiel's parents whom she had never met before. Aqiel agreed. It was time he got serious with his life he thought. He sent an e-mail, "Hei guys, see you next weekend.........I am briging a 'friend'."

As soon as Datin Bibi received the e-mail she was curious.....is he married or coming with a 'friend'? He could not be married as he definitely wanted to get our blessings!

"Abang, dia datang dengan kawan dia! (He is coming with a friend, love!) atau dia nak dapat menantu 'Mat Salleh' nampaknya! (Or he is bringing back our daughter-in-law!).

"Tak kan dia hendak bawa kawan lelaki, mesti teman wanitanya!" (Can't be his male friend, must be his girl friend!) replied Datuk.

It was Sunday, and Datuk Khalid and Datin were at the Kuala Lumpur International Airport waiting for the arrival of Aqiel from LA. Soon the airport announced the arrival of MAS flight from LA.

"It will take at least another 45 minutes before clearance by the Immigration and Customs," said Datuk.

After close to 40 minutes Aqiel appeared with 'Daniella' and their baggage. Datin was thrill to see 'Daniella' who was a typical American blond. She hugged both Aqiel and 'Daniella' before Aqiel got the chance to introduce them.

"Mak, this is not Daniella but Rachel, a friend we met on the plane. Daniella just went to the restroom for a while. She asked me to meet you both first....I think she is feeling a bit jittery to meet her future in-laws. She should be out soon."

Datin was a bit embarrassed and apologised to Rachel, but Datuk remained cool and calm. In fact down deep inside Datuk was more anxious than ever.

Rachel excused herself as her boyfriend was waiting for her at the entrance in the car. "We will see you again....please contact me....Daniella has my number. My best regards to her, Aqiel. Mak Chik, Pak Chik jumpa lagi OK? Bye." said Rachel. Datin was very impressed as Rachel can speak Malay. "Dia selalu datang keMalaysia.....ayah dia seorang consultant diPetronas, emak," replied Aqiel. Datin asked Aqiel about his studies and life in the States. Aqiel answered that he had a few more years before he is ready to come back. After five minutes, Daniella appeared, a beautiful young lady with the Latino look. Aqiel lovingly held her hand and introduced her to his parents. She kissed their hands according to the Malay custom but Datin could not help but hugged Daniella lovingly. It was a clear sign of 'motherly' approval.

They chatted for a while at the airport and Daniella conveyed her parents' best regards to Datuk and Datin. An American couple approached them and the wife hugged Daniella. He was Daniella's uncle, Mr. Roger and wife, Martha, who worked in the American Embassy.

"I thought you are coming to stay with us. Your room is ready, Daniella," said Datin.

"Thank you so much, but my dad and mum insisted I stay with my uncle. You know, Malay custom...it will not look very nice," Daniella replied, looking sheepishly at Aqiel. They all laughed.

"This must be Aqiel's arrangement.......to please us. Anyway I am having a small home coming reception for Aqiel on Saturday night, so Mr. and Mrs. Roger....please join us. You too Daniella, don't forget to come," joked Datuk.

Aqiel and Daniella excused themselves and stepped aside for a private chat for a while before saying good bye. Daniella and Aqiel then followed her uncle to the car as he wanted to see her off. She kept on looking lovingly at Aqiel, hoping he insisted on her staying with his family.

# CHAPTER 46

In the car Datin could not help but smiled all the way. Datuk glanced at her and said,

"Seronok nampaknya.....ada apa-apa ke?" (You look happy.......any good reason)?

Datin just ignored. She was pleased with his choice and was looking forward to having beautiful grand children.

"How serious are you about her, Aqiel? We.....I have no objection to your choice but she must understand that she has to convert to Islam and not you convert to Christianity! Nowadays we have a lot of problem amongst teenagers regarding religion. Islam is very strict on this and whoever intends to marry a Muslim must convert to our religion and practised it religiously," said Datin.

"I have explained to her what needed to be done if we were to get married. She has agreed and her parents too did not object to it. The important thing to them was that she was happy. Any religion to them was good as long as there was no force or compulsion," said Aqiel.

"Do you pray five times a day back in the States, Aqiel?" asked Datuk. "Sometimes, ayah, when I have the time," replied Aqiel. "What.....when you have the time? You must make time as without religion you are a lost soul!" Datuk said angrily. "Sudah....sudah lah abang......anak kita baru balik.....dah kena marah!" (Cool dear our son just arrived and now he gets a scolding from you). Datuk kept quiet throughout the whole journey to the house. Datin who was sitting at the rear seat together with Aqiel held his hand to show his love for him. She whispered a few loving words to Aqiel to cheer him up. At times Datuk, who was very moody, heard them laughing quietly at the back. By the time they reached home Datuk was no more in a bad mood but tried to please Aqiel by saying, "Remember you mentioned in your letter a few years back that you wanted to have a fish pond right in front of your bedroom......well we had it built about two years ago," said Datuk. "Thanks abah," said Aqiel. He grabbed his luggage and rushed to his bedroom on the ground floor to view the fish pond. As soon as he entered his bedroom he was very impressed as through the big glass door was the double tiered fish pond that he wanted. It was most soothing to the ears to hear the the water falling from endlessly from the top to the first tier and then overflowed to the second pond. He opened the glass sliding door and went to have a look at the pond and the fish. I was exquisitely well designed. On the top was the unique typical big Malay traditional vase where the water was pumped in and dropped onto the first and second ponds.

Many gold fishes of different varieties and colour were seen swimming merrily on the top pond and the second, which was much bigger, were seen the Japanese carps of various sizes and colour. "Those fish are of so many varieties....giving us so many beautiful colours for us to appreciate," Aqiel was startled as Datuk suddenly appeared behind him. "They are beautiful dad....I can just sit here all day long reading a book or just engrossed with my laptop. Thank you, dad. "Your mum is preparing some 'goring pisang' (fried bananas) so please join us when you ready." "I would like to stay a bit longer to see those fishes, dad," said Aqiel. While sitting near the pond Aqiel was contemplating on how happy the fish are just swimming around in the pond without caring for the outside world. They just eat, swim and probably sleep for a while until the day they have to go. They don't have any religion, there was no need to pray and no rules and regulations to follow. They enjoy free sex, there is no jealousy, hatred and everybody is equal except for a few rogue fish, however, in this pond they are all equal. Maybe the rule of jungle law, 'the survival of the fittest' still existed. Aqiel continued to dream about the simple life of a fish and was suddenly jerked from those pleasant dreams by a call from his mum. "Aqiel....Aqiel....come and join us for some coffee," called Datin.

# CHAPTER 47

$A$t the dining table they talked casually about America. Then they discussed about his marriage. "Is she willing to stay in Malaysia, Aqiel?" asked Datuk.

"She does if she can employment here. She has qualifications so if she has to stay home in no time she may get bored," replied Aqiel.

"The government today is quite relaxed on this matter and qualified spouses are allowed to work and given citizenship without much fuss. We can work that out once both of you are married," answered Datuk. You must be tired....you know 'jet-lag' after a long trip so it is best you rest after this.

After the coffee Aqiel excused himself and retired in his bedroom. He was dead tired, probably jet lagged as his dad said, due to the long flight from LA to Kuala Lumpur. He immediately fell asleep.

He was sleeping soundly when suddenly his cell phone rang.......he just ignored it but the phone kept on ringing. He was upset,

"Please leave me alone!" and put down the phone.

He felt he had just slept for a few minutes.....He had actually slept for more than four hours. When the phone started to ring again, he was shaken..... Daniella was on the line. He thought he was still in LA and never realised that he was backed in Kuala Lumpur!

"Hello? Who? Daniella.... Are you still at the office? What?.....Oh... so sorry. I was supposed to pick you up at 7.00 pm? You're kidding me.... Now is 7.30? Where? China Town? Oh.....Sorry, I thought we are still in LA. Oh.... At Shah Alam. Okay...kkkk.. Give me 20 minutes. I am so sorry, sweetheart, I overslept.....Yes.... That was a very long flight. I will be there in 20 minutes.....I will take you for a very special dinner at an exclusive place. Bye...I love you."

He rushed to the bathroom, had a quick bath, dress casually in jeans and T-shirt and rushed downstairs. Many of his relatives were waiting, including his uncles, aunts, sister Wawa and husband, Adam.

"Hai there... I am in a rush...see you later," he waved to them.

Everybody was perplexed and puzzled. Datin immediately stopped him in his path,

"Aqiel!…...come and meet your relatives first……they are here to join you for a family BBQ tonight. This is a surprise BBQ for you, Aqiel. You cannot leave them just like that."

Aqiel immediately stopped dead and thought that this was really a surprise. He was thinking how best he could resolve the problem with his family and Daniella. He knew he had to come up with something original to please his parents, relatives and also Daniella. While going round greeting all those present he came up with a brilliant idea after Wawa asked him about Daniella.

"Where is Daniella….. Aqiel?" "Oh, ya…I thought she was already here… okay…..I am going to fetch her right now to join this BBQ…..Just give me about 40 minutes, Okay?"

Before anybody could answer he was off. He quickly made a getaway and asked, Pak Man, Datuk's chauffeur to drive him to Shah Alam.

Within 23 minutes he was at Mr. Roger's house. He rang the doorbell and Mr. Roger appeared inviting him into the house. Aqiel came in but declined to sit down as he said he was in a hurry. He waited for Daniella who was upstairs. Aqiel invited Mr. Roger and his wife to join the BBQ but he declined as they were expecting some guests at home. He sent his best regards to Datuk and Datin. Daniella came down stairs gracefully, looking so resplendent in her 'kaftans' and gorgeous with her lovely smile. She gave Aqiel a kiss on the cheek and request permission from her uncle and aunty to go out.

"Don't be late, dear, take care," said her aunty.

They excused themselves and jumped into the waiting car.

"Where are we going, dear?" asked Daniella.

"If I had my way we are not going anywhere tonight sweetheart. That perfume just turns me on. I will asked my chauffeur to leave and we can spend a few hours in the car, alone, just admiring you, okay?" answered Aqiel.

"I would love that, but how do we get your chauffeur to leave?" they both laughed.

"By the way my parents and relatives have organised an impromptu BBQ for you…. So, we will have our private dinner some other nights, okay?" "Right," replied Daniella.

On the way to his house, Aqiel briefed Daniella on the dos and don'ts in Malay customs,

"You got to give a good first impression, sweetheart."

# CHAPTER 48

As soon as they arrived most of the relatives were around the swimming pool chatting while some Aqiel's cousins were busy at the BBQ. Children were running around, giggling and enjoying themselves. Aqiel introduced Daniella to all his relatives that were there. Daniella loved the tradition and the attention she got, especially from the ladies.

"Dah besar kau Aqiel dan tunang kau macam bintang filemlah, Aqiel. (You have grown up Aqiel and your fiancée is like a movie star, Aqiel)", said one of his aunts."Belum bertunang lagi, ada jodoh jadilah, Mak Ngah (We are not engaged yet, with luck we will, Aunty), replied Aqiel."

"Okay……cukup…..cukup……mari kita makan, ni banyak makanan Bibi sedia untuk sambut bakal'menantu'dia",(Okay….enough…enough…Let us eat, there's so much food prepared by Bibi to welcome her future 'daughter-in-law') interjected Datuk Khalid.

One of the uncles in jest said, "Bibi dah lama tunggu nak timang cucu 'Amerika' tu!" (Bibi had been waiting very long to cuddle her 'American' grandchild).

Everybody in the house were laughing, enjoying each other's company.

"Come Daniella, let me show our Malaysian style of BBQ…..we have salad, baked potatoes, cucumber and some herbs, it is all 'rojak' (mixed), beef, mutton, rabbit, chicken, fish, squids, crabs, and whatever we can roast but no pork. That stuff is forbidden to Muslims. We also have 'satay' and 'ketupat', local favourite delicacies. You must be famished Daniella?" said Datuk.

"Wow……so much food to choose. I am very hungry and so is Aqiel, as we hardly touched any food during the flight…..it was so boring and tiring, Datuk."

"Don't call me Datuk, just 'Daddy' will do!"

"Amboi…amboi….belum apa-apa dah suruh panggil 'Daddy'…… tunggulah dulu!" (Oh…oh…..pull yourself together…..too early to call you 'Daddy), Datin interjected.

Everybody enjoyed the exchange of witty quips by Datuk and Datin. It was eat, drink and fun until late in the night for everybody. Some of the children, dead tired with the running around, were sleeping on the sofa or on their mothers' laps while the men were still enjoying the night. Wawa and husband sought permission from her parents to leave for home as she was not feeling well. She gave Aqiel and Daniella a hug, and invited them for a private dinner before they leave for the States. She had been very close with Aqiel since childhood. Just before midnight Aqiel decided to send Daniella home.

"Your aunty must be worried. You better give her a call before she makes a Police report of a missing young American 'chick'!" Aqiel joked. They both smiled. On the way home Daniella spoke about Aqiel's family and how she felt she can easily adjust to life in Malaysia "There so many expatriates here, especially in Kuala Lumpur, you know. If you work here you can easily fit into the local crowd here and join them at the club to play golf, tennis, swimming or even aerobic classes. Life will be just like America except that here is sunshine all year round!" added Aqiel. "I love the weather here, always sunny with the occasional rain.....no tornados, typhoons, hurricanes, earthquakes or big floods that can be very devastating to our lives," said Daniella. "We do have floods all over the country but comparatively these are mild like what some parts of the States are experiencing......we are talking about financial compensations of about 12-13 million ringgit annually, dear, not much really," said Aqiel. Pak Man who was driving the car pretended not to hear the conversation as most obedient drivers would do.

# CHAPTER 49

The next morning Aqiel after breakfast left the house to meet Daniella. He wanted Daniella to see some of the tourists' attractions around Kuala Lumpur and Selangor. Pak Man, chauffeured them around, he was as good as any tourist guide in Kuala Lumpur, being very knowledgeable on the local tourism attractions. He also spoke with a reasonably good command of English, which helped him to bring around many of Datuk's foreign clients for a quick spin.

On the way, Pak Man told them a joke that he came across in the Readers' Digest. He said there was this snobbish American tourist, a Texan, who flew into London. Being filthy rich he took a limousine tour of London. The chauffeur first showed him the white Tower at the Tower of London. "The building was constructed in 1078 and completed in 1087, almost 9 years to complete," said the chauffeur.

"A little tower like that? In Houston, we'd have that up in a year," said the tourist proudly.

Then they passed the House of Parliament, started in 1834, and completed in 1852, which took more than 18 years.

"We got a bigger building in Dallas, and it only took a month," said the Texan puffing his cigar.

As they passed the Westminster Abbey, the fuming chauffeur remained silent. "Wow, what's that?" asked the Texan.

"Don't know," replied the cabbie. "It wasn't here yesterday!"

They all laughed at the story. Aqiel said to Daniella,

"Pak Man is hinting to you not to behave like the Texan, sweetheart." Pak Man smiled.

First, they went to Putra Jaya, Malaysia's capital of administration, where the Prime Minister and most Ministers had their offices. It was completely out of this world, with a touch of serenity and grandeur. The administrative buildings were unique, with the touch of the beautiful Taj Mahal of India combined with the intricate Malay traditional architecture. The manmade lakes gave the area an added 'cooling' effect. Daniella was impressed but posed a very pertinent question to Aqiel.

"Why are the structures of the buildings here strictly based on the Malay architecture? I thought Malaysia is a multiracial and multicultural country. It would have been brilliant and unique if those buildings depicted the multicultural architecture of your nation."

It was a mind boggling question that made Aqiel lost for words for a few minutes.

"Probably, no one thought about it and at times decisions were made by one person, honey. I don't know....I really felt it would have been better for Putra Jaya to reflect a picture of a true Malaysia," replied Aqiel.

Daniella sarcastically said, "I feel very much at home here, darling."

"Why?" asked Aqiel.

"Don't you notice? They used the term 'Precinct' over here just like back home?" Daniella said.

"Really?" replied Aqiel "I did not notice that.....I don't know, probably someone in power loves America so much!"

"I thought the leaders here hate Americans. Maybe they hate Bush but not America. I am sure you have many beautiful Malaysian names to call your roads or whatever...Malaysians should think as true Malaysians.....I think your leaders are still entrenched with the colonial mindset! Sad, so very sad," she said and smiled sarcastically.

They passed by the King's Palace, Istana Melawati and also the residence of the Prime Minister, on the way out.

"The Palace is so huge. The Queen must be feeling very lonely when the King is away out of town. That's why they always follow their husband outstation, I suppose." she joked.

"The Queen is the pillar of strength for the King, kind of advisor.....without them the King cannot think straight...too many distractions," joked Aqiel.

"You're kidding me, sweetheart. I remember Margaret Thatcher said, "If you want something said, get a man, if you want something done, asked a woman!" interjected Daniella.

"Alright...alright let me rephrase my words....... 'a man, without a woman is nothing' or rather 'a man without a woman, is nothing'......satisfied?"

"I am more confused now," said Daniella.

"I too am confused now, so, let us not get into the intricacies of these jargon....forget all that and let us just enjoy the awesome sight here, darling" Aqiel said.

Pak Man was feeling very confused not because of the conversation of the couple but because of the complicated sign boards. "I am sorry Aqiel....I feel I have passed this area a couple of times just by following the signs up there. The problem with these people is that the Engineer must have given the draft and the sign boards done by the contractors who had no idea where these sign boards were to be installed. In the end what we see in Putrajaya are sign boards that are not friendly to motorists but confused them more. Many were taken on a merry-go-round. Fortunately there is no toll around this area if it had then the Putrajaya toll booths will top the monthly collections in Malaysia!" "I noticed you have been going round and round but since you are a veteran driver I dare not comment.....I saw the sign boards were very confusing," added Aqiel. "I wanted to get out of Putrajaya so I followed the road sign indicating Jalan Tun Razak. The moment you take that turn you are totally loss as there is no more Jalan Tun Razak to follow. I did not realise until I came back to that point again. You know I spend more than half an hour trying to get out of this area. It is time for some smart elite in Putrajaya Board to sit down to sought out the road signs system so that the motorists especially to outstation drivers are not taken on a wild goose chase so to say!" Aqiel added. "Actually what we need badly here is more petrol kiosks for the lost motorists like us," added Pak Man.

# CHAPTER 50

They decided to go for a quick drive to see Cyber Jaya, the heart of Malaysia's Multimedia Super Corridor. Passing through there was like passing through a concrete jungle....buildings and lots of buildings where many multinational companies, from all over the world, invested billions on hardware and software to establish another 'Silicon Valley'.

"It would be nice if this area has more greenery and artificial lakes as landscaping. It would be more pleasant to the eyes" said Daniella.

"Yes, in Malaysia it is a common tendency for contractors to cut down all the big trees during the development....to them it was much easier to build up the buildings and later they look into the landscaping and replanting of the trees. Our leaders never learn from the style of development of the British. They always maintained the big trees as shade and built the buildings around the area. It is definitely a cost saving exercise. It would be more cooling to the area. There will be more Multimedia Super Corridors in Malaysia to cater for the East Coast of Malaysia, Southern Malaysia and Northern Malaysia and eventually in East Malaysia, Sabah and Sarawak. All these projects are supposed to benefit the local people in that area. What I fear is that as in the past these projects only benefitted a certain section of the people leaving the majority in the lurch. There is so much money involved here and if not properly monitored and implemented only than 70% of the total amount expended would filter down to the people," remarked Aqiel. "What happen to the 30%, honey," asked Daniella. "God knows....!" replied Aqiel.

"By the way the next time we are back here we will visit Sabah and Sarawak. Frankly, sweetheart, many Malaysians including me had not been there. We ignore our own tourist spots but feel proud to tell friends of the foreign places we visited. Whenever we tell our friends that we are visiting places in Malaysia they are just not interested even if they themselves have not been there. However, if we mention overseas they have all ears for you!" added Aqiel.

"What a shame," smiled Daniella.

"I have seen more of America and Europe than Malaysia. I have to put that right soon. Anyway this time around we will go to Langkawi Island for a few days before we leave for LA, ok?" said Aqiel.

"What's in Langkawi?" asked Daniella. "Langkawi, honey.....is the most beautiful legendary island in the world, nice resorts....something like Hawaii Islands. Legend has it that a Princess 'Mahsuri', who was pregnant, was brutally killed by local chiefs out of jealousy. Before she died she cursed the island for the next seven generations... the island will not see any development during that period. It really happened. Anyway that curse is now over and the island is slowly being developed for tourists," said Aqiel.

"Why did she curse the island and not the local chiefs that stabbed her? Is it safe to go now? Are the generations of the local chiefs still around?" Daniella suddenly felt rather insecure.

"I agree with you the local chiefs and all those involved should have been cursed not the innocent islanders. It is all over now.....seven generations have passed. The government is turning that island as the tourists' destination in this part of the world. Anyway, as they say the natural beauty of the island is beyond words to describe. They are constructing the cable cars and also the skywalk as additional tourists' attractions. We will see all that when we arrived there. Frankly I have not seen the latest development including the cable cars and skywalk!" smiled Aqiel. "Where are going next Pak Man?" asked Aqiel. "How about the Batu Caves?" said Pak Man. "OK," said Aqiel.

# CHAPTER 51

As soon as they arrived at Batu Caves Daniella was surprised to see thousands of devotees thronging the area. Pak Man dropped them at the entrance and promised to join them after parking the car. Aqiel and Daniella moved slowly following the crowd. Daniella felt safe as there were so many tourists from all over the world taking photographs and climbing the steps into the caves. "What is the big occasion today anyway?" asked Daniella. "Thaipusam.....a religious festival for the Hindus," Aqiel replied, shouting on top of his voice due to the din in that area. The long procession consisting of devotees carrying the kavadis and the chariot of the various Gods started from the Hindu temple in the centre of the city took almost 9 hours to reach Batu Caves. Daniella watched in awe at the many devotees who carried 'kavadis' of various sizes up the 272 steps by 'helped' by the God of Murugan to the top where they have the Hindu temple. "Thai" is the months (January-February) while "Pusam" is the star. Aqiel and Daniella too followed the devotees climbing the steps to the drum beats of their supporters. It was very daunting and taxing if you were to go up alone but following the large crowd and devotees dancing to the drum beats made the climb much effortless. Coming down was a pleasure. When they came down they still could not see Pak Man and Aqiel led Daniella to a stall where they offered coconut water.

That was the first time Daniella tasted coconut water and she just adored it. She requested for a second coconut as it was a very hot day. They then moved to the entrance and only then saw Pak Man desperately looking for them. "I dared not go in because I miss both of you. It took me almost one hour to find an empty car space about two miles from here. Shall I bring the car here Aqiel?" asked Pak Man. "No Pak Man, we will walk with you to the car after all Daniella was once a marathon swimmer and runner!" Aqiel quipped. Daniella just shrugged her shoulders and followed Pak Man though Aqiel knew she was tired after the long climb.

In the car Aqiel explained that the celebration for celebration is held once a year, just for a day. "The biggest celebration in Malaysia is here at Batu Caves as almost one million came to celebrate including about 10,000 tourists Penang came in second besides Negri Sembilan and probably Johore. In the other states the celebration is rather moderate as Indians are a minority group here, round about 8 millions only. In other parts of the world especially in India the celebration is just majestic. But Thaipusam is celebrated on a big scale in Southern India such as in Palani, Kerala including in Sri Langka and many states of which I have lost count.

They then went back to the city to catch a glimpse of the Telecom Tower on Bukit Nanas. Due to the school holidays there was a very long queue. Majority of the crowd made up of tourists from Singapore, China and Japan. They had to queue and it was only after 45 minutes that they got the chance to go into the lift that took them right to the top of the tower. The view from the top was magnificent as it was a very sunny day and the sky was clear. "This is the Eiffel Tower of Malaysia!" said Aqiel.

"On a cloudy day you hardly see anything from up here," Aqiel overheard a tourists guide telling the group of Japanese tourists.

After about 30 minutes of watching the surrounding areas through the telescope they decided to move on to the Twin Tower of PETRONAS or Kuala Lumpur Convention Centre (KLCC). As they were very hungry Aqiel went looking for a suitable place to have lunch first, before exploring the Twin Tower of PETRONAS. Pak Man initially refused to join them for lunch but Aqiel and Daniella insisted. Daniella whispered to Aqiel whether it was the Malaysian custom to invite the chauffeur to join them on the same table.

"We sit with our chauffeur on the same table for breakfast or lunch here, unless it is a breakfast or business lunch with our clients. I believe that we are all humans.....some are more fortunate than others, that's all. An activist once said, "Today we are masters and they are your slaves, one day, they maybe your masters and you their slaves!"

"I love that attitude, sweetheart.....at home the Americans do not practised that! In certain places they don't want to eat in the same restaurant as the blacks," said Daniella.

"I hate Americans, so arrogant and stupid.....sorry.....I don't mean you or all Americans but some, especially those in power. I can still remember that incident in the restaurant vividly, dear. I was eating with my Chinese and Indian friends when a group of corporate Americans asked us to move to another table to give more space and security to some VIPs who came to lunch there. We refused to budge and their bodyguards threatened us. There was nearly a fight, but fortunately, two Police Officers, from a nearby Police Precinct, who were alerted by the restaurant owner, came in and everything cool down. Anyway, the group left the restaurant leaving us to eat in peace. I could not confirm whether they were from the local Mafia group, FBI or CIA officials......they all behave and look the same."

# CHAPTER 52

$A$t the KLCC they opted for a fast food restaurant – 'Kenny Rogers'. Aqiel and Daniella just loved those dishes. Pak Man never did like fast food, he preferred a rice stall. However, having tasted 'Kenny Rogers', he agreed it was a very delicious dish, but "too expensive for me and my family," he said. Pak Man excused himself, as he wanted to say his prayers at the KLCC mosque. He asked Aqiel whether he would want to join him for prayers but Aqiel declined sheepishly. Aqiel and Daniella went to the bookstall located a few floors at the KLCC. Aqiel and Daniella bought a few books they spotted to bring back home. They found the books much cheaper than in America. By 2.15 pm Pak Man joined them and they decided to go to the Putra World Trade Centre, where an exhibition on the latest electronic equipment and gadgets were held. Aqiel's cell phone rang,

"Hello, oh....Ayah....Aqiel ada di KLCC ni......datang keoffice ayah? Sekarang? Lusa bolih ayah? Besok hendak bawak Daniella keMelaka. Okaylah......besok pagi saya datang office dan tengah hari saya pergi Melaka. Bye." (Hello....dad...I am at PWTC now..come to your office? Now? The following day dad? Tomorrow I am going to Malacca with Daniella. Okay.... tomorrow morning I will see you at the office and we will leave for Malacca at midday. Bye."

"Who was that?" asked Daniella.

"My dad, he wants to see me now. Anyway, I managed to convince him to see him tomorrow to which he agreed," answered Aqiel. "Convinced him.....it is more like 'con' him Aqiel," remarked Daniella. "Whatever....anyway after that we can proceed to Malacca. If we are 'forced' to stay in Malacca overnight, I don't mind........" said Aqiel, smiling.

Daniella just stared at him..... "Don't even think for a second......we will sleep in separate rooms. I will get Pak Man to sleep in my room......".

Pak Man heard his name being mentioned asked, "What is it?"

Aqiel replied, "Nothing.....Daniella says there was no need for you to go to Malacca tomorrow since we have to stay overnight......you have a family at home."

"Aqiel......I did not say that. You are too much......Pak Man we thought you might want to go to Malacca and stay overnight there," said Daniella.

"No problem, I love Malacca. My children are all adults, they take care of my wife when I travel outstation, said Pak Man."

"Habis peluang aku!" (That ends my chance!) Aqiel responded with a slap on his forehead.

"But" added Pak Man, "I can stay at my sister's house."

Aqiel smiled and Daniella gave Aqiel a 'pinch' on his thigh. At the PWTC they went straight to the exhibition hall. There were so many new electronic products being introduced and at a very good discounts. He bought a new cell phone set to give away as present to Wawa. Daniella bought a new digital camera to bring to Malacca and Langkawi Island later. Before 5.00 pm they decided to go home. It was a rush hour as most office workers left the office for home. Pak Man, with 20 years of experience driving in the city brought them through the back lanes to avoid the traffic jams.

# CHAPTER 53

At 9.46 am the next morning Aqiel and Daniella were standing in front of the impressive 20-storey building of Bibi Sdn. Bhd. They took a lift up to the 20th floor where his dad's office was located. The secretary told him to take seat as the Chairman was busy, and they sat in the waiting room, browsing through some local magazines. His dad was having a discussion with Alan. After waiting for about half an hour, Alan emerged from Datuk's office. Aqiel greeted Alan and introduced Daniella to him. They chatted for a while before Alan excused himself as he had another meeting to attend. Before Alan left he invited Aqiel and Daniella for dinner before they leave for LA to which they accepted willingly. Aqiel entered Datuk's office leaving Daniella in the waiting room with the secretary. He sat down as Datuk was on the line with a client. It's not that often that he had the chance to come into Datuk's room and he observed a number of photos of Datuk with a number of VVIPs. There was his photo with the Prime Minister of South Africa and behind him a picture when he received the Datukship from the Sultan of Selangor. As soon as Datuk put down his phone he focused his attention on Aqiel.

"How is your work in LA Aqiel? Happy?"

"O.K. dad," replied Aqiel.

"You know I have been working for almost 35 years….I mean really work to see that our business are still competitive and relevant until today. Your uncle Mawi has helped me a lot in the initial stages of the company's growth. Zamani as you know has been appointed as a Judge and is not keen to join the company even after his retirement. As he put it,

"I am no businessman, so I have no business trying to mess up the family business."

"Zamani intends to write novels on crime fictions when he decides to retire. So I decided to just leave him with what he loves best to do," said Datuk. "We found the challenge and responsibility in the corporate world too much for both of us to manage now…so we got Alan to join us. He brought our company to a higher level by going global…with more qualified staffs to assist us. I am actually tired today and your uncle Mawi is no corporate man. We intend to take the back seat and watch the new generation manage the company. Actually Aqiel, I wish you to decide whether you want to come back to help me realise this dream…..that too if you wish to do so. If you feel comfortable working in LA I have no objection as there is no obligation for you to come back."

"How about Uncle Alan, Ayah? He is a very trustworthy and competent person I noticed," said Aqiel.

"He is, Aqiel….someone I can trust with my life. Yes, a very responsible and trustworthy, but, I am looking for a person to understudy him. Alan is in his prime but he needs a good assistance…..so we need a second liner to back him up. Here is my plan. I will remain in the company as non Executive Chairman…."

He rattled on as what he had discussed with his wife.

"When I leave…..Alan will be the Executive Chairman and you take over as the MD…..and eventually, you will be the Executive Chairman and others in the next generation will hopefully help to keep the company going for generations to come."

"I like the idea, dad, but I have to……." replied Aqiel.

"Take your time, think it over…maybe even talk with Daniella…then let me know before you go back to LA," said Datuk.

"Thank you, dad, I will do just that….I won't disappoint you. I got to go now to Malacca and should be back tomorrow evening."

"You are staying overnight in Malacca?" asked Datuk.

"Yes, it will be a rush if we come back on the same day….there is so much to explore there, Abah!"

"Explore?" questioned Datuk.

"No….no…visits…..Abah. Daniella likes to visit historical places you know….she is in the waiting room now," Aqiel stood up to leave.

"Whatever you do, remember you are not in America and…….." Before his dad could finish his advice, Aqiel was out of the room……."

"Bye", he waved to his dad, who quickly followed him to the waiting room. He wanted to say hello to Daniella. Before Aqiel could pulled Daniella out of the office Datuk was behind him.

"Hello Daniella? How are you this morning?" greeted Datuk.

"Fine Datuk, how are you?" replied Daniella.

"OK....I did not know you were out here waiting for Aqiel....you could have come in to join the discussion. Were you served any coffee?"

"Yes, your secretary is very efficient and kept me company while Aqiel was with you. Your office is very impressive and this building is a landmark in KL.!" Datuk just smiled with satisfaction on the compliment given by Daniella.

"We have to go, Abah, or we will be very late in Malacca," interjected Aqiel.

"Okay....by the way where are staying in Malacca? You can get 30% discount if you stay at the Renaissance.....just mention my name......anyway have a good time and buy some 'cincalok' for your mum."

"We have not book any hotel as yet....there should be rooms there as it is not a weekends or school holidays. I will get the 'cincalok' for mum....bye," assured Aqiel.

"Bye Datuk," said Daniella.

# CHAPTER 54

"So….what is 'sinsalok'?…. and….why were you summoned by your dad?" asked Daniella in the car.

"'Cincalok' not 'sinsalok', dear….oh…that's my mum's favourite dish….it is actually some fermented shrimp. If I don't get back with a bottle of 'cincalok' I better stay out of her way for the next one week….she would not forget or forgive me for forgetting her favourite dish! Regarding my dad….well he was feeling lonely…. it is nothing actually….he told me to get married as he was looking forward to cuddle a grandchild…. So I told him we are on our way to……I mean get married in Malacca!" Aqiel jokingly told Daniella.

"Come on, sweetheart, be serious," begged Daniella.

"Okay….okay….my dad want me to join his company and eventually to take over from him. I am not keen to come back here but hope to make my fortune in America and now my dad needs me to help him…..that is something I have to think seriously. He built that company from scratch with a small capital and only 2 employees about 40 years ago and looked at it today. Who would ever believe that this company had such a humble beginnings. He expected me to take over and expand the company further," replied Aqiel.

"That's a very good proposition. Aren't you accepting it? You are the eldest and definitely qualified to run it….so?" said Daniella. "You know I would not mind to stay here if we get married….this is a nice place to work and stay, Aqiel," Daniella said.

"I said I will think about it as I still feel I need to better equip myself before I come back," said Aqiel.

Pak Man who was listening to their conversation interjected,

"Excuse me Aqiel. I know it is not my place to give advice to you. Who am I…"

"Tak apa Pak Man…..you are like my own uncle. From a baby you brought me up like your own son….gave me encouragement and confidence when I feel low….go ahead Pak Man….say what you want to say though it might hurt me," encouraged Aqiel.

"Okay.....you are an adult now and should be getting married to Daniella......I married much younger than you, you know. My wife was only 13 when we got married."

"Wow....so young," interjected Daniella.

"Yes Daniella, but that was our custom then. Today the girls get married rather too late.....sometimes even after 30! Anyway Aqiel, your dad and mum, lately, always talked about you, your future and the company. They had high hopes that you take over as soon as possible. They are both old and tired..... it had been a long struggle for both of them and thanked Allah they have achieved beyond their dreams. You know I have been with them through good and bad times, I know the sufferings they had gone through. They badly need the rest, Aqiel. Now is the time for you to join the company. Uncle Alan is there to guide you and later I hope you and Daniella will keep the company together."

"Thank you Pak Man....thank you."

# CHAPTER 55

For the rest of the journey to Malacca, Aqiel was very quiet, deep in his thoughts about his future. Daniella took a quick nap. Pak Man, man of few words just drove the car without uttering a single word after that though in his head he had so much to say to both Aqiel and Daniella. Though he had only met Daniella recently Pak Man felt down deep inside that he could trust her to be a good wife for Aqiel. After an hour's drive they were at the butterfly and crocodile farms. They took their time to enjoy the places and later checked in at one of the hotels in the city. They told Pak Man to take the car to his sister's house, as they did not need the car that night. They intended to explore the city of history and culture by trishaw or just walking around.

"That should be fun," said Daniella. "If it rains then it would be more fun," said Aqiel. "Why?" Daniella asked innocently. "We can get to sleep early, love," Aqiel quipped. "Aqiel, Aqiel...let us focus on Malacca ok?" Daniella said.

After checking into the hotel they rested for a while, feeling fresh, they changed and went out looking for some food stalls to eat. They were looking for local delicacies. They went to the stalls near the beach at Kota Melaka. It was a beautiful night stroll as the city was well lighted up and many tourists walking around. Malacca is really a fabulous city for tourists to visit. The old buildings had been gazetted as historical heritage and were very well maintained and colourful. The lighting at night made the buildings more majestic. After a dinner of 'nasi goreng China', 'ikan bakar' and other local delicacies they walked back to their hotel. They sat at the lounge where a husband and wife, sang many beautiful melodies of the yesteryears and the current top hits. They also invited patrons to come forward and sing with them. Aqiel, being a singer, needed no persuasion to step to the microphone and sang a few songs including his favourite, "I just call to say I love you". Just before midnight they decided to call it a day and adjourned for bed. They were both dead tired.

The next morning after breakfast they met Pak Man at the porch of the hotel.

"Dah minum pagi Pak Man? (Had your breakfast Pak Man?) asked Aqiel.

"Sudah, kenyang ni......Mak Chik buat nasi lemak dan roti canai lagi. Semalam kena nasi durian....sedap Aqiel!" (Yes, I am full...Aunty prepared 'nasi lemak' and 'roti canai'. Last night she served rice with durian.... delicious Aqiel).

"Selamat pagi, Pak Man," smiled Daniella.

"Selamat pagi....Oh....you can speak Malay now.....just after three nights in Malaysia," replied Pak Man.

"I have been learning Malay from Aqiel for the past three months......tapi malu mau cakap," (but shy to talk) said Daniella.

"Jangan......lagi banyak cakap lagi cepat pandai. Sekarang hendak cakap dengan Daniella dalam bahasa Melayu saja, Okay? (Don't be shy...the more you speak the more proficient you be....now I intend to speak in Malay okay?) If an uneducated person like me can speak English, you should not have any difficulty in mastering the Malay language," said Pak Man.

"O.K." replied Daniella timidly.

# CHAPTER 56

They went for a drive around the outskirts of city to see some of the traditional Malay villages. Malacca is one of the states where the houses in the villages were very well maintained and the house compounds very clean. The housewives swept their house compounds every morning without fail. They cannot bear to see a single leaf lying in their compound in the morning! They stopped by at a stall at Tanjong Kling to buy the local delicacies 'cincalok' (fermented prawns).

"This is 'cincalok', and you eat it with chilli, salted fish and rice. "It's very delicious.....that's my mum's favourite." said Aqiel.

On the way there they saw many bullock carts pulled by bulls or cows on the road. Daniella told Aqiel that she would love to take a ride on one of the bullock carts. Back in the city they took a bullock cart ride and Daniella said it reminded her of the days she went to her uncle's ranch and took a cart ride driven by two horses.

"That was a much faster ride. I will take you there one weekend when we are back. The ranch is just two hour's drive from LA," she said.

"I'll love that," replied Aqiel.

"Pak Man cari makan kedai, saya lapar sekarang," (Pak Man look for a stall food).

"Kedai makan…. Daniella, not makan kedai!" (It's not 'stall food'…. 'food stall', Daniella!)

Aqiel turned his face away from Daniella……laughing quietly…..Daniella quickly put her palm across Aqiel's lips to stop him from laughing.

"I am not laughing at you……I was looking at the antics of little kids playing out there, behaving just like Mr. Bean" said Aqiel.

"Don't you dare……" Daniella said lovingly, hugging Aqiel.

They stopped at a local food court and Daniella tasted some 'gado-gado', 'wan-tan mee' and 'ice kacang'. Pak Man opted for chicken rice and 'teh tarik' while Aqiel ate 'nasi bryani kambing' which was his favourite and 'cendol'. After lunch they checked out from the hotel and returned to Kuala Lumpur. All the way back Aqiel and Daniella were sleeping soundly. Pak Man was thinking to himself,

"These two must be are dead tired….they did not sleep last night, I think, they must have be watching 'Discovery' all night long…..I hope so…."

By 6.15 p.m. they were back in Kuala Lumpur and Aqiel sent Daniella back to Shah Alam. "Tomorrow night is the reception at my house, please remind your uncle and aunty to attend…..including you…." said Aqiel. "You are coming with your uncle Okay? I will send you back after the dinner… bye."

Back in the house her aunty was waiting for her.

"Did you have a lovely time, Daniella? Malacca is a beautiful city right?"

"Oh, yes…..such a fabulous time we had….we should have stayed longer, aunty. There were many exciting places we did not have the time to go. Malacca has many splendid golf courses…the next time we will bring our golf sets for a few rounds of golf there."

"Your uncle has played golf there a couple of times and he enjoys the course," replied the aunty. Do you want any tea, dear?"

"No thanks, we had too much to eat in Malacca. I wonder whether I can join you for dinner tonight," said Daniella.

"Your uncle is attending a dinner reception at the embassy…so it is just you and I. We can have something very light, Okay?"

"Right. I need to take a shower now, aunty, and a little rest. I will come down before six," replied Daniella.

# CHAPTER 57

Daniella was having a quiet dinner with her aunty.

"Are you serious with Aqiel, dear? I find him a very polite and intelligent young man. Not that I have known him that long, but my first impression is that he is someone you can trust, though he looks playful at times," the aunty started the conversation.

"Yes, Martha, I am……..we have been together for almost three years now and I enjoy his company. We are thinking of getting married soon and…… eventually to move here. Mum and dad just adore him. His dad had asked him to help with the business…...he is thinking seriously of coming back. I like Malaysia and just hope I can land a job here once I am married to him."

"That's nice; we hope you made the right choice. We all want to see you happy, dear. Malaysia is a wonderful place to settle. In fact, Uncle Roger is contemplating of getting his Permanent Resident status and to retire here. Our kids are all adults now and Rina wants to work in Australia, while Bill is seriously thinking of working in Germany. We love the sun, so Malaysia is our choice."

"I believe that's a wise decision, aunty. Many foreigners have made Malaysia their second home initially but their final destination when they retire," added Daniella.

It was Saturday night, Roger, Martha and Daniella were dressing up for the dinner at Datuk Khalid's house. Roger was waiting impatiently for the two ladies downstairs. After waiting for half an hour they came down looking gorgeous and pretty. "It was worth the waiting," he thought to himself smiling. "What!" said Martha when she saw the expression and smile on Roger's boyish face. "Nothing," replied Roger who kept on smiling while walking to his car. He was lucky as there were very few cars on the road and they reached the house just before 8.15 p.m. There were already many guests enjoying their drinks and tit bits. Aqiel was anxiously waiting for them at the porch.

When Roger's car arrived at the house Aqiel opened the door for Martha and Daniella while Roger went to park his car. He gave Daniella a kiss on the cheek and guided them into the house to meet his mum. He left them there and went back to the porch to wait for Roger. As soon as Roger emerged, they shook hands and went in to meet his dad and mum. Aqiel, excused himself, then pulled Daniella aside and brought her to meet some of the clients and the office staffs. Alan and Judy were there, so were Mawi and Siti, Nasir, Wong, and many new staffs. Judy came over and said to Aqiel that she wanted to bring Daniella, her uncle and aunty to see the exclusive paintings in the library.

"You mingle with the guests, this is your party, they want to meet the 'heir' to the throne of Bibi Sdn. Bhd. Enjoy yourself, Aqiel. Let me show Daniella the collections and I promise you she will be back with you, say, in fifteen minutes from now!" said Judy.

"That's too long aunty......how about five minutes........you know, I am lost without her around," begged Aqiel.

"Men....that's what they say before they are married, Daniella.....after marriage, they sneaked behind your back.......meeting......meeting....for all you know it is mating...." said Judy. They both laughed.

Judy and Daniella had just met but they'd quickly bonded when they discovered they shared the same passion - paintings. They left Aqiel looking amused. Aqiel followed Alan who introduced him to most of the clients and they casually talk about the local politics and business opportunities. It was a buffet dinner, near the swimming pool, so everybody helped themselves to the local food and drinks. After more than forty minutes Daniella was still nowhere to be seen. Aqiel was getting restless and feeling anxious and just could not focussed his mind on his dad's clients. He was about to go into the house when he saw Daniella and Judy emerged laughing. He excused himself and went straight to them.

"What were you two up to?" asked Aqiel, "Aunty you promised me 15 minutes now it's almost 45 minutes....."

"Sorry," said Judy, "we completely forgot about you......Daniella just told me a joke.....for women's ears only....it's definitely not for you."

"Okay....Okay....if you will excuse us Aunty Judy.....I want to spend some time with Daniella.....alone please. Uncle Alan has been looking all over for you.....I last saw him chatting with a gorgeous sexy lady....I think they went into my bedroom....," joked Aqiel.

"Really?" Judy smiled understandingly and went looking for Alan in the crowd. It was a lovely night, rather cooling and most importantly good company.

# CHAPTER 58

"How do you like my dad's collections of art?" asked Aqiel.

"Impressive!......and I am also impressed with his collection of books. You can find almost any books from science to fictions. I can spend hours in that room everyday, Aqiel. It is amazing for such a man to have the time to read all those books," said Daniella.

"That's over forty five years of collection, sweetheart.......he did not have the opportunity to further his studies in his younger days, so reading those books was his way of catching up with what he missed out," explained Aqiel.

"I believed he would have been a great scholar, architect or engineer had he been given the opportunity," said Daniella.

"I agree, right now with my MBA and working experience, I noticed he is more knowledgeable than me in the business world. He talks to doctors and engineers like he was one of them......fantastic! A few local universities and business alumni had invited him to deliver business talks on a number of occasions. He did and more universities like his approach as his tips were very practical and merely common sense on doing business. The lecturers and students gained much from those lectures. I said to him, one day, you may be bestowed with an Honorary Doctorate by a university."

Datuk laughed and said,

"Without even a first degree I get an Honorary doctorate that will be a great achievement for me!"

"So watch out what you say in front of him," said Aqiel to Daniella.

At 11.15 pm Roger and Martha came over. They said they had to leave. Aqiel said he would send Daniella home.

"The night is still young.....I like to show Daniella, Kuala Lumpur by night.....like the 'Bintang Walk', and 'Bangsar'. She should be back by three in the morning," explained Aqiel.

"Right then......you take this key to the front door Daniella.......take care....good night to both of you," said Roger.

"Good night," replied both of them.

"Mr. Roger, in case it is too late, Daniella may put up here for the night.......will that be alright?" asked Aqiel.

Roger looked at Martha, both hesitated, but Datin who overheard the conversation said,

"Yes, that should be fine......Daniella can used my 'sarong' and 'Kedah dress' to sleep."

"Tak payah emak.......Daniella tu bukan pakai apa pun bila tidur......saya tau lah! (No need, mum Daniella doesn't wear anything to bed.....I know that!).

"Kau ni Aqiel, kalau dia orang faham bahasa kita, marah nanti dia," (If they understand our language they will be angry), quipped Datin.

Roger, Martha and Daniella, not having any inkling of what was said between mother and son, just smiled. Roger said,

"Okay then.......we have to go, bye!"

# CHAPTER 59

Aqiel and Daniella were walking at the famous 'Bintang Walk', which was crowded though the time was about 0200 hrs. Many couples were enjoying drinks and food at the café some were shopping around while others just came to join the crowd. There were many tourists. There were no 'peep-shows' like at 'Soho' in London or in Sydney. Everybody came to enjoy and forget their worries...... 'don't worry, be happy' was the motto. Aqiel and Daniella stopped at one of the café and ordered a cup of capuccino each while watching the crowd passed by. They left at 3.45 am and it was too late to go to 'Bangsar', the city food centre. They left for Aqiel's house and were home by 4.30 am. Datin was still downstairs, waiting for them. She was tired and sleepy, but had to wait to make sure Aqiel kept strictly to the house 'code of ethics'....sleep in his room...alone....until he is legally married. Datin knew if she did not wait for them, Aqiel would lure Daniella into his bedroom. They said goodnight downstairs and Datin, smiling, led Daniella upstairs to her bedroom. Daniella looked at Aqiel and just shrugged her shoulders. Aqiel, looking gloomy, went into his bedroom downstairs.

The next morning Datuk and Datin were having breakfast but Aqiel and Daniella were still fast asleep. Datuk was reading the Sunday morning papers around 10.00 am when Aqiel came out from his room followed by Daniella. Daniella was wearing 'Baju Kedah' and a sarong (Casual Malay dress for women). Both Datuk and Datin were stunt to see both of them emerging from Aqiel's room. Datin for one was more shocked as she had waited and personally put Daniella into the guest's room upstairs earlier. Datuk's disapproval looked made Datin very uncomfortable.

"Macam mana ni?" (What happened here?) asked Datuk.

"Tak tau," (I don't know) replied Datin.

Aqiel who was at the breakfast table with Daniella overheard the conversation. He cheekily replied,

"Daniella ni selalu 'sleep walking' emak. Aqiel bangun pagi tadi tengok tengok dia ada sebelah! Tak ada apa apa pun!" (Daniella used to walk in her sleep, when I woke up this morning she was sleeping on the bed! Nothing happen!)

Datuk could not control his smile over Aqiel's smart remarks and soon Datin was laughing,

"Engkau ni lah Aqiel, ada ada saja! (You, Aqiel, always have a ready answer!) Daniella, not knowing what was said, joined the laugh.

After taking their bath, Aqiel requested for permission from his parents to send Daniella home.

"We are thinking of going to Langkawi Island for a few nights. We had already made reservations for the flight and hotel. We love if both of you can join us but the hotels and flights are fully booked, so perhaps the next time, emak....ayah."

Datuk looked at Datin and said, "We can drive down by car and take the boat from Kuala Perlis, no problem, and I can get a room at your hotel through my contact. Aqiel can share a room with me and Daniella with your mother..."

Aqiel became restless......"but since I have urgent things to attend .......we will not join you this time", added Datuk. Aqiel sighed with relief.

That evening Aqiel and Daniella went to Istana Hotel to keep their dinner date with Alan and Judy. Alan and Judy remembered their stay overseas and believed Aqiel and Daniella must be experiencing the same bliss in LA. Judy asked Daniella,

"How do you like Malaysia now that you have seen Malacca and around the city of Kuala Lumpur and PutraJaya?"

"Seriously, it is a beautiful country with amazingly friendly people. We intend to go Langkawi Island for a few days and Aqiel promised me that the island is just like 'Fantasy Island'," answered Daniella.

"It's Daniella....you will love that island. So many spots to explore, both historical and tourists' attractions and you do not feel like coming back to Kuala Lumpur after that visit! The weather maybe a bit too warm most of the time but I think you can adjust to that better than facing winter," said Judy.

"I just dread winter.....especially when you get 2 to 3 feet of snow. The whole city is paralysed at times. Here I understand you do not experience extreme change in weather like cyclones, typhoons, earthquakes and floods. In Malaysia very mild floods and winds hit you. I hate all that because the natural disasters are recurring annually and the damage to the people is tremendous with devastating effect on their lives notwithstanding the rebuilding of the cities and homes, which costs billions to the governments and taxpayers. Like the recent Katrina typhoon…..the people until today have not recovered from the trauma from that phenomenon, which was very real and devastating," replied Daniella.

# CHAPTER 60

"Both of you had stayed so long overseas and may realise that the people there are totally different from here," said Aqiel. "We do not discuss too much about the US administration but are more focussed on our own jobs and ambitions. Business opportunities in US are simply abundant and it was entirely up to the individual to go for it. The purchasing power of the people is enormous so any good idea can make big money. Success stories from rags to riches like Michael Dell and his PC computers, Eli Broad in homebuilding, the amazing Chris Gardner success from an apprentice to proud owner of stock brokerage company and Kyle MacDonald idea of swapping a paper clip for a house, are all inspiring stories to hear. You can make good money in the US if you can translate your good ideas into reality. If my dad does not have a business to run here probably I would stay in US to build my future. Business opportunities there are for everybody....the sky is the limit you know."

"I would have done the same thing if I did not think about Datuk and Datin. Anyway, after being here helping Datuk, I have no regrets but a feeling of fulfilment," said Alan.

"I was born in US and making Malaysia my home is not a bad idea. It would be different if the economy here is bad, then I would urged Aqiel to stay in US," added Daniella.

"Doing business here and overseas are totally two different scenarios......" said Alan, but he did not elaborate. "By the way do you play golf Aqiel? Alan asked Aqiel..

"I never did like that game Alan.....though I love watching basketball, baseball and American football," replied Aqiel.

"Any special reason why you do not like golf?" asked Judy.

"Well a number of good reasons actually. Firstly, from what I read in the medical journal, golf is not a very good form of exercise though you walk for miles. Today you do not get the chance to walk as you are required to use the buggy! It is very time consuming...imagine spending almost 5 hours hitting that small stationary ball! You can spend less than 1 hour at squash or badminton and get much better results physically.....or even jog for 6 or 7 miles three times a week around the neighbourhood. Swimming and cycling would be very good alternatives.

Secondly, and to me most importantly, we deprive the homeless from getting cheap homes. Even desolate land in the rural areas is sold by the square foot…too expensive for the rural folks to purchase and encouraging those with land to part with it. Too many premium agricultural land in the rural areas have been converted into golf courses…..reducing the fertile agricultural land to be developed with varieties of crops…..rearing of animal stocks….food for the nation….making us less dependants on imports of foodstuff and savings of billions of ringgit on foreign exchange. Golf courses only benefitted a handful of golfers and imported foreign workers besides the filthy rich owners of the club! This is just absurd and ridiculous! So back in US I prefer to jog or just go to the gym thrice a week," said Aqiel.

"That's a mindboggling reasons, Aqiel. I never thought of golf in that perspective…….I play golf to get business contacts. However, I noticed today not many successful business leaders are playing golf………too time consuming to them, they say……you see them only during charity golf tournaments," said Alan.

"I have told Alan how I felt about golf, Aqiel, but he insisted that it was good for his business. Frankly golf has not given us quality time to spend with the family…..Alan is away on the golf course almost every weekend! In fact he has his mini gym at home but sadly never could find time to exercise there. Sonny and I are the one that utilised the gym," Judy lamented.

"Actually I have that mini gym for you and Sonny to sweat it out," smiled Alan. "I don't mind if we exercise together….that would be fun!" Judy laughed cheekily.

"I agree with you that today in Malaysia there are too many golf courses…. the Klang Valley itself has more than 50 courses today. Not all are being utilised daily except for a few golf clubs like the Subang Golf Course…. practically fully booked daily!" Aqiel added.

Alan interjected, "I read somewhere about Kevin Costner who said, "Sex and golf are the only two things you can enjoy even if you are not good at them!" Everybody had a good laugh over it.

# CHAPTER 61

O n Tuesday morning Pak Man sent Aqiel and Daniella to the airport to take the flight Langkawi Island. They went to check in and suddenly there was a commotion at the ticket counter. Daniella saw people panicking at the ticket counter. A little girl was crying and some people were trying to help a man who had fallen down. Aqiel came to her side and said that a man had fainted. An ambulance arrived to take him to the nearest medical centre. After waiting for a few minutes the airport announced the departure of their flight to Langkawi Island. It was a short flight, barely forty minutes. From the flight Daniella who was so impressed with the view, seeing so many little islands, the corals and the deep blue sea said,

"This place is more beautiful than Hawaii or the Bahamas, sweetheart."

"I told you so remember….the most beautiful resort in the world! We can go cruising or fishing and later go sightseeing around the island. I love to ride on a motorbike for two….more fun," Aqiel said excitedly.

At the airport they took a cab to the Hotel Pelangi, at Pantai Cenang. It was a beautiful hotel by the beach. They checked in and rested for a while. Aqiel was trying to get a quick nap. Daniella did not sleep, but was watching the local TV station. Suddenly there were scenes at the airport where they witnessed the incident earlier. She could not understand what was narrated in Malay so she woke up Aqiel to listen to the announcement. Aqiel, rubbing his eyes, feeling strained, tried to focus on the announcement.

"Oh, dear……remember the commotion at the ticket counter…..one of the passengers coming to Langkawi Island died of heart attack. He was our local TV personality. He was only 41 years old, dear. The little girl we saw crying was the daughter, it is so sad to lose your dad at such a tender age."

"What about her mother?" asked Daniella.

"She has a mother….separated from him a few years earlier. But, she is closer with her dad, I heard" replied Aqiel.

"Thank God…..she has a mother" said Daniella.

"What time is it?" asked Aqiel.

"1.15 p.m. dear, I am very hungry….must be the weather," said Daniella.

The restaurant was crowded when they came in. They were ushered to an empty table near the window, overlooking the beach. The beach here was not the best, but crowded with tourists, who came to water ski, ride the water jet scooters or try parasailing.

Aqiel said, "There are better beaches at the smaller islands, quiet and isolated".

He led Daniella by her hand to see the local dishes that were displayed at the buffet corner. Western food was abundant. Since both felt very hungry they opted for buffet lunch. There was just too much food to choose, too lavish. Aqiel advised Daniella to try to taste a little bit of everything.....that will satisfy her curiosity.

She said she wanted to savour local dishes only..... "You cannot get that back in America!"

"Good choice," replied Aqiel. "What's your drink?" asked Aqiel.

"Fresh coconut water, sweetheart," replied Daniella.

"Waiter, two fresh coconuts please.......table number 9," Aqiel whispered to the waiter who was standing close by.

After lunch they decided to go for a walk on the beach, "to help digest the food," she said. It was a very warm day and many tourists were sunbathing while the kids were happily running around, some building sandcastles, while others trying to catch tiny crawling crabs in the sand. There were many on water scooters. Some couples just lazed around enjoying the sea breeze. There were many fishing boats taking tourists for deep fishing experience. Whatever it was the atmosphere here was one of fun and relaxation, ideal for those in need of complete rest. Aqiel and Daniella walked and walked, talking about their future and dreams until they came to a dead end, the rocky part of the beach. There they explored the rocks for fish trapped in the hollow part of the beach. There were many colourful small fishes swimming. It was fun to try to catch them. They found some nice shells on the beach but decided not to pick any shell, as they had no real need of it.

# CHAPTER 62

They turned back to the hotel and on the way met with a few fishermen who just came back from the sea. They were busy classifying their catch, of all sizes and variety, into separate baskets such as crabs, squids, prawns and fishes.

Aqiel greeted them and inquired whether they had a good their catch that morning. They replied "Very good catch…..more than expected. Would you like some prawns, squids or crabs?" It was a very tempting offer and would be ideal if they were camping at the beach. They had to decline the offer as Aqiel felt they needed them more than him. They just squatted down and watched the fishermen busy putting their catch in different baskets. "Are you selling it to the middle men?" asked Aqiel. "No……we used to but the middle men con us and made more money than us. Now what we had done was to form our own cooperative, buy a small old van and sell to market or 'pasar tani'….it was more lucrative!" they said. "Yes….a very good idea. What the government should do is to give grants or easy payment loans," said Aqiel. "We agree to that idea, in fact for years our grandfathers and fathers had been fighting to get these grants or loans but their promises remained promises. We wanted to be independent. For example in agriculture where products like padi, fruits, eggs and vegetables are produce through the hard effort of the rural people and the middlemen come in with their vans from the town and sell the products 6-10 times above the prices they bought. They gave excuses that the transport costs had gone up and many other reasons to convince the individual farmers that they should sell cheaper. The government formed FAMA to help the rural people to sell their products but even FAMA has its own agenda," one of the fisherman said..

"We, who had been fishermen for ages and today we are still facing the same problems. We risked our lives for days and nights in the rough sea. When we returned to land we are subjected to the demands of our middlemen. They have ice factories, lorries and wholesalers to back them up. We are paid a meagre sum for our effort because the fishing boats are also owned by them…… we are just mere workers!" another fisherman said. Daniella looked at Aqiel as she could barely understand what they were discussing. Aqiel understand the plight of the farmers and fishermen but until today the government treated these problems very lightly. What is the government's agenda on this matter? Aqiel believed that given the right encouragement these farmers and fishermen would be able to stand on their two feet and totally eliminate these middlemen concept as they have the products. Today we have many Malays in our markets selling fish, meat, vegetables eggs and many other agricultural products but these products are again sold by the middlemen or in towns they are known as wholesalers. They just set-up a shop in town and completely control the agricultural products, distributing them to retailers at much higher price. "We do not have the money to buy the big boats and the fishing equipments neither can we afford to build an ice factory or buy lorries. We are the genuine workers but why are we still struggling to make ends meet? Some drastic measures must be taken by the government if they want bumiputra to be respected in the business world. If the government still feels that by giving subsidies for padi fields or diesel to the fishermen would be of great help they are totally mistaken. The middlemen are enjoying these subsidies and the only way to genuinely help the farmers and fishermen is by forming strong cooperatives that can eliminate these unscrupulous middlemen. If the government still persists to continue with the old system the farmers and fishermen will continue asking for subsidies for the next 50 years......probably that is what the government wants," lamented one of the fishermen. Aqiel was quiet and after shaking hands with them bid them goodbye.

# CHAPTER 63

While walking back to the hotel Daniella asked Aqiel, "What was that about?" Aqiel, initially was reluctant to discuss the matter with her but soon relented. "This is about poor opportunities in my country, honey.....the government after hearing their complaints, is, to me, not solving the problems hands on." "What do you mean?" asked Daniella. The farmers and the fishermen are the one who toil the land and catch the fish but they remain poor forever. The middlemen who just wait at the jetty gets richer and richer by expanding their business," said Aqiel. "So?" continued Daniella. "The hard work is done by these poor people but the middlemen get wealthy......that is why they are not happy. The fisherman have no resources to buy boats, ice factories or lorries and the farmers lie the padi planters cannot dream of building a rice mill. My contention here is why don't the government build these facilities and let their cooperatives run the business from A-Z.....totally eliminating the middlemen?" replied Aqiel. "If the government continues with these policies then the economy of the poor farmers and fishermen will remain as it is today.....always waiting for subsidies!" added Aqiel. "You know the government has so much money from the income of petroleum, timber, palm oil and many others but some of this income has been misappropriated by unscrupulous leaders. The fate of these farmers and fishermen can drastically change if that billions of ringgit misappropriated are channelled to uplift the economy of these poor rural folks. Remember they are the one who supply food daily on our table," said Aqiel. "Now I understand why through the conversation you had with the fishermen they suddenly became serious, darling," said Daniella.

Back at the hotel they decided to take a swim in the hotel pool. After changing into proper swimming attire they went to the pool. There were not many guests around. They choose a secluded spot to put their things. As soon as Daniella took her towel away Aqiel who was watching her in her two piece swimming suit, made a whistle,

"What?" asked Daniella.

"You look stunning in that two piece suits...let us get back to our room, sweetheart....swimming in the pool is a waste of time! I can lose more calories in the bedroom!" said Aqiel.

Daniella, who was a college swimmer, waved her hand to Aqiel, and said,

"Catch me if you can…...see you later", quickly she jumped into the pool followed by Aqiel.

Aqiel struggled to catch up with her…she had very strong effortless strokes, keeping Aqiel far behind. Daniella took pity on him, so she swam back to meet Aqiel. Aqiel gasping above the water asked her,

"Wow….you really can swim….where did you learn to swim like that, sweetheart?"

"Long story," said Daniella. "I am not going anyway, love," said Aqiel. "OK…..I started seriously when I was five years old. I had ambition to swim in the Olympics, but I lost out in the trials when I was 16 years old. Those selected were really great swimmers…..they spend more time in the pool than in bed….all on their own initiatives. The trainers only trained them in the evening for four hours daily. I did not have the time and actually no initiative to do that as I wanted to do well also in my academics. Anyway, I won a couple of local schools and college championship before I retired from competitions. No regrets…I made my choice. Where did you learn swimming?"

"Me? Well, I started jumping into the river behind my granddad's house in the village at the age of nine…no swimming lessons….purely my 'kampong' strokes….my granddad tried to teach me…..but he himself could barely keep afloat…..so I just wriggle my body, throw my arms and legs, like Tarzen, and try to stay afloat….," laughed Aqiel. "No wonder…. sweetheart, your swimming style is so unique…..you should move forwards……..not…..backwards" joked Daniella. Aqiel splashed her with some water. "Actually in Malaysia there is not much emphasis put in schools on swimming. So we have no local competitions regularly. Not many towns have standard public swimming pools, even now. Though we are surrounded by water the culture is not there as the youths prefer other forms of exercises such as badminton, basketball, football and other games where the facilities are easily available. The kids go into the water during picnics…..so nothing serious. I believe if the public swimming pools can be free of charge to school kids then more kids will be interested in swimming." "Anyway they need qualified coaches, with due respect not your grandfather, to teach them to swim…..forwards not backwards Aqiel," Daniella laughed. Aqiel too smiled, "Today most of the swimmers started on their own in streams and rivers behind their villages as a form of recreation rather than anything serious.

If more emphasis is given then swimming can be part of our sports. Doctors say that swimming is the best form of exercise."

"I noticed that….you swim with your head above the water, gasping for air all the time…..that is not the way to do it. You use too much energy, lose speed and tire fast. With that style you will need lots of stamina and even trying to swim 5 metres will take a great effort. You will start gulping lots of this unhygienic water before you reach the other end of the pool! If we have more swimmers like you then before the day is over half the water in this pool will be gone! Come let me show you how it is done," said Daniella.

"Okay….I hope before we get back to Kuala Lumpur I can beat you in the 50 metres free style, Daniella!" laughed Aqiel.

"It may take you more time than that…probably in a hundred years, if you are lucky!" said Daniella giggling like a little girl.

Aqiel eventually relented, "Okay….alright…teach me lesson number one………"

So Daniella taught Aqiel the right breathing exercise and proper strokes and kicks to move forward while holding on to the edge of the pool. "You must keep on doing that until I asked you to stop, OK?" ordered Daniella. Aqiel nodded his head in the water. Daniella kept on Aqiel doing the basic exercise until Aqiel got bored when he suddenly grabbed her and they both went down under the swimming pool for almost two minutes. The other swimmers who saw them went down were watching anxiously but were very relieved when their heads popped out of the water. Both came out gasping for breath.

"Aqiel…….you are not too bad under water…..you swim like a fish and have very good breathing rhythm," laughed Daniella. "Do you know that many long distant swimmers swim 5-6 hours everyday non-stop for days a week. Probably, since you can stay long under water you should take up long distance swimming," smiled Daniella.

After a while they got out of the pool and ordered some refreshments. While relaxing on the beach chair they talk again about his idea of moving back to Kuala Lumpur.

"Whatever you decide, sweetheart, I want to be married to you before you move back. I want to be with you always…..promise me, please," pleaded Daniella.

"I am not coming back without you, Daniella, not after all we had gone through. I don't want to wake up in the morning and find a different person besides me."

# CHAPTER 64

The next day Aqiel rented a motor bike (a Honda cub) and they took a tour around the island. They first went to Padang Matsirat to see the Mausoleum where Princess Mahsuri was laid to rest. It was a small place and nearby was the area where there was the legendary 'beras terbakar', (burnt rice), had for centuries been found in the sandy area. They then proceeded to the cable car that took them to the one of the highest peak on the island. From there they took a walk on the Sky Walk and admired the scenery around Langkawi Island.

"The scenery from the top of that hill was just phenomenal and panoramic!" said Daniella.

Later they took a long trek up another hill to the 'seven wells' (telaga tujuh), a waterfall picnic spot with 7 wells going down the hills all the way through a tunnel to the sea. Nobody had survived that slide down the waterfalls from the top of the hill. There had been reported cases of accidents when some adventurous tourists ventured too far to the edge of the waterfall. They fell into the ravine into the waterfall and their bodies were never recovered. It is not a dangerous picnic spot if the swimmers confine themselves within the safety zone of the seven wells. On the way out they stopped at other interesting places before stopping at the famous Hot Springs where Aqiel tried the traditional reflexology. It was quite painful initially but more relaxing after a while. After that they explore the shopping centres in the town of Kuah before they adjourned for lunch. "Do you know that this is a duty free island?" asked Aqiel. "Really? No wonder the electrical goods, chocolates and many other items are much cheaper than in Kuala Lumpur," said Daniella. "It is not only those items, even cars and motorbikes are tax free!" said Aqiel. "Then we should buy a car or motorbike here and bring it to Kuala Lumpur," said Daniella cheerfully. "Hold it.....it is not that easy......if you buy a car or motorbikes you have to keep it here for 5 years before you can it to the mainland. For small items you must stay overnight on this island for at least 3 nights if I am mistaken," Aqiel explained. "Oh, I see, let us drop the idea then," said Daniella.

After lunch they decided to buy some local souvenirs for their friends in America at the handicraft centre. Here one can find not only handicrafts from Kedah but also from other parts of Malaysia. There were numerous souvenirs to choose but Daniella was attracted to the local 'batiks' and Selangor pewter items. After walking around the small town of Kuah they decided to have a drink. They stopped at a stall and Daniella order two coconuts. "Ehhh.....bolih tolong beri saya dua kepala muda." The stall owner smiled and Aqiel could not help laughing. "What is wrong?" asked Daniella. "Kelapa not kepala, honey, kelapa is coconut and kelapa is head!" answered Aqiel. Daniella was embarrassed. After they had their drink they soon decided to return to the hotel to rest. In the coffeehouse at the hotel they met some tourists who mentioned places that interest Daniella. These places included the book village, the National Art Centre, the restaurant in the crocodile swamp, an island known as 'Pulau Dayang Bunting' (Island of the Pregnant Concubine) and many others.

"We will try to visit those places tomorrow if time permits," said Aqiel, "but I will not take you to Pulau Dayang Bunting because you should not get pregnant before we are married!"

"Why? Why do you say that?" inquired Daniella.

"That island is special, especially to the ladies!" replied Aqiel.

"I don't understand, honey?" said Daniella.

"I will explain to you later in our room!" laughed Aqiel while giving a loving hug to Daniella.

# CHAPTER 65

In the evening after dinner they sat at the hotel lounge to enjoy the local musicians entertaining the guests. Aqiel really enjoy this kind of entertainment as they played local Malay and international songs. They met a couple from Australia, a rancher, who joined their table for the night. The Australians, a very friendly couple proudly talked about their cattle and horse ranch. They owned about 2,500 acres of land to breed the cattle and horses. They also grew some grapes, apples, oranges and mangoes. Once a year they took time for about two weeks to 'see the world', they said. The husband reminded Aqiel of the famous Australian character 'Crocodile Dundee', and his wife like Karrie Webb, the famous Australian golf champion!

On the second day they visited the book village which was temporarily closed.

Daniella said, "I hope they do not close the book village permanently. This is a very good concept as the village being located on a paradise island gives more time for parents and their children to devote quality time reading books. It's a good way to cultivate the good habit of reading among children."

"Malaysians barely read a book a year, I was told, so the former Chief Minister of Kedah, an avid reader himself, wanted to inculcate the good habit of reading. I hope, whoever takes over the government will continue this good cause…..put aside their political or personal differences!" said Aqiel.

They proceeded to the National Art Centre. Here were displayed paintings from Malaysia's top artists and painters for tourists to view. Some of the paintings were up for sale.

"I noticed that you have many talented artists in Malaysia. If they were born during the time of John Constable, Michelangelo, Leonardo da Vinci, Claude Monet or Pablo Picasso, I am sure some of them will achieve fame as those European artists did. It's actually a question of timing, dear," said Daniella.

"Maybe and maybe not…..those living in the Malay Archipelago then were considered as uncivilised in the eyes of the Europeans. Art as you know is the visual expression of civilisation and Europe for centuries was at the peak of her civilisation. Islamic paintings and architecture, however, were idolised by the Europeans because the Islamic world were more civilised than the Europeans then," admitted Aqiel.

They then proceeded to see the Underwater World (Fish aquarium) that boasts of so many salt-water fish and mammals. Daniella was not very impressed with the aquarium, as she had seen much better 'Underwater World' back in America.

"This aquarium actually is to cater for the local tourists as foreign tourists had seen better ones elsewhere," quipped Aqiel.

By midday they decided to return to the hotel due to the extreme heat. They had a quick lunch and rested in their air-conditioned room to beat the heat. Aqiel, who was exhausted, soon fell asleep. Daniella, who was still very excited with the local environment, turned on the local TV station to learn more about the country. It was later in the evening that they went for a stroll on the beach when the atmosphere was quite cooling and breezy. There were many other couples sitting around on the beach absorbing the beauty of the sunset. They sat down for a while, chatting listlessly, and watching the beauty created by Allah right across the blue sea. The brilliant mixed of colours splashing in the sky as the sun went down slowly was just amazing sight to watch. The cool breeze caressing their faces made Daniella quivered and she snuggled closer to Aqiel. The evening was getting cooler so they decided to go back to the hotel.

# CHAPTER 66

O̲n the third day Daniella and Aqiel went for a walk on the beach. Daniella was fascinated with the facilities available so she decided to try her skill on the Jet ski, wind surfing and parasailing where a number of operators were waiting for tourists. So immediately after breakfast they went to the beach and hired a jet ski each. Aqiel had a motorbike licence but Daniella was a beginner. So this time around Aqiel showed off his mastery in riding the jet ski. Daniella, anyway, tried her hand on riding the jet ski with Aqiel closeby on another jet ski. Initially it could be quite testing for a beginner but with some guidance from Aqiel she was able to control the throttle of the jet ski. Aqiel, however, caution her not to stay too close to the beach where there are many swimmers as it could be very dangerous. He told about an incident he saw on the beach in Bali when two girls on a jet ski went out of control and hit one of the swimmers right on the head. It was a fatal accident but could have been avoided if the jet ski stayed away from the crowded beach. Having tried riding the jet ski she abandoned the idea of riding by herself and jumped on to Aqiel's jet ski as the pillion rider. It was a more romantic ride.

Though scared when Aqiel came up with some heroic stunts she soon felt very comfortable holding on to him. Aqiel next tried his skill on wind surfing while Daniella too tried it but without much success. She was in the water more than surfing over it. The balancing act and the wind were crucial factors that Daniella had to quickly adjust. Both factors played very important roles ensuring of enjoying parasailing. Very soon she gave up and decided to try parasailing of which she had some experience previously. She had some experience on hand gliding back home in the country, so she took to the sky like an eagle. After more than 25 minutes hovering around she came down and told Aqiel of the beautiful feeling to be up there.

"It was like flying without wings," she said. "The scenery was just absolutely terrific with the blue sea on the left and on the right the lush green of the Langkawi Island. I saw you from up there, so small and helpless, on the white beach close to the vast blue sea. Suddenly, I started to imagine about the tsunami that hit this part of the world. Imagine the angry 30-foot waves hitting onto the beach bringing down trees, houses and buildings almost three miles into the inland. The thought of the tsunami brought me down fast."

Aqiel added, "I never thought about it until now.....what a nightmare for those who survived the ordeal and lost their loved ones. The underwater earthquakes are still going on in Indonesia…this is a unique phenomenon that was unheard of during our lifetime".

Aqiel while was watching her like a hawk though he was wind surfing. He was scared of the danger if she got stuck in the trees or the buildings near the beach. "I was terrified seeing you hovering up there. I once saw a man, who was enjoying parasailing got entangled to a tall coconut tree in Batu Ferringhi, Penang. It was just his bad luck as suddenly a gush of strong wind through him off balance and pushed his parachute to a coconut tree where he got stuck. Fortunately, he was not hurt but his ego was bruised. Imagine being stuck between the leaves of the coconut tree for nearly 60 minutes with the Sunday crowd watching him before the local fire brigade managed to bring him down safely. Anyway the holiday makers applauded him when he reached the ground. He was so embarrassed and soon was seen running towards the hotel nearby…. and that evening that incident was shown on the local TV again," said Aqiel. "You know what darling?" said Daniella. "What?" asked Aqiel. "I would like to try water skiing," she answered. "It is late now as we have to catch a flight back to Kuala Lumpur in a few hours time. Probably we can do that when we go for our honeymoon in the Caribbeans," said Aqiel. "OK," said Daniella lovingly.

# CHAPTER 67

After resting in the afternoon they took a flight back to Kuala Lumpur. At the airport they got acquainted with a young couple from Germany. They said they extended their two-day to five-day stay, as there was so much to discover at the Berjaya Langkawi Beach & Spa Resort, Burau Bay. The travel agency in Munich recommended the resort which offered to tourists with a difference.... the water chalets.

"We saw the brochure, a beautiful resort with traditional Malay wooden bungalows built over the sea on stilts, and we love it. The gentle sea breeze and lapping sound of the waves under the chalet will lull you to sleep. Privacy is assured as each bungalow has space for its own private balcony with deck chairs, separate shower with a view of the Andaman Sea. Security is guaranteed as they had security guards and frequent Marine Police rounds at the resort. There are so many choices of sports and recreation activities organised, such as jungle trekking, golf at Gunung Raya Golf Club or the Datai Golf Club, island tour, island hopping, fishing and snorkelling. They arranged group day and sunset cruises whenever there is a request. That's a very exclusive resort," the young couple told Aqiel.

Daniella was very impressed and said to Aqiel that the next time around in Langkawi Island, Berjaya Langkawi Beach & Spa Resort will be her first choice.

They realised how tired they felt when they reached home. Office mates in America advised their friends to go for a holiday when they are mentally tired.......the truth is....you get extremely more tired physically and financially, though, possibly, very refreshed....mentally. It takes another few days before you can fully recover! Aqiel and Daniella made up their mind to take a flight back to LA on Sunday night and were fortunate there were seats available.

Aqiel decided to take Daniella for a quick drive to his home town Seremban the next morning. Aqiel arrived early at Daniella's place that morning. "I have a surprise for you today. We are going to take a trip to where my grandfather was born, a very small village, known as 'Pantai' (Beach), not touched by development until now. 'Pantai?' isn't that a beach? Is the place near the beach, dear," Daniella asked. "No...no...there is no beach or sea close by but you will notice that the ground in that village is sandy, just like the beach. Probably thousands of years ago that area must be underwater or close to the sea. We need world renowned geologists to do a thorough study here to determine the truth. However, there must be a good reason for naming that village 'Pantai', dear," explained Aqiel. Actually I want to show you a very unique architecture of the famous Minangkabau house in those days. Unique because there is not a single nail were used in the construction of that house. In Negri Sembilan there were many houses and one of these houses is my grandfather's. From there we proceed go for a short visit to my grandmother's village completely isolated from any development since the first time I set my eyes on it.

If we have the time we may spend sometimes at Port Dickson, a small resort town by the sea," Aqiel explained. "Today there is no Pak Man, so you will have to just trust my driving. Anyway it is a very short drive to these places," Aqiel added. Daniella was happy just to be alone with Aqiel and it did not really matter where he took here even to the moon! She just smiled and Aqiel having a quick glance at her puzzled looked and was curious why Daniella was so amused. "You look cheerful this morning, love.....care to share with me?" Aqiel asked. Daniella just shrugged her shoulders and smiled. Aqiel drove the BMW 5 Series onto the highway to Seremban. "Both my dad's and mum's families have their roots in Negri Sembilan, a state just 45 minutes drive from Kuala Lumpur. In those days before the highway was constructed it took us almost 2 hours to get there.

One thing I like about the old road, though it was small, the environment was very scenic and very much cooling because of the huge trees lining up the roads. Most of my relatives are staying all over Negri Sembilan except for the younger generations who today worked all over Malaysia in search greener pastures. However, I believe more than 60% of them I have not met only some of the elderly relatives like my uncles and aunts. After driving for a while Aqiel explained to Daniella that on the left is Putrajaya/Cyberjaya where she saw the new administrative centre of Malaysia yesterday. Later after a few minutes of driving Aqiel said, "We are turning towards KLIA where we landed from LA. That is the one of the old roads to Seremban. That old country roads though very small through KLIA can be very interesting to tourists as we will be passing by many rural development areas like the Felda schemes." Daniella was curious about Felda, "What is Felda?" "It was an ingenious idea of our

2nd PM who wanted to open up the vast waste land in the jungle and make it productive for the nation through abundant labour force in form of those landless hardworking Malays.

In those days, I understand not many landless Malays were willing to sacrifice their lives in these settlements. They had been so used to the security of doing odd jobs in the villages enough for their day to day survival. Those fishermen who had been in that industry for generations were more difficult to convince. They felt lost working on land and what more in the jungle. The early settlers had to struggle as government assistance was very limited. They had to build their own homes, felled the jungle, prepare the land, plant the rubber seedlings and survived on supply of water and food from the rivers or animals in the jungle. The settlers were paid by Felda a nominal sum in return for their effort. They built their own makeshift homes and had no schools for the kids. It was only later that the houses and rubber plantations were contracted out and the settlers came in to the scheme when all the infrastructures were ready. Schools, mini shops, Police posts, clinic, water supplies, electricity, mosques were some of the facilities ready. It was a new self contained village in the middle of nowhere. The success story of Felda spread far and wide and soon more Malays applied to be settlers including the ex-servicemen. More land was opened including in the interior of East Malaysia.

# CHAPTER 68

Today Felda is the cash cow and 'fixed deposit'of the government and more areas are now planted with palm oil. Believe me Daniella, there are so many millionaires in Felda schemes today......imagine from being landless and poor to proud rich landowners," related Aqiel. "Wow....it sounds like the Wild....Wild West, but in those days the rich get richer," exclaimed Daniella. "During those early years no other country in the world ever started any rural development scheme systematically like Felda. Each settler (family man) is given a small house with a reasonable plot of land including about 10 acres of rubber, oil palm and some land for orchards and fish ponds. Schools, sundry shops, mosque, electricity, water and many other amenities were built for their convenience. Initially it was so difficult to get the landless to move into these schemes as they had been used to easy lives by doing odd jobs in the villages. Once they joined as settlers they had to follow strictly the regulations just as practised in most rubber estates then.

The landless Malays never like the word 'work' and 'discipline' as those were dirty words in their vocabulary. Many left the Felda schemes as they could not adapt to the new way of life. It was only later when their rubber trees and oil palm became productive that they appreciated what the government had done to their lives. Today they earned a few thousand ringgit monthly and living in luxury renovated houses. Many drive in cars which they never could dream before. Now in every state Felda schemes have changed the lives of the poor landless people in Malaysia. Do you know that today Malaysia is one of the leading exporter of oil palm and rubber. Felda is one of the most successful land schemes in this world and its investments all over the world are very substantial....over billions of dollars. I should have shown you the landmark building near the KLCC of Felda," explained Aqiel. "You know dear I have never heard about Felda until now. That is very innovative thinking by your previous PM......a man of vision," said Daniella. "Yes, he was indeed; a man in a hurry as he knew he was seriously ill and sadly he died young," replied Aqiel. "I noticed that great men and women die young like Alexander the Great, James Dean, Bruce Lee, Jose Rizal and many others including the greatest entertainer Michael Jackson.

Only rogues who became leaders lived long to do more damage to our world! Fortunately for the world American Presidents can only be elected for two terms....you cannot just imagine the atrocities they can do if they are to rule indefinitely like what had happened all over the world today!" lamented Daniella. "Some famous entertainers here like P. Ramlee and Sudirman including our famous film director Yasmin died young," lamented Aqiel. Slowly they passed through rows of houses mostly renovated and further down the rubber plantations managed by the settlers. "That's one of the Felda schemes known as Sendayan that I mentioned to you earlier. Those are some of the settlers who are not only hard working but spent their money wisely by renovating their old homes. Some settlers still leave in their old houses as they indulged in gambling and some 'get rich quick' schemes. Some settlers get a second wife as soon as the plantations are in production. However, the saddest part was when the settler divorced their first wife to bring in the second wife into the scheme. Imagine after having shared with the first wife and kids through thick and thin and she is dumped by him when the rubber trees are in production!" Daniella felt so miserable hearing the wives being treated like 'rubbish sheets' by the men when they enjoyed a slightly higher standard of living. "It is a pity women are still being treated as second class citizen here...... so much for women's rights!" Daniella said. However, she was very impressed with the effort of the government to help thousands of the landless including their next generations benefitted from the programme. "These landless rural folks must be very grateful to be given a second chance to live a decent life. Other Asian countries should adopt the system dear," Daniella said. "Many countries came to study the scheme, like it and some tried to implement it but as many failed as you need very dedicated staffs and settlers to make the project a great success," replied Aqiel.

# CHAPTER 69

After passing through the Felda schemes Daniella was lost in her own thoughts. "A penny for your thoughts, dear," Aqiel said while having a quick glance at her. "Oh...sorry. I was thinking about the natives of Brazil and whether the government can apply the Felda concept there," Daniella replied. "Actually if given a proper brief I see no reasons why the Amazons cannot accept the new way of life. The government must first start on a small scale and let the others 'beg' to be settlers....only then can the project be successful. If the government just 'forced' their ideas on the Amazons I am sure the idea will be rejected," said Aqiel.

Soon they drove into the town of Seremban. "Welcome to my town, dear. What do you think about the town," Aqiel asked. "Frankly, do you want to hear the good news first or the bad news?" Daniella asked. "The good news," replied Aqiel. "The road system in this town is chaotic and congested......you know the traffic flow is not systematic and there are too many traffic lights. Do you know that studies have shown traffic lights caused more congestions than roundabouts. Traffic lights do justice financially for the manufacturers and suppliers but in most cities they prefer to improve the traffic flow by having roundabouts. It is definitely hazardous and nerve wrecking to drive in this town!" Daniella said. "OK.....what is the good news, dear?" asked Aqiel. "Sadly there is no good news about your hometown," Daniella laughed. "OK, I agree with you though I feel sad about it. I understand the former Menteri Besar tried to improve the traffic flow, without much success, but the more changes he made the more chaotic it became. Formerly the centre of the town was a-two way traffic flow but he turned it into a one way traffic flow and that resulted in more commotions. The next Menteri Besar wanted to undo it but had no idea how to undo it as many major changes needed to be done which can be very costly to the taxpayers," Aqiel replied. "You should stand for the general election and be the next Menteri Besar, Aqiel," she quipped. "I have thought about it but the problem is nobody in politics wants a smart elite like me," replied Aqiel smiling sheepishly while driving along the road leading to the town of Jelebu.

All along the way were Malay villages with rice fields, buffaloes and fruit trees. At the 9th milestone Aqiel slowed down and turned into a driveway leading to a big Minangkabau shaped house. He drove in and Aqiel was met by his grand aunty and his son, Lazim. Daniella came out of the car and stood with awe at the magnificent structure in front of her. "This is Pantai.... here are my grand aunty and his son," Aqiel introduced her to both of them. "Masuklah, jangan takut.....ini rumah lamo tapi kuet lagi," (Come in, don't be afraid....this is an old house but still very steady). Before Aqiel could lead her into the house Daniella who was so fascinated with the large wooden house was walking slowly admiring at the workmanship of the old craftsmen.

Aqiel excused himself and followed Daniella who was admiring the old structure. Aqiel realised then as a local he took for granted the magnificent workmanship of the early Malays unlike a foreigner, Daniella, who was mesmerised with the architecture. Daniella took a couple of pictures to show to his parents and her professors at the university. "You know Aqiel in America this type of building will be gazetted as a 'national heritage' where the government will maintained this house as tourist's attractions," "I heard there was some attempt to do that but my feeling is that Malaysian leaders still do not appreciate or understand the true meaning of 'national heritage'. So when new leaders took over they have new priorities of their own," Aqiel said.

# CHAPTER 70

After spending for more than half an hour on the ground around the house Daniella decided to see the interior. Aqiel sought permission from his grand aunty as he wanted to take her explore the interior of the house. "Dio ni gilo dokek rumah lamo-lamo!" Aqiel said to his grand aunty. (She is just mad about antic homes).

They walked slowly through the living room, then the dining room and the main hall which was about 50 yards long. Aqiel explained to Daniella that in Malay customs there were no furniture at all in the house unlike the homes of the rich in America and England. "Here we sit down on the floor for breakfast, lunch and dinner. The atmosphere then was very cordial and friendly as everyone sat on the floor. What you see today like the settee, dining table and chairs and beds are influence from the West!" Then Aqiel took her up the attics where young maidens are required to stay when there were marriages and other celebrations. Now they used that place for hanging and drying clothings. It was another huge large hall where more than 100 people can comfortably sit on the floor. These attics would keep the maiden safe from the goggling eyes of the men looking for a younger wife wives especially during weddings or feast. You know many wealthy old men then were always on the watch out for a second, third or even fourth wives!," "Corrections Aqiel....not only wealthy but filthy and dirty old men," Daniella giggled.

"The floor, sadly is dusty today as very seldom it is used by my grand aunty....in fact the place has become the homes for the birds!" added Aqiel. "I notice that....so many birds' droppings everywhere," said Daniela. Aqiel took her to the windows and showed her a house. "Do you know whose house is that?" She shook her. "That is the house of the mother-in-law of the Menteri Besar of Kedah, Dato' Mukhriz Mahathir. That young politician will go a long way in politics if he plays his cards right and he is ear marked to be the next Prime Minister of Malaysia if Barisan Nasional stays in power. Anyway this was where my grandfather was born almost 90 years old! The craftsmen then were very smart and innovative. Imagine building a house of this size without a single nail.....it is fantastic!" "You know Aqiel the craftsmanship in the early years were just unbelievable. They built houses to last forever but today the contractors cut corners and costs to make profit at the expense of the owners. They have no pride in their work and I believe rightly why the earlier builders are known as craftsmen and the modern era builders as contractors," added Daniella. "The builders in those days take pride in their workmanship and were sought by the wealthy to build their homes. Actually they guard sacredly their reputations," Aqiel added. After some tea and biscuits Aqiel and Daniella took leave as they were in a hurry to go to his grandmother's birth place.

# CHAPTER 71

On the way to his grandmother's village Daniella commented, "Now I have some good news about your hometown." "Really? What is the good news?" "Your grandfather's house is so impressive....one of its kind in this world!" replied Daniella. Aqiel kissed Daniella on her cheek and said, "Thank you..... thank you. At least there is something you like about my 'heritage'!" he said Daniella then said to herself that, "That was a very unique piece of antics and deserved to be classified as 'a National Heritage'.

They had to pass through the town again and after driving through some rubber estates and several villages Aqiel stopped the car by the roadside. "This very small village with barely 30 houses then and only one small sundry shop was where my grandmother was born. Everybody in this village are related to us......they are other my aunties, uncles or cousins etc. That shop used to sell just the basic needs for the villagers such as rice, sugar, salt, coffee and other essential items. For fish, meat, eggs or other necessities the villagers had to take a bus to the nearest small town which passed the village every 3 hours daily, that too if you are lucky!" smiled Aqiel while relating the story to Daniella and Pak Man. "It must be very lonely to stay here," said Daniella. "Not really..... during those days most households have big families and during the school holidays when we come back there was always bound to be wedding feasts! It was a very lively village as the children moved around in groups doing their own chores. Furthermore my parents came back here during the fruit seasons......durians, rambutans, mangoes, mangosteen and many other fruits. It is just like in Western countries where you do your own pickings," Aqiel said.

"There used to be some paddy fields around here and a plot of small holders rubber at the back of the house. The house was built right on top of the hill, surrounded by the fruits trees, strategically overlooking this whole small village. It was a very simple kampong bungalow with 2 bedrooms and a very large living room where you can easily sit 60 men, on the floor, I mean.. The dining room can comfortably sit another 30 ladies. The original building was which was attached to the main building had another room and a kitchen. You must be thinking where the toilet or bathroom was. Actually, there was none indoors......all were done during the day fifty yards away near the well!" "What happens if you feel you need to leak or whatever?" asked Daniella. "Well, my granddad will accompany you to the well with his kerosene lamp as others were scared of the dark. Unfortunately the whole building caught fire one evening when everybody was asleep as one of their kerosene lamps fell on the wooden floor and caught fire. My grandmother and family were lucky to escape the fire unscathed but they lost everything. It took almost more then 1 hour before the fire brigade arrived.....due to the distance, I suppose. After that incident the site where the house was burnt was just left abandoned as we believe it was bad luck to build a new structure there. The wooden house had concrete pillars and you can still see them if you walk up the hill," said Aqiel. Daniella was sad just looking at the condition of the site.

# CHAPTER 72

As there was not much to see around the village Aqiel decided to proceed straight on to Port Dickson, another famous seaside resort on the west coast of the peninsula. It was just about 20 minutes drive from the town of Seremban. On reaching the small town of Port Dickson, Daniella was very impressed with the change of scenery for throughout their drive along the coastal lines were many huge hotels and resorts. The sea looked blue and the beach was very inviting. They drove down for lunch at the Hilton Hotel. "Darling.....why not we have some lunch at these food stalls, I am sure the food here are tasty and much, much cheaper than at the hotel," said Daniella. "Thought Mek Salleh only eats at expensive places, said Aqiel to himself. "Beg your pardon.......what did you said, darling?" asked Daniella. "Really nothing.......just that I once have a friend here by the name of Mat Salleh......wonder where he is now!" answered Aqiel smiling." "This place is just glorious and beautiful," declared Daniella, "I like to stay here for a few days Aqiel." "Yes, Port Dickson has been the weekend's getaway for residents from Kuala Lumpur and the surrounding areas as it is just 45 minutes drive from Kuala Lumpur. Maybe on our next trip we will make reservations to stay here overnight, darling," added Aqiel. They walked on the beach for a while before they drove back to Kuala Lumpur.

"You have not seen the views and beaches in the East coast....the sea is much more cruel as we are facing directly the China Sea. "Should be a welcome sight for surfers as the waves will be quite high," remarked Daniella. "Not really that challenging as the waves you see in Hawaii or along the beaches of California. Malaysians are still far behind time as far as surfing or competitive boating is concerned. If we had then we would have produced many world class surfers from Kelantan and Trengganu!" replied Aqiel. "Recently some interests had been shown by the State Government of Terengganu to host the boat race known as 'the Monsoon Cup' near one of the island. However, the race was mainly to attract tourism and foreigners to the East coast of the Peninsula. We Malaysians are mere spectators. "Probably such boat race is a good start for better times in the future.....I mean create interests among the locals to participate," said Daniella. "It is a very expensive sport for the locals and I believe there are many other affordable water sports that locals can participate and excel.

There are so many medals to be won at the Asian and Olympics Games in various categories of boat races which the Ministry of Sports should support. We have so many natural rivers, artificial lakes and canals all over the country which can be used by the State Sports officials to promote these sports," added Aqiel. "You should propose to the Minister of Sports on this matter, dear," smiled Daniella. "I think I will ask my dad to propose that as they will listen to him rather than a young dude like me!" retorted Aqiel which made Daniella smiled. Before long they were safely back in KL.

The next day in Kuala Lumpur was spent following Datin to the various shopping malls.......lunches and window shopping. It was when they were at one of the shopping malls that a snatch thief snatched Datin's handbag. She was admiring some batik dress in one of the boutique when a young man snatched her handbag. She was lucky because the handbag had no strap and was tucked under her arm. She let the handbag go and screamed for help. There had been cases when the victims suffered nasty falls on the floor or the road because their handbags were strapped to their shoulders. These snatched thieves are so ruthless and would do anything to the victims to get the bags.

Aqiel and Daniella were on the opposite shop looking at some perfumes when they heard the scream and saw the commotion at the adjacent shop. When he turned around Aqiel saw his mum shrieking for help and a young man burst out from the boutique running away with her handbag. Without giving a second thought Aqiel gave chase followed by a few other customers at the mall. They gave chase right to the exit of the mall where the thief's accomplice was waiting on a motorbike with the engine running. Many of the patrons however, were too scared to help or they were not aware what was really happening. It was only when Datin and Daniella came running shouting 'thief! thief!' did the crowd realised what actually was happening. The thief was about to jumped on to the waiting motorbike when Aqiel decided to make a rugby tackle at his legs. He was lucky as one of his hands managed to catch one of the ankles of the thief who fell right on top of his waiting accomplice. The motorbike fell and they all collapsed on top of one another. One of them pulled out a knife and threatened Aqiel but as an expert exponent of karate he expertly kicked the knife from the assailant hand and knocked him out with a chop. Some of onlookers who were close by came to his assistance to subdue the two culprits.

Daniella heard the crowd whispered, "Like Steven Seagall lah.....no more like Van Damn. Both of you are wrong. I think it was more like Bruce Lee!" Aqiel smiled when he heard those remarks. A few bystanders shook his hands for his gallant effort. A Police patrol car that happened to pass by arrested the thieves who were brought to the nearest Police station. Immediately his mum and Daniella arrived looking worried and anxious. On seeing the culprits being handcuffed by the Policemen and Aqiel shaking hands with the crowd, Datin and Daniella were relieved. Aqiel's arms were bruised and his trousers torn due to the daring stunt he made on the suspects.

"My hero!" shouted Daniella rushing to Aqiel.

# CHAPTER 73

$H$e was embarrassed as there was such a big crowd gathering in front of the mall. Anyway, the crowd like anywhere in the world bonded together when they were faced with a common adversary and they gave a rousing appreciation to Aqiel's daring feat and those who assisted in apprehending the suspects. Later Datin, Aqiel and Daniella went to the Police station to give their statements. The Police thanked Aqiel and those who gave support to nab the snatch thieves and hoped that in future more of the public would come forward to help reduced crimes in this country. The Police Officer at the Police station said,

"We want many others in the society to react like you En. Aqiel, then Malaysia would be a safer place to live in. Thieves and robbers would think 10 times before they even dare to think about committing these crimes!"

Datin told Daniella about 35 years ago Datuk came to her rescue when an enraged man came to her office and tried to attack her. He overpowered the intruder with his bare hands. "Today Aqiel did it," Datin said..

"It's in the blood, mum," replied Aqiel proudly.

On the way home Daniella told of her experience in the city of Chicago with her mother. They went there to see her aunty who had an operation in one of the hospitals. On the way back to the hotel they took a taxi but were driven to through the back lane as the driver said it was faster. It was a dark night and the cabbie suddenly stopped and another of his accomplice came out in the shadows. "We knew we were cornered and told the cabbie to take our valuables. He wanted more. We were dragged out of the cab by the 2 rogues. While struggling to get loose we started shouting for help but the place being very isolated and notorious no help was forthcoming.

Suddenly, out of nowhere this old Chinese man came to the srescue. He told the two rogues to stand down and leave. Seeing this frail old man of about 80 years old they just smiled and asked him to just leave before he got hurt. The old Chinese man repeated his request. Seeing the old man was not about to go quietly one of the rogues took a swing at the old man. The old man side stepped and threw him hard onto the ground where he never recovered from that fall." The other rogue took out his knife and said, "You, grandpa need to be taught a lesson......do not try to interfere with the hobbies of the younger generations......I will cut you down into small pieces and feed them to the wild dogs." Daniella continued, "We were watching there with fear and dared not move. The rogue with the knife attacked him viciously and we both closed our eyes. We heard some 'ughs' and 'ahhs' and before long it was so silent." She heard the old man said, "Yes, I am a grandpa but there is so much a young man can learn from me." Then the old man said, "Now you can open your eyes and go home."

We wanted to give him some money for him or his family but he just refused saying that God had been kind to him and his family. "Go....go now as this place is dangerous for women. Take a cab at the main road up there." "Mother, however, was unhappy and she left some money in his hand before we left. We said thank you and took a cab back to the hotel. We never got to know who that old Chinese man was," ended Daniella. "Consider him as your modern saviour....just like Superman or Batman in the old days! You and your mother are lucky to escape unscathed. Thought you learn Judo, Daniella?" Aqiel quipped. "That was long ago when I was in the kindergarten," she laughed.

# CHAPTER 74

In the evening Aqiel, though slightly in pain after the morning 'drama', went with Daniella to one of the discos in the city, the 'Hard Rock Café'. Aqiel told Daniella,

"In Phuket, Thailand, they have a place known as "Rock Hard Café", no.... no...it's nothing like what you have in mind....here a group of transvestites staged a clean stage show, singing and dancing just like the musical theatre 'New York, New York', but not with such grandeur. These shows were, however, well patronised by tourists...almost full house every night".

They left the disco just before 1 am, as Aqiel felt so tired after the ordeal in the afternoon.

On the final night in Kuala Lumpur, they went for dinner hosted by Wawa and husband. Initially the dinner was supposed to be held at her home but being pregnant she decided to give them a treat at seafood restaurant at Kelana Jaya. Datuk and Datin joined them for the evening. During dinner Datuk reminisced about his younger days and how he struggled alone to build the company.

"I got my strength from, Bibi....she was my advisor, friend and most importantly my lover....." he said, kissing the tips of her hand.

Daniella spontaneously remarked, "How romantic, Datuk...from a pauper to a tycoon,".

Daniella loved the seafood, which was served in Chinese style, 'Steamboat', where they just throw their picks like, squids, prawns, crabs, vegetables, noodles into the hot soup in the steamboat and start retrieving the sea food, noodles and vegetables after a few minutes before others 'recover' to satisfy their tummies. It was a kind of fun family 'mind game', where they try to outwit the others the whole night. Daniella, who had never experience a steamboat dinner, enjoyed the food that night.

She said to Wawa, "When Aqiel told me we were going for the 'steamboat' tonight I thought we were going on a steamboat ride and have dinner on board the boat, like they did on the Mississippi river. This is a totally new experience for me......sharing together our food in a very hygienic and healthy way with friends and relations, Wawa.

Thank you for the delicious dinner Wawa, Adam."

"You are most welcome

'Sis'," replied Wawa, smiling at Aqiel. Adam just smiled. "Actually in Islam they encourage the 4 men or 4 women to share one tray of food for lunch or dinner using the fingers as sign of comradeship. Would you like to try that, Daniella?" asked Aqiel. Daniella rolled her eyes up and just smile.

That night before Aqiel retired for bed, his dad and mum called him into the living room to discuss some personal matters. "Happiness in this world is short lived and can be meaningless if we do not prepare ourselves for the hereafter. Today we are young but eventually we will get old and everybody dies," Datuk started the conversation that night. "Tomorrow you will back to the States for a few more years so a few words of advice should be in order I think, "he said. Then he looked at his wife to continue with the motherly advice. "Kami nampak yang kau cukup mesra dengan Daniella dan kami pun suka dia, (We notice that you love Daniela and we too like her), added his mother. "We noticed that you tend to take Islam not seriously......you are an adult and adult has the responsibility to diligently practised Islam.

Getting married is everybody's dreams but when you marry a convert the responsibility is greater. As a husband you must lead your wife to be a good Muslim or you have failed in your duty as a husband," said her mother. Datuk then have this to say, "The most important thing in marriage is not only because of love but also both of you have deep admiration and respect for each other. If you do not have that sacred combinations then your marriage is doomed for failure," advised Datuk. Aqiel just nodded his head in agreement. As a young boy he attended quran classes, prayed 5 times a day and knew about the do(s) and don't(s) in Islam but he failed to practised what he had been taught when he went to the States about 8 years ago. He had to repent and practised religiously Islam if he wanted to get married. That is the only way one can achieve true happiness and lead one's wife to heaven.

That night while in bed tears suddenly appeared in Aqiel's eyes when he recalled the advice from both of his parents. He knew he had to make these changes because he was no more the young Aqiel who can play delinquent on this serious matter. He wanted to get married and to do so he must behave like an adult.......a good Muslim, a model for his future wife and kids.

# CHAPTER 75

On Sunday night Aqiel and Daniella took the flight to LA. Datuk, Datin, Wawa and her husband were at the airport to send them off. Daniella's uncle and aunty could not make it, as they had to attend a diplomatic function at one of the hotels. Datuk reminded Aqiel to think seriously about their advice and offer. Aqiel promised to think seriously about the offer and hope to be back in December.........together with Daniella.

"Emak carilah nama Islam sesuai untuk Daniella. Sekarang Jabatan Ugama larang banyak nama yang tak sesuai!" (please choose a suitable Muslim name for Daniella. Now the Islamic Department is very particular about names!).

"Panggil Teratai, Chempaka atau Intan kan manis," (Just call her Teratai, Chempaka or Intan.....that should be sweet), replied Datin. 'Teratai' and Chempaka' are names of famous Malaysian flowers while 'Intan' is the precious stone, diamond.

"I like the name Mahsuri," said Aqiel.

"No...please...no.. not that name. Not after what you told me about her fate!" cried Daniella.

"Kekalkan nama Daniella tu, kan istimewa. Nanti tukar nama rasa macam kahwin dengan orang lain pulak!" (Retain the name Daniella, it's a beautiful name. If you change the name it's like marrying another person!) quipped Wawa.

"You Wawa....always the person to rely on.....my sweet sister, that's why I love you, sis. Its Daniella then!" replied Aqiel.

Aqiel and Daniella hugged Datuk, Datin and Wawa and shook hands with Azman before they entered the departure hall. Datin could not help but shed some tears as she was going to miss Aqiel and now also Daniella. On the plane both Aqiel and Daniella were quiet for a few hours. Both were lost for words as they kept thinking about the wonderful family they had just left behind. It was only when the stewardess served dinner on the flight that they slowly managed to regain their composure. Daniella started chatting about their trip to Langkawi Island and Putra Jaya. Soon they both forget about Kuala Lumpur and looked forward to start work in LA. Their plane stopped over at Tokyo for about 45 minutes before proceeding to Honolulu and LA.

Half way through their journey to LA Aqiel had a serious talk with Daniella. "Now let me I explain to you this concept of marriage in Islam. Firstly darling, in Islam for a couple to get married both must be Muslims. So in our case you must first convert to Islam, adopt the religion. However, one salient point to know is that the conversion to Islam is not for your love of another person or to fulfil your wish to get married but for the love of Allah SWT. If your reason to convert to Islam is to get married and not for the love of Allah SWT then that is a bad decision." Daniella looked puzzled and confused because to her whatever she did was entirely her love for Aqiel. "The concept of love in Islam is to love Allah SWT and then to any human being dearest to you," said Aqiel.

This was new to her and did not make any sense. Aqiel knew he had not managed to get the message through to Daniella and he felt he was not the right person to explain to her. "OK.....let us do it this way. First you must talk with your parents on your intention to convert to Islam and the marriage. Your friends too must be aware of your intentions so that they don't have to hear all these from a third party. Your parents may object initially or they might not. Either they agree or not the choice is yours as you are of age. If you are prepared we will proceed with the next step that is to introduce you to the Islamic centre in LA. There you will be taught what Islam is really about. I am sure you will meet with many American Muslims there whom you can communicate and hopefully get the right answers. You will need to attend a number of sessions to really appreciate and understand the message they want to convey to you. Do you understand what I mean?" asked Aqiel.

Daniella was feeling very depressed from her facial expression as conversion to another religion was a major decision she had to make. Aqiel knew how she felt as it was going to completely change her lifestyle to be a good Muslim. "OK....let me do this Aqiel. I will meet with my parents this weekend and I hope to make them understand what I have to do to be a good Muslim. Then on Tuesday together we will go to the Islamic centre and meet the Ustadz there for further clarification. What do think?" Daniella suggested. "Fine.... agreed.....we will do just that, darling," replied Aqiel.

# CHAPTER 76

$B$ack at the airport, Datuk and Datin were in the car driven by Pak Man. Realising both Datuk and Datin were rather quiet seated at the back, Pak Man decided to break the silence,

"Daniella is a nice lady, Datin…..when I drove them to Malacca and other places she was so easy to please. She does not behave like a westerner but like an Asian lady, very polite and shy. I like her and I believed Aqiel has made a very good choice."

"I like her from the moment I saw her at the airport, Pak Man. After more than two weeks with her I know I had made the right decision ....it is not a mistake…..she is the right lady for my Aqiel," said Datin.

Datuk just sat there quietly. In a lighter mood she said,

"Datuk, himself is in love with her…..he loves her more than his own children…..in his sleep sometimes he called out her name!" laughed Datin.

"Please….please….Bibi is just pulling your leg Pak Man…..yes, I too am very happy that Aqiel has made the right choice as his life partner. We are all children of Allah SWT so to us race is of no importance but she has to convert to Islam to marry Aqiel. I want to see my children happy with their choices. We are old…they have many years ahead and my hope is they find happiness in building up their own family life. Many Malaysians brought home foreign wives and many ended in divorces….such a pity…..they just could not adjust to our local ways. I hope Daniella can change her lifestyle to our Malaysian way of life," said Datuk. "Sometimes it is not really the faults of the foreign wives but their husbands. It is really difficult to adjust to our Muslim's way of life as it can be terrifying to them. We noticed that foreign wives married to non-Muslims can easily adjust to Malaysian way of life. In the case of Malay husbands it is their duties to see that their foreign wives gradually fit into the Malay society. It is when the husband failed to do so that the wives are lost and gradually led to divorces," said Datin. Datuk nodded in agreement, "Yes, both parties have to give and take and whoever comes to our country will have to adapt to our way of life," added Datuk.

Pak Man who had been listening to the conversation interjected, "Datuk, Datin.......Daniella seorang wanita yang cukup baik dan saya percaya dia bolih mengimbangkan diri dan jadi seorang menantu yang baik untuk Datuk dan Datin, insyaallah." (Daniella is a very nice lady and I believe she can adjust her life to be a good daughter-in-law to Datuk and Datin, God willing) "Insyaallah," said Datuk. Datuk pick up the 'The New Straits Times' and started reading it. Datin on the other hand was lost in her own thoughts while Pak Man listened to the music in car radio to keep him company.

# CHAPTER 77

Business in Malaysia picked up under the Ninth Malaysia Plan. There was a slight hic-up before the general elections because the Opposition had managed to garner strong support for their move to take over Putrajaya especially from the urban voters. The rural folks were still adamant that the ruling party must be retained in power as only these leaders cared for them. There were many good and sincere leaders in the ruling party and the Opposition and Datuk only wished was that these good leaders get together to rule the country. The society was not happy with the abuse of power, mismanagement in public spending, corruption in the hands of a few leaders. The big 'fish', as they say, got away with millions of ringgit but only the poor small fish are charge in court and put behind bars. Those in power misunderstood the good intentions of society as they thought that society was against them for no reasons but in actual fact society wanted the 'rogues' in the government to be punished leaving the good leaders to lead the country. Racism, especially, has no place in our country. For the good or bad of the country the ruling party won the general elections but not convincingly. So the ruling party found it difficult to peacefully rule the country. A veteran politician said, "This is good for the country as the ruling party cannot arbitrarily implement policies and spend the budget as they like. The close scrutiny by the Opposition is good in our contexts!" The government moved cautiously and slowly in implementing the various projects and programmes. Genuine businessmen were happy with the new approach of the government to ensure projects were completed within specific period at the lowest costs. All construction projects of the government were under the direct supervision of the Ministry of Works and no more under various Ministries as practised before. Only on completion of these projects would these projects be handed over to the other Ministries. Maintenance too came under the direct supervision of the Ministry of Works. This was a very good move as then only one Ministry, though the manpower increased, is directly in charge of the country's development.

Other Ministries were directed to concentrate and focus implementing their policies and not waste time in supervising the physical construction of structures or buildings. Before each Ministry was more concerned in the award of tenders were then the priorities of each Ministry and they had no expertise to supervise the construction works. Construction works were delayed, abandoned or poorly constructed. Even private developers played havoc with the house buyers due to very poor government enforcement and widespread corruption'.

"The coming years looks very promising as the new Prime Minister has made a bold statement to eradicate corruption in the country. He said, "I am the Prime Minister, I make the decisions. We all hope he is brave and strong enough to do that," said Datuk.

"Malaysia now has a Prime Minister who makes decisions based on what he thinks is right for the Malaysian people rather than to please the party or for political gain. Malaysians today can trust someone who is not afraid to back up what he says," commented Alan to the members of the Board of Bibi Sdn. Bhd.

"Alan is right there. The new PM is concerned for the whole nation rather than making a 'selected' group rich. Previously, the genuine businessmen were ignored but the young cronies without expertise awarded projects. That resulted in the failure of the earlier Malaysia Plans. The Prime Minister realised only a transparent government can make the nation move together. The most important decision he made was telling the politicians to stick to politics and let the businessmen beef up the economy. He once spoke at a lunch talk, 'Politics and business should never intertwine as it will breed 'corruption' in society. You either stay a politician or businessman full time.' Politicians will not agree with that statement but there is a lot of truth in it. Every genuine hard working and innovative Malaysians are now happy to come forward and do their part in nation building irrespective of race, religion, political inclinations or gender......the Prime Minister wants Malaysians to work together for their future generations," said Datuk Khalid. He then said, "If you are not strong then you must be smart to attain your dreams."

Margaret Fuller, an American journalist and social critic said, "It is astonishing what force, purity, and wisdom it requires for a human being to keep clear of falsehoods."

# CHAPTER 78

Over the weekend Daniella came over and stayed overnight at her parents' home. She at last found the right time to talk to both of them after dinner. Her mother, Monica, knew from her body language that Daniella wanted to have a serious talk with both of them. She could feel the energy coming from Daniella as she had known her daughter since birth. Daniella' mother whispered to Bush, her husband that their daughter needed to talk to them. Daniella was then busy in the kitchen washing the plates. Earlier she told them to just sit down in the living room while she cleared the table. After half an hour she appeared from the kitchen with 3 cups of coffee. "Sit down, Daniella. We know you want to talk to us, so let us talk ok?" said her father. "Right.... now where do I begin? By the way Uncle Roger, Aunty Martha and Aqiel's parents send their best regards to you. My visit to Malaysia recently where I met Aqiel's parents had helped me to make up my mind about marriage. Aqiel had proposed and I have accepted to be his wife. Before the marriage I have to convert my religion to Islam," Daniella explained.

She looked into the eyes of her parents and waited for them to voice their opinions. Monica looked at Bush and slowly Bush spoke to Daniella. "We knew this was coming, that is you will want to marry Aqiel and in doing so must convert to Islam. Daniella, your mum and I have no objection at all and we are happy for you as we feel you made the right decision. However, you must remember that being a Muslim here can be quite testing.....eh.....challenging to you and the family. Americans, especially the Christians, right now, look at Muslims as terrorists. In certain cities or parts of America the residents are more tolerant but certain groups can be very nasty towards Muslims. 9/11 are still very fresh in their minds especially those who lost their loved ones in that attack. Anyway that is just an advice, honey. Do what you need to do and what is best for you. Being a Muslim will not stop you from being our baby as all we want is to see you happy." Daniella and her mum were both in tears when she hugged both of them. Even her father could not help from wiping his teary eyes. She sat between her parents on the settee just like when she was three years old. Her mother hugged her tightly and her father just wrapped his arms around them. Daniella then just related her stay in Malaysia and the many places she visited.

"You know Aqiel has an elder sister by the name of Wawa. One day she told me that she wanted to give a 'steam boat' dinner. I said marvellous. I asked her 'Where and what do I wear for the dinner?' She asked, 'Why?' Since we are going on a boat it would not be appropriate to wear an evening dress,' I said. "No...no....Daniella....we are not going sailing. Dressed as you like, because, we are having it in a nice posh restaurant in town. Anyway, let me explain it this way. 'Steam boat' is the Chinese sea food dinner where you have to serve yourself....we just dump in all the sea food like fish, prawns, squids, eggs, noodles plus vegetables in a steaming bowl.....when these are ready we eat it by using chop sticks or whatever is convenient to you. It's kind of an eating competition....who eats faster gets to eat more.' she laughed. They all smiled at how naive Americans can be about oriental food.

Just before midnight she said gave good night kiss to her parents went to her bedroom. Actually she was so excited and upon reaching the door of her bedroom she immediately called Aqiel from her cell phone. "Sorry darling, are you asleep?" she asked. "Asleep? This is LA darling......the night is still young especially on a Saturday night! I am at the night club with a few chicks to keep me happy," replied Aqiel. "Aqiel......stop joking.....listen to me ok?" "I am serious.....right now I am at the 'Hard Rock Cafe' in the city with.....eh.... eh....Maria Sharapova! Can you hear the hot music?" Aqiel asked. "Aqiel.... be serious for once," begged Daniella. "Anyway Maria Sharapova is too tall for you, listen, listen....I had just spoken to my parents and they gave their blessings, darling!" "They did? Now what do I do with Maria? Sorry....they agreed? Thank God! Where are you now?" asked Aqiel. "At my parents home of course......where are you?" Daniella asked. "At home......I was watching this sad movie about a very lonely man whose girl friend has gone home to her parents. On the serious note I was just about to go to bed after reading this very interesting novel 'Yesterday, tomorrow......sharing my thoughts' which we bought at KLCC in Kuala Lumpur, remember? It is by a Malaysian writer known only as 'Tokman'. Tell you what....when are you coming back honey?" asked Aqiel. "Probably by Monday," answered Daniella. "OK....when you back in the city, call me, and we meet for breakfast somewhere to discuss about our meeting with the Ustadz at the Islamic centre." "OK.....see you on Monday then, Good night," Daniella ended the call.

# CHAPTER 79

On Monday morning Daniella met Aqiel for breakfast at the McDonald outlet near Aqiel's office. Daniella told Aqiel that her parents did not object but was very happy with her decision to get married to Aqiel. "In that case the next step is for us to meet the Ustaz tomorrow at the Islamic centre. There are so many things I want to ask not only for you but for myself. I know I personally need to attend many classes here to increase my knowledge of Islam. I need to improve on the right way to read the Quran. They will teach about the ways of a Muslim lady including the 5 daily prayers and reading the Quran. It is going to be lots of hard work for both of us for the next 1 year, darling. Your dress code too has to change....no more skirts and shorts.....those beautiful legs are only meant for me to see," Aqiel said. Daniella pinch him on the thigh as she did not want other customers to see. "Ouch....remember you can always refer to me when in doubts because in Islam one must never have the feeling of dubiety at all." Daniella was eager to meet the Ustadz or Ustadzah at the Islamic centre.

They then took the bus to go to the mosque of Los Angeles which was one of the biggest mosque in LA. "I have never noticed this mosque before though I passed this road so often daily," said Daniella. "I did but never had the chance to pray in this mosque even on Fridays......now I really regretted for not doing that," lamented Aqiel. "The London Central Mosque or known as The Regent's Park Mosque is much bigger than this. During one of my trip there I had the opportunity to see and enter the mosque. The hall can accommodate about 5000 worshippers and there is still room for about 2000 ladies to pray on the balcony. The land was donated by King George V1 and the mosque was completed in 1978 under the renowned architect Sir Frederick Gibberd. There are many other huge and beautiful mosques around the world like in Bahrain, Qatar, Turkey, Pakistan, Iraq, Iran and many others. However, we must never forget the Holy Mosque in Mecca, the Holy Mosque of Medina and the one in Palestine, the Al-Aqsa mosque. These are holy mosques where Muslims are encouraged to visit. Anyway when we go for our Hajj, insyaallah, we will visit both the Holy Mosques in Mecca and the mosque in Medina," said Aqiel.

They walked by the side of the mosque and were looking for somebody to ask for any official of the mosque. There were many tourists but nobody had any idea on how to go about to contact the officials of the mosque. Aqiel and Daniella felt lost and luckily Aqiel saw a man reading the Quran in the hall. He approached the man who, however, was not an official there but was kind enough to show him to the office of the Imam. He knocked the door and went in and after a few minutes signalled to Aqiel and Daniella to enter the room. There he spoke with an elderly Ustaz for a while who signalled Aqiel and Daniella to step in.

The gentleman wished them 'Assalamualaikum', smiled and left the office. Aqiel replied 'Alaikumsalam'. The Ustaz greeted both of them with the normal Arabic greetings, and they shook hands while he gave a smiled at Daniella. He invited them to sit down. "I am Ustaz Mohammed El-Karim, the Imam of this mosque. You are.........?" "I am Aqiel and this is Daniella," said Aqiel. "I am a Malaysian, Muslim by birth and intend to get married to Daniella, a Christian." The Ustaz took a long look at Daniella and smiled. "I was born a Christian, a black Christian but at the age of 18 I realised there was something missing in my life. A few Muslim friends told me to try to get closer to Islam. Before I convert I learned to read the Quran and try to understand it. I compared the Bible to the Quran and gradually it occurs to me that Islam will lead me to the right path.

My parents, a devout Catholics, initially objected strongly to my idea but after some persuasions they finally gave their blessings. I told them they will not lose a son as I am with them until death do us part. As my love for Islam is deep after conversion I decided to pursue further on Islam and managed to get enrolled at the AlAzhar University until I got my doctorate. Alhamdulillah...... today I am back here and blessed as they appointed me as the Imam here. My wife, like you Daniella expressed her wished to be a Muslim so I advised her to follow the Ustaz. I told her if you love the way of Islam then we will convert you. After 3 months she decided to be a Muslimah. We like each other and decided to get married and 'Alhamdulillah' today we are blessed with three kids........2 boys and a girl."

# CHAPTER 80

"Alhamdulillah" said Aqiel. "Daniella here has voluntarily decided to convert to Islam and we seek your advice as to how to get it done before our marriage." "Alhamdulillah.......and congratulation to you Daniella for choosing Islam," he said. There is so much to do in such a short time. First we must get you Daniella converted to Islam and if possible to bring both your parents to see this simple ceremony. It will take just a few minutes but we like parents and relations to attend it, if possible. The next phase is the more difficult phase of your life...... learning and practising the way of life of a Muslim lady.

Your dress code has to be changed and so is your American lifestyle. We have daily or weekly classes that conduct the teachings of Muhammad SWT by the Ustazah for the females and Ustaz for the males. We do not charge any fees but those who like to donate are welcome. So when do you intend to get converted?" asked the Imam. "I will have to talk with my parents and see whether they would like to come to the simple ceremony," looking anxiously at Aqiel. Right here are forms that you need to fill and if you are underage, which I believe you are not, the consent of your parents, are needed. So when you have decided to get converted to a Muslimah, give me a call at this number," the Imam handed over a call card to Aqiel. "Can I ask you a question, sir?" asked Daniella. "I mean no offence to Aqiel," she said. Aqiel looked puzzled and confused. "I have heard so much Muslim men marrying more than one..... is this true?" she asked.

The Imam smiled, "**Surah 4(3) An-Nisa' in the Quran** has been misunderstood and wrongly interpreted by many Ulamas. Our Prophet has four wives when he practised Islam religiously. In the Quran it is clearly stated, **"And if you fear that you shall not be able to deal with the orphan-girls, then marry (other) women of your choice, two or three, or four but if you fear that that you shall not be able to be deal justly (with them), then only one or (captives and the slaves) that your right hands possess. That is the nearer to prevent you from doing injustice."** Why did not the Quran says marry one, two, three or four and be fair to all, because Allah SWT knew we, men, have our weaknesses and we definitely are not capable of being fair and just like our Prophet Muhammad SWT. Further there were many other reasons whereby Muslim men are allowed to marry more than one wife. Unfortunately, those reasons are what most Ulamas just ignore completely. Some of the more pertinent conditions were that your first wife is childless, a widow and many others. You will learn this when you are seriously engaged in learning the religion. So to me many Ulamas sadly misinterpreted the Surah and encouraged Muslim men to follow the 'sunnah' of our Prophet Muhammad SWT. Do you have any other questions, Daniella?" She shook her head and smiled.

He shook hands with Aqiel, a nod to Daniella and said, "Assalamualaikum." Aqiel replied "Alaikumsalam." On the way out of the mosque Daniella was intrigue with the charisma of the Imam. "You must be shocked when I asked about polygamy in Islam, Aqiel?" asked Daniella. "Not quite," answered Aqiel "as I too wanted to ask the same question to the Imam. In Malaysia whenever you meet Ulamas it is natural to hear them say, "Tonight, I will be with my third wife".......it is more or less accepted that to be an Ulama you must marry more than one," said Aqiel. Aqiel casually related to Daniella that Islam is such a beautiful complete religion since our Prophet Muhammad SWT preached to the world about it. However, after he died there were so many Imams and today we have so many sects like Shias and Sunnis. They slaughter one another in Syria. Actually in many parts of the world Zionis bomb Muslims, Islam kills Christians, Buddhist slaughter Muslims and vice versa. These fanatics make the various religions look bad.

Besides that there are so many teachings that are considered unislamic and misleading. Do you know that 'Islam' has been in existence since the time of Adam and Eve. Though humans were introducedto 'Islam' by various names like Judaism and Christianity basically the teachings are that of 'Islam'. It was only when the Prophet Muhammad SAW spread the teachings of the Al-Quran that 'Islam' became a religion that is complete and pure that spread all over the world. So those who professed the old 'Testaments' strictly were practising 'Islam' then. Today Islam has been condemned as a religion for terrorists by the western world especially after the 9/11 incident. Muslims and even Hindus are being despised by Christians here. It is not actually the religion of Islam but like any other religions there are bound to be 'fanatics' and these are the people who used religions like Islam, Christianity or Judaism as the platform to launch their attacks on others. They hope to get the blessing of others from the same religion. This ridiculous act, however, do not easily sway the literate citizens of the world to support them.

Just like the leaders of America they have their own agenda which they hope the Americans will give full support. They targeted Islamic leaders like Saddam Hussein, Gadaffi, Osama Ben Ladin as big threats to the security of America. The American leaders find excuses to invade and attack these countries on pretext of looking for nuclear or biological weapons. Actually they are interested to take control of the huge volume of petroleum and gas in those countries. So actually terrorism works both ways.

Daniella was finally converted to Islam in front of her parents and Aqiel. It was simple ceremony as promised by the Imam. From then on every Sundays Aqiel and Daniella attended the religious classes conducted by the mosque. They abstained from many of the forbidden acts as taught to them like free sex, drinking liquor, eating animals that were not slaughtered and many don'ts under the Islamic law. Initially Daniella found adopting the Islamic religion as too rigorous and strict by slowly through the months she began to appreciate the Islamic way of life.

Initially she was very conscious of her change in dress code where she had to cover her head, neck and long sleeves though she still wore long pants for work. Her office mates adjusted well to her new looks as Daniella told them about her conversion. Nothing has changed in her working environment. When she walked to her office daily there were slur remarks from some passerbys but ignoring them was the best way to deal with this problem. Overall the Americans were not racists or anti-Islam and carrying on with your own business would ensure safety.

# CHAPTER 81

$A$lan was obsessed with his feeling of searching for his parents. A few months after he had a chat with Datin Bibi, he went to the orphanage hoping to get more information about his history. He met with the lady who was then the head of the organisation, Che Lat. Che Lat was very helpful and went through the records she had in the office. The records were, however, rather sketchy, with a footnote stating 'Alan was abandoned at the front door of the orphanage and found by the gate keeper, Pak Hussein'. There was a handwritten note, believed to be hand written by a woman, 'Please take care of my baby. God bless you'. Pak Hussein had already retired and was living with his wife in Taiping. Che Lat told Alan that probably Pak Hussein was the only one who can shed some clues as to Alan's real parents.

Alan took leave to take a trip to Taiping after getting the address of Pak Hussein's house. He did not bring his chauffeur, Pak Mat, as he was on a rather 'sensitive' mission. He came to small village in Taiping, known as Kampong Pokok Assam and stopped at one of the local stalls to ask for directions. The stall owner told him it was about 500 metres down the kampong path. A boy, who lived near Pak Hussein's house volunteered to show him the house. He jumped into Alan's car and brought him to a wooden house. Alan alighted from the car and the boy ran to the door and called out,

"Assalamualaikum……Tok….Tok….ada orang cari Tok!" (Peace be with you…..Tok…..Tok …..somebody is looking for you!).

The wooden old door slowly opened and an old ailing man popped out his head.

"Siapa tu? (Who's that?).

"Alan.." replied Alan… "Pak Hussein tak ingat saya….dulu saya tinggal dirumah anak yatim Bibi."(You don't remember me Pak Hussein…..I was at the Bibi's Orphanage).

On hearing the name of the orphanage, Pak Hussein's face suddenly lighted up and he immediately opened the door. He was happy to meet anybody from the orphanage, the place where he spent most of his active life.

"Oh….. sila masuk…"(Oh…. Come in..). "Ohh….engkau Atan pun ada," said Pak Hussein.

Alan and the boy entered the hut that had two bedrooms, a kitchen and the living room. The toilet was outside the house.

"Siapa nama anak sekali lagi?"(What's your name again?)

"Alan……dulu dari rumah anak yatim Bibi, Pak Hussein".

"Alan…ya…..ya…saya baru ingat….awak lah baby yang saya jumpa depan pintu tu. Apa khabar, sihat nampaknya. Apa khabar Datuk dan Datin?" "(Alan…Yes….I remember…you were the baby I found at the front door. How are you, you look well. How are Datuk and Datin?" "Sihat semuanya."(Everybody is alright).

Pak Hussein related that he owned this piece of land of about 2 acres and the house, which he bought with the retirement benefits given by Datuk Khalid. Most of the area was planted with fruit trees such as durian, rambutan, mango, jackfruit, coconut and a few papaya and banana trees. It was initially not meant for commercial benefits but when there was a bumper crop he leased out the trees to interested parties. Part of the land was utilised with 5 units of small huts, which were rented out to the lower income group. The rental was his monthly income, which was sufficient for his simple life style. He now lived with his wife, Mak Jah who had gone to the nearby shop to buy some groceries. His only son, Razak, now married, was serving in the Army in Sarawak.

"Pak Hussein…..saya datang kesini hendak tanya sikit pasal keluarga saya…..siapa ibu bapa saya….kalau Pak bolih bantu."(Pak Hussein I came to ask you about my family…..who my parents…if you can help) asked Alan.

Pak Hussein was silent…..he was very quiet for a very long time. There was that faraway look in his eyes, just blank….. without uttering a single word. Tears welled in his eyes. He was in deep thoughts. Alan did not know what to do and he too remained quiet. Suddenly, Mak Jah, came home.

# CHAPTER 82

"Ingat tak ada orang….sunyi aje," she said. (I thought there was nobody in…..so quiet).

Pak Hussein immediately wiped the tears away, and responded by saying,
"Teringat kisah dulu..dulu…..Jah. (Thinking about old times, Jah). Jah…..ni Alan…..dulu dia ni tinggal rumah anak yatim Datuk Khalid tu." (This Jah is Alan….he was once in Datuk Khalid's orphanage.)

"Ingat….siapa tadi…….rupa-rupanya Alan, wah…..dah berjaya sekarang….kereta besar…syukur alhamdudillah," said Mak Jah. (Thought it was somebody else…..so it is you Alan…well…..you are successful now…big car…thank God).

Rezeki, Mak Jah. (God's will, Mak Jah).

"Duduklah dulu Mak Jah nak buat kopi ni." (Have a sit, Mak Jah will prepare coffee.)

"Jangan susah-susah Mak Jak….saya baru minum dikedai," replied Alan. (Don't worry, I just had a drink at the stall.)

Mak Jah just ignored the reply and went straight to the kitchen to make coffee. From the kitchen she shouted to Atan,

"Kau nak kopi Atan?" (You want coffee Atan?)

"Coca-cola atau Pepsi, bolihlah Nenek?" (Coca-Cola or Pepsi will do Granny?) joked Atan.

"Engkau ni Atan….mengada-ada aje, ingat ni kedai kopi ke?" (You are kidding Atan…….this is not a coffee shop?) Mak Jah replied.

"Lawak aje nek". (Just joking granny), replied Atan.

Pak Hussein and Alan joined the laugh. Pak Hussein looked into the eyes of Alan for quite a while before he said,

"I did not tell the truth to Datuk about you. I had to lie because your mother begged me to do so. She will not leave you with me if I did not promise to keep this a secret. I did not want her to give you to some other orphanage, as I know Datuk and Datin loved children. In fact in that year I brought two babies of my Chinese friends to the orphanage. I have to seek their permission first before I can reveal the truth. I can only disclose whom your real parents

173

are after I have contacted them and that they agree to let me do so. One thing you should know…..they are still alive….and you have two younger siblings, a boy and a girl. Give me your contact number and I will call you in ten days time. If all goes well you will know your real family then," said Pak Hussein.

Alan was surprised he spoke good English. "Can't we just go over to the house and surprise them, Pak Hussein? Are they here or in Kuala Lumpur?" asked Alan.

"That's not a good idea…they had no idea about you, where you are and what happened to you, they regretted giving you away though, as they missed you so much…..they just wanted to forget that sad episode in their life," Pak Hussein said. "I'll try to contact them. The last time I met them was about 9 years ago, just before I retired from the orphanage. They came over to my house in Kuala Lumpur and inquired about you. They said they were then staying in Sitiawan, Perak, and had no permanent place to call home. From time to time they did call me and I expect them to call me anytime soon…..just to say hello. Give me 10 days and if everything works well you will meet them."

"Thank you Pak Hussein…..thank you Mak Jah, Atan……I am glad I made this trip today. Can I have your phone number please, Pak Hussein?" asked Alan.

"Of course, 019-2399399, I don't have a house phone as the cell phone is very convenient. Even Mak Jah knows how to send SMS." joked Pak Hussein.

Alan asked, "Atan hendak tumpang uncle Alan kekedai ke….ambil basikal yang tinggal disitu?" (Do you want a lift from uncle Alan back to the stall, Atan, to get your bicycle that you left there?)

"Tak ape….uncle Alan…Atan nanti jalan kaki….dekat aje." (No need…… Uncle Alan….I will walk there….it's near).

"Ni….kopi bujang ni….minum lah dulu Alan…..Atan, ni Coca Cola kau yang hitam ni!" Mak Jah smiled to Atan. (Have some coffee first Alan and Atan here is your Coca Cola in black).

# CHAPTER 83

$A$lan drove back to Kuala Lumpur......feeling relief to know his parents are both still alive. He wanted so much to meet them again and be part of that family. He stopped at a stall in Ipoh that was selling his favourite 'noodles' with chicken, mushrooms and abalone. The old man and his elderly wife were serving strings of customers that were queuing at the stall. A young man assisted them. There was something peculiar about the young man, the way he talked and his body language, something that reminded Alan of his twins. He just shrugged it away and enjoyed his dish with a glass of star fruit juice at one of the tables. After a quick lunch he proceeded home. At home he related his fruitful visit to Taiping. He promised to take Judy on his next trip....hopefully to meet his real parents. Judy was happy that Alan knew his parents were still alive and that gave him hope to meet them, Gods willing.

That weekend they went for lunch at Judy's parents' house in Port Dickson, Negri Sembilan. Judy's parents, Pandian and Violet, both pensioners, were eagerly waiting for their return. Judy's younger sister, Michelle, and brother, Mark, who studied at the local universities, came back with them. Sonny enjoyed the company of both Michelle and Mark. Pandian had a house near the beach, which he bought in the 60s. On arrival the parents hugged their children, Sonny and Alan. The three teenagers immediately changed into their swimming outfits and rushed to the beach.

"Look at that.....before we could even say hello they are running off to the beach.......they missed the beautiful beach more than they missed us, Violet," said Pandian smiling.

"Hello....be back early for your lunch or you will miss your favourite dishes," called out Violet to her children.

Whenever they came home on weekends, they always asked their mother to prepare their favourite dishes or cakes. Mark looked forward to her mother's chappati with tandoori chicken, while Michelle, who was health conscious preferred spring rolls (poppiah). Their father, Pandian, however, was a die-hard 'thosai' freak. Alan always enjoyed his weekends here as he got to enjoy local

Indian dishes cooked by his mother-in-law for a change. He once jokingly said to Violet in front of Judy,

"It is not very often I get to enjoy Indian dishes on weekends as Judy has no flair to cook Indian dishes. She is now more 'westernised' than the westerners."

"You…Alan…..you told me you never did enjoy Indian dishes……too hotlah….blah….blah…blah…..and now you are telling my mum you missed Indian dishes!"

She immediately pounced and wrestled with Alan on the sofa in front of the family. Everybody had a good laugh. Pandian asked Alan about his job. Alan said he was happier now that the company was moving well and most of her joint venture projects got off to a good start. The herbal project is slow taking off and it will take time to establish the brand in the market, locally and overseas. He related his trip to Taiping in his quest to find his real parents. Violet was happy that there was still someone who knew Alan's parents.

"Without Pak Hussein it would be just impossible to find them as there was no record to follow up. Furthermore, even if someone claims to be my mother, I would need to check her DNA to be certain whether it is true," said Alan.

"We wish you the best and would be looking forward to meet them… hopefully soon," said Pandian.

Pandian, once the angry young court interpreter, had now turned sober. He was unhappy as he could not fulfil his ambition to join the Judiciary. However, when one of his children got admitted into the local varsity and the other send overseas on study loan, he changed his mind about the government. Though he missed his opportunity in life he was grateful to God that his two children were given the privilege to pursue their tertiary education. His wife, Violet, said that during those early years scholarships were limited and the government had to give priority to others. She, however, was happy as she started her career as a student nurse and retired as a Matron the highest level achievable in the nursing world. After his retirement Pandian wanted to pursue his law studies again but found that poor health would hinder his studies and his family advised him to drop the idea.

At 12.30 pm Mark, Michelle and Sonny came racing back to the house, all 'tan and dark' from the sun. They were so excited to be at home.

"Go and take your bath and get ready for lunch," Violet instructed them.

Pandian stepped in and said, "The sea water is almost contaminated, kids, so you all better take a good bath before you come down for lunch."

"We want to go back........do we need to change? asked Mark.

"Do as your mum tells you.....we are all hungry now," said Pandian.

# CHAPTER 84

The three teens rushed upstairs and within five minutes were downstairs.

"That sure was fast...did you three take your bath together?" Judy joked with her siblings.

"Me? Yulk! No way....only both of them were fighting to get under the shower!" replied Michelle. Violet asked, "How did you know that......were you also in there?" "No...no....never...I just heard their voices while waiting in the bedroom!" replied Michelle.

"No wonder I can still smell the sea water," laughed Pandian. "The three of you did not even have time to soap your body!"

"That's the smell of the sea out there, dad, not us," replied Michelle.

"Okay.....Okay.....let's eat," said the Violet.

As expected there was 'thosai', 'chappati', 'tandoori', 'fried poppiah', chicken and 'dhal' curry. Unlike the rest in the family Sonny loved all the food laid on the table.

"Sonny is like a empty rubbish bin....everything is delicious," laughed Mark.

"I need the strength to stay fit and score more goals!" joked Sonny.

"Just eat Sonny...don't bother about Mark....soon you will grow stronger and bigger than your uncle!" said Violet.

"So Mark how do you like law studies? You are in the second year right?" asked Alan.

"So....so...lah brother. I need to put in more effort this year.......no more fooling around...no girls....no carrom....no girls...no girls," replied Mark smiling. Alan just laughed it off saying, "That is the most hazardous challenge while trying to study in a university!" "Not hazards lah brother but more of 'perks' in varsity life!" interjected Mark.

Michelle winked her eye at her mum, Judy smiled but his dad pretended not to hear.

"How about you Michelle?" asked Alan.

"I am finishing my accountancy by end of this year and looking for a place to work in March next year," said Michelle.

"Why not come and join us, we need another accountant by next year," said Alan.

"Not now.....I prefer to get exposure in the banking sectors before joining any company or government. I need to understand better the 'mentality' and 'work culture' of our bankers before I do business with them. Anyway I'll think about the offer," replied Michelle.

"That's a good idea, Michelle, there is nothing like a good exposure in organisations like the banks before joining the companies. Accountants are professionals and are accountable not only to the company they work but also to the government and public at large," said Judy.

"The same principle applies to lawyers.....they should work first in the Judiciary before they decide to practice. They then can be sure to be on the right footing from day one," added Pandian looking at his son Mark.

Mark nodded his head in agreement. "Get to know the Judges before you state your case...right dad?" said Mark.

"Sure......there is nothing better in the life of a lawyer if the Judge is on his side! Makes life easy all the way." added Pandian.

After lunch the three teens rushed off to the beach. "Don't swim when your tummy is still full," shouted Pandian to the trio.

# CHAPTER 85

Alan and Judy helped Violet to clear the table, while Pandian watched soccer on TV. Alan decided to take a short nap and went straight into the bedroom. Having rested for a while Alan and Judy took a walk on the beach. There was quite a big crowd on the beach….mostly families having their picnic together. Alan always enjoys the walk on the beach as that gave him plenty of time alone with Judy. They just talk about their three kids, her family and the future.

At 6.30 pm they came back to the house and decided to leave for Kuala Lumpur. Michelle and Mark stayed back for another night as they had no lectures on Monday. As usual the trip back to Kuala Lumpur took much longer due to the heavy traffic of holidaymakers. They arrived home close to 8.45 pm and realised they were all dead tired. They just had a light dinner, 'instant noodles' and some fresh fruits. After dinner they watched a movie on Astro while Sonny decided to go to bed early. Alan and wife too decided to turn in by 11.00 pm It had been a long day. At 11.45 pm Alan's cell phone rang. He woke up, took the phone and was surprised to hear the voice of Mak Jah, Pak Hussein's wife.

"Alan ke tu….ni Mak Jah….(she was sobbing)….Alan…..Pak Hussein kena serang sakit jantung…..sekarang ni ada dihospital Taiping…..dia coma…" (Is that Alan….this is Mak Jah ….sobbing…..Pak Hussein had a heart attack… he is now in Taiping hospital…in coma).

"Ya, Alan ni Mak Jah…..terima kasih ….saya akan datang segera," replied Alan. (Yes, this is Alan, thanks Mak Jah….I will come now).

Alan woke Judy from her sleep and phoned Datuk to inform that he was going to Taiping tonight. Judy insisted on following him to Taiping and Alan was thankful as he needed a friend to keep him company….it was a long drive at night to Taiping. They informed Sonny they had to go to Taiping on an urgent matter.

They left just after midnight and were in Taiping before 1.30 am. They headed straight to the hospital and were told by the nurses that Pak Hussein was in the ICU. At the entrance of the ICU Mak Jah, relatives and friends of Pak Hussein met Alan and Judy. Mak Jak related to them that Pak Hussein collapsed at about 10.00 pm in the house while watching a soccer match. The neighbour called an ambulance and he went into coma on the way to the hospital. The doctors confirmed it was a heart attack and admitted him into the ICU for observation. He was still not out of danger yet. Mak Jah was so grateful that Alan came. Alan consoled her not to worry too much and that Datuk had agreed to foot the hospital bill though he was no more an employee. Alan requested the hospital to upgrade Pak Hussein to first class ward after he was discharged from the ICU and decided to stay on for a few days in Taiping to see the progress of Pak Hussein. They stayed at the Hotel Malaysia. Mak Jah stayed back at the hospital to be close to her husband.

In the morning after breakfast Alan and Judy went to the hospital and was relief to hear Pak Hussein was now conscious and will be moved to the First class ward in the afternoon. They were allowed to see Pak Hussein, who was awake and looking cheerful when he saw Alan. They chatted for a few minutes and told Pak Hussein not to worry. Alan at the corridor met with one of the doctors who explained about some symptoms of heart attacks. "I am sure Pak Hussein must have heard from the other doctors about it. Anyway, there are many symptoms or signs of a heart attack. The major symptom is angina, an oppressive, heavy pressure sensation in the chest. It may not necessarily be in the chest but pain can be elsewhere like in the neck, in the throat, in the jaw or in the arm. Other symptoms include dizziness, fatigue, even sweating and difficulty in breathing. A heart attack can also occur because of a blockage of one of the arteries due to build-up of cholesterol and plaque. However, about 20% of our patients died of the 'silent' heart attacks where the patients experience no pain," said the doctor. When the doctor was explaining these symptoms Alan looked at Judy as at times he did experience those symptoms. The doctor looked at him and said, "Don't worry....you are still young and those pains could be just muscle pains due to golf, tennis or badminton." Alan suddenly felt relief as he did play tennis and golf when he had the time.

# CHAPTER 86

$A$lan kept Datuk informed on Pak Hussein's progress. They sent Mak Jah to her house as she needed to change and take some essential items for Pak Hussein. Later they send her back to the hospital. At the hospital Alan left her some money before they left for Kuala Lumpur.

It was almost 12.00 noon when they arrived in Ipoh and Alan decided to take Judy for lunch at his favourite stall. As usual the place was crowded but they managed to get a table. Judy had chicken rice, Hainanese style while Alan tried 'Loh Mai Kai', steamed glutinous rice for a change. Both ordered fresh coconut water, Malaysia's most healthy drink.

The old man (towkay) was not around but the frail old lady and his son were serving the customers. When the young man brought their dishes Alan asked him what was his name.

He replied, "Tat Meng….Wong Tat Meng."

Judy looked at Tat Meng and noticed there was something peculiar about him that reminded her of her twins. She did not mention it to Alan. While they were eating the old man came back and greeted all his customers with a big smile. Again Judy noticed something peculiar in his smile, but she could not recall where she had seen such a pleasant smile. His friends called him 'Uncle Wong' and they all seemed warm to his friendly gesture.

"No wonder he has so many customers daily," whispered Judy whispered to Alan, "his public relation is just superb!"

"PR alone will not do, his wife cooks delicious par excellence food......that gave the edge…..she is what we should call 'Chef Diva'," replied Alan.

'Uncle Wong' came to their table, as he did with other customers, and said, "You two must be new here. How's the food?"

"Very delicious, Uncle," replied Alan, "but I am not new here, Uncle, this is my fifth time. My wife Judy is a first timer here…she loves your cooking. We are on our way back to Kuala Lumpur from Taiping."

"Sorry if I did not notice you when you came here before, but this time around I could not help but notice your beautiful wife here. Is Taiping your hometown ......or you just came visiting. We were from Taiping, long, long time ago," said Uncle Wong.

"We went to visit a friend, Pak Hussein, who had a heart attack last night," said Alan.

"Pak Hussein? Which Pak Hussein....is he from Kampong Pokok Assam.....his wife's..... Mak Jah?" asked Uncle Wong.

"Yes....yes that's right! You know them?" asked Alan.

"How is he...is he alright? He is a very good friend of ours.... Mei Lin, my wife, and I knew him a long time ago. Is he still in the hospital?" asked Uncle Wong.

"Yes, he had recovered and should be out of ICU by this afternoon," replied Judy.

"Thank you......thank you.....excuse me....thank you," said Uncle Wong.

He went straight to the kitchen to his wife where they were seen engrossed in a discussion over some issues. His son joined in the conversation but soon left the kitchen to attend to the customers. Both Alan and Judy watched the couple for a while before they left the stall. Alan was wondering about the relationship of Pak Hussein and Uncle Wong while he took a slow drive back to Kuala Lumpur. Alan could not help but kept thinking about Wong Tat Meng, Wong's son......reminded him so much about his twins.

# CHAPTER 87

The next morning at the office, Datuk called a meeting with Mawi and Alan. Alan briefed them about Pak Hussein and Datuk told them the company would bear all medical expenses at the hospital. He told them he would be going with Datin in the afternoon to see Pak Hussein. Mawi said he would go down on Friday. Datuk meantime also mentioned that he was interested to look into developing the potential of solar energy in a big way to replace electricity for industries, lighting up highways, rural areas, cities and housings and not nuclear power. Nuclear power was just to alien to him. He had met with some local expertise from the universities and Japanese scientists who were interested in developing the idea when he went with some local scientists to Japan recently.

Mawi on the other hand mentioned about the company going into the business of super or hypermarkets. He felt there was still room despite the competitions from Carrefour, Giants and Tesco. Malaysia is ready to welcome a few more of these super or hypermarkets, especially in states like Perlis, Kedah, Kelantan, Terengganu and Pahang. Datuk agreed and asked Mawi to make a survey and submit a paper for the next board meeting. He had already invited two scientists to brief the board at that meeting. His priority now, however, was to see Pak Hussein was well taken care of.

When Datuk and Datin arrived at the Taiping hospital there were several people in Pak Hussein's room. Pak Hussein was very pleased when he saw both of them walked into the room. He proudly told those in the room that this was his former boss and wife. They chatted about the good old times and Pak Hussein introduced his visitors to both Datuk and Datin. Uncle Wong and Mei Lin were there and so were another old couple, Uncle Lim and wife, Mew Choo. Datuk conveyed the company's staffs 'get well' message to him and told him that all medical expenses will be taken care of by the company. Datuk granted this for his loyalty to the company while in service. Pak Hussein shed tears of joy as he knew the expenses for his health care would be high from now on.

Many of his friends, mostly pensioners and those on EPF (Employees Provident Fund) could not pay for their medical expenses which came to close RM 800.00 monthly. Datuk said the government should looked into other alternatives, kind of health insurance subsidy, whereby the poor get good medical treatment despite of being incapable to pay the medical fees. The government is capable to allocate a reasonable sum every year in the annual budget for this purpose if there is a will. The public can only donate so much and sometimes corporations donated because they had to as they have 'shotguns' pointed at their heads! One fine day the public may not response to the call anymore. Uncle Wong and wife excused themselves, as they wanted to catch a bus to Ipoh before it was too late. Datuk and Datin invited Uncle Wong and wife to join them as they were on their way to Kuala Lumpur. Uncle Wong and wife were reluctant to take the lift but Datuk coaxed him by saying,

"Apa hendak segan....kita semua sama.....hari ini awak perlu bantuan, mungkin esok saya pula!" (There no need to feel shy.....we are all the same..... today you need my help, tomorrow I may need yours!)

Reluctantly, Uncle Wong agreed, after Pak Hussein urged him to do so.

Pak Hussein said, "Wong, Datuk orang baik....satu hari awak akan tahu!" (Wong, Datuk is a good person.....one day you will know!).

Wong and Lim had a few private words before they departed. Mew Choo and Mei Lin hugged each other as they had been friends since their schooling days.

# CHAPTER 88

In the car, Wong sat with Datuk who was driving and Mei Lin sat with Datin at the back seat. Mei Lin and Wong looked very uncomfortable in the car but Datuk and Datin were very gracious, spoke in Malay with them to make them relax. Datin asked Mei Lin how they got acquainted with Pak Hussein. Mei Lin looked rather confused and so Wong came to her rescue.

"Long time ago Datin.....when we were in Taiping. We were neighbours...... my wife, I mean. When his first wife, Mak Yam, died Pak Hussein went to Kuala Lumpur to find work and we kept in touch with each other. We moved to many small towns to open up a small food stall, in Sitiawan, Pusing, Lumut and now in Ipoh."

"Oh......yes, Pak Hussein came to work at our orphanage.....I saw something good in him and employed him as our security guard," added Datin.

"How many children do you have Mei Lin?" asked Datin.

Again Mei Lin was looking for help from Wong.....Datin felt she had infringed into Mei Lin private matter...she apologised. Wong explained that Mei Lin 'lost' her first child and now had a teenage son and daughter. She had always been sad about that incident. Datin was sorry to hear about the 'loss' and decided not to pursue her conversation on family affairs. Wong related about his business in the many small towns he went and the problems he encountered with the local authorities demanding monthly 'coffee money' which they had to abide to. It was only in Ipoh that he managed to operate a decent food stall without unnecessary interference from anybody. They were happy with the response from the customers....he said probably the 'fung sui' was good. However, their monthly collections were not enough to send his children for further studies. He said they had a very special relationship with Lim and wife....more than just friends. He did not elaborate.

Upon reaching Ipoh, Datuk dropped Wong and Mei Lin at their stall, which was closed for the day. Datuk and Datin proceeded to Kuala Lumpur. All the way to Kuala Lumpur Datin kept on thinking about Mei Lin. She looked sad and burdened by something heavy on her shoulder.

"I wanted to ask her, in case we could help, but she seems recluse and wanted to be left alone," said Datin.

"There are certain things that are best left alone......we will help if they come forward," said Datuk. "By the way, regarding Wong ....there is something about him that looks familiar to me.....was it the smile or the laugh....I have seen that somewhere," added Datuk.

"I felt the same thing......" Datin interjected.

Meanwhile at the hospital, Pak Hussein was preparing to go to bed. He told Mak Jah,

"Datuk and Datin are very caring and understanding.....even when I am no longer in service. They were always very tactful in handling their staffs, treat us like a family. They came up the hard way, struggling to make ends meet. It is difficult to get bosses whose staffs 'will die for them', today. Today we get bosses, who thinks they know everything......rude, arrogant, insulting and in short behave like little Napoleon. The employees work just for the salary...nothing more or less......and the success of the company is not their concern. Look at Datuk Halim's company here, the monthly turnover of his staffs.... just beyond comprehension....though he offers them good salaries. He is young but rude and offensive, unlike his late father, whom the employees respected. That was once a very successful company.....now it is slowly losing good business and clients."

"Datin Halimah, his wife, is also very egoistic......always showing off her shoes, clothing and jewelleries to us.....bought in London, Paris, New York......whenever we meet at the surau. We came to learn about Fardu 'Ain and Fardu Kifayah......she joined our group to tell us about her visits, cruising and trips overseas. Who are we.....we cannot even afford to buy decent food daily!" said Mak Jah. "Most of the Datins in Taiping cannot tolerate her behaviour......that's why she came to join us......the lower income group."

"I pity them....they lose their directions... all because of wealth and power,.....they do not see the right path shown by Allah, lets pray they realised their follies before it is too late," added Pak Hussein.

# CHAPTER 89

$P$ak Hussein was discharged from the hospital after five days and he was told to get a good rest. At home he was watching TV when he remembered he needed to make some calls. Using his cell phone he dialled a number.

"Hello....hello. How are you? I am Okay. Now.....yes, discharged yesterday. Come over when you are free. Where is your husband? Where? Playing mahjong.....he should stop gambling. Anyway I called you to discuss a very urgent matter. Remember the son that you gave away to the orphanage about 40 years ago, he is doing great. What? No...no...no....he is married and now has two sons studying overseas......yes....yes....... you have two grandsons now. I know.....now...now..... please don't cry.......I know you are very happy. The big question now is whether are you prepared to meet your son? Yes....yes......his name is Alan.....just Alan. He came to see me recently and asked about both of you....he wants to meet you both. Yes....I told him both of you are still alive and I need your permission to arrange the meeting... we got 4 days to come back to him. Pardon? My advice....well my advice is to meet him......he will understand why he was abandoned then. Okay.......you need to discuss with your husband first and come back to me, say in two days time? Okay......bye."

Pak Hussein felt relieved after the telephone call, as he wanted so much to fulfil Alan's request. Mak Jah came out from the kitchen with a glass of warm water and asked Pak Hussein inquired about the phone call.

"You remember Alan.....I just called his mother to try and arrange a meeting between them......she said she needed to discuss with her husband first".

"Let us hope Alan gets his wish to meet them both. Like us, his parents are old.....so why delay," said Mak Jah.

Meantime Alan was waiting anxiously for the call from Pak Hussein. The 10 days he promised was over but Alan gave him additional time as he was admitted to the hospital for 6 days. One Friday night he received a call from Pak Hussein. The meeting had been arranged on Sunday morning at his house. Pak Hussein did not reveal the name of his parents......'surprise', he said. Alan was so excited about the news and so was his wife, Judy. He could not concentrate on his work neither could he sleep well at night. On Saturday evening he drove to Taiping with his wife and put up at Hotel Malaysia. On arriving at Taiping he took a drive near Pak Hussein' house hoping to get a glimpse of his real parents in case they were there. There was no car, just Pak Hussein's motor bike and the house was quiet. Alan went to check in at the hotel. That evening Alan and Judy went to bed early as they were both so excited about the family reunion tomorrow.

First thing tomorrow morning Alan and Judy had an early breakfast and by 8.30 am was at the door of Pak Hussein's house. Pak Hussein and Mak Jah were surprised when they saw Alan and Judy standing at the porch.

"You are early Alan......they are suppose to be here only at 10.00 am." said Mak Jah.

"Have you had your breakfast yet.....we have some nasi lemak if you care to join us," Pak Hussein invited them in.

"We had an early breakfast Pak Hussein, thanks. It's better to be early than late, Mak Jah," said Alan.

They chatted about the good times Pak Hussein had at the orphanage. At 10.15 am, a taxi came in. Alan got so excited when he saw a Chinese man alighted from the taxi. Pak Hussein invited him in and introduced him as Uncle Tan, an old friend. They casually talked about his health. Tan brought some fruits and said his wife Ah Soo could not come because she had to take care of her granddaughters. By 10.30 am there was no sign that anybody else is coming to the house. Alan guessed Uncle Tan must be his father. Pak Hussein, however, looked very relaxed and never did indicate that Tan was the man they were waiting. Alan could not resist anymore and wanted to switch the conversation.....when the phone suddenly rang. Pak Hussein took the phone,

"Yes, where are you? You cannot make it today.......she is not feeling well...I understand....Okay....yes.....we will fix another day....alright.... thanks for calling."

Tan asked Pak Hussein whom he was speaking over the phone. Pak Hussein replied a friend. Alan was then more confused.....so was Judy. Pak Hussein informed Alan the meeting was cancelled and he will try to fix another day.... soon. Alan was disappointed.....Tan was confused...."

Am I interrupting something here?" asked Tan.

"No......Alan wanted to meet a friend but he is not able to make it today," replied Pak Hussein.

Alan suspected that Tan could not be his father. Tan said he had to leave to help his wife and Alan offered him a lift as he too decided to return early. Tan was so grateful. They left Pak Hussein's house at 11.30 am.

# CHAPTER 90

The next morning Alan could not but felt that the person who called the Pak Hussein's house must be his parents. How he wished Pak Hussein would tell him where to locate them. He did not want to pressure the old man but to let him do it his way. Judy told Alan,

"Pak Hussein knows what he is doing."

Alan had to go overseas on Saturday for a week with Datuk and he told his wife to standby in case Pak Hussein called. While in Geneva Judy called saying a meeting had been fixed for Sunday, as Alan should be back by Saturday. Alan agreed and asked Judy to reconfirm the meeting with Pak Hussein. On Saturday afternoon Alan arrived home and told Judy they will go over to Taiping on Sunday morning, as he was still tired from the trip.

Early in the morning Alan and Judy went to Taiping. When they arrived at Pak Hussein's house there were so many people gathering inside and outside the house. They went in and saw Mak Jah crying, consoled by her relatives and friends. Pak Hussein had died early this morning from massive heart attack. Soon many of his relatives and friends arrived, including Uncle Wong and wife, Uncle Lim and wife and many others. Alan informed Datuk about the sad news and Datuk said he would be there before the funeral. He asked Alan to take care of all the funeral expenses. Alan sat with Uncle Wong and Uncle Lim. Wong asked Alan,

"How did you arrive so early from Kuala Lumpur?"

Alan replied, "Pak Hussein arranged a meeting here this morning......family matters."

Uncle Wong overheard the conversation and asked, "Are you Alan?" Alan nodded.

"Then we have to meet after this......this was Pak Hussein's last wish," said Uncle Wong. Alan agreed but he had to attend Pak Hussein's funeral first.

Alan went in and told Mak Jah that all expenses will be taken care by Datuk including the three nights 'tahlil' (religious gathering). Pak Hussein's son, Razak, and family from Sarawak were fortunate to be home because they were back for a holiday. He took time off to be with his father after his heart attack.

Datuk and Datin arrived just before the funeral, together with Mawi and Siti. After the funeral, Uncle Lim invited Wong, Mei Lin, Alan and Judy to his house. Datuk and Datin decided to leave for home as they had other matters they had to attend to. Uncle Lim gave a simple lunch prepared by Mew Choo. Throughout lunch Uncle Wong reminisced about his long relationship with Pak Hussein. He was full of praised for Pak Hussein, "He was a simple man but one with a very, very warm heart. He was very trustworthy though at that time he was just a Security Guard at the Bibi Orphanage. I will miss him dearly and my visit today was because of his request. He must have something important to tell me......" Wong said with teary eyes. "I came this morning hoping to receive some good news from him.......now that will remain his secrets forever," Alan said.

"If we have more Malaysians like Hussein, Malaysia will be a very much better place to stay," said Uncle Wong.

"He was just a face in society but was a great man to me. He helped my wife and me on many occasions though he himself could barely make ends meet. He shares what little he had with his neighbours. I remember when we were in Kuala Lumpur, we barely had any food to eat, as we could not get any job, Hussein gave us some money from his meagre salary for months. His friendship had no boundaries....religious, racial or political...... all are Malaysians...... "we are all humans" he used to say. I just wonder what Malaysia would be like today if he was the Prime Minister," said Uncle Lim. He went into deep thoughts for a while. There were tears building up in his eyes as he tried to control his emotions. His wife came to his side and consoled him, rubbing his back gently.

Uncle Wong quickly defused the situation and said, "Hussein was my close friend too, as he helped us though he was only a Security guard."

Mei Lin suddenly was sobbing uncontrollably......Mew Choo immediately sat near her to give her strength. Everybody was shocked as to why she was crying. Wong had no choice but to come out with the truth,

"Before Hussein died I was at his house two days ago. We had a long chat.....talking about the days when life was dark.....the future bleak. We had a son when we were young......our marriage was not blessed by both our parents as we had no job. In fact our parents disowned us and we moved out to Pak

Hussein's village. I did not know him but his parents took pity and allowed us to stay in one of the vacant huts. That was when my friendship with Hussein started. His father arranged some odd jobs for my wife and me….she help at the local food stall. In fact Hussein called a meeting this morning to discuss some matters."

# CHAPTER 91

"My first son was given to Pak Hussein around 1977......we were not able to give him a proper home and education," Lim blurted out.

Suddenly Alan felt dizzy........ "Oh.....my God.......Uncle Lim did Pak Hussein send the baby to Datuk orphanage?" asked Alan.

"Yes......yes.....that was what he told me......why.....why?

"Oh my God.........," interrupted Uncle Wong. "Anything Uncle Wong?" asked Alan.

"Yes......yes......my first son was also given out for adoption and Pak Hussein arranged it. We had to give him away as my wife was so sick after the delivery and I was doing odd jobs. There was no one to take care of him. So we gave to Pak Hussein for adoption. When we had our second son and daughter we could manage our lives because the food stall business was doing well," said Wong. Alan became more confused. He thought to himself that one of this 'Uncles' must be his father.

All these while Judy was seated there dumbfounded and equally confused.

"I am confused now.......one of you must be my parents......but whom? Now that Pak Hussein is no more around.......who can help us to reveal the truth. I remember the other Chinese boy, Jimmy, was adopted by an Indian family from Penang and the other by a Malay family. Both are now successful in lives, Jimmy is working as an accountant in a bank and Eddy, an engineer, is in Petronas. We have been in touch with each other lately," said Alan.

"Thank God......at least we know how to contact them," said Lim.

Mew Choo said, "Maybe Mak Jah knows something about you Alan...... she was a helper there, I understand."

"Yes, I am sure she can throw some light to us," added Mei Lin anxiously.

"We cannot disturb her these few days......she is mourning.....give her a few weeks before we see her, Okay?" said Wong, "meantime if we need to know fast we can all go for DNA test."

"Let us first wait and hear what Mak Jah has to say and if we are still not convinced then we can go for DNA tests....." said Lim, "after all we are not claiming back our sons.....but just want to know who are our sons."

"I will call you when Mak Jah is ready to meet us......Okay?" said Lim.

After having some tea they all dispersed. Alan and Judy gave Wong and Mei Lin a lift to Ipoh. It was a long drive for Alan.......thinking about his real parents which was still a mystery. Wong too was deep in his own thoughts and both Judy and Mei Lin felt asleep at the back. On reaching Ipoh they shook hands and Mei Lin hugged Judy good bye.

What had transpired that day turned Alan into a recluse. He lost his sense of belonging and direction. The DNA tests would be conclusive but he needed assurance from someone who really knew what happened on that day. Besides Pak Hussein only Mak Jah can clear the mystery. He had no choice but to wait.

Alan was on the phone with Jimmy the next day.

"Yes......I met two old Chinese couples yesterday and chances are good that one of them could be your parents. Are you interested to meet them?" asked Alan. "Things can get messy for both my adopted parents and me," replied Jimmy. "Pardon? I know......things can get a bit messy for your adopted parents and you but why not you just have a chat with them on this matter. Maybe they too would like to meet them....after all you already have a family of your own......it will not in any way affect your relationship with them. Discuss with them and let me know....Okay? The next time you are in Kuala Lumpur drop in my office......I'll buy you lunch," Alan advised. "Let me think about it. By the way have you contacted Eddy? One of them could be his own real family.......don't you think so?" said Jimmy. "Could be.....I will just do that tonight because he is now on one of the rig in Terengganu. Send my regards to Susie and your kids.......bye," Alan replied.

# CHAPTER 92

Business was as usual at the office and the e-mails and faxes received from overseas were encouraging. Datuk told the management team that they now had to monitor the progress of each business thoroughly and ensure any problem was nib in the bud immediately. Take good care of the staffs and they will take care of the business well. Datuk decided to visit his business partner in Europe and a week break in London with Datin. Alan excused himself as he had unfinished family business to attend to.

After almost three weeks Lim made up his mind to see Mak Jah. He went to the house with Mew Choo. Mak Jah was alone cleaning the house compound. She was so happy to see Lim and Mew Choo…..old friends, whom she could relate to Pak Hussein. They together had gone through the good and bad times, which strongly bonded their relationship. Lim and Mew Choo spoke in Malay with her.

"How are you Mak Jah?" asked Mew Choo. "Trying to cope with life without Hussein…….Okay……but at times I miss him," replied Mak Jah, "come in…...let's have some coffee."

They went in and Mak Jah went straight to the kitchen to boil some water. She then came back and sat down in the living room with Lim and wife. Mak Jah told them that Atan came over to accompany her almost every night…… that helped to ease her pain. At times even Atan's two elder sisters came to stay overnight being very friendly neighbours and coming from a big family of ten…….. She heard the kettle whistled in the kitchen and quickly went in to prepare some coffee. She came out with a tray and three small coffee mugs.

"Have a drink Lim, Mew Choo…….sorry, no cookies today," said Mak Jah.

"It's alright…..we came, hopefully to seek your help Mak Jah," said Lim.

"Glad to be of help, Lim, if I can….what's it all about?"

"It's like this …….you remember Hussein arranged for us to meet our son on the day he passed away…..remember? Well, now that he is not around we feel you are the best person to help us in this matter," said Lim.

"Yes…yes, I can still remember that fateful day. Both of you came to our house in Kuala Lumpur that evening with your baby boy. You pleaded with us to take care of the baby as you were not able to support him. We told you we too were not able to feed another mouth but could arrange your baby to be taken care of by the orphanage where we were working. You agreed and told us not to tell anyone about both of you. We had not told anyone, even to Datuk and Datin," said Mak Jah.

Mah Jah was quiet for a moment and later said, "Wong too gave us a baby boy to put under the orphanage. So I am uncertain as to who is your son.... Alan, Jimmy or Eddy and a few other Chinese families. Alan came looking for his parents and we need to run some kind of tests at the hospital to determine this, I understand."

"Yes.....yes, I think they call it Deoxyribonucleic acid tests in short DNA tests....I remember watching the movie series 'CSI – Miami' and many crime stories in Astro", said Lim.

"Yes, DNA would be the conclusive tests to determine the dilemma we are facing now according to Doctor Aru," added Mew Choo.

Mak Jah said, "We must get Wong and Alan to undergo the tests together with you and Lim or the whole exercise would be simply futile."

"I will contact Wong and Alan and we will fix a date to come to the Taiping hospital for the tests. The sooner we get this done the better for all of us.....you know we are all old....we don't know who is next on the list to get invited to heaven!" said Lim, jokingly.

"We should all meet here to get a unanimous agreement from all parties, say in a few days time," said Mak Jah. Lim agreed to make all the necessary arrangement.

# CHAPTER 93

On Saturday morning they all gathered at Mak Jah's house. Uncle Lim, Uncle Wong, Alan and their wives were all there. While having coffee they were listening attentively while Mak Jah recollected her version of the story about the adoptions. "Both of you, Lim and Mew Choo came to our house in Kuala Lumpur that evening with your baby boy. You pleaded with us to take care of the baby and we said we could arrange your baby to be under the care of the orphanage where we were working. You agreed and the next morning I send the baby to the orphanage. After three days Wong came to see us…..Wong too wanted his baby son to be sent to the orphanage for a better future there. There were others. You know all babies looked the same……cute and chubby! They were all of almost of the same age. Datin named one Alan, the other Jimmy and another as Eddy if my memory is correct…….and they had wrists name tags as identification," said Mak Jah. "After a week I was not sure…… who is who….the name tags came loose….I mean between Alan, Eddy and Jimmy," added Mak Jah. "Jimmy was adopted by an Indian family…….he is now in Penang, I understand. Eddy and Alan remained at the orphanage until they start living on their own. All are happily married, you know,"

"So Alan……who…..whose son is he?" asked Lim anxiously.

"I don't know," replied Mak Jah, "but could be yours or Wong maybe Eddy or Jimmy could be yours. Whatever it is you must be prepared to accept the truth through the DNA tests," said Mak Mah.

Lim and Wong looked at each other, so did Mew Choo and Mei Lin. Alan stood up and walked towards the window to relax and look for answers. Then he remembered about the notes left by his parents.

"I was told by Datin that there was a simple note left by my parents….. who left that note with the baby?" asked Alan. Both Lim and Wong could not remember about any note. After a while he sat down and said to them,

"We have no choice but to go for DNA Paternity tests…..that's the only way……are you all agreeable?" said Alan. "How about Jimmy and Eddy?" asked Lim. "They have yet to make up their minds……they will let me know when they are ready, I suppose," replied Alan.

Without any hesitation they all agreed and Alan called the hospital to make arrangement for the DNA tests. The Taiping General Hospital advised that the arrangement can only be conducted on next Monday morning. Under the DNA Paternity tests there was no necessity to take the mother's DNA sample. They all agreed to meet on Monday morning at the Taiping hospital before they departed for home.

Early on Monday morning they all met again at the hospital canteen for a quick breakfast. By 9.30 am they proceeded to the doctor's room to undergo the DNA Paternity tests. "The whole procedure is simple and not painful.... so I want all of you to just relax while I take your blood," advised the doctor. The doctor took 2ml blood sample of Wong, Lim and Alan.

The doctor said, "If blood was not available I can take buccal swabs (from the inside of the cheek) as sample, anyway I prefer blood samples".

The doctor told them it would take a few weeks before they can get the results as the samples would be sent to a Chemistry Department's DNA laboratory in Petaling Jaya, Selangor. Alan asked the doctor for more details on the DNA tests.

The doctor said, "The DNA test has an accuracy of 99.99%. Samples are sent to the Biological Laboratory in Petaling Jaya and the DNA is extracted from the samples. It is amplified in a machine known as thermalcycler, which makes millions of copies of the genetic material. This goes into the genetic analyser, which produces a genetic profile of each individual. Comparisons are then made of genes found on 16 specific DNA segments. Paternity is established if all 16 segments match."

What happened if some segments do not match?" asked Alan.

"Further testings are carried out as these differences could be due to mutation. If there are more than two mismatches, then the man is not the father. It normally takes 4 to 5 days to come up with the results and in emergency cases within 24 hours. Since we are away from Kuala Lumpur I expect the results to be back in about 2 weeks."

# CHAPTER 94

$A$lan thanked the doctor and left the hospital with great expectation. Alan offered Wong and Mei Lin a lift to Ipoh and they parted with Lim and Mew Choo at the Hospital. In the car Alan was happy that his searched for his real parents was coming to an end soon. He could then focus all his energy on his career. In Ipoh Wong offered Alan free lunch which he accepted without any resistance…….he just love the food cooked by Mei Lin. He left the stall after lunch and went back straight to his home to rest. He opened up a bottle of cool beer, Anchor beer, his favourite brand and watched the Astro while waiting for his wife, Judy, to return from office. He opened up a packet of groundnuts, which he bought in Ipoh. While enjoying his groundnuts, his cell phone rang. He picked it up and answered.

"Hello……Alan here……who? Oh….Jimmy. No…no…..I am at home now….just back from Taiping. Yes…..yes…. we all underwent the DNA tests. Oh….no….it will take a few weeks before they can verify the results. Yes…it will be conclusive…..yes, I will let you know the outcome of the tests. Okay, I will do that. Anyway I suggest you take your DNA tests in Penang and bring the results here. Can you do that and come down to Taiping when the doctor calls us to announce the results. It would be nice if you can ……Okay …..I will keep you inform," said Alan. "Were you able to contact Eddy?" asked Jimmy. "Yes…..but he was not very interested," answered Alan. "OK then ……..bye," said Jimmy.

While watching a movie on Astro he soon fell asleep….not realising he was exhausted and very tired due to the anxiety from the trip to Taiping. He woke up when he heard his main door opened and his beautiful wife walked in. He looked at his watch…it was 6.45 pm.

"Hello darling……how was your day at the office?' asked Alan.

"Oh…...some very disturbing news, dear. There is talk that the company may be forced into a merger or worse taken over by another company. Whatever it is we are sure many of the senior staffs, especially, will be offered VSS, voluntarily resigned from the company."

"Wow…..that's serious……" said Alan.

"Even if I stay I will have to face a new boss or transfer to another department......I hate to think about that," replied Judy, "you know they will always bring in their trusted team to take over control of the company......I am seriously contemplating of applying for another job."

"Your company is doing well......what went wrong? Alan asked.

"Exactly, there is nothing wrong with the company....in fact we are about to be awarded a new 70 million dollar contract overseas......that's it... somebody up there is up to no good," said Judy.

"You decide what you want to do, I do not really understand your corporate culture.....you know better. If you feel you can progress further in your company, stay on......why leave. However, if you feel you are not up to it......to handle idiosyncrasies of the new bosses then by all means......leave the company," advised Alan.

"My company has all along been professionally managed......by qualified professionals. But this new company, interested in the merger, is too politically link and most of the directors are politicians, though some are qualified." "Those qualified politicians are the ones that you must really watch out as they are all out to make quick bucks while still in power," said Alan. Judy was quiet all the time. "Judy......are you still with me?" "Yes, love.....I.....I was just thinking.....actually I am quite confuse with the new development. I understand the new group that intend to take over are closely tied to the ruling political party.....good as the company will get more projects but bad as these projects might not be executed efficiently and resulting in lots of leakages. Decisions made must never be politically motivated..... once that happened the CEO of the company would face an uphill task to run the company economically. We have seen so many multibillion companies went bust due to political interference!" said Judy.

"Look at Bibi Sdn. Bhd......all major decisions is professionally decided by the Board and the directors are focus on business not political gains. Datuk is so professional in his work.......even his own brother he kept away from the company's operation as Mawi wants to mix business with politics," remarked Alan. "Well sweetheart the best you can do now is just put your office problems at the back of your mind and sleep it off. Hopefully you feel a better and stronger person by tomorrow morning. Do not rush into making decisions.....fate can do wonders to us when we least expect it to happen. Remember when I nearly resigned from the company after the 'attack' from

En.Mawi? Have faith in God....He is always there to look after us......good people," said Alan.

"O.K......I will see it through.......and.....will only tender my resignation if I have no choice," said Judy.

"That's my girl......come here," said Alan.

"No...no.....no.....not now........let me prepare your dinner first......," replied Judy. She gave a cheeky and sexy look at Alan while walking briskly into the bedroom. Alan stood up and gave her a chase right into the bedroom!

# CHAPTER 95

While having lunch at the office with Datuk, Alan received a phone call from Lim requesting him to come down to Taiping Hospital on Friday. That was two weeks after they had the DNA tests. Alan informed Datuk who wished him the best of luck. Alan phoned Wong and offered them a ride to Taiping, which they agreed.

Early the next morning Alan and his wife took the ride to Taiping to resolve his parentage. In Ipoh they picked up Wong and Mei Lin. They greeted one another but each was occupied in their own thoughts all the way to Taiping. Alan sensed the tension in Wong and Mei Lin as they were the biological parents of either Alan or Jimmy. On arrival at the hospital Lim and Mew Choo were there waiting at the lobby. They greeted each other and went to see the doctor. The nurse at the counter informed that the doctor was on his normal morning rounds at the wards and will be back at about 9.30 am. So as to reduce the tension and waiting time Alan invited them to have some drinks at the hospital cafeteria. They all agreed and took a short walk to the cafeteria. The place was busy with outpatients and staffs but some light refreshments would be good to all of them. They then went back to meet the doctor. At 9.45 a.m. the doctor came back from the ward and invited them into his room.

After some preliminaries the doctor said, "We received a very positive report from the laboratory a few days back. It is confirmed, beyond any reasonable doubt that Alan is the biological son of......Mr. Wong."

Everybody was stunned for few minutes. Mei Lin began to sob and so did Mew Choo. Alan looked at Wong and Mei Lin and spontaneously came down on his knees and clung to Mei Lin. Tears of joy came down his cheeks and Mei Lin was now crying uncontrollably. Wong too was overcome by the situation and he came over to Mei Lin and Alan......the three embraced each other. Judy could not help herself and she too came over to console her-in-laws and Alan.

After being able to take control of the situation Alan asked the doctor whether there was any DNA report he received from Penang in particular from his friend Jimmy. The doctor said there was none. Lim and Mew Choo accepted the decision of the tests in good faith and joined in the rest in rejoicing the good news to Wong's family. After a few minutes and having taken control of themselves, Alan thanked the doctor and they left his room. Lim, though sad that Alan was not his son, invited them to his house to commemorate the reunion. Alan was thankful to God for bringing his biological parents in his life.

At Lim's house, Wong related to Alan about the fateful day that he and Mei Lin decided to give him away to the orphanage. "We were very young when we met and decided to get married. It was not the spirit of nationalism and independence that urged us to get married but the love for each other. Mei Lin and I were jobless and without proper education getting a job was difficult. Her parents were against the marriage…..We understand now why…..but at that time we only think of ourselves…to be together……we left the house and that was when we met Pak Man, Pak Hussein's father. He was not a rich man but inherited some land in the village where he built two huts for rent to the poor. He was a man with the heart of gold…….he took us in and gave us shelter and food. He refused when we wanted to pay our monthly rental and Pak Hussein, then a young man, became my good friend. I did some odd jobs in the village and Mei Lin help to wash dishes and clothes at a few houses. Our income was not even enough to put some decent food on the table… fortunately, Pak Man told us not to pay any rental, water and electricity. He knew we could not afford to do so."

Tears were swelling in the eyes of Wong…..his voice quivered and Mei Lin kept on sobbing.

"Mei Lin got pregnant after 3 years of marriage and we were in a dilemma as to what we had to do to keep the baby…. you…Alan. We knew we could not even buy you milk and food regularly….what more to give you education. Mei Lin was not well after the delivery so we went to see Mei Lin's family who turned us away; though her mother was sympathetic she could not do much as her father remained adamant. I had no family of my own and we decided it best to give you away for adoption. We knew we would not able to offer you a good home, education and most importantly…..future. Fortunately, Pak Hussein got a job as Security guard at the orphanage in Kuala Lumpur then and we decided to seek his help. We knew you would be in good hands at the orphanage….and we were right…….you have turned out to be a very responsible young man. We are proud of you…very, very proud. We have never forgotten you….your mother always cry when she speaks about you even after we had your brother and sister. We felt the family was incomplete without you. We are so happy of you.....for what you are now......Datuk had given so much to you...we are so grateful to him.... please forgive us......"

Alan hugged to his father and said, "There is nothing to forgive, Pa, Ma......I understand....I really understand. That's the reason I wanted to meet you both....if I was angry I would not be here......you both are not at fault...... it's fated....destiny! From what I understand about any religion......whatever happen to us is fated.....and nobody is to be blame......we must never blame anybody for whatever happen to us...God's will!"

# CHAPTER 96

"Okay….Okay….." Lim tried to defuse the sad mood, "let us have some drinks now…..now that all is well…….but I still need to know who is my biological son……I thought it was you….Alan. I am happy for Wong and Mei Lin. Now that you know your parents, take good care of them. How do you feel?"

"Wow…..great…..just great…..my own mother, father, brother and a sister…..what more can a man asked?" replied Alan. "By the way I promised I will help you to find your son……and I believe he is Jimmy. I will call him later and persuade him to come to do the DNA tests here."

Later Alan and his family decided to take leave……it had been a long fruitful weeks for Alan. Before they left Taiping they dropped at Mak Jah's house to thank her for all the assistance she and the late Pak Hussein had done. Mak Jah was so happy that all went well and Alan was back in the fold of his biological parents.

"Take care of your parents, Alan, they are old and need your love. Your brother and sister need your help too……they are very bright youngsters…see that they get the chance to further their studies," advised Mak Jah.

"Thank you Mak Jah….without you and Pak Hussein I can never dream of meeting my real parents. We have plans for my siblings…..but we need to discuss with them first," replied Alan who gave some money to Mak Jah.

On the way back to Ipoh Alan asked lots of questions from his parents, trying to catch up for the lost time. His parents obliged and related their days when they were young after having given away Alan for adoption and how they started the noodle business, from one town to another in Perak. They started in Taiping but decided to move to other towns in Perak. Life was so harsh, there were times they could not afford a day's meal as what little they earned went to payment of rent, electricity. Later when your siblings Tat Meng and Sui Leng were born our lives turned for the better by the will of God. We could afford to send them to school though financially it was tough. They, however, sacrificed and ensured that the kids were always happy and had their meal everyday. Mei Lin's parents cut her off from her family and she had not seen them since we left the house in Sitiawan, Perak. Alan just listened when his parents related the sad episode. He did not realised tears rolled down his cheeks, it was dark in the car and nobody saw him crying. He felt sad, as he was not there to give them a helping hand and share their sorrow. Judy was watching the happy reunion quietly. Alan suddenly realised Judy had been very quiet and asked her,

"You are extra quiet today, honey......anything?"

"Oh.... I was so thrilled with what happened today......and I now realised that's why Uncle Wong......sorry Papa reminded us of our sons. Both our sons and Alan inherited your smile and laugh, Papa. Alan and I spoke about it the last time we met you and we just could not pin point the identical characteristics between Papa and Alan!" replied Judy.

Mei Lin smiled and said, "I noticed that the first time I saw Alan but kept it to myself."

When they reached Ipoh, Alan was so excited and decided to stay overnight in his parents' house as it was a weekend, "to get to know his brother and sister better", he said to Judy. Judy said she did not bring any spare clothing but Wong said both of them could wear his siblings' clothing overnight.

"They are about your size, you know," said Mei Lin.

"Okay...we can get our toothbrushes and under wears at 7-Eleven and the supermarket across the street," said Alan.

The food stall was very busy when they arrived. It was evening and many of Wong's faithful patrons were there. Judy asked Mei Lin,

"Who cooks when you are not around?"

"Sui Lin and Tat Meng.....are both excellent cooks........my customers keep telling me that," replied Mei Lin smiling.

As soon as they got down, Alan rushed into the stall and rushed to hug his brother who was serving some customers. Everybody was surprised, especially Tat Meng. Alan could not say a word to Tat Meng but just hanged on to his brother. He then went into the kitchen and tried to hug his sister who took off screaming. She could only just take a few steps before Alan caught her. She screamed and struggled to free herself but Alan held on tightly to her before she could run. Some customers were shocked on hearing the commotion in the kitchen. She was screaming at the top of her voice until her parents came in, laughing, and explained to her about Alan. Both Tat Meng and his sister stood confused for a few minutes before they come to their senses. This must be the long lost big brother they overheard discussed by their parents a few months ago. They were shocked but happy that he was Alan.

The customers at the stall joined in the reunion party and Alan gave the customers for the night free dinner and drinks. Judy also hugged Tat Meng and Sui Lin who were then both in tears. It was laughter and joy until midnight together with the customers. After the customers left, they sat for supper. Under a more sombre atmosphere, Alan talked about his life as an orphan, student and how he met Judy. He told them about his twins and he knew they would be looking forward to meet their grandparents from Alan's family. The rest in the family just listened to Alan, though from time to time Mei Lin was seen wiping tears but consoled by Wong.

# CHAPTER 97

After supper Alan went to purchase the toothbrushes and other necessities at a nearby shop. When he returned to the shop the whole family were gathered upstairs. Judy had just taken her bath and was wearing Sui Lin pyjama. They were chatting happily about their early days. Alan quickly excused himself and went to take his bath. He put on the pyjama given by Tat Meng, the trousers were a bit too short as he was slightly taller than Tat Meng, and he looked 'funny' in it. Judy tried to control her laughter and so were the rest in the family.

In the end Alan was the one who started laughing, "I look like a clown, right?" he said, and everybody burst into laughter.

Alan, however, was unconcerned, as he was so happy to have found his long lost family at last. Wong and Sui Lin never felt so happy and complete now that the whole family is together at last. Wong talked about his life to them and explained why Alan was given away to the orphanage to Tat Meng and Sui Lan. He wanted them to understand and accept whatever happened was fated. At times he choked when he related how Mei Lin could not sleep for weeks thinking about Alan. Mei Lin was crying silently but Alan was by her side to comfort her. In a lighter mood Wong told his family that Alan was actually named 'Wong Peng Soon' after the legendary badminton king of the 50s.

"I idolised Wong Peng Soon for his prowess, skill and mental strength. Nobody came close to beating him in the singles during his heydays. So when Alan came along he decided to name him after his idol 'Wong Peng Soon'.

"I do play badminton for pastime but to name me after the legend…..that's a great honour. I need to improve my game soon…..probably invite Datuk Lee Chong Wei to be my sparring partner!

"Fat hopes Alan Wong!" Sui Lin cheekily remarked. Everybody in the family laughed at Alan.

"Okay….okay….not Datuk Lee…..probably Datin Wong Mew Chew!" joked Alan.

"That's more like it……but you need Datuk Lee's permission first!" added Sui Lin.

Again everybody had a good laugh over Sui Lin's remark.

Wong continued to relate his sad story to his family.

"I did not give Alan's birth certificate to Pak Hussein when he gave him to the orphanage. Datuk must have decided to call him Alan, as it was very easy to remember at the orphanage," said Wong.

They were all not sleepy that night probably due to the excitement and carried on chatting until dawn. Late at dawn everybody felt sleepy and they all slept together in the living room, too tired to move into the bedrooms. At noon some customers knocked on the door to buy some food. They were all still feeling groggy due to the late night and took sometime before realising some customers had arrived to have their lunch. It was a weekend and the customers usually brought along their families to eat out. Alan suddenly realised it was almost noon. The customers had arrived and the kitchen was not ready. Wong rushed downstairs and opened the main door and apologising to them that he had a late night. He told them about his new found son and they joined in his excitement. Wong apologised again and promised that the kitchen would be ready in an hour's time. Some left very disappointed but having known Wong for a long time they said they would come back later. A few opted to wait in the stall and ordered coffee or ice tea. Meanwhile Mei Lin rushed to the bathrooms to get ready to go to the kitchen. Tat Meng and Sui Lin took turns to go into the bathroom. Within 25 minutes they were all busy taking orders from the customers and cooking in the kitchen. Alan and Judy came down to help his parents serving the customers. The customers were overheard talking about the family reunion and they were happy for the family.

One of the customers remarked, "I hope Uncle Wong will not close down the business in Ipoh!"

"No…no…whatever it is, Ipoh has given me everything…I will not abandon this town," replied Wong.

Alan told some of the customers that he was very grateful to God for Ipoh gave him this food business, brought in many loyal customers and most importantly brought Alan back to his family. He was contemplating of buying the shop lot and to continue doing his business in Ipoh. However, this was subject to the price being reasonable, otherwise he had to look for an alternative shop lot.

"There is nothing like having your own shop lot and home to do business," said the father, smiling.

Before 2.00 p.m. many customers got to enjoy their late lunch due to the concerted effort of the whole family. By 3.00 p.m. most of the regular customers had left and Alan and Judy decided to go home to Kuala Lumpur late in the evening. He promised to come back over the coming weekends to discuss on the educational future of both his siblings. He wanted them to complete their tertiary education.

# CHAPTER 98

Back at the office the next day Datuk Khalid was the first person to walk into Alan's room to congratulate him on finding his parents and siblings. Alan was taken by surprise, as he had not informed anybody yet about his meeting with his parents. Datuk Khalid casually said, "There is no secret in our office here…..I am kept well informed, though I am seldom in the office now. Watch out, I have so many spies in the office you know. Actually a 'bird' came and whispered to me about it." He laughed. Alan was puzzled and asked Datuk who really told him about it. "Mak Jah gave me a call as soon as you left Taiping….she is so happy for you…..and so are we. Now that you are settled down with your family matters I am sure you can now really focus on your job". "Thank you for your support and understanding Datuk……you are always there to stand by me when I feel low. Thank you, Datuk."

On the following weekends Alan and Judy took a drive to Ipoh to visit his family. He wanted to discuss with Tat Meng dan Sui Lin on how he could help to finance their studies. As usual the food stall was busy when he arrived at about 10.45 am. Customers were enjoying their favourite dishes with their families since it was a weekend. Some came to enjoy late breakfast and a few for their early lunch. Alan and Judy went upstairs to meet his siblings after greeting his parents in the kitchen. Tat Meng and Sui Lin were waiting for him upstairs. Alan wanted to see their 'A' level results to suggest about the various options they had to further their studies. Physics, chemistry, biology and additional mathematics had been Tat Meng favourite subjects while Sui Lin, however, loved the arts subjects, in particular English, English literature and history. Anyway, she had the niche on mathematics and accounting. Alan and Judy started by explaining to both of them that they hope to help both Tat Meng and Sui Lin to achieve their ambitions. They would finance their studies in the field they were interested to pursue. Tat Meng was keen in pursuing his dream of becoming an Accountant and Sui Lin a lecturer in English. However, Tat Meng now almost 30 years old will pursue his ambition at a local institution in Ipoh. He loved cooking and would like to continue to help his parents during his free time.

Sui Lin in jest said, "Tat Meng is scared to leave his girlfriend, Leng Leng here...that's why he wants to stay in Ipoh."

Tat Meng just blushed and was unable to rebut his sister's remarks. He was going steady with one of the local girls here, a teacher, whom he hoped to marry soon. Anyway, now that he got a chance to pursue his ambition he intended to do just that first. Sui Lin being more ambitious agreed to apply for a place at one of the centre of higher learning in Kuala Lumpur. Alan told them to keep him informed of their applications. His only advice was to study hard and do not let their parents down. Tat Meng and Sui Lin were overjoyed that their big brother had given them hope and opportunities to better themselves.

They then all adjourned downstairs to help their parents served the customers. Alan noticed that his parents had established a very large loyal group of customers and it would be a shame if his parents had to move out to a new location. He was hoping that the shop owner would agree to his terms of purchase of the building. Weekends had always been a busy day said his parents. The crowd kept on coming until midnight. Alan and Judy decided to stay overnight at his parents' home as it was too late to drive back to Kuala Lumpur. That night Alan sat with his parents to discuss on the future of his two siblings. Judy and Alan's two siblings were asleep by then. He told his parents about his proposals and in case they had to leave home his parents could consider employing part time maids or helpers to assist them. Wong told Alan that from time to time there were many youths who came to offer assistance when they were busy on weekends. Wong casually related his early days in the food business,

"After 2 years staying in the kampong and saving some money we decided to start a small food business in Taiping town. Business was very competitive but we were harassed by the local councils, though we were licensed to operate the food stall. It became very expensive to operate in Taiping and after two years we moved to Lumut. We were still in the business we were familiar with.....Chinese food. In Lumut business, was rather slow, though we had a more stable life. A customer from Ipoh who came to eat at our stall advised us to operate our business in Ipoh where there were more customers."

The customer said, "Your dishes are unique and tasty and Ipoh Chinese loved delicious Chinese food....you can make more money there. I can help you to find a shop to rent...very good location for customers."

"One weekend we went to see him in Ipoh and took a look at the shop he proposed. The rental was reasonable, as the wooden building though old had sufficient space for a kitchen, a toilet and eating space for customers. There were three rooms upstairs, a toilet and a small living room. We were initially given a five-year tenancy. This is the shop lot I am talking about. We have been operating here for almost 15 years and the rental has been kept to a very reasonable rate. We always kept in touch with Pak Hussein to inquire about you but he just told us you were doing well and not adopted by anybody. We love this place and we have many loyal customers, old and young. If this was our own shop I will not hesitate to slightly renovate the kitchen and eating space to give more comfort to the customers. The owner, Kah Chong, passed away a few years ago and the family is contemplating of selling this property," said Wong.

# CHAPTER 99

"How much are they thinking about, dad?" asked Alan.

"Probably about RM 300,000-00…it is negotiable as we had known them a long time," replied Wong.

"I would like to buy this property for you and mum as a gift for you and mum. I will discuss with the owner tomorrow and if the price is right we will close the deal."

"I don't know what to say, Alan, we do not want to impose on you after what we had done to you. But today we are both most grateful and proud to have a son like you," said Wong who gave his son a big hug.

Alan in return kissed his mum on the cheek saying, "I want to see both of you happy now, after what you had gone through."

Wong said he had some savings for the rainy day but it was not enough to finance Tat Meng and Sui Lin's further education.

"We both felt so sad when Tat Meng and Sui Lin could not further their studies after having achieved very good results in their Grade 'A' level. Scholarships were out of question and getting loans were as difficult for people like us.

"Dad use to say, others are given opportunities on the silver platters, but we have to earn it," said Judy.

"Both Tat Meng and Sui Lin decided to help us in the kitchen while trying to secure a job in the public or private sector. There were many jobs that they applied but getting calls for interviews were very few. They were not successful at any of the interviews. However, we thank God for He had given us good health and prosperity. Tat Meng and Sui Lin are now very good cook and that they can survive by operating the food stall when we have to go. And we are happy that you are giving them both opportunities to further their studies. I pray that they will be as successful as you in their lives. Depriving anybody from pursuing further education to me is a big sin when we are short of professionals in many fields today. What they do with their lives after getting tertiary education is something they have to decide. They cannot blame anybody," lamented Wong.

Alan agreed that getting good education is very competitive today and each has got to struggle to achieve his ambition. By 3.00 in the morning they were all feeling sleepy and decided to call it a day.

Early the next morning breakfast, Wong and Alan went to meet the late Kah Chong's eldest son, Kelvin. Kelvin, a teacher by profession, was at home doing some gardening with his wife, Patricia. They had a nice home near the Tambun area. They were greeted warmly by Kelvin and Patricia as they arrived at the house gate. "Come in Uncle Wong, come in. This must be your son Alan that you had been telling me all this while," said Kelvin. "Yes, this is Alan. Alan this is Kelvin and his wife Patricia."

Kelvin had known Wong since he was a young boy and he was very attached to Tat Meng and Sui Lin. In his younger days he spent most of his free time at the shop and on weekends even slept there.

"We had no children then, so Kelvin was like a son to us...even now. When Tat Meng and Sui Lin came into our lives they too were very close to Kelvin. That was how they got free tuition from Kelvin," laughed Wong.

Kelvin humbly said, "They were like a family to me....that was no tuition just giving some tips!"

Alan noticed that Kelvin was about his age. He graduated from the local university in Physics and became a full time teacher in Ipoh. His wife was a nurse at the local hospital.

**"Come in...come in..." said Patricia, but Wong insisted to discuss matters in the garden.**

**"It is very nice out here...under the cool morning sun once a while,"** he said.

**Patricia went in and Kelvin invited them to sit at the garden chairs. Alan casually asked Kelvin about life in Ipoh in particular and the development of the state of Perak in general. Wong, who was eager to finalise the deal, signalled to Alan to discuss on the sale of the shop lot. He had waited so long to own his own place and the time was now right. Alan immediately asked Kelvin whether the shop lot was still for sale.**

# CHAPTER 100

K elvin replied, "Yes, and we would like to give Uncle Wong the first choice. It is only when he rejects the offer that we will look for other buyers probably let the real estate firm to handle it. There had been no offer from other parties to purchase the shop lot as yet."

"What is your asking price Kelvin? Give me a fair deal," said Wong.

"I went to the Land Office and also inquired about the market price for such property and was told it was in a region of RM 400,000-00. It is an old building but 'rock steady' they said built by very responsible contractors during those days," said Kelvin.

"Yes, the building is still solid and needed just some minor renovations, here and there. I love the shop and the location….very ideal for my business," said Wong.

"Uncle Wong, I am not going to make profit from you on this property, in fact if my dad was still alive he would give you the best deal. I am prepared to part with this property to you for RM 300,000-00 only. How is that?" asked Kelvin.

Wong was taken by surprise. He expected above RM 300,000-00.

"To the other purchasers my opening price will be above RM 400,000-00, but for Uncle, we feel it is just not fair. You and Aunty are now like a family to us, now that my dad and mum are no more with us," said Kelvin.

Wong was still stunt with such a generous offer and did not realise that tears were swelling in his eyes. Everybody was silent for a few seconds. Alan whispered into his dad's ear and Wong after wiping the tears away, nodded at Alan and said,

"I will take it at RM 320,000." "Thank you Uncle, I always knew you are a man with a golden heart," said Kelvin.

"Now that we have all agreed on the price I will arranged for a lawyer to handle the transfer okay? Probably you will need a lawyer too Kelvin?" remarked Alan.

"Agreed……my lawyer will contact your lawyer to finalise the deal. It is nice to do business with Uncle," said Kelvin shaking hands with Wong and Alan.

Patricia brought out a jug of ice cool lemonade and some cookies.

"Come Uncle…Alan…..here are some drinks and homemade cookies," said Patricia.

Wong said to Alan, "Patricia is also a very good cook and loves making cookies!"

"Not as good as Uncle Wong…you are chef par excellence! Patricia had been getting professional tips from uncle and aunty but somehow she said the taste is never the same!" said Kelvin.

"Perfection comes with time…a long time," replied Wong. They all laughed.

"Judy would be happy to meet you…..she too loves making cookies," said Alan.

"I am looking forward to meet her, Alan," replied Patricia.

They chatted for while before Wong and Alan decided to take leave.

"Aunty will be worried why I am still not back, Patricia!" Wong joked.

"Drop in again Uncle Wong, and bring your wife along the next time you come around…..let us know so that we can prepare something special," said Patricia.

"Oh…..no…….don't trouble yourself by preparing special dishes for us. We are very simple people……..Chinese tea will do," Wong replied smiling. Alan said, "Why don't you bring your family for a dinner tonight as we are still around. Let us celebrate together the deal that we just concluded."

"I'll never turn down an invitation from the best Chinese restaurant in Ipoh," quipped Kelvin.

"That's a brilliant idea we will be expecting all of you there….say before 7.00 p.m. okay?" said Alan.

"By the way, who is cooking," asked Kelvin.

"Of course me….specially for your family," replied Wong smiling.

# CHAPTER 101

On the way home Alan asked his dad why he reduced the price to RM320,000 when he whispered to him for RM 350,000. "Kelvin indicated a figure of RM 300,000 when the market price was above RM 400,000….so I thought RM 320,000 would be a very fair price. I am saving you RM 80,000 you know," Wong joked.

Wong phoned Mei Lin and informed her that he had agreed on the terms of offer for the shop lot. It was a good deal. Mei Lin was happy as they now have a place of their own at last. He told her that he was going to the wet market to buy some vegetables, fish and prawns as he had invited Kelvin and family for a dinner. Back home Mei Lin told Tat Meng and Sui Ling of the good news. Mei Lin shed tears of happiness, as she never dreamt of owning her own shop after what they had gone through after marriage. Doing odd jobs with combined earnings insufficient to pay any rental but just their daily food was not their way of living. They wanted to at least have sufficient money to pay the house rent, though it was only RM 30-00 a month. Pak Man told them to pay only if they could afford. When they started their business in Lumut they paid monthly to Pak Man whenever they could. Pak Man returned the money and told them to keep it for the 'rainy days'. Pak Man died many years ago and we attended his funeral. Until today they were most grateful to Pak Man and family until today. It was God's will that Alan came back into their lives and now they have a home of their own.

That evening Kelvin and family came for dinner at the shop and both families had a great time. Tat Meng and Sui Lin, however, had to cook and entertain the other customers. They alternately joined the dinner to celebrate the occasion. Patricia and Judy enjoyed their new relationship and were chatting away about their children, beauty and health care. Judy promised to see Patricia the next time she was in Ipoh.

Later in the evening, after Kelvin and family left, Alan and wife departed for Kuala Lumpur. On the way back Alan confessed to his wife that he had never felt so happy in his life until today. Helping his parents to own their own home cum shoplot plus making the dreams of his siblings to pursue further studies were the pinnacle of his achievement…nothing can ever eclipsed that. He had some savings in the bank and hopefully he could close the deal by the coming weekends. Judy was happy and fully supported his move.

Alan was in his office when he received a phone call from Jimmy.

"Hello, yes, Jimmy, anything I can do for you?" asked Alan.

"I have been contemplating about the DNA tests and the meeting with my biological parents. I am seriously in a dilemma and very confused. I have not told my…..my parents as yet. I did not want them to feel dejected because they hoped that I would never look for my biological parents. They feel that things can be rather complicated and that they will lose my loyalty and love for them. I am seriously thinking whether I should pursue with these tests or just forget the whole thing and let it be. Things may turn nasty and confusion may reign if I proceed with this idea," lamented Jimmy.

"Think positive, Jimmy. This, I believe is good for you, your biological parents and your….your adopted parents. You never know Jimmy….but I felt it best you resolved your parentage rather than try to ignore the issue….it will not go away, you know. You are now an adult, settled down with a nice family and I believe ready to face the reality of life. I know there is a shadow hanging over you so why not face and erase it from your nightmares you have been having for so long. It is not going to hurt you, your family and I believe even your adopted parents. I know your feeling for being sent to the orphanage, just like me, but no parents want to do that unless they have to….they love us and they want a better future for us, a future they could not offer. I have the same feeling as you initially, but I realised I just cannot keep on running from learning the truth. When I met them I was not angry but instead sympathised with them to have to make such sacrifices…for our future. It was a gamble, but they knew they took the right step. Give it a try Jimmy, for all you know you will love them just like your adopted parents…..but most importantly, you make them happy to know their long lost son had survived and doing well in life. God is great, you know, He created enough space for us to love everybody…each in its own way. Let it go, Jimmy…what has passed is over. Think about it, talk to your wife and explain to your adopted parents…you got to…it is not only for you but the future of your family."

Jimmy was silent on the other line. "Hello Jimmy, are you still there?" asked Alan.

"Ya......I am still here.....okay......I will discuss with my wife and I need your help if I decide to go for the tests and eventually meet my biological parents," replied Jimmy.

"Anytime, Jimmy...you know we are like brothers, so you can always depend on me. I tell you what...whatever you decide, please let me know, okay?"

"Okay, I will do just that. Bye and thanks," said Jimmy.

"Bye", replied Alan "thanks for the call".

# CHAPTER 102

Two weeks after his meeting with Kelvin, Wong had finalised the sales and purchased agreement drawn up by the two lawyers. Alan had given the cheque for RM 320,000-00 through his lawyer to Kelvin. It was now up to the Land Office to issue the new title to Wong. The shop lot was unofficially his property now. With his savings he wanted to renovate the shop lot with additional toilet and bedroom upstairs. A facelift was badly needed downstairs in the dining hall and the kitchen.

"A minor renovation and a coat of paint would do much good to your shop," said Alan to his father.

"Not too colourful, dad," said Sui Lin, "the customers might mistake the shop for KFC!" they all laughed.

"No....just plain light grey will do for me and a new sign board – 'Restoran Wong dan keluarga' (Wong & family restaurant) should do it," said Wong. "What is important we must maintain the quality of the food served, improve our service but maintained the price at reasonable rates. If we can maintain our present customers we should be okay," he added.

Meantime Alan had to go on a trip overseas for a few weeks with Datuk. He phoned up his father and said he was depositing the amount of RM 50,000-00 into his father's bank account in case the two siblings had to register themselves at the higher institutions when he was not around.

One morning Alan received a call from Jimmy. He sounded very excited over the phone.

"Alan....I know my biological parents now....oh....I am so glad I did it. You know 6 weeks ago I went for my DNA tests in Penang hospital and when the doctor compared the results from Taiping General Hospital it is confirmed that my parents are Lim and Mew Choo. I have met secretly with Lim and my mother Mew Choo yesterday but have yet to tell my adopted parents. It is so difficult to approach this sensitive subject. Alan."

"You have to Jimmy, as they deserved to know. Nothing much will change as you are now a family man and like me it is good to have two parents to turn to. We are matured Jimmy, and so are your parents, so tell them....it is just a question of how you approach it. I am sure they will be happy for you too," advised Alan. "After that you should bring your biological parents to meet your adopted parents…I believe everyone will be happy in the end. Congratulations, Jimmy…….that was good news to Judy and me. Keep in touch and bye."

"Alan…hold on….it is not that easy as you think…I don't have the guts to face my adopted parents as I had promised never to mention about my real parents to them…..I…..I….am worried….." said Jimmy.

"Jimmy….Jimmy….hold on….are you there…Jimmy……Jimmy…." shouted Alan into the phone.

"Darling…darling….Alan….wake up….wake up….you are having a nightmare!" Judy tried to wake up her husband.

Suddenly Alan woke up from his sleep and realised he had a dream about Jimmy. It was just 3.45 am….very early in the morning and Judy was wide awake besides him.

"What was all that about, darling? You mentioned the name of Jimmy in your sleep!" asked Judy.

"Oh dear…it was Jimmy….I had a dream talking to him over the phone. Anyway, it was just a bad dream!" replied Alan. "Sorry I woke you up, dear…. just a bad dream!"

Suddenly he remembered he had to catch a flight with Datuk to London this morning on his way to Brazil.

"Let us go back to sleep as I have to be at the airport first thing tomorrow morning," said Alan.

# CHAPTER 103

Alan met Datuk at the airport early in the morning and they had a cup of coffee at the cafeteria.

"You looked worn out this morning Alan? I hope you did not have late sleep last night!" asked Datuk.

"No Datuk….we went to bed early but I had a bad dream about Jimmy last night. My wife woke me up at about night 3.45 am and after that it was just difficult to close my eyes. I kept thinking about him," replied Alan.

Datuk just nodded his head after apologising to Alan. After a good lunch on the plane Alan fell asleep while Datuk was engrossed on his laptop. Datuk and Alan landed at the Heathrow Airport after about 7 hours' direct flight from Kuala Lumpur. They were in London for 2 nights before they flew to Rio de Janeiro Airport. Datuk made a courtesy call on the Malaysian Ambassador and the Trade Commissioner in Brazil to foster closer relationships and get first hand information from them. The Ambassador gave them dinner in Rio before they flew to Sao Paolo. He wanted to follow Datuk to meet the busineesmen in Sao Paolo but was unable to do so as he had a number of official functions to attend in Brasilia, the centre of administration in Brazil, just like Putrajaya

"I would like to see more businessmen from Malaysia doing business here. The opportunities are tremendous!" the Ambassador said during dinner. "Many Malaysian businessmen came here and ignored us and quietly went on their own to secure business here. They came looking for our help when they got into some trouble. By then it was too late for our office to do anything. What I am most unhappy is that they then blamed us for not helping them when they get home! They painted a negative picture that we in the Embassy and Trade office overseas are here on a long holiday! They did not realised that we are here to help Malaysians feel safe and secure when they are here, whether for holidays, study or on business. If the businessmen approach us before they meet with their counterparts here we may be able to give some useful guidance and advice to them."

Azarai, the Trade Commissioner, was free and he helped to organise meetings with the relevant businessmen in both Rio and Sao Paolo. He explained over lunch in Rio, "The opportunities were there......as there were many large corporations trying to penetrate the market in Asean and Asian countries. Malaysian is seen as an ideal country to sell their goods to these Asian and Asean countries. We have a very good reputation as being reliable especially having a very stable government and politically very stable. BN ruling the country for over 55 years without a break is really impressive and a great achievement."

He arranged for business meetings both in Rio and Sao Paolo. Brazil, as said by Azarai, is a big country that offered tremendous business opportunities and it was a matter of striking up with the 'right' and trustworthy partners before venturing into it. A major part of Brazil was still unexplored and the country is quite advanced in the sugar cane, petroleum and heavy industries. Datuk intend to explore seriously into the petroleum and heavy industries. He noticed that many of the successful industrialists here were Italians.

"We agree not all businessmen in this world are genuine. Many are just out to make some quick bucks!" said Alan.

"Let me relate to you an incident, which happened to me, though not directly," said Datuk. "I had this experience once when I was in the First Class section from Kota Kinabalu to Kuala Lumpur. A well-dressed gentleman sat beside me. As soon as he was settled we struck a conversation. He introduced himself and asked where I was going and where I was working. I did not tell him my real profession but told him I was doing some small business in Penang. He was supposed to be in the toy business from Sabah and was expanding his business overseas, as there was great demand for his products from overseas. Actually his core business was logging. He gave me his business card, which I saw had the name of a holding company, address and telephone numbers. Behind the card were about 20 subsidiaries, which made things, looked very impressive. He tried to impress me with his 10-year business plans and his expansion to China and India. "That is where the economy will be soon," he said. "That is very impressive," Datuk remarked.

"After chatting with him for while he said that he was looking for a reliable partner to invest in his expansion programme and asked whether I was interested. He stressed that he needed to get the answer within a week. Then, he opened his brief case, which was on his lap and took out a bottle of medicine. Being very suspicious and curious I took a quick peep in his brief case from the corner of my eyes (which I should not have done) and was

225

surprised to see one old sarong and T-shirt instead of files or plans. He then continued and said he would be in Kuala Lumpur the next day at a certain hotel after finalising his business in Penang. He requested me to call him when I got back in Kuala Lumpur. He gave me his cell phone number," said Datuk.

"Though he was well dressed and spoke good English, the old sarong and T-shirt made me very suspicious. We parted at the airport and that evening I phoned my uncle, who was a businessman and told him about the character I met on the flight. I said I do not trust him but my uncle wanted to meet up with this character. So I gave him all the particulars and where to meet him. The first thing I did the next morning was to give a call to his office in Sabah. There was no such number. I call my business friends in Sabah and was told he had not heard of such a company there. I got more suspicious and informed my uncle to be extra cautious when he met with this character. I then phoned the businessman and said that my uncle, who was my partner, was interested to meet him. The next evening my uncle got an appointment to see the businessman at the hotel. He was met at the lobby but he insisted they met in his suite where they can have more privacy instead of the coffeehouse or the lobby," continued Datuk.

# CHAPTER 104

"My uncle, though scared, made his way and proceeded to the suite. Another businessman, his partner, met him at the door. After introducing himself my uncle entered the suite. In the living room were two other characters who were gambling away. On the bed was a brief case, which was deliberately partly opened containing cash in one hundreds and fifties notes. My uncle anticipated there were a few hundred thousand in the brief case. The gamblers invited him to join in but he opted to just watch. In the meantime the businessman was on the phone contacting his colleagues to discuss the partnership. The businessman briefed my uncle about the company's long term plans and as usual the bottom line was very, very impressive. Meanwhile plenty of cash was changing hands between the gambling duos.

After about fifteen minutes the 'Boss' came in. He was supposed to be the Chairman of the company and they addressed him as Tan Sri. After the introduction Tan Sri scratched his head and told his partner that the overseas clients wanted an additional 100,000 ringgit to be deposited into their accounts immediately to close the deal. They were short of cash and turned to my uncle whether he could contribute that amount and in doing so sealed his partnership in the company. Fortunately my uncle had no such money and he also sensed that these characters were out to con him by creating such a crisis. Even if he had such large sum of money he would not part with it before he had seen the business in Sabah personally. Further, he insisted things should be legally binding. The businessmen said they could go down to Sabah to meet their lawyers after resolving this immediate problem. My uncle said he can arranged for telegraphic transfer, bank draft or some other banking transactions but they insisted he came back with the cash only by the next day if he wanted to be a director of the company. My uncle promised to come back early the next morning after withdrawing the money from the bank, but in fact he had no intention to do so." Datuk added.

"He met a friend, a Police officer, and related the whole incident to him. The Police Officer said that he had received a number of reports on such scam. The Police Officer after reporting to his superior officer, with a few of his men that evening followed my uncle and went over to the hotel. The four characters must have sensed that my uncle was up to trap them and so went missing. A check at the front desk showed that they had checked out from the hotel at 6.00 p.m. A quick check by the Police at the airport showed they were still in the city. Probably they were still in the hotel if the front desk staffs were in cahoots with them. His cell phone, which was operating using the prepaid, proved useless. They must have sensed that they could not con their prospective 'victims' for that day and decided to clear out fast. On checking the registration desk the Police found that the four characters came with false passports. According to Police this was not the first case he had come across.

The conmen 'modus operandi' was similar in many cases. They met with unsuspecting victims telling them they represent large companies overseas looking for partners. The meetings were held at hotels and normally in the bedrooms. A few parted with their money in their greed to get rich quick while others managed to keep their money intact by reporting to the Police. There were still many con men from the African countries that need to transfer their gold or money to Malaysia promising of hefty commissions to those 'helpful' caring Malaysians. The conmen never stayed long in one place for fear of getting caught. The Police Officer told us that the 'victims' should report to the Police when approached by such shady characters," Datuk ended his story.

"In the case of business overseas, it would be best to go through our Trade Commissioners' office.....you reduce the chances of being cheated or suspicion from your prospective partners," said the Trade Commissioner as they are there to help Malaysian businessmen seal genuine contracts overseas and not come back home frustrated and disappointed.

Datuk and Alan had a very good business trip to Brazil through the good office of the Trade Commissioner. Bibi Sdn. Bhd. had to be competitive to gain a fair share of projects under the 9th Malaysia Plan. Datuk's trip to Brazil was to look for willing partners that have the expertise to help Bibi Sdn. Bhd. gained advantage over other contractors. Malaysia's economy was booming and those in the construction industry had the lion's share of the budget. However, the local car industry was struggling to survive due to the very competitive nature of the business. Consumers were not happy with the local cars as the imported models very of very high standard though slightly expensive. Consumers wanted, if possible, maintenance free cars and not be bothered with teething problems every now and then.

Datuk and Alan came back after a successful one week business trip. Datuk had so many ideas that he hope he could bring home to bring the economy of Malaysia to greater heights.

# Chapter 105

$B$ack home Alan and Judy went to Port Dickson to spend the weekends again with Judy's family. They arrived there in the morning and her parents, Pandian and Violet, were glad to have them for the weekends as the other children were away for the weekends. After unpacking their things Alan and Judy went for walk on the beach. While passing a group of young man sunbathing they overheard a conversation between a Malay man and his Chinese friend about the sea being contaminated by waste water from about 60 illegal hog's farm rearing almost 170,000 pigs. The wastewater was let out into the sea through one of the small stream. Tourists stayed away from that beach as the water was polluted, contaminated and smelly. The Malay gentleman said,

"With due respect, Lam, I am not against Chinese rearing pigs in Malaysia but these farmers should have respect for the other races. Firstly, get the proper approval and licence to operate such a farm from the local authorities. Secondly, the farm must have proper sewage system including approved effluent ponds to filter the wastewater and not just let it loose into the river and into the sea. The river is a source of various activities to those residing along the river and so is the sea."

Lam replied, "I love eating pork, Syed, but after what I saw on TV on how the farmers breed the pigs here, pork does not appeal to me anymore….not so much as a protest but I lost my appetite because the farm was so filthy!"

"What really irked me is that there is no attempt from the authorities to take action on these illegal hogs' farms that had been operating for almost 30 years! Complaints from the local residents for ages had no effect on the authorities. But why wait for years before the authorities decided to step in? It was only when a local TV station highlighted the problem that those in power started to come out with the usual lame excuses. It was so pathetic to hear them saying that the matter is so sensitive to the Chinese community so they just did not know how to resolve it. If they had checked the problem 30 years ago then it won't be a sensitive issue today. My answer is simple…..resign and let others who can handle it run the state!" retorted Syed.

Lam related his experience to Syed, "I was in UK previously for a few years and had to visit my landlord once a month whose house was located in a hog farm....quite a big one....as he was then the hog farm boss. My visit there was not to join him for any pork BBQ but to pay my monthly rental to him. On a number of occasions I was invited to enter the enclosed dorm, and you know what..... the place was so clean and hygienic with minimal stench. The dorm was cleaned twice a day. Again in Taiwan during my visit there the situation was the same. The hog farms were well maintained, with proper drainage and very hygienic. What I came to know was that these farms were licence and frequently checked by both by the Health department and the local veterinary officers. The farm was out of bound to outsiders and they maintained very strict security on the farm so as not to infect the place with diseases or viruses. To maintain that level of hygiene and control at our local hog farms here both the farmers and the authorities must change their 'lackadaisical' attitude first. There is definitely something not right if a farm can operate illegally for 30 years!"

"I agree with you and am very angry at the 'power-that-be' for deliberately closing one eye for whatever reasons," added Syed.

Alan and Judy just looked at each other and walked on pretending they did not here the conversation. When they were out of hearing Alan said,

"You see Judy our locals now are very smart, aware and concerned about the environment and they expect those in authorities to execute their job efficiently and effectively. It's not easy to be an elected representative today.... you'll have to always maintained a very high energy level, honesty, and especially full of integrity!"

"Very demanding attributes to have!" said Judy, however, from what I heard from my office mates, many of the rural folks are still with the 1950s' mentality.....unwilling to change or to take up the new challenges of the 21st century! That's sad.... they got to quickly 'wake up' from their deep slumber before they experienced coma." They both smiled.

# CHAPTER 106

Alan and Judy then stopped at a nearby 'nasi lemak' stall to take a few home. Many young men were playing beach soccer near the stall and others were sitting watching the game. One of the spectators remarked,

"If our national team play more beach soccer probably they can learn to control and hold on to the ball more confidently rather than panicked and hurriedly pass the ball recklessly. Being able to dribble the ball well and control it gives a player more self confidence, which is good for the game. Look at Ronaldhino and Messi...they took up the game from small and they put so much emphasis on dribbling. Dribbling thus comes natural to them during the game."

"The same is true with the other world class players like Pele, Maradonna, Zinedine Zidan, Ronaldo and many others," added his friend.

Alan smiled at Judy and after they left the stall said, "What they said is very true. Even our son, Sonny, knows about that. When I went with Datuk to Brazil recently, we saw the young boys playing beach soccer all the time… morning, afternoon and in the evening. It was a kind of obsession and the quest to master the art of dribbling and ball control amongst the youth there. When I brought the matter casually during lunch with our clients there they admitted that was the secret of their success in world soccer. The boys did all this on their own time in pursuit of greatness. No one forced them to do it but since the soccer mania in that country is so competitive they have to master those skills to have a chance to play at even local leagues. It pays well to be skilful."

"In Latin America soccer is so competitive and it's like religion to them!" said Judy.

"True. The craze is not only in Brazil but also by at all the South American countries. We must be crazy like them to achieve greatness! Our players today do not aspire to be world beaters….their benchmark, sadly, is to be the top team in South East Asia, which they are struggling to achieve as even the Philippines, Myanmar and Singapore are hard nuts to crack. Look at our once arch rivals like Japan, South Korea, China and North Korea….they are playing soccer at the world stage now. Their players are in great demand in European and English leagues. State Associations today just organised a 3-day selection to choose the players for the various age groups. It is not a good omen to have the 'pyramid' standing upside down. There is no short cut to reach world class achievement. The players should stop blaming the management but instead focus on practice, practice and practice.....until they reached perfection.....the coaches can only guide them."

"Lee Chong Wei (badminton), Azizul (cycling) and Nicol David (squash) are three Malaysians that should be excellent icons to emulate," said Judy proudly.

When they reached the house, Judy's mum was seen outside planting some plants. Judy helped her mum in the garden while Alan went straight in to have his bath. After lunch Alan took a nap while Judy was busy helping her mum in the kitchen preparing some cookies. During tea Judy served some puddings and cookies for the family. After tea they all watched some movies on Astro and later decided to see a piece of property by the beach, which was for sale. Alan was interested to own a piece of land in Port Dickson after his retirement, as he loved the sea and the slow pace of life here. He hoped to own a small vessel to go cruising and fishing after his retirement.

"Kuala Lumpur is too hectic for a retiree, and that is the reason the rich and the famous buy homes at Janda Baik and the highlands," he said.

The land for sale had a beach close by but the price was just too exorbitant.

The evening was just fabulous when Judy's dad and mum reminisced on their young days before Merdeka (Independence). They were still students and were schooling in the same town.

"We had a lot of respect for teachers then....we were even scared to meet them. The Headmaster then was like a Semi-God, highly acknowledgeable and respected by the teachers and students. Today, all these had change drastically....many parents interfered in the administration of the school and teachers are just scared stiff of the pupils because of the parents. So to be on the safe side they try not to get involved in the problems of the students, which resulted in assaults and bullies," remarked Violet.

"I was a temporary teacher in the 60s after my Senior Cambridge and was teaching in a Primary school. I disciplined my students by cracking their knuckles, just enough to hurt their ego, and never had any problem from the parents. In fact I told the parents about their children when they came to fetch their children or when I met them in town or at some functions. You know what the parents said to me? Caned them if you must......if they are naughty or lazy in school disciplined them and I will give additional caning if they complained to me!" laughed Pandian.

"You do that now dad, you might land up in hospital or be sued by the parents," smiled Judy.

"Parents are too protective of their kids today. They do not trust the teachers to discipline their kids in schools," said Alan.

"Most parents are educated now, many are even smarter than the teachers... so when they checked their kids school work and find errors, the confidence on them just simply eroded," replied Judy.

# CHAPTER 107

$\text{A}$lan related his informal discussion during lunch with some officials from the Ministry of Education. The topic of school bullies and teachers were brought up by one of his friends.

"Today we read in press daily about school bullies and teachers trying to 'discipline' their students their innovative ways. Teachers before during my time were very innovative but there were no negative reactions from the parents. Put it this way, we deserve to be treated that way. Parents then were with the teachers. Today parents are well educated and they talked about psychology…the healthy way to educate the kids. The western books on child psychology are readily accepted by the parents not realising that the West is facing more serious problems with their kids in schools today," said an official.

"Then again teachers today are asked to attend endless courses and meetings away in other states. When I asked them what the courses or seminar were all about….the standard answer was 'familiarisation on new policies'," said Alan.

"I know for sure that some school meetings are held outstation when it could be conducted in the school itself. Everyday 4 or 5 teachers are attending meetings or courses, somewhere. It is just not fair to the students and parents. Anyway it is not the fault of the teachers…they are directed to attend," said Osman, a former teacher.

"I do not know who is to be blame, teachers, parents or the Ministry of Education. Everybody has a role to play to get back to the proper way of managing schools," Alan said.

"I specifically mentioned the word 'managing' as schools should not only be properly administered but 'managed' like the business sectors. Head teachers and their Senior Assistants must think out of the box and behave like managers in the private sectors. Head of Departments of the various Departments in the various ministries too must change their attitudes and approach as a business costs centre like those in the private sectors. We need 'professionals' to manage the schools efficiently, not just promote any senior teachers who are about to retire to head the schools or departments so as to continue the tradition. These senior teachers are no more productive and interested in their jobs," added Alan.

"Promotions should not be based on seniority and other negative criteria. There are teachers who are good in imparting their knowledge and others capable and good leaders. If we can classify them into two broad categories then schools will be well managed and students will be taught by dedicated teachers. We must do away with the civil servants' attitude which for ages had been very stereotyped. The teachers should see how the banks and big conglomerate managed their 'business' efficiently," added one of the officials.

"The current terminology such as teachers, counsellors, senior teachers, Senior Assistants, Headmasters and up to Director General may not be suitable anymore as the posts do not reflect the actual role they need to play in modern educational system today. Just like any big corporations, the Director General should be known as the Chief Executive Officer and others down the line of management known appropriately as Executive Directors, General Managers, Managers and Senior Executives. The management system should undergo major 'decentralisation'. 'Decentralisation' here means that Executive Directors are appointed to head each zone. The whole nation can be divided into 5 main zones....North (Perlis, Kedah and Penang), Central (Selangor, Kuala Lumpur), South (Negri Sembilan, Malacca and Johore), East (Kelantan, Terengganu and Pahang) and East Malaysia (Sabah and Sarawak). Each hierarchy is given adequate power to manage responsibly. The Executive Directors of each zone will only refer to the Ministry on major policies only as they are answerable to all major decisions in their zones. At the State level, the Directors of Education are known as General Managers, and Headmasters upgraded to Managers. They make decisions at that level. Today even 'bully' cases are brought to the notice of the Minister for decision!

At each school level there will be 2 Senior teachers who will oversee the other ordinary teachers each. We need to create such an atmosphere and hierarchy in this huge educational system to make it more vibrant and attractive for professionals and qualified Malaysians to join the teaching line. All teachers are disciplinary and counselling teachers in the school. This is a major restructuring and reengineering but to me that is the only way out to leap frog and enhance the teaching profession to a new respectable level. The proposal will work subject to we stick strictly to the policy of meritocracy, which will attract more professionals from all races to join the educational profession," said Alan.

"In short you are saying that the government needs to corporatise the Ministry, Alan?" said another official.

"Exactly, Jeffrey….without political interference only then can they moved on to a new level," replied Alan.

"The Ministry should also stop 'experimenting' and introducing too many new policies to schools but make do and improvise what have been implemented. The gap between the city schools and urban schools are widening and it is sad just to think about the schools in the rural areas. Not only the teachers are confused but the students and parents are upset!" said Osman. What Alan was suggesting was a very drastic overhauling of the educational system and it will take a government with lots of political will and inner strength to implement it.

Alan said to Pandian, "We will need people with leadership qualities not just bosses in this country. Some Malaysians leaders are not very sincere, as they do things just to be in the media. Just watch the TV closely and you see both the politicians and sponsors posing to the media when they donated money! That is against the Islamic teachings according to Datuk Khalid."

# CHAPTER 108

"What do you think about this policy of having 'Vision Schools', 'Clustered asked Pandian. "Frankly, I am against such a policy simply because we segregate the students into categories just like eggs, fish, fruits and many other commodities in factories. These kids are not commodities but human beings that we need to nurture and educate. If we start segregating them from the early years then these slow beginners and the less intelligent will have very low esteem on themselves and in the long run lose self confidence in life. I remember reading a study made by some educationists on this matter. They put two students, an intelligent student and an average student into two separate classes under the same teacher. The teacher was told the opposite that is the intelligent student was the average of the two. The teacher with that knowledge in mind treated the students accordingly and the intelligent student soon lost out as he lost interest in his studies. The average student became motivated as he was treated likewise. So my simple analysis is that if students are graded in classes where there is a mixed group then the average students will benefit in the presence of the intelligent students. The teachers too are motivated and enjoy teaching in these classes as they see the average students progressing well in their studies. The important thing is that the mindset of the teachers.....they must treat all students as equal and the slow learner not to be left behind or ridiculed. Today teachers who are teaching in the less 'fortunate' classes tend to take things easy.....they became less motivated because their teaching skills are not recognised. Before the year ends they were not able to complete the syllabus and the students fared badly in their examinations due partly to the incomplete syllabus. The teachers teaching a group of intelligent students enjoyed their work as the syllabus are completed well before time. They even had time to do revision in class with the teachers. At the end of the year their classes produced the best results, as expected. Their teachers are well rewarded and considered as exemplary teaching staff. The Ministry of Education should seriously reconsider that policy so that no students are left behind." "The problem today is that the Ministry put too much emphasis on straight 'As' to show to the rakyat that they are a producing first class students annually.....actually students with third class mentality!" said Pandian. "I pity these students as when I interviewed them I realised they were taught to learn by hard but not to understand and question the facts," added Alan. They discussed on other aspects of education comparing the new with the old system where the older generations with just a Malaysian Certificate of Education can discuss intelligently with teaching professors in universities. "Now even some university graduates are unable to express themselves well what more to sit in a forum," lamented Alan.

Pandian talked about the security of the country. "It is safer to live in the smaller towns or villages than in the cities. Here if anything happens the whole community will come to assist.....race and religion never come into play," he said. "True....very true, dad.....I had a very bad experience recently near my home in Kuala Lumpur," Alan explained. "An average man on the street would not want to lift a finger if you are in trouble unless the victim is your relatives. You heard of so many cases of victims of snatch thieves and hijacking of cars in the city shouting for help in vain as no one responded to the call for help. This attitude encouraged the thieves and robbers to increase their activities," added Pandian.

Judy came out from the kitchen after helping her mother, sat down and was soon listening attentively to the conversations between her dad and Alan. "You know dad I read this very touching story in the local mass media about a Malaysian by the name of Mr. Raven Murugesan who sincerely displayed an act of kindness at a busy food outlet. He was shopping at a busy supermarket when he heard the azan was in the air and it was time to breakfast. He entered a fast food outlet and saw there was only one counter operating with a very long queue and the counter girl went on working without taking a break. When it was his turn at the counter he asked her 'puasa?' (fasting?). With a charming smile she said, 'ya uncle' (yes uncle). Her eyes evidently showed that she was tired. He quickly took the Tropicana Twister and biscuits which she had just scanned and offered to her and said, 'Adik minum dan makan sekeping biskut ini dulu. Tak apa kami bolih tunggu'. She looked at the Chinese man behind him who sportingly nodded. She took the drink and the biscuits and sat beneath the counter. It was not even 30 seconds when she resumed her work. There were tears in her eyes. I salute to Mr. Raven Murugesan and the Chinese man in the queue who showed compassion in the incident. The moral of the story to me was that there has always been the touch of 1Malaysia in the country from before as displayed by these gentlemen but politics has done irreparable damage to our society. There is no point in stressing for society to respect each other and live peacefully when the political leaders are always at each other's necks!

"True very true," added Pandian, "those good old days, the days that we do not see each other as Indians, Chinese or Malays but as our friends are definitely gone. It is so sad." "Actually we still have that feeling in the present society but certain leaders just overplayed the situation hoping for political mileage," said Alan. "There is not much we can do as certain race feels they are far more superior than others like the Nazi race after the second world war," Pandian ended the discussions.

# CHAPTER 109

Alan related an incident one evening on the busy road of USJ Subang Jaya. It was about 6 p.m when the traffic flow was very busy. The cars were slowly queuing up to the many traffic lights along the street. About 100 yards in front he saw by the roadside an elderly man and a young man exchanging insults. All of a sudden the young man threw punches and karate kicks at the elderly man who fell on the roadside. The old man, in his sixties, was not about to retaliate, but the young man kept on kicking him on the road. Nobody bothered to stop the fight. It was like this was a common daily scene in our big city. If this incident had happened in the smaller towns in Malaysia, hundreds of locals would have immediately separated the two 'street fighters'! Not in Kuala Lumpur, everybody likes to keep their noses and hands clean unless it happened to their own family members.

"I took pity on the old man, who was badly in need of help, as he was desperately looking at the passing cars for familiar faces. Though I was scared, I stopped my car nearby, got out and approached the two men. I was hoping that other cars would also stop and assist me to stop the fight. I was wrong as nobody wanted to get involved in the disputes or care for others in time of needs. The incident was taking place in the urban city not in a village and I was just appauled at the 'caring attitude' of our citizens who treated the dispute between the two men as a daily norm in the city. To them the two men fighting were just two faceless persons on the street. I quickly dialled to the Subang Jaya Police Station before trying to help the old man to his feet. I then tried to talk some sense and reason out with the young man." Initially the young man agreed to stop but as soon as the old man turned his back the young man became aggressive again and gave the old man who was walking to his van another karate kick on the back. The old man felled again and this time he lost his temper, got up by himself and ran to his van. He came back with a long screwdriver to defend himself. The young man panic and he went to his car and brought out his car steering lock. They were ready to fight it out.

"I talked to the old man and persuaded him to get back into his van and drive off to the nearest Police Station as I knew he was going to lose out facing a young active man. He agreed. He was slightly hurt, as there was blood flowing on his right cheek. He was, to me, a very reasonable person and proceeded to his van but the young man tried to kick the old man again while he was limping slowly to the van. I shouted to the old man who immediately turned and warded off the kick. The old man had no choice then but to fight back.... he refused to listen to me and his eyes showed that he was determined to make his stand no matter what the eventuality. I knew this was a dangerous situation so I had no choice but to call again, using my cell phone, the Subang Jaya Police Station for help. It was such a great relief to me when within a few minutes a patrol car arrived at the scene. I did not want the old man to be a victim just because of a minor misunderstanding. The two Policemen took control of the situation and brought them to the Police Station. I was asked to give a statement about the incident. At the Police Station I came to learn that a near collision between the two led to the street fighting. As the evening traffic was very heavy going into USJ Subang Jaya there was nearly a collision between the van and the young man's car. The young man overtook the van dangerously and the old man reacted by 'honking' him a couple of times. Being egoistic, the young man was unhappy and decided to block the van and both ended parking and arguing at the roadside. It was a simple case of road bully and the young man picked an old man to show his 'macho'."

"Road bullies normally choose women and the elderly drivers to show their 'rudeness' on the road but I was surprised at the latest incident in Kuantan. The elderly Chinese man accidentally knocked the Malay young lady's new car. It was a very minor accident as the trffic in town was heavy. She came out in a rage with the steering lock in her hand and threatened the old man. She hit the bonnet of his car a number of times and broke the old man's car window while literally scolded the cool old man. You know what Alan.....there were so many people watching the argument and nobody wanted to stop the lady from verbally abuse the old man. It was on Youtube. Did you see it?" added Pandian. "No, I miss that. Road bullies are getting more daring just like the car thieves......getting more daring each day. These days they steal cars in front of the drivers and public. Cars were stolen at night before, now in broad daylight!" lamented Alan.

"Yes I have read so many of such cases in the newspapers especially in Kuala Lumpur," said Pandian. "Now they targetted the elderly and women," added Alan. "In a recent incident a woman was about to open her house gate manually and the thieves who had been following her on a motorbike, pounced and threatened her with a parang and drove the car away. Her handbags, cell phone and many important documents were all lost." Pandian then related an incident that he saw with his own eyes at the beach in Port Dickson. "This couple was having their swim and I was with Violet nearby enjoying the morning sun while watching the Sunday beachcombers. We heard a car window being smashed and when we turned to look these two car thieves were entering the car and trying to start the car. We shouted to alert the couple swimming in the sea. The crowd dared not take any action as they were scared the thieves might be armed. I phoned the Police immediately while the couple awiftly swam back to the shore in time to see their cars driven away by the thieves. They phoned the Police again using my cell phone but the car just disappeared in thin air." "I believed this is the work of a syndicate and having road blocks will not work, dad," replied Alan. "They must have a workshop somewhere in the estates where within a few hours the stolen cars are cannibalised and ready to be sold as spare parts," added Alan. "Yes.....I think that is their modus operandi," Pandian said.

# CHAPTER 110

Pandian then told Alan that he made some inquiries about the land the company wanted to purchase for some projects further up the town of Port Dickson.

"Oh, yes, dad….our company wanted to opened up a refinery and storage installations for quite a large volume of oil palm…...it's a joint venture project by the way," said Alan.

"Well, there are some villagers who had parcels of land near the beach now grown with coconuts. You may be able to purchase over 600 acres in total from my own estimation. However, if you are to purchase please negotiate discreetly and buy directly from them and not through a third party. There are so many so-called local leaders who are shrewd 'negotiators' in the villages. I have seen many cases when I was working in the court where unscrupulous characters made tons of money at the expense of the landowners. When these rich rogues, through inside informers, came to know that a mega project is targeted to be launched in a certain area these rogues, usually in collusion with certain financial institutions, will purchase the land at a very minimal premium, say RM 2 per square foot. The landowners will part with the land thinking they made a good sale as they either inherited the land from their forefathers or bought it cheap then. They are not interested in developing the areas but just make quick money from the transactions. Within a year or two, they knew the mega project will be approved and the interested party will need to purchase that piece of land. From a purchase price of RM 2 that same land is now sold, probably, at RM 22 per square foot! Remember the Port Klang Free Trade Zone case? All these profits made within a matter of a few years and by these rich rogues. So my advice is if your company is genuinely interested in purchasing these parcels of land please negotiate directly with them and buy at the market price. Being fair to them will please God who will ensure prosperity and protection to your company for a long time," said Pandian.

"Thanks for the advice, dad, we will deal with the villagers discreetly and directly. In fact we are not only purchasing their land but utilised them as our permanent workers based on their qualifications. We want the locals to be employed there, as they will help to keep the area secure from outsiders. We have other plans to help the locals like building home stays and simple restaurants.....basically we are into community development too. With the project in full swing the economic spin off in that area will be tremendous," said Alan.

Jimmy, at home, was toying with the idea of going for the DNA tests. He was curious who his biological parents are though he was scared to find out the truth. He had always felt his adopted parents were his biological parents and did not know how to handle the situation having another two persons coming into his life. He phoned up Alan and spoke with him to get his final advice.

"Hello, Alan.....yes, Jimmy here. How are you.....your family? Good. We are okay .....in fact I call you to seek your advice on the DNA tests to find my biological parents. You had gone through it and I suppose you are the best man to consult....besides being my best friend. Please tell me whether I should go ahead with it.....right now I am a happy family man but felt something was missing."

"Have you spoken with your adopted parents? Talk to them seriously and tell them why you need to know your roots. Don't make them feel hurt.....tell them nothing is going to change after this including your love for them. No part of your love to them is taken away because God has given us 'love' that can be given to all and everybody in this world.....so loving your biological parents after this DNA tests will not reduce your love for them....not a bit. I still love Datuk and Datin as my parents even though I now have my real parents. I will defend Datuk and Datin with my life if anybody wanted to endanger them. So my advice to you Jimmy is to go for the tests and be done with it. Once you have identified your biological parents your mind is completely at rest and you can get on with your life Jimmy. Hey....having two sets of parents are just great....not many people get that chance in their lifetime!" said Alan.

"Alright, I think the first thing I have to do is to meet with my adopted parents tomorrow and seriously discuss with them on this matter. If there is no objection from them then I will contact you to help me arrange the tests with Uncle Lim. By the way, I have not met him.....does he look like me?" asked Jimmy.

"Not really, but you have some mannerisms of Aunty Sui Lan, Jimmy" replied Alan.

"Ok....I will call you again tomorrow Alan......bye," said Jimmy.

# CHAPTER 111

Jimmy sat down on the sofa for quite a while until his wife came out from the bathroom. His wife, Susie, asked him what was wrong….he would normally be watching the TV and always in a very jovial mood.

"I just spoke with Jimmy and he encouraged me to go for the DNA tests as soon as possible. What do you think, dear?" asked Jimmy.

"This is your life and I think Alan is right…..you should go ahead and get it over with………I noticed lately you did not sleep well and I believed your mind is too preoccupied, probably thinking about your real parents. You have a stable job, a happy family and it is time to face the truth. Find your real parents….be strong and go to meet them. Whatever happened in the past accept it as fated and you will come out more forgiving and strong. Meet them and explained to them why you need to do this. They will understand though they may feel hurt…..initially," said Susie.

"I think I will do just that tomorrow…..I need you to come along Susie…. your support would give me the strength to face whatever eventualities," said Jimmy.

"Sure…..I will come along, dear," replied Susie.

Jimmy lifted up the phone and called his mother. "Hello, mum….Jimmy here….will you be in tomorrow evening? Yes…..we would like to come for dinner at your place. No….no….there is no need to cook anything….we'll buy some fast food like KFC and McDonald burger for dinner….ok?…..see you tomorrow then….bye," said Jimmy.

Krishnan, Jimmy's adopted father asked his wife, Maya, who was on the phone.

"It was Jimmy…..they are coming for dinner here tomorrow night," said Maya.

"So what are you cooking tomorrow?" asked Krishnan.

"No cooking….they told me they are buying some KFC and McDonald burger for dinner," replied Maya.

"That sounds appetising for a change......I need a change from your 'thosai', dear," said Krishnan.

"I know......I too am fed up of making 'thosai' almost every night......at my age now I just do not know what to cook!" lamented Maya.

The next day before 6.30 pm Jimmy and his family arrived at his parents' home. They brought down the KFC and McDonald burgers into the kitchen. Jimmy sat down to watch TV while his wife was busy in the kitchen with her mother-in-law preparing for the dinner. Jimmy and his dad talked casually about the express bus accidents that happened regularly on the road. Krishnan mentioned that the authorities were too lackadaisical in exercising their powers on these buses.

"Letting drivers on drugs and numerous summonses to drive the buses and risking public lives are tantamount to criminal negligence by the bus companies and the authorities. There are too many express bus companies with over 9000 buses competing for the daily long distances travelling here. The bus companies further have to compete with the trains and aeroplanes to maintain their profit margin." "I would suggest the number of licences issued be reduced and merged the many companies into a number of consortiums. Maybe the Licensing Board need only approve five consortiums to ply the main route from Kuala Lumpur to Johore Baru, KL to Kota Baru and from KL to Kangar. Any other diversions from the main route within that region will come under the jurisdiction of one of the consortiums approved for the main route. The bus operators can be better control under this system by the Licensing Board, Police and Road Transport Department as only a few consortiums are involved instead of about 200 operators now. I am just wondering why the Police or Road Transport Department did not initiate any action on the bus companies after nearly 70,000 summonses were issued from 1999."

"The beauty of our country is that if you failed to pay your summons for speed trap for 4-5 years you are still free to drive around but limited to just 6 months road tax! And if you dare to delay the payment of these summonses you get a discount of about 30%.......so why pay the full amount early when you can get a much better deal (discount) for late payment!" added Krishnan.

"It is simply crazy to me for the relevant departments to allow such a thing to happen after 50 years of independence. Heads should roll here, dad. The transport consortiums should be able to employ professionals to organise better internal management system to monitor the drivers, buses and remuneration inclusive of EPF and Socso. It is only when the bus companies are well organised with disciplined drivers can the government allow them to drive public transport," said Jimmy."

"The important thing is that the buses are also given sufficient and proper maintenance daily and the drivers must have adequate rests and emolument. You can only have discipline drivers when there is mutual respect between the management and employees. Only big consortiums can maintain a proper workshop and qualified engineers and mechanics. I remember a friend of mine who used to work in a conglomerate with a large fleet of lorries. Though the company had a proper workshop with qualified mechanics and engineers the lorries frequently broke down. The drivers were reckless and abused the lorries because of their dissatisfaction with the management…so good management-employees relationship is crucial in any business enterprise, Jimmy," said Krishnan.

# CHAPTER 112

They were discussing about other current issues when Susie shouted, "Dinner is served, come and get it!"

All the kids rushed to the dining table to pick their favourite pieces of chicken, but Susie told them to wash their hands first, then take their seats and allow their grandparents to have their pick first. When everybody was seated Jimmy said a few words of praise to God for the peace the harmony in the family, good health and abundance of food on the table daily. The kids looked forward to fast food and really enjoyed the dinner because they were brought up with fast food unlike the older generations. In no time all the chickens were ate up by the kids. Next the kids 'attacked' the burgers, and that too were cleared within a few minutes. Susie then brought in some ice creams and fruits as desserts. The ice creams were the kids favourite but none touched the fruits. Maya told them to each take a piece of the mango, rock melon and rambutan. She said fruits are excellent for growing kids..... make them more intelligent and smart! The kids reluctantly took their share of the fruits and ate them without much enthusiasm. They made faces at each other while trying hard to finish the fruits. Only then were they allowed to leave the dining table by their granddad. They scooted off into the TV room after consuming fruits. After dinner Jimmy adjourned to the living room with his parents. Susie was preparing coffee. The kids went into the TV room to play their favourite game on the Play station 3.

"I am glad, Jimmy, that you never took up smoking like many other young executives. It's really a waste of good money, I know because I have gone through it," said Krishnan.

"I don't know, dad, but smoking was never my idea of passing the time. Some of my friends said they have to smoke after lunch or dinner....to complete the course, so to say. Others say without cigarettes they cannot think properly, and the most ridiculous excuse I have ever heard is that, cigarettes 'rejuvenate' them physically and mentally," replied Jimmy.

Krishnan lamented that, "I used to smoke after my 'O' level and carried on smoking for a few years. This was a result of moving around with smokers.

I used to blame them but I soon realised it was not them….It was me, why blame others when I was the one that smoke the cigarettes! I was not forced to smoke by them, though they kept offering cigarettes to me all the time, but I could still remained their friend if I did not smoke. Friendship is not about smoking together and moving together all the time…..it is about respecting each other. So through my own initiative and will power I slowly reduced and stopped smoking. A very bad flu and cough before I reached my 40th birthday helped to end my smoking days."

Maya who overheard the conversation said, "Kissing him when we were dating and before he stopped smoking was like kissing an ash tray! But, anyway I did not complaint."

Krishnan laughed heartily at her remarks, "but the best thing was she always asked for a goodnight kiss before we parted…..that was before we got married!"

Maya who was sitting beside Krishnan pinched his thigh and Krishnan jokingly shouted in pain. Susie who was in the kitchen rushed out to see what the commotion was all about and the three kids out of curiosity popped their heads at the door of the TV room. When they saw their grandparents joking and laughing they went back into the TV room and Susie continued with her chores in the kitchen.

"Dad…mum….I would like to ask your permission….huh….I hope you do not feel hurt to what I am about to ask," said Jimmy.

"What is wrong Jimmy? It is not about your family……?" asked Maya, who suddenly looked worried.

Krishnan was more composed but also became a bit tensed.

"It is like this dad….mum…. I am all grown up now and after discussing with Alan, my good friend, I have the urge to find who my biological parents are," said Jimmy.

At that point Susie came in with two cups of coffee, one each for Krishnan and Jimmy. She knew what was going on so she just put the cups on the table and sat beside Maya. Maya and Krishnan looked at each other for a while before he said,

"Jimmy…..you are now a much matured young man. We are proud of you since the day we adopted you from the foster home. We knew that one day you might want to search for your real parents. Your mum and I had discussed this and expected this to happen one day. So…..though we feel slightly hurt, we give you our full blessings to go and find your real parents. Fulfil your desire to do so....we support your wish to meet your real parents, maybe they too are looking forward to meet you," said Krishnan.

"Thank God......it was so difficult to make this decision, dad, but your words have given me the courage to proceed with my wish. Mum....dad.... nothing is going to change between us after I meet my real parents.....I promise you both," said Jimmy.

Susie who sat besides Maya held her hands and hugged her for she knew Maya was overcome by emotions as a mother always did.

"So when do you intend to do this, Jimmy?" asked Krishnan.

"I hope within these few days, dad. Alan had done some preliminary investigations and chances are one of the Chinese families in Taiping could be my parents. His findings are based on information from those who were working at the foster home at that time. The gentleman and I would have to undergo DNA tests at the Taiping hospital soon and the results would take about 2 weeks. Alan is helping me to undergo these tests. I will let you know when the date for the tests is confirmed," replied Jimmy.

"Would you like us to come along Jimmy?" asked Krishnan.

"Not right now dad, probably when the DNA results are out. I would like mum and dad to meet them then.....okay? Jimmy said.

"Fine, Jimmy.....we pray to God everything will work out fine for you, son," said Krishnan.

Jimmy then went to his mother and kissed her on her cheek and then to his father.

# CHAPTER 113

$T$he next morning he phoned up Alan as soon as he reached his office.

"Hello Alan.....ya...Jimmy here. At last I managed to sit down and talk with my parents last night about the DNA tests. They consented to my request.....I am happy to have settled amicably with them about the tests. Yes...they are looking forward to meet my biological parents....yes.....that would be great if they can bond together....makes my life simpler, right? So..... when can you arrange for the tests?" asked Jimmy.

Alan said, "Thank God....that's good news Jimmy. Uncle Lim has already done the DNA tests earlier so the records are still at the Taiping General Hospital. So I suggest you do the tests in Penang..." before Alan could finished Jimmy interrupted, "No.....no.....it is better the test be done at Taiping Genral Hospital by the same doctor, right? Further he has all the records of Uncle Lim." "OK......good idea. Tell you what.... I will contact the doctor today and I should be able to confirm the date for the tests. Glad you are willing to travel to Taiping for the tests?" said Alan.

"Fine with me as Penang is less than 2 hours drive from Taiping and I want to meet Uncle Lim immaterial whether he is my dad or not. I will be waiting for your call Alan.....thanks," replied Jimmy.

Jimmy, an accountant, had left the bank and now set up his own auditing firm in the city of Penang. He went about his work and attended meetings in the morning but his mind was never focussed on the job. He was waiting anxiously for the call from Alan. His lady partner, Anita, knew Jimmy was not performing on that day. She came to his room and asked him what was keeping his mind occupied. She knew he had always been an inspiration in the organisation.

"I am in the midst of looking for my biological parents. You know I grew up in the orphanage when I was young and I feel it is time to look up for my biological parents. A good friend is helping me to sort out my problem and today I am waiting for his call to confirm the date for the DNA tests," explained Jimmy.

"Oh, I see…..why don't you take a day off today and relax your mind. I know how it feels, the agony of waiting for the call on such an important matter. My advice is go home for the day…..after all today we have no meetings to attend and not much paper work to be done, right? You deserve a break anyway," said Anita.

After lunch Jimmy went home and dozed off on the sofa while watching a movie on Astro. He woke up when he heard his cell phone rang.

It was Alan, "Hello Jimmy….I contacted your office but Anita told me you had gone home for the day. Are you all right? Anyway, I have contacted Uncle Lim and managed to make an appointment for your DNA tests this Monday the 15th. Is that day suitable for you?" asked Alan.

'Great….just great…..at what time is it?" asked Jimmy.

"Normally it is about 9.00 am but if you can be here by 8.30 am that will be fine. I will bring Uncle Lim to the hospital….okay?" answered Alan.

"Thanks Alan….I will see you in Taiping on Monday then….thanks again."

# CHAPTER 114

Early Monday morning Jimmy and Susie left Penang for Taiping in his car. He was very excited with the idea of seeing his 'biological parents', if they really are. He believed they must be from the Chinese community as his features are more Chinese rather than from an Indian descendant. They reached Taiping early as there was very little traffic on the highway and so they decided to have for a quick breakfast at one of the restaurants. After breakfast they left for the hospital just before 8.15 am and arrived at the car park by 8.30 am.

They walked to the lobby and saw Alan and Judy talking to an old Chinese couple. Jimmy's heart stopped beating for a few seconds and he nearly fainted. He managed to hold on to Susie who was a bit shaken by the episode. They stopped for a while before proceeding to where Alan and the rest were seated. Judy noticed them from a distance and both Alan and Judy came over to greet Jimmy and his wife. Uncle Lim and his wife waited anxiously for them to come over. Alan then led Jimmy and Susie to meet Uncle Lim and his wife. They shook hands and exchanged greetings. Jimmy said he was surprised to see Uncle Lim and wife at the hospital as he thought they might be waiting at home. Uncle Lim said, "I like to take a stroll every morning with my wife in Taiping….it is so cooling and relaxing, so this morning we decided to take a stroll to the hospital but met Alan half way here."

While waiting for the doctor Uncle Lim casually talked to Alan and Jimmy about his life. He did not complete his education and started working in a bicycle shop helping an old man. It was a small shop and his income was just enough to pay for his daily expenses. His father died in a house fire when he was just two years old and his mother was working as an 'amah' at the Rest House. Like Uncle Wong, his mother too passed away when he was still struggling to survive. He went to stay with his 'towkay' who lived alone in a small hut. He continued working, as an apprentice in the bicycle shop and that was the time he first met Uncle Wong. "We were young, homeless and trying to survive in this very competitive world. We met often after work to discuss on ways to step out of this extreme poverty. Wong was in love then….

that made the situation worse for him. In my case my 'towkay' wanted to close shop because he was tired and getting old.

I begged my 'towkay' to allow me to manage the bicycle shop but instead he told me to take over the business. He was alone and had no relatives who cared for him. Running the business gave me sufficient income to lead a decent living. The old man died and I inherited his business. Then Aunty Sui Lan came along and we got married about the same time as Uncle Wong. Initially business picked up but soon the bicycle business slowed down. Aunty was pregnant and I could barely feed the two of us, as I had to pay rental for the shop besides the electricity and water bills. When our child was born we had no choice then but to give him up to the orphanage arranged by Pak Hussein.

A few years later the business picked up again and aunty was working as a cleaner at one of the supermarkets here. Aunty never did want to have another child, as she never could forgive herself for giving away her first child. After three years we went to see Pak Hussein but he was not able to identify our child. Many had been adopted and we thought Alan was the child we 'lost'. Business was down again during the recession and we completely dropped the idea of looking for our child. We knew that wherever he is, he must be in very good hands.

The bicycle business picked up when new models were introduced… especially with the introduction of mountain bikes. People became health conscious and cycling became the favourite pastime for families and the teenagers. I made some money and was able to expand my own shop, which until today is doing reasonably well. We have our home upstairs and the bicycle shop downstairs….it is a very convenient and a perfect arrangement to me. Now I have 2 assistants to help me. It is only of late that when I met Uncle Wong that we wanted to at least meet with the sons we gave away for adoption. Wong is happy now to know Alan is his son, healthy with a happy family. Now aunty and I need to know who our real son is….whether he is happy and well? We know he may not be happy to see us for what we did in the past to him but we just want to see him once," said Lim.

"I am sure whoever is your son would love to meet both of you. He would not hold any grudge against both of you as it was fated that they had to part in that manner," said Jimmy.

# CHAPTER 115

A nurse approached them and asked Jimmy to follow her into the doctor's room. The doctor explained the procedures to Jimmy and that the DNA results would be known within a few weeks.

After 20 minutes Jimmy came out of the room. They then adjourned to the hospital canteen for a drink before they departed. Jimmy and wife wanted to send Uncle Lim and wife back to their house but they declined, as they wanted to talk with Alan and Judy for a while. While driving to Penang Jimmy asked Susie about Uncle Lim and his wife.

"Aunty has a lot of common features with you, Jimmy.....her smile and her eyes......it is you in her. Again your walk and gestures are like Uncle Lim too.....so chances are they maybe your biological parents. I like both of them after this first meeting.....very friendly and easy to converse. It's in their eyes, Jimmy. I felt very comfortable around them you know," said Susie.

"I noticed that too......I......like....love... both of them, Susie. I know for sure that the old man and his wife are my dad and mum the moment they spoke to me. I felt I have heard those voices before....a long, long time ago."

Tears started to roll down his cheeks and Susie gently touched his shoulder to console and calmed him down. She too was in tears. Both were very quiet for a while until Jimmy broke the silence and said,

"Let us go to my dad's house. I am sure they are eager to know about our trip to Taiping," said Jimmy.

"No objection......you are driving....just drive me there!" replied Susie.

"Ok, boss," said Jimmy, smiling.

On the 10th day (Tuesday) after taking the DNA tests Jimmy received a call from Alan.

"The doctor has received the tests and wants you and Uncle Lim to come down to the hospital this Thursday morning. Can you make it.....you must as without you he will not revealed the results," said Alan.

"Definitely! I will be there together with my dad and mum....I would appreciate them to be here to meet Uncle Lim and aunty if they are my biological parents," replied Jimmy.

"I will bring Uncle Lim and Aunty to the hospital, say by 10.00 am. Ok?" said Alan.

Jimmy rang up his wife Susie who was having a meeting in her office. He then phoned up his dad and mum and told them that they are coming along to Taiping on Thursday morning. On Wednesday he attended a number of meetings but by afternoon after lunch he told Anita, his partner, he had to leave for home. He then told his wife, dad and mum that he wanted to drive to Taiping that evening as he did not want to be late the next morning. They all agreed, as they too did not want to rush to Taiping early in the morning. It was raining heavily when they left the Penang Bridge at about 9.00 pm. Jimmy was driving very carefully as the vision ahead of the car was barely 50 metres because of the rain. Susie was in the front seat with him while Krishnan and Maya were at the back. It was a pleasant drive on the highway as the traffic flow was smooth.

"Fortunately though it rains heavily today there are very few vehicles on the road. Anyway I prefer driving in the rain then through the haze at night..... remember when we had to go to Malacca last June, darling?" said Jimmy. "Yes," answered Susie, "that was a very bad haze from our neighbouring country and it was during the day. We could barely see more than 70 metres and the API was just shocking, above 600! I could scarcely breathe......luckily modern days cars have are equipped with air-con. This seems like an annual event without that country making any effort to control or stopped it from happening..... definitely open burning on a large scale can be very hazardous. Why don't the leaders slapped whatever laws they have on these culprits?" Jimmy was reluctant to comment as he was so focussed on his driving due to the bad weather. Krishnan, who was very quiet and sleepy throughout the journey, suddenly, opened his eyes wide when he heard the topic of interest to him.....haze.

"I had a lot of experience on haze when I working in the private estate before. Actually, countries like Malaysia and Indonesia are all guilty of what is happening today. For many years Malaysia had allowed our workers in the agricultural sector to practise open burning in the name of rural development. Opening burning is definitely cheap for the operators but caused health hazards to the neighbouring areas. I used to travel to Kedah and Perlis after the harvesting seasons and the kampong folks burnt the field causing haze across the country. Accidents on the road resulting in deaths had happened due to this haze but the authorities just closed one eye. Then the haze became more serious when jungles were cut and burnt to start large estates for rubber, palm oil and other crops. Our government did nothing to control these open burnings though other countries were affected environmentally. Actually our citizens then were not really concerned about such haze.....they treated it as part and parcel of their lives." "What happened then?" asked Jimmy. "Well...... when the citizens were happy the government did nothing.....as you know changes in this country will take place when the citizens start complaining!" answered Krishnan.

"True, very true.....our leaders are very slow to react when they have some vested interests in any incident. Actually we are fed-up with this haze which occurred annually. From year to year we are given the standard answer from both governments!" added Susie. "There is not much we can do, dear, because Indonesia is doing what we did a few years ago.....opening burnings. Now we have opened up all the jungle with plantations and Felda settlements.....there is no more jungle to burn. We have now moved to Indonesia to look for riches and most of the companies took the advantage of open burninsg there to save costs. So our Government is very slow in pointing fingers unlike Singapore!" said Krishnan. All the way it was raining and it was much heavier when they reach the Taiping district.

# CHAPTER 116

On leaving the highway and entering into the junction to Taiping his car slowed down as the other cars in front of him had stop. An express bus that was speeding behind him suddenly went out of control and knocked his car that had almost come to a dead stop. There was no way Jimmy could have avoided the collision as the bus came roaring straight behind his car. All Jimmy could say was, "Oh...my God!" and rest in car could only scream helplessly. The car spun a number of times and hit the divider before landing in the ditch. The bus hit other cars too before it hit a tree. Jimmy and his wife were trapped in the wreckage while Krishnan and wife, who were in the back seat miraculously escaped with minor injuries. The bus after colliding with the car skidded and hit a tree. Some passengers in the bus were injured and the bus driver suffered a broken leg. It took the fire brigade more than an hour to extricate Jimmy and Susie. Both were in coma probably due to the massive head injuries and were rushed to the Taiping General Hospital by two ambulances that arrived in a matter of a few minutes. The doctors did their best to revive Jimmy and Susie and after 8 hours they were both admitted into the Intensive Care Unit but the chances of survival were very slim.

The next morning Alan and his wife arrived at the hospital together with Uncle Lim and wife. They did know about the accident. They waited and called his cell phone but there was no answer. The doctor called Uncle Lim and they all entered his room. The results were positive......Jimmy is Uncle Lim's biological son. He and his wife were so delighted and could not wait to see Jimmy. In the meantime Krishnan, who was treated as an outpatient and still in a daze, went looking for Alan in the hospital as he knew he must be waiting for Jimmy. The nurses knew Krishnan was in distressed and it was impossible for him to find the DNA's room. They took pity on him and one of the nurses at the hospital immediately asked him to follow her into the doctor's room. He knocked at the door and without waiting for an answer immediately went in. In the room he saw a Chinese family rejoicing, smiling and laughing. He slowly closed the door and asked,

"Excuse me....are you the doctor that did the DNA tests for Jimmy?"

"You look very distress.….please take a seat. Yes, I am the doctor, anyway who are you?" asked the doctor.

Everybody in the room looked at him. He was in tears, looked shattered and depressed,

"I.…..I.…..I am.…Krish.…Krishnan…Jimmy's adopted father from Penang," replied Krishnan. "My wife Maya is in ward 6.…..…we met with an accident on the way here.….."

"Oh.…...you must be uncle Krishnan. Jimmy has spoken well about you.… where is he uncle.…we have very good news for him.…...is he outside?" asked Alan who had never met uncle Krishnan but heard that he was the father-in-law of Jimmy.

"We came last night and our car was hit by a speeding bus fom behind.…. it was a very nasty accident with a bus.…...near the junction towards Taiping. Jimmy.…..... and Susie.….. had serious head injuries and both are in very critical conditions," said Krishnan.

Alan asked, "Where is he now?" "In the ICU .…..…I came here because I knew you are all waiting for him. Both are still in coma," Krishnan said. Uncle Lim and his wife looked at each other and without any delay rushed to the ICU followed by the others. They all went into the ICU with the help of a doctor. Mew Chooi slowly approached his bed, held Jimmy's hand and kissed his forehead.… he was on life support and tears were rolling down his cheeks. Mew Chooi, who was in tears softly spoke to him, "You are our son Jimmy.….. our long lost son..….." and she cried openly. Lim and the rest in the room could not control their emotions too. Mew Chooi suddenly went into hysteria and suddenly collapsed. A doctor and Alan quickly grabbed her and carried her to a room next door accompanied by Maya and Judy. Uncle Lim was crying too and Krishnan hugged him to give him strength. He too was in mental anguish, "He is a great kid, unselfish and full of compassion.….you have a very good son, Mr. Lim," said Krishnan who was also overcome emotionally.

Shortly afterwards the ICU ward turned frenzy when the doctors had to attend to Jimmy whose condition had deteriorated. They were all asked to leave the room as the doctors desperately tried to revive him. The doctors did their best to keep Jimmy alive but after an hour he was declared dead by the doctor in charge. Mew Chooi collapsed again and both Krishnan and Lim hugged each other trying to console each other. Alan was standing at one corner of the ICU feeling so sad and depressed. He cried like a kid. Krishnan hugged

Uncle Lim and told him that all this was fated. He blamed himself for this accident, as he was the one who encouraged Jimmy to go through this entire 'senseless' search for his real parents. If not for his persistent in coaxing Jimmy to go through with the search Jimmy would still be alive today. Uncle Lim could not utter a single word but just hold on to Krishnan.

The doctor, meanwhile, brought Lim and Mew Chooi to see Susie who was a few beds away from where Jimmy was in the ICU. The doctor said her condition was very stable and he expected her to come out of the coma any time today, God willing.

"She broke her right leg, three ribs and her shoulder blade. Fortunately there is no serious injury to her head or her internal organs. She suffered mainly concussion."

# CHAPTER 117

It was suppose to be a happy family reunion but fate had it that it had to end in a sad tragedy. Jimmy had fulfilled his wish to meet his biological parents though it was just for a few minutes. Alan helped to make all the necessary arrangement for the burial in Taiping as requested by Uncle Lim. Krishnan agreed that he should be buried in the Chinese cemetery under Chinese religious customs, as he was never converted to practice Hinduism when he was adopted by Krishnan. Susie recovered from the accident but life was never the same without Jimmy. Uncle Lim said to Krishnan,

"I am happy because we were given the opportunity by God to at least have the chance to meet him......but our only regret was that we never got the chance to hear him call us dad or mum...or hear him response when we call him 'son'. At least I know who was my son and had spoken to him when we first met to take the DNA tests."

"You and I lost a wonderful son, Uncle Lim, but we have to be strong for our loving daughter-in-law, two great grand sons and a beautiful granddaughter. They need us now and together, God willing, r we can get over this tragedy and emerged stronger."

Krishnan, Uncle Lim and their wives wept uncontrollably throughout the funeral. Datuk, Datin, Mawi and many of his office friends attended the sad ceremony.

Meantime in LA, Aqiel and Daniella after her conversion to Islam continued to attend classes at the Mosque. She had changed her dress code permanently to that of a Muslim lady as advised by her Ustazah. After 1 1/2 years since her last visit she was back in Kuala Lumpur for her wedding as her parents wanted her to experience a traditional Malay wedding. The wedding was solemnised at the Federal Territory Mosque where she agreed to recite a few verses of the Quran to the guests which included her parents. They were all surprised that this American lady can read the Al-Quran fluently. Aqiel's parents were proud that her daughter-in-law had taken the initiative to seriously embrace Islam.

In the evening Datuk hosted a grand wedding at the Shangri-La Hotel for Aqiel and his radiant bride, Daniella. A crowd of almost 1000 guests were present including Daniella's parents, Bush and Martha, and close relatives from US. Among the guests that Datuk specially invited were Krishnan, Lim, Wong and their spouses. Susie came with her three children and so did Mak Jah. There was a small 'bersanding ceremony' where selected guests including their parents from both the bride and the groom went on stage to bless the wedding couple.

Aqiel and Daniella went for a short honeymoon to Bali, Indonesia. "Why Bali, honey," asked Daniella. "In this part of the world that is the land of paradise, romance and fertility," Aqiel replied. "Fertility?" continued Daniella. "Yes...eh...umph....the land on that island is so fertile because of the volcanic ashes that acts as fertilisers for the rice fields that can grow well even on the terraces, I guess!" answered Aqiel. They flew to Bali, Indonesia on the next day and soon landed at the new Ngurah Rai International Airport in Jimbaran. They then took a cab to the Ramayana Resort & Spa in the heart of the town of Kuta. Besides being one of the best renown resort there the place was also near to the famous Kuta Square, Kuta Galleria, Art Market and most importantly to the long white sandy beach. "Tourism has always and will always remain the number one source of its foreign exchange revenues. Both nature and cultural heritage are major components of Balinese tourism. Hinduism was the first religion in Bali followed by Islam and Christianity hat came much later. Hinduism, however, remain as the religion for the Balinese though under Majapahit Empire rule the Javanese influence on local art, dance, architecture, sculpture, painting and puppet theatre are then accepted as the culture of Bali. They spent their honeymoon there for five days and four nights going around the island to see the temples and places of interests on a rented motorbike. That was the most convenient and interesting way of exploring the island on your own time. In fact most of the young European and Australian tourists prefer that mode of transport as they enjoy the fresh air and breeze that swept across their faces and hair. Most of the evenings they spent their time window shopping or relax at the night clubs in Kuta. They never miss scuba diving and many other sea sports.

# CHAPTER 118

Upon returning from the honeymoon Aqiel rested for two days in his dad's house before he moved to a new bungalow, which his dad bought as a wedding present. It was after three days that he got down to some serious business at Bibi Holdings. Datuk initially assigned him to the post of a Special Executive Officer to the MD so as to expose him to all aspects of the job in the company. As he had a few years of working experience in US he was put on attachment to the various divisions of the company for a year before he became the General Manager of the company. He got to know the job better as he was exposed thoroughly to the overall business of the company. Being a very simple gentleman he was well liked by his staffs. In the meantime Daniella was offered a job as a lecturer at a local tertiary institution. Being an active person she got involved in a number of voluntary organisations on Saturdays, which kept her busy and happy. Alan was appointed as the new Managing Director of the company when Mawi was asked to retire. Datuk remained as a non-Executive Chairman of the company. The new arrangement gave Alan the opportunity, with the consent of Datuk, to slightly restructure the company to meet the present global challenges they had to face currently and the near future. He knew the future of the company was bright but he had to tread cautiously to reach his goal.

Aqiel, being an active person was deeply involved in the company's management. In his job he came into contact with other corporate figures who advised him that besides hard work a corporate figure must always be in touch with those in power such as those in the government service or in politics.

"Never try to affiliate yourself with one camp in politics, as politicians tend to jump from one party to another at their own convenience. When they do that then as businessmen we are left in a lurch," advised a friend. "That's the last thing you should do! Your dad had done the right thing and that's the reason he is so successful! He is respected by both his enemies and friends."

Aqiel kept focussed on his business and all he wanted was to expand his business into other fields that he knew best. Alan was doing well in the other areas and it was timely that the company moved into other sectors. He was keen to move into two of the major branch of the mass communication emphasising on advertising and the motion pictures, which were very much interlinked with the musical world. He took over and restructured an ailing advertising agency, 'One Magic Touch Advertising Sdn. Bhd.' with a group of very creative staffs to stay competitive with the other well known firms in the country. In the film industry, Aqiel, who had about 3 years experience in movie making in the US got a few friends in Los Angeles who were willing to help him set up a studio in Malaysia. He formed the company 'Sight and Sound Sdn. Bhd.' and equipped the studio with the latest 'state-of- the-art' technology and staffs his organisation with expertise from both locals and overseas. In both these new ventures he gave an extra value added X-factors to be different from those in these businesses to capture the market. He had to import 'expertise' to move to a much higher bench mark, at least equivalent to that of the Hong Kong and Bollywood productions. Both new investments were big in terms of the revenue to the companies.

Aqiel managed to get a big piece of land at Cyberjaya, Selangor where he set up his own film and recording studios under one roof. Alan focussed on his 'One Magic Touch Advertising Sdn. Bhd.' which was set up in the city of Kuala Lumpur where most of the clients had their offices. His advertising agency went on an aggressive marketing to introduce the company in the vibrant market and within a year, after having gone through many presentations they were successful in getting a number of clients. Alan asked him to keep focussed on the new companies as the others were very well established. Initially his advertising agency was involved in the print and broadcast advertisements. Besides producing jingles aggressively the company was also producing commercials and teasers for the TV stations. Aqiel was very cautious in looking at the motion pictures production as he needed to get a good script, actors and actresses to screen his first movie.

"First impression is very essential to any audience," Aqiel said to his staffs.

Alan's advertising agency kicked off very well but Aqiel's first attempt at producing a motion picture that could create public interest was unsuccessful. However, that did not deter Aqiel from pursuing to produce more movies. It was only after his fifth attempt that his movie 'The Silent Revolution' hit the USD20 million marks, which was good for Malaysian standard. From then on he knew that his movies had managed to capture Malaysians from all walks of life and also accepted in the international market. His recording studio was fully booked all year round and as the rates were very competitive he managed to attract producers from Hong Kong, Indonesia and the neighbouring countries. Part of the studio was also utilised as a dubbing studio for the local movies. From then on Aqiel's new setups were moving on the right tracks. Both the advertising agencies and the production houses were under the Bibi's Holdings.

# CHAPTER 119

In the meantime Roger and Martha had decided to settle in Malaysia for good. Roger bought a piece of property near the beach in Port Dickson where he renovated the old building and planted up the surrounding area with fruit trees. He managed to purchase the 1 acre land at RM 20 per square foot. He had another two years of service before he retired. He told Datuk Khalid at one of his functions that he just loved Malaysia for its weather, political stability and friendly people.

"You cannot get a better combination then that anywhere else in this world!" said Roger.

Roger came across an article in the Time magazine on Norman Foster, a British architect's dream of building the eco city in Abu Dhabi known as Masdar City. It was a radically innovative development powered entirely by renewable energy. It is a multibillion project in Abu Dhabi but what Roger intended to do was just for his own bungalow only. However, he expected the small project to cost him at least USD 2 millions. It may be quite a high initial cost to many people but in the long run it was going to be very cheap to own that bungalow. He briefly explained to his wife about the new concept. "Another very good alternative and I think will be much cheaper is the invention of a very young lady, Cynthia Lam, now studying in Melbourne, Australia, who invented a new device known as H2Pro that uses sunlight to purify water while generating electricity. This is a very revolutionised concept and if implemented nation wide will close NEB and all the IPPs! The invention is still in its infancy stage but once approved by SIRIM will be very popular alternative in the rural areas," explained Roger.

"Right now electricity in our houses is derived from the National Electricity Board, which needed to utilise oil to run the generators. The price of this commodity fluctuates and I believe will keep on increasing though the government is trying to help the end users by subsidising the product. Subsidising end users actually means using the rakyat's money, so it is really a vicious circle. There will come a time when oil productions will decrease and the government will have to look for other alternative energy like the solar, wind, nuclear and many others. In our case we intend to tap the solar energy a renewable energy source that could ultimately be as powerful as oil. I am looking for the right architect and engineer to build and install the right kind of photovoltaic technology that will work best for our house. I am also hoping to have my own tube-well water for drinking and bathing, and store rain water for washing purposes and hopefully we can be self sufficient in a small way. Once all these facilities are installed and in placed there will be no more monthly bills to burden us. I am trying to tap the solar energy as Malaysia has abundant rainfall and lots of sunshine."

"That's a brilliant idea, darling," replied his wife.

There was no local expertise in these fields as yet so Roger contacted his colleagues in England to help him out in this matter. He also invited a local engineer to work closely with the English architect. He was very happy as he managed to get a very meticulous local artisan to build his home according to the specifications by the architect. The bungalow was duly completed after almost 8 months of trial and error. Roger and his wife had after furnishing the house to their tastes, moved in with a house warming party. Datuk, Datin, Aqiel, Daniella and some friends were invited for the BBQ party. The guests moved around freely to see the new home that was self sufficient and with very low maintenance costs. Aqiel was so impressed with the idea and told Daniella that he intended to build one at Janda Baik soon. Datuk, however, was thinking seriously on a much bigger scale.....building a prestigious housing project based on the same concept for the elite. Later if the project was viable he would proceed to build a housing project for the middle class residents.

"The project is viable as in due time the cost of installing of these concepts will be much cheaper.....just like the cell phones and computers!" said Roger. "I don't mind being your local consultant!" Roger joked.

"Wouldn't this affect the NEB and The Water Board," asked Aqiel. "Well, actually the NEB and the Water Board have their hands full as they are fully utilised by the other consumers. We now have Independent Contractors who supply electricity to NEB and water supply to homes. Frankly speaking both NEB and Water Board should be thankful for this innovative ideas that help to keep Malaysian homes cheap to maintain.

"Actually I need a consultant if I was to go into this project and since you are no more in service I am prepared to consider the idea," said Datuk seriously. "Just wait for my letter of offer, okay?"

Roger was delighted with the offer and he said, "Thanks Datuk. That's very kind of you!"

Roger and Martha, had prepared a BBQ on the lawn facing the seaside. The weather was beautiful with a slight breeze and they enjoyed the evening at Roger's bungalow.

# CHAPTER 120

Aqiel during his free time had developed a new hobby, which was dangerous to Daniella. Though he played badminton in the evening three times a week he just loved to go on either his big bike or his 4-wheel drive trekking into the dense jungle with a couple of his close friends once a month. In the case of his love for big bike he usually would leave home early on Saturday morning and back home by Sunday evening. He and a group of 10-15 big bikers will ride to the north, or south even to the East coast from Kuala Lumpur. They will stay overnight in a hotel and host a BBQ for the local big bikers. By doing that they engaged themselves with the local activities, visit a few tourist attractions and developed a healthy form of outside activity. "From Kuala Lumpur, on the big bike we can reach Perlis within 3-4 hours, if we do not get the speed traps. It will take about the same time to Johore. It would be slightly longer in the case of Kelantan. We have gone to Chieng Mai, Thailand, last year and planning to tour Sabah and Sarawak soon," said Aqiel to his father. "Daniella never like this hobby though a few riders do bring their wives or girl friends during this week ends' rides," he added.

"Another one of his 'dangerous' hobby was trekking in the thick jungles in his 4-wheel drive with a few close friends. He liked to venture into the jungles of Terengganu, Pahang, Kelantan and Perak. He plans to explore the jungles in Sabah and Sarawak which they say was more challenging. When he went trekking in his 4-wheel drive it would be more than 2 days and he would be required to camp in the jungle to sleep with the leeches and mosquitoes instead of a 5-star hotels!" remarked Daniella. Aqiel, however, had a serious accident during one of his 4-wheel drive trekking in the thick jungle in Pahang. Trekking with friends on weekends in his 4-wheel drive was a new hobby and normally Daniella will be his navigator. This is one dangerous hobby that Daniella too enjoyed and like to share. Daniella never missed such trips as she loved trekking which she told Aqiel as 'so thrilling'! Fortunately, his wife, Daniella did not follow him on that trip. He went with another friend as his navigator with three other 4-wheel drives. His Land Rover was following the other three 4-wheel drives. They were manoeuvring on the muddy slippery trek along the mountain slopes and it was raining steadily. To the left was the mountain edge and on the right the steep slope or gorge with bamboo and many wild trees with a fall of almost 300-350 feet if they made any mistake! The other three drivers being experienced under such conditions were driving steadily as they had to reach their destination before it got dark.

Aqiel was following them cautiously when he suddenly lost control of his Land Rover as the back wheel slipped at the edge of the gorge and within seconds sent the Land Rover toppling over the steep slope. The Land Rover turned turtle a couple of times while plunging down but had a lucky break as the bamboo and tree tops broke the fall half way down before the Land Rover got stuck on one of the tree tops. Had they not get stuck there then the Land Rover would have landed on the solid rock. His vehicle dropped to almost 100 feet and both Aqiel and his navigator were knocked around like dolls on the way down. Aqiel and his navigator were unconscious and their friends in the other vehicles did not realise what had happened until they stopped and waited for his vehicle during a short break near a small brook.

# CHAPTER 121

They waited patiently for Aqiel to arrive but after awhile there was still no sound of Aqiel's Land Rover and they suspected his Land Rover must be experiencing some kind of mishaps as they received no answer using the satellite telephone or the ham radio. As the track was very narrow they used only one vehicle to retrace the way back leaving the vehicle and a team member to stay on guard. After travelling for about half an hour they saw traces of Land Rover's tyres on the track. Looking down they were shocked to see Aqiel's Land Rover hanging precariously on the tree tops. They shouted to Aqiel and his navigator but there was no response. They then called using the 'ham' radio and satellite phone again but they did not receive any answer. The team leader and another friend decided to go down by using the ropes to where the vehicle was hanging precariously to assess the real situation as it was barely visible. One of his team mates contacted the Army rescue team via the nearest Police station. It was getting dark but with the help of the torch lights they managed to get close to the vehicle and saw both Aqiel and the navigator were both bleeding and motionless. Testing the stability of the vehicle the team leader decided to get closer to both of his friends in the Land Rover. He gently shook Aqiel and saw that he was conscious but was moving in great pain. His left leg was fractured and one of his shoulders looked dislocated. His navigator, however, was unconscious and he too had a fractured right hand. His head, however, was bleeding profusely.

The team leader contacted his team mates on the slope to let down two more ropes so that they can haul Aqiel and the navigator up. He decided to do so as the wind was getting stronger and the rain heavier. He knew that the Land Rover could at any time topple down further posing more danger to the two occupants. When the ropes were let down the team leader expertly tied the ropes each to Aqiel and the navigator. Fortunately by that time the navigator was also conscious. They were informed that the rescue team from the Army was on the way by helicopter.

The team leader directed his team mate to slowly haul them up using the automatic winch with each of them aiding the injured Aqiel and his navigator so that they did not get knocked onto the sharp edges of the gorge. Aqiel and the navigator were in such excruciating pain but the team leader had no choice as it was already very dark and the wind was blowing stronger. They were lucky for as soon as they left the Land Rover, a sudden gush of strong wind tipped the vehicle, which plunged downwards and in a few seconds hit the bottom of the gorge exploding into flames.

As soon as they reached the top of the slopes the helicopter arrived. They drove to an opening where the helicopter lowered down a stretcher and the injured were individually lifted up into the helicopter and immediately transported to the General hospital in Kuantan. The rest of the team went to their camp site for the night to rest before proceeding to Kuantan on the next day. Aqiel's Land Rover was never recovered as to salvage the vehicle was a total wreck and rather risky!

At the hospital the next day Datuk Khalid and family were waiting anxiously for the doctor's report. Daniella, who was 3 months pregnant, was sobbing softly consoled by Wawa.

"I begged him not to go, Wawa, as the weather has been very wet lately. He, however, insisted on going since he had already made the necessary plans with his friends" said Daniella.

Wawa could not say anything as she too was feeling so depressd as to what had happened to her brother. She just kept quiet but kept on consoling her sister-in-law. Aqiel and the navigator underwent a number of operations. His navigator was in a more serious condition because of his head injury. Aqiel after the operation was out of danger but his navigator was sent to the ICU for observations for a few days. Datuk and his family were so grateful to hear about the good news and prayed for a quick recovery of both Aqiel and his navigator. Datuk listened attentively to the team leader, who arrived later on the second day, about the rescue operations. He could not explain how the incident happened as they right infront and Aqiel and his friend were right at the back of the convoy. "Only Aqiel and his navigator knew how they met with the accident. Datuk and his family stayed at one of the hotels in the town for a few days so as to stay close to Aqiel. Daniella was from morning until night at the hospital every now and then watching the progress of Aqiel's........ giving him morale support for a fast recovery.

After a few days Aqiel was completely out of danger and he said to Daniella, "You know I am contemplating whether to continue with my hobby after this......what do you think, honey?"

"I have no objections.....your navigator has recovered but after I deliver our first baby I will come along on these trips......agreed?" asked Daniella smiling lovingly.

Aqiel looked for a long time at Daniella and said, "Are you serious, darling.......I would love to have you as my navigator again!" "Sorry no deal.…... you are gong to be my navigator, I am driving," Daniella joked.

"How about starting tomorrow then?" said Aqiel. They both burst into laughter.

# CHAPTER 122

Aqiel after a few weeks was able to walk using his crutches and went to see his navigator who had also recovered in the other ward with his family.

"I am so sorry for what had happen on that day. I just lost control of the vehicle at a crucial time.......I am so sorry for what you have to endure for my stupid mistake!" said Aqiel.

"Aqiel," said his navigator who was still in pain, "It was not your mistake alone. I too did not inform you of the treacherous danger along that stretch, as I had more experience in this 4-wheel drives trekking. I am sorry for not giving you the right tips however, what is more important is that we are both alive today. This episode will, hopefully, turn us into much wiser persons, insyaallah!" answered the navigator.

Aqiel hugged his navigator and spoke quietly to his wife and his two young kids before he left the room.

Aqiel was discharged on the 3rd week and his navigator was transferred to a private hospital in Kuala Lumpur with all expenses paid by Aqiel. Aqiel recuperated at home for 3 weeks before he went to his office again.

He was warmly welcomed by his staffs when he went to the office. He directly went into Alan's room. Alan shook hands with him and asked, "Are you sure you are ready to be back at the office?" "Yes, it is so boring to stay at home alone surfing the Internet......or reading through the face book!" said Aqiel. "By the way are you still serious with your trekking and big bike?" inquired Alan. "Oh yes....these are my hobbies and as long as I am healthy I intend to do so......dangerous these hobbies maybe, Alan, but I just love living dangerously," Aqiel laughed.

In the meantime, Lily a teacher in Taiping, was always in touch with Mei Lin, her cousin, since she left home. Lily had always been in contact with Gan Cheng Hwa's family and kept Mei Lin updated about her family in Taiping. Lily on her part was kept secretly informed of Mei Lin's mother, Swee Lan and her family. Swee Lan had always had Mei Lin in her mind ever since she left home. As they say mother's love is forever. She kept remembering of the time Mei Lin was just a baby and later grew up to be a beautiful young girl.

They spent many happy moments together until Mei Lin left the house when she was still schooling. Though she too objected to Mei Lin's decision to get married at such a tender age, she did not expect Mei Lin to leave the house. Gan Cheng Hwa was however, adamant and for a few months did not want to hear the name of Mei Lin being mentioned in his house. It was only on the eve of the Chinese New Year that he broke down during dinner when he thought about Mei Lin.

From that day he was always thinking about her and hoping she came back home. He was ready to forgive her, however, he never told his wife or anyone about it. Swee Lan knew about Mei Lin's eldest son being given away but she did not know to whom. She was also informed of the other children Mei Lin had and missed all of them so much. She wished that Mei Lin and family would call on them every time there was a long holiday. She knew her husband Gan Cheng Hwa was ready to accept Mei Lin back into the family but she needed someone close to Mei Lin to convince her. As fate played a major role in our lives on 29th August 2010, Lily and her husband called over at Mei Lin's shop in Ipoh. It was a pleasant surprise to both Wong and Mei Lin whom they had not met for almost 7 years. After having lunch Lily spoke about Mei Lin's father and mother.

"How are they, Lily…..my parents, sisters and brothers? asked Mei Lin.

"Your brothers and sisters are all fine and their children doing well in education. But your parents…..they are both old and frail. Your father is very sick and I came to know he is undergoing treatment for prostate cancer. Whenever I dropped in to see them your mother always mentioned your name. Your father as usual remained silent and pretended not to hear what your mother was talking about. Of late I noticed your father is not in the best of health and my wish is that you and your family visit him while he is still around. It would be a great gesture if you can do that and make them happy before they pass on. They are longing to see you, I know that for sure. They have forgiven you a long time ago, and what stop them from contacting you are their egos…..especially your father, I mean. Your mother never had any grudge against you but was too scared to hurt the feeling of your father. They do not have much time left and I sincerely feel you, Mei Lin, as the daughter should take the first big step to reconcile the family ties. After all it was you, Mei Lin, who rebelled against them….I know you were young and innocent then, but what you did hurt them. They wanted you to have a good future right from the time you were born. But as it turned out.....fate took its course. They are not angry with you anymore.....they never did for they love you so much, Mei Lin. What happened then was just a natural reaction from caring parents. Do not blame them for the past, you must be ready to forgive and forget.....let the past slip by. It is not too late, Mei Lin, and I suggest you think seriously about it with Wong. A family reunion now would be most timely."

Mei Lin suddenly felt very sad and tears were swelling in her eyes. Wong knew Mei Lin was on the verge of crying so he quickly came over and held her. It was such a comfort to have your husband by your side in time of need. For the first time Wong spoke, "August 31st is a holiday and I suggest the whole family go down to Taiping to see your parents. I think it is high time our children meet their grandparents."

"What if they chased us out?" asked Mei Lin.

"I believe they are now more forgiving and just waiting for us to make the first move, Mei Lin" said Wong.

"Yes," interjected Lily, "They have changed and now wished to meet all of you....seriously....go to Taiping, you have nothing to lose but all to gain!"

# CHAPTER 123

By 3.20 p.m. Lily and husband decided to return to Taiping. Wong and Mei Lin thanked both of them for their advice and they should be in Taiping on the morning of August 31st.

"We will see you after that Lily," said Mei Lin.

After Lily and husband left Wong gave a call to Alan, who was still in the office.

"Hello Alan....this is your dad...are you busy?"

"No....not for you, dad....how is everybody at home?"

"They are all fine," Wong replied.

"Is there anything you want to tell me, dad?"

"We have never really sat down and talk about your grandparents. Now is the time to do that, Alan. You remember Aunty Lily and husband? They came for a visit here this morning and had just left after lunch. They told us about your grandparents and we feel that now is the time to visit them. So we intend to go there on the morning of August 31st that is this coming Monday. We would like you and your family to come along if you...that is if you want too."

"Definitely, dad, I love to.....for a long time I have wanted to meet them but dared not suggest to both of you.....in case you might feel offended. I will be there before 8.00 am, dad."

"That's great...so I see you and the family then, bye and send my love to Judy and Sonny."

"I'll do that....bye and my love to all at home," said Alan.

Alan was in a daze for a moment after the phone call for he never thought such a family reunion was possible. He just hoped everything would just turn out fine.

"Merdeka! Merdeka! Merdeka!" were the shouts of independence from the first Prime Minister, Tunku Abdul Rahman that Alan heard on his car radio while driving to Ipoh. Independence did not mean much to him.....even today. There is so much hyped by the government to rally the people to celebrate independence together but to the younger generation the call for celebration revolved amongst the politicians only. The mass media depicted the fight for independence was by the politicians and not the masses. The politicians went ahead highlighting only one political party and one race fought for independence. The people, especially the younger generation, felt divorced and had no reason to celebrate independence though they are Malaysians. Alan felt that the government should get all political parties and NGOs to sit on the Merdeka committee at Federal and state level. That will get all Malaysians from all walks of life celebrate Merdeka together as they felt that they or their older generations had played a part in achieving independence.

Judy and Sonny were dozing off as they watched a movie until late at night. It was a movie about how Malaya achieved her independence....but with a difference. Alan was impressed that a young brave movie director gave a totally new perspective on how we achieved independence......depicting that the whole nation was involved and not just a few political parties and sections of society as depicted in most documentaries and history books. That approach evoked the spirit of nationalism throughout the nation as the government recognised that everybody played a major part in the fight for independence. The movie depicted that fighting for independence was about being self-reliance, building a strong economy, self-rule and most importantly living together in peace and harmony. Our forefathers had practised that spirit, way back from the great era of the Malacca Sultanate. The Malays, Arabs, Chinese, Indians and many other races were working and living together maintaining the highest form of tolerance ever dreamt by any multiracial community in a cosmopolitan city.

"That movie is great....just the right and best recipe educating Malaysians that we are equal and must always stay united," said Alan to Judy last night.

Before 8.00 am they were in Ipoh in front of his dad's shop. His family was eagerly waiting for his arrival downstairs. They all packed into his brand new KIA MPV and proceeded directly to Taiping.

"Did you inform grandma that we are coming, mum?" asked Alan.

"No.....we are not sure of their response so we thought best we just give them a surprise visit," replied his mother. "Let us keep our fingers crossed that everything will turned out fine. By the way, we will stop at the wet market to buy some fish, meat and vegetables to take there as your dad has volunteered to be the chef today!"

"No problem....this is a special day for your mum you know, I like cooking and you definitely want to spend more time with them today.....they are your parents you know ….. we have so much to catch up, dear! I understand your dad just love tom yum prawn soup….so that will be one of the top dish," said Wong.

"My mum used to love sweet sour fried fish….but her taste may have changed over the years," said Mei Lin, "but I am not sure about May Loh and her kids…..I have never met them. I was told my younger sister, May Loh, after her marriage, stays in England and has two kids, Mei Mei and brother, Moh Toi. I understand they returned to Malaysia very often …..wonder if they are back here today."

Alan remarked that Taiping is one of the wettest town in Malaysia, "It rains almost every afternoon here……that is why the surrounding areas are so cooling." The rest in the car were very quiet, full of anxiety and expectancy. Mei Lin, specially was deep in her own thoughts. Sonny however, was so engrossed in his own world…..the digital game, a new IPod.

All the way from Ipoh to Taiping the weather was sunny and the traffic flow quite heavy as it was during the school holidays. They arrived in Taiping by 9.15 am and went straight to the wet market. Alan followed his parents into the market and the rest of the family waited at a nearby restaurant. Judy went looking for the famous steamed groundnuts at one of the stalls. The groundnuts were exceptionally big and tasty and found only in Taiping.

Judy never missed to buy the groundnuts when she was in Taiping….. "She just goes 'nutty' over that 'nuts'…..in short she cannot survive without that 'nuts'!" Alan laughed.

After purchasing all the essential items they needed they came back to the MPV. Sonny was missing. Nobody knew where he went or when he left. Alan and Tat Meng went desperately looking for him in the shops nearby. After quite a while he emerged smiling from the nearby hypermarket.

"Where did you go Sonny? All of us were worried for you…..we nearly reported to the Police," said Alan.

"It was boring waiting in the restaurant so I decided to go to the cyber café and send an e-mail to Alex and Michael in UK!" said Sonny.

"It is okay but inform us where you want to go….just don't disappear like that," said Judy. "So in future let us know first before you leave so that we know where you are, okay?"

"Okay, sorry dad…mum…everybody" replied Sonny timidly.

They then got into the MPV and proceeded to the housing area close to the lake.

# CHAPTER 124

"Cool…Taiping is really cool….grandda's house must be very near to the lake mum….I think I would like to come here during the next school holidays. Can I come here mum?" asked Sonny.

"Of course, but first your great grandparents must agree to your request…. if you behave today, probably they will grant your request," said Judy.

"You will have to help great grandma around the house when you stay here, Sonny…..then they will love you!" remarked Mei Lin.

"Hurray! I am coming to Taiping during my school holidays…hurray!" shouted Sonny.

"Don't be too happy Sonny, I heard great grandpa is a very strict man," joked Tat Meng.

When they saw the old double storey house everybody was quiet….Mei Lin and Wong suddenly felt tensed and Wong held his wife's hands tightly. On entering the main gate they realised the house and its compound was not properly maintained but there were many fruit trees.

Sonny shouted, "Look grandma….mangoes! durians! rambutans! Rambutans were in season and all the trees were bearing delicious fruits…. red, orange and yellow."

The durian trees too were bearing fruits and Wong saw quite a number of the ripe fruits down there waiting to be picked.

"Looked, grandpa…..durians over there…there and there….so many dad…..I love durian…wow!" shouted Sonny with joy.

"Nobody is picking the fruits….it's such a shame. Sonny can help Tat Meng to pick those fruits after we seek permission from your great grandparents, Sonny" said Wong.

There was a white Proton Waja parked under the porch and Alan decided to park under the trees nearby to keep his MPV under the cool shade. They all walked cautiously to the main door of the house. Sonny pressed the door bell….once, twice….but there was no answer. The house was so quiet and Wong thought they might not be in. Sonny was about to press for the third time when the door opened and a maid appeared.

Stepping aside right behind her was Mei Lin's father, Gan Cheng Hwa, a very sick looking old man on a wheel chair and her mother, Swee Lan, standing by his side. They looked at them dumbfounded and confused but not surprised at all. Suddenly Mei Lin's mother with tears in her eyes smiled and opened her arms to welcome all of them into the house. Mei Lin and Wong rushed in to hug both of them. Tears flowed freely and everybody asked for forgiveness from each other. The household, which had been under the cloak of wilderness and sadness, suddenly felt the 'veil' lifted by invisible hands, giving new hopes of happiness and prosperity to the family. Everything was forgotten as if nothing had happened for the past 40 years. It was a day of celebration not only to commemorate 50 years of Merdeka but also to rejoice the reunion of the family that was separated 40 years ago due to a misunderstanding. Mei Lin and Wong thanked God, quietly, for bringing them back to the family. Mei Lin asked her mother where whether her sister May Loh and family came back. "May Loh is in England only Mei Mei and Moh Toi are here. Oh....they woke up late and went to celebrate 'Merdeka' at a friend's house. In fact they just arrived from KL last night. They should be back soon after lunch" replied her mother.

After everybody had settled down, Wong and his daughter, Sui Lin, went to the kitchen to help the maid cook lunch. Mei Lin remained with her parents to catch up on the 40 years of separation. She had so much to tell and they listened attentively to her. Alan, Tat Meng and Sonny went out to pick some rambutans and durians for the family. Mei Lin's mother phoned the other siblings and family members to join the lunch.... "it is like Chinese New Year," said one of Sonny's cousins, "Cool," Sonny added, "like Christmas mum!"

# CHAPTER 125

After lunch the whole family sat around the family room and listened to Mei Lin's parents relating their lonely times without her during the 40 years of separation. Gan Cheng Hwa said, "Mei Lin is our baby girl in the family and we wanted her to reach the sky in her education. We knew she could as she was one smart baby and always top the class in primary school. We did not want to listen to her at all and thought as parents we know best and was always right. We stood firm and wanted her to complete her studies. She loved Wong since her early school days, though he was from a very poor family. When he was in Standard 6 his father died and he had to leave school to help his mother who was then a domestic helper at one of the houses here. Within a year his mother passed away due to dengue. Mei Lin wanted us to help Wong see through his education. We were too conceited and arrogant and wanted Mei Lin to stop her relationship with this boy from a poor family.

An uncle who owned a bicycle repair shop, took him in but treated him like a slave in the house to the disliked of his Aunty. However, she could not do much because her husband was one stubborn person. He was not allowed to continue his schooling, though like Mei Ling, he was an intelligent and bright kid. However, besides keeping the house clean, helping in the kitchen he had to do the washing and then helped in the repair works. After a few years his uncle had a heart attack and he had to take care of everything in the shop house with his Aunty. Life then was more relaxed but by then it was too late for him to continue his studies in school."

Meanwhile Mei Lin was still in touch with him secretly after school. We did not know about the relationship as we thought after his parents died that they went their separate ways. It was after sitting for her Lower Certificate of Education that Mei Lin became rebellious and emotional. We did not know what was wrong with her until one day she told her mother that she wanted to marry Wong. We could not allow that and no parents in their right frame of minds would allow that to happen. We wanted her to finish school first. She obtained 8 A's in that examinations," said Gan Cheng Hwa.

"Your father wanted you to abide to his wishes. I could do nothing to appease him. Swee Lan was a rebellious young girl then," added Swee Lan.

"I lost my temper and chased her out of the house. It was a very rash and harsh decision which I later regretted….very much later. I was deeply disappointed and felt she had brought shame and disrepute to my family. She left the house and my wife never forgave me for that. Initially we went looking for her but to no avail. We heard she married and followed Wong to live in one of the villages. When she came for help I turned her away again and that was the last time I saw her though friends informed us of her whereabouts. Swee Lan became very emotional after Mei Lin left the house. She was admitted to the hospital here and nearly landed at the Tanjong Rambutan hospital for the mentally sick patients. Fortunately she recovered and came home for a few years without talking to me. It was only after 2 years when we had another child, May Loh, that Swee Lan recovered. May Loh, like Mei Mei is a very smart student and obtained a scholarship to study overseas in England. She obtained her degree and got married to a Briton. She is now working there and during Chinese New Year will be back here with her husband and two kids, Mei Mei and Moh Toi, for a week. Both kids are graduates now so Mei Mei is now working with a bank and Moh Toi with an architect firm. Both regularly come back during summer holidays since their younger days. Now that they are working they take leave every year to be with us," related Gan Cheng Hwa. Until today, she never stopped thinking about you Mei Lin. Every Chinese New Year eve she cried just before the family dinner. I knew her thoughts were for you, Mei Lin. There were many times that I wanted to drive down to your home in Sitiawan and later in Ipoh to seek your forgiveness but I had too much pride and…………. stupidity." "One evening he was already in front of your shop in Sitiawan but at the last minute he chickened out. I wanted to go in but he stopped me as you might turned defiant and turned hysterical in front of everybody.... though we maybe shamed but that incident would be bad for Wong's business too," Sui Lan said.

"We went home unhappy as our attempt to reconcile with you failed miserably. Not only your mother who was affected emotionally, I, too suffered insomnia and ill health since you left. It was about 3 years ago that I was diagnosed for prostate cancer and only God knows how much time I still have with you all. Today, the August 31$^{st}$, I feel relieved and extremely happy that Mei Lin and family are home with us again. Her returned had brightened up the house again, which used to be quiet, gloomy and shrouded with sadness," said the frail looking old man in between sobs.

Wong decided he wanted to say a few words, "Eh....umph....all that happened were actually my fault. I should have never even looked at Mei Lin as she was from a very rich family. She went to school by car while I walked to school daily without pocket money or breakfast." Everybody was silent and looked down. Everybody could see that Wong's eyes became teary though Mei Lin was already in tears. Wong tried to control his emotions and eventually continued with his story. "I did not really want to marry with Mei Lin after her LCE but when she was chased out of the house I had to take the full responsibility. If I had also rejected her then things would turned worst for her. I knew she would leave Taiping and only God knows what would happen to her. Yes, I love her and we decided to get married though at a very young age. We survived by doing odd jobs and Pak Hussein was a tower of strength during those early years. Our first child, Alan, was taken care of by Pak Hussein at the orphanage. We were lucky as the orphanage run by Datin was well managed and had no racial discrimination. My past experience as a cook under the tutelage of my aunty helped me to further develop my skill in cooking. When our business improved I attended adult classes then Mei Lin joined me to attend classes up to Senior Cambridge level. We sat together as expected she performed much better than me." Everybody in the room laughed lightly to reduce tension. We were happy to have achieved our ambition to complete or education......nobody knew about this except the two of us until today," ended Wong. "Wow......Ah Kong.....never knew you and grandma have Senior Cambridge Certificate.....very well educated cooks!" The whole family laughed at that remarks.

# CHAPTER 126

Mei Lin hugged her father and begged again for his forgiveness because whatever had happened was because of her. At that moment a car drove into the porch. "That must be Mei Mei and Moh Toi," said Gan Cheng Hwa. They were chattering all the way in and asked their mother who came to the house. Before Sui Lan could answer they had both reached the living room. They stopped dead and looked at the visitors in the room. "Whose MPV is that downstairs, grandpa?" asked Moh Toi. "Do you recognise them, Mei Mei....Moh Toi?" asked Gan Cheng Hwa. They looked at the faces but knew these were not familiar faces but one looked just like their mother. "Are you Mei Lin.......my Aunty?" asked Mei Mei. Mei Lin could not answer but extend her arms to hug both her niece and nephew both of whom she had not met. She was again in tears when both kissed and hugged her and everybody in the room could not help being teary eyes. "You look just like my mother," said Moh Toi. "Mother has been talking about you and every time we came back we went searching for you but to no avail. Grandpa and grandma were just reluctant to talk about you. We only saw pictures of you, Aunty, in the family album. Even when we came back this time around she asked us to try to meet you and family and get Mei Lin to come home. My mother loves you so much though she has never met you. She has heard so much about you from grandma and said whatever has happened has to be forgiven and forgotten," Mei Mei added. "We are back now and back for good," said Mei Lin. "By the way this is your Uncle Wong," (They hugged him), this is your cousins Alan, Tat Meng and Sui Lan. Judy, is Alan's wife and Sonny here is your naughty nephew!" introduced Mei Lin.

"I have two elder sons, in fact twins, studying in UK......Michael and Alex. Both are doing their 'O' level at Rochester Independent College in Medway Towns in the County of Kent, just East of London. You know the college is quite close to University of Greenwich and University of Kent where I hope they will qualify to get admissions," said Alan. "Oh yes.....we know the college.....very prestigious and not easy to get admitted. When we are back we may pop in to see them on weekends," said Moh Toi. "That will be nice," added Judy. "By the way when is your next trip to UK Alan?" asked Mei Mei. "Well.....we have actually planned during the coming summer holidays so that we can spend more time with those two boys, probably take them for a drive to Scotland," replied Alan. "Yes!" said Moh Toi, "probably we can tag along if you rent a caravan!" "Why not," said Judy, "it will be interesting and a pleasure to have both of you as our travelling companions......remember, both of you have to cook as we are both on holidays!" "OK," replied Mei Mei, "as long as we have free meals and roof over our heads." Everybody in the room laughed. "Actually I am very eager to see the famous Loch Ness Monster, "Nessie" as they called it," voiced Sonny.

Judy looked at Alan and Moh Toi took the initiative to explain to Sonny. "Loch Ness is the second largest lake above sea level in the highlands of Scotland. It is about 23 miles long. What I understand from our lecturer was that the scientific community regards the Loch Ness monster as a modern day myths. The myth started way back in the 6th century with various sightings by officials of the church then. In 1933/34 were the years where many sightings of this creature on land by many travellers were reported. The most reliable one was the report from one George Spicer and wife who saw the creature crossed the road when he was driving there. The creature immediately dived into the Loch Ness though there were tell tale signs on the grass of a big creature crossing the road leading to the lake. It was a kind of plesiosaur according to the reports. Then Dr. Wilson in 1934 photographed the monster in the lake showing the neck and head only. Some experts believed that the photos were faked. There were also videos and films images that most experts rejected. Scientists from all over the world came over to use modern equipment like the sonar images but to no avail. The myth has slowly lost its interest until someone created or come up with a new sighting!" "Probably they are looking at the wrong place because the monster could be spending most of her time on land in the highlands and only swim in Loch Ness for food!" said Sonny. "You may be right, Sonny," replied Mei Mei, "food is excessive in the lake." "Your theory makes sense Sonny," added Alan, "so we should explore the highlands rather than the lake!" Everybody laughed at that remark. "You know I would love to have the opportunity to Wimbledon tennis for once," said Judy. "What tennis? It is better to spend money to watch EPL football matches.....more thrilling and exciting!" "Yes...both are very expensive..... with that kind of money we can travel to Paris," said Alan. "Agreed," said both Judy and Sonny. Again they all laughed at their reactions.

# CHAPTER 127

Everybody was happy and Swee Lan expertly put them in a more jovial the mood by diverting their attention to the fruits in front of them,

"Hey.....what are we waiting for.....an invitation to eat? Let us all now enjoy the fruits of 'labour' of Alan, Tat Meng and Sonny in the orchards.

They spend so many long hours to pick these fruits. It must be real hard work as I noticed Sonny was sweating through and through!" "Alan interjected "The sweating was not because of laborious work.....he was running around the compound and only Tat Meng and I were actually doing the hard work!" Sonny, smiling, hid behind his mother. "But before all of you enjoy the fruits you must thank your grandfather who had the vision to plant those trees years ago. This is the third year the trees are bearing fruits but for whatever reasons this season the fruits are plentiful."

Gan Cheng Hwa could not help but smile with pride and said, "Your grandmother had a big part to play. Initially I did not want to plant these fruits trees as I told your grandmother probably we will not be around to enjoy the fruits. She said to me that even if we are not around then the squirrels, birds, civets and others could still enjoy the fruits and every religion believed that at every single bite made by these creations of God, God would in return blessed the person who planted the fruit trees. Your grandmother in turn contributed by making sure that these fruit trees grow strong and productive by applying every year with fertilisers." "What fertiliser did she used granddad," asked Sonny. Granddad looked at his wife who replied, "Cow dung!" "No wonder the fruits are so big and sweet," said Tat Meng and everybody laughed.

Alan, Tat Meng and Sonny looked amused and everybody smiled at them and suddenly the kids scrambled for the fruits in the trays down on the floor. Alan and Tat Meng later went to pick more fruits as their grandfather said if they leave the fruit there they will just rot away or the squirrels will have a field day! "Your grandmother and me are just too old to pick the fruits as we do not enjoy eating them anymore," said his grandfather. "You know when I asked your grandmother to pick some durians......before she leaves the house I told her to write it down. She said "Don't worry....I can remember!" After half an hour she came back with some rambutans. I asked her what happened to the mangosteens. She said "What? I thought you said you wanted the rambutans!" They all laughed at the humour. "Frankly, we are both so forgetful......it is only Mei Lin that we always remember," said Gan Cheng Hwa sadly. Mei Lin could not help herself but hugged the old man lovingly.

Before they left Mei Lin promised her parents that they would be back soon to sleep there a few nights. This time around they were unsure of the situation so nobody brought any luggage to stay overnight. Alan said he liked Taiping as the place was very relaxing and cooling. He had been here before to visit the zoo and on the way to Bukit Maxwell for holidays. He and his family would definitely come more often to Taiping now that he had a 'home' to return. His grandfather welcomed the idea as they felt they would feel lonely now that they know they have a big family around.

In the evening on the way back Mei Lin told the family that her parents were not surprised about the visit because Lily had told them earlier. "We knew that because they were actually waiting for us to knock on the door. The look of shock on their faces was because 40 years has been a very long time and they never expected to see Mei Ling and Wong again right at their doorstep! Lily reunited us, mum, and we are all glad it all turned out so well," said Alan.

Mei Lin said, "God bless her and her husband for bringing us all back together." She looked at her husband, Wong and said, "People used to say, 'Family - is God's greatest gift to mankind', those words were meaningless to me then but today......that family reunion change my whole perspective about life." Alan related a story he read recently in a book. "The great Mahatma Gandhi said, if we are to reach peace in this world and if we are to carry a real war against war, we shall have to begin with children; and if they grow up in their natural innocence, we won't have the struggle, we won't have to pass idle resolutions, but shall go for love to love and peace to peace, until at last all the corners of the world are covered with that peace and love for which consciously or unconsciously, the world is hungering."

"Gandhi was a great leader and left us many legacies that mankind can practise until today. Gandhi did what he preached unlike many leaders of today such as politicians, religious heads, teachers and parents who failed to live up to the expectations of the younger generations," said Wong.

There was an incident whereby a mother who could no longer bear to see her son eating too many sweets turned to Gandhi for advised. "Please Bapu, will you tell my boy to stop eating sweets. He simply eats too much of it and will not stop." Gandhi told the mother to come back with her son in three days. The mother returned after three days with her son and Gandhi said to the son, "Young man, stop eating sweets. They are not good for you." The mother was perplexed and decided to ask Gandhi, "Bapu, why didn't you tell my son that when we first came to see you? I don't understand." Gandhi said to her, "Three days ago, I, too was eating sweets. I could not ask him to stop eating sweets as long as I continued to do so." The great Gandhi once said, "I am a leader so I must follow my people." This was just opposite to what most leaders will say," I am a leader so the people must do what I tell them to do and not do what I do."

AUTHOR: <u>TOK MAN</u>
Aman Shah Khalid

Acknowledgement: To my beloved wife, Salomi, for giving me ideas while spending so much time helping me to edit and read my final draft. At times we 'disagree' over certain issues but in the end I have to agree with her not because I am scared of her but because she is right!

Photos in the books are merely illustrative.

Printed in the United States
By Bookmasters